THIS BOOK SHOULD BE RETURNED ON OR BEFORE THE LATEST
DATE SHOWN TO THE LIBRARY FROM WHICH IT WAS BORROWED

AUTHOR		CLASS
	FULLERTON, A.	A F G

TITLE   Stark realities

8

Alexander Fullerton, born in Suffolk and brought up in France, spent the years 1938–41 at the RN College, Dartmouth, and the rest of the war at sea — mostly under it. His first novel — *Surface!*, based on his experiences as gunnery and torpedo officer of HM Submarine *Seadog* in the Far East, 1944–5, in which capacity he was mentioned in despatches for distinguished service — was published in 1953. It became an immediate bestseller, with five reprints in six weeks. He has lived solely on his writing since 1967, and he likes to recall that, working for a Swedish shipping company at the time, he wrote *Surface!* in office hours, on the backs of old cargo manifests.

STARK REALITIES

October, 1918: Germany is suing for peace, terms for an armistice are being negotiated and all U-boats have been ordered home from patrol. Among them is UB81, commanded by Oberleutnant zu See Otto von Mettendorff: he's young, dynamic and infatuated with a new girlfriend. However, before he can reach Germany, the UB81 is 'holed' by a destroyer off the Eddystone lighthouse and sent to the bottom. Meanwhile in London, Anne Laurie, a young war widow now being courted by an American naval officer, and employed in the Intelligence Division of the Royal Navy, learns of Otto's death. It jolts memories of a pre-war weekend in Berlin in the summer of 1913 . . .

Books by Alexander Fullerton
Published by The House of Ulverscroft:

LAST LIFT FROM CRETE
ALL THE DROWNING SEAS
THE TORCH BEARERS
REGENESIS
A SHARE OF HONOUR
THE GATECRASHERS
STORM FORCE TO NARVIK
THE APHRODITE CARGO
SPECIAL DELIVERANCE
THE BLOODING OF THE GUNS
SIXTY MINUTES FOR ST. GEORGE
PATROL TO THE GOLDEN HORN
SPECIAL DYNAMIC
SPECIAL DECEPTION
IN AT THE KILL
THE FLOATING MADHOUSE
SINGLE TO PARIS
FLIGHT TO MONS
WESTBOUND, WARBOUND

ALEXANDER FULLERTON

STARK REALITIES

Complete and Unabridged

CHARNWOOD
Leicester

First published in Great Britain in 2004 by
Time Warner Books, London

First Charnwood Edition
published 2004
by arrangement with
Time Warner Books
an imprint of
Time Warner Book Group UK, London

The moral right of the author has been asserted

British Library CIP Data

Fullerton, Alexander, *1924 –*
    Stark realities.—Large print ed.—
Charnwood library series
1. World War, *1914–1918*—Naval operations—
Submarine—Fiction 2. War stories
3. Large type books
I. Title
823.9′14 [F]

ISBN 1–84395–831–7

Published by
F. A. Thorpe (Publishing)
Anstey, Leicestershire
Set by Words & Graphics Ltd.
Anstey, Leicestershire
Printed and bound in Great Britain by
T. J. International Ltd., Padstow, Cornwall

This book is printed on acid-free paper

Our war aim, apart from destroying the English Fleet as the principal means by which Britain controls its Empire, is to reduce its total economy in the quickest possible time, bringing Great Britain to sue for unconditional peace. To achieve this it will be necessary:

(a)   To cut off all trade routes to and from the British Isles,

(b)   To cripple in all the seven seas, all ships flying the British flag and all ships under neutral flag plying to and from Great Britain,

(c)   To destroy military and economic resources and by means of air attack disrupt the trade and commerce in the British Isles, showing its population quite mercilessly the stark realities of war.

German Naval Staff memorandum to the Kaiser,
6 January 1916

For a woman, lying is a protection. She protects the truth, so she protects her chastity.

John le Carré, The Little Drummer Girl

Man has always found it easier to sacrifice his life than to learn the multiplication table.

W. Somerset Maugham,
Mr Harrington's Washing

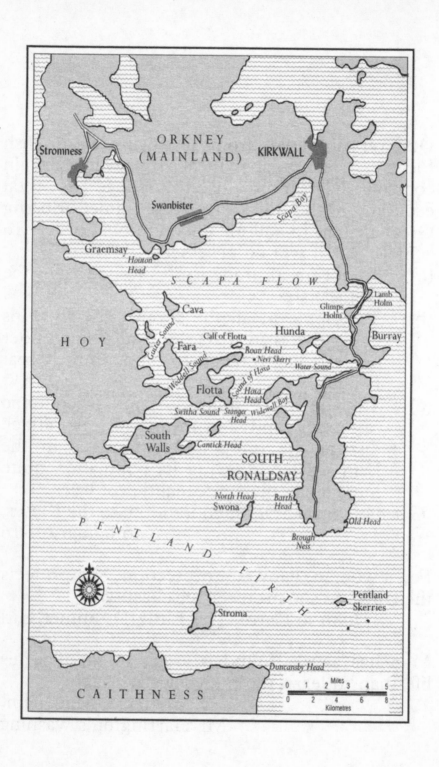

1

'Down, you two!'

The lookouts had been expecting it, were already tumbling into the open, brass-rimmed hatch, their wet, oilskin-wrapped bodies temporarily occluding the soft glow of light in the tower below; von Mettendorff stooping to the voicepipe to call down, 'Break the charge, stop engines, prepare to dive!' UB81 battering eastward through black, white-streaked, pre-dawn sea — English sea, Lizard Point roughly fifteen nautical miles abaft the beam to port. She'd been making about six knots throughout the hours of darkness — her best surface speed being nine, nine-and-a-quarter, but had spent the night on one diesel only, the other's power going into the necessary re-charging of her batteries; was losing way now, pitching and rolling more wildly as engine-power fell off and the sea did its best to take charge. Get down into it, in a minute you'd have peace and quiet; in fact he was diving about a quarter-hour sooner than he might have done, being this close to the enemy coast and — well, Falmouth, Plymouth; it was only a matter of common sense to sacrifice a couple of miles of faster eastward progress for a better chance of bringing his ship home intact. Meanwhile, one last binocular search of the most obvious danger-sector, from right ahead back to the port quarter: 81's skipper a tall, lean figure bulked out by oilskins shining wet in the still near-total darkness, his Zeiss glasses gripped one-handed and sweeping slowly, steadily. Needing the other hand for hanging on with. No engine racket now, only the wind's howl and the sea's roar and the noise she made throwing herself around. And — nothing there, so all right, duck under . . . Stooping to the pipe, yelling down, 'Motors half ahead, open main vents!', hearing the start of acknowledgement of that order from below and cutting it short by dragging shut the voicepipe cock: thuds of the vents dropping open, rush of escaping air, Oberleutnant zu See Otto von Mettendorff by this time in the hatch — unhurried but not wasting any seconds either — dragging the heavy lid shut above his head and jamming a clip on, calling down to Claus Stahl to stop her at fifteen metres. Thinking, *Some chartwork now, then breakfast* . . . Both clips on: clambering down the ladder into the control-room. Time/date 0648, 22 October 1918.

★ ★ ★

Stahl, UB81's first lieutenant, put down his coffee mug and looked at his skipper across the wardroom table. The messman had just left them.

'Wilhelmshaven? And 'merchant vessels not to be attacked'. A *general* recall — cessation of operations, in other words? Evacuating Flanders, maybe? There was a rumour of that, wasn't there, before we sailed? But recalling boats from

2

everywhere else as well — bloody *surrender?*'

Otto shook his head, glancing through into the control-room. 'Keep your voice down, man. In any case, evacuation of the Flanders bases does *not* necessarily mean surrender.'

They'd had the signal last night via Nauen, the German Navy's long-range wireless transmitter. Long-range transmission being needed of course because it *was* a general recall of U-boats from patrol — some in mid-Atlantic and the Mediterranean, as well as in the Channel and North Sea. And Stahl was right — evacuation of Bruges, this boat's Flanders base, had been on the cards before they'd left for this patrol. Hence presumably their recall now to Wilhelmshaven, the main fleet base, home to the High Seas Fleet.

Background hum of electric motors; atmosphere soporific in the warmth they generated and the stillness of the boat rock-steady at her depth of fifteen metres. To use the periscope she'd have to be at less than ten: in this sort of weather more like eight for that top lens to reach above the waves. In any case it was still dark up there, you weren't missing anything. Anything that *was* there — please God — you'd pick up on the hydrophones.

Gasse or Schuchardt would, whichever of them was on watch.

Wilhelmshaven, though: Helena was at Wilhelmshaven, and on his September visit there she'd promised . . . Otto with his eyes shut, hands over his face, promising *himself* that whatever the hell this recall was going to lead to,

3

the first free minute he had he'd be on the line to her.

Which was — something else entirely. Something — to put it mildly — thrilling. Nothing to do with the questions crowding his mind and Stahl's. Stahl's darkly unshaven, rather pudgy face creased with foreboding as he muttered, 'Those whispers about the Army beaten to its knees — '

'Oh, come on . . . '

'Run out of steam, then. Either way, ourselves as the only weapon could pull chestnuts out of the fire.'

'If the war's lost, Stahl, *we* didn't lose it. And the Army is *not* 'beaten to its knees'.' Skipper almost whispering. 'Over-extended lines of communication is one thing — and exhaustion, look at the distance we've advanced since April — and the damned Americans in it now is something else again. Guessing's no help though, Stahl, nor's defeatism. Or listening to propaganda from our enemies, including left-wing politicians and revolutionaries. Anyway, looking on a very much brighter side, I must say the prospect of a spell in Wilhelmshaven — *well* . . . ' A smile suddenly on his blond-bearded face, hands lifting as if in — what, revelation, hope? 'Tell you frankly, far as *I'm* concerned — '

'Wilhelmshaven by way of the Dover mine barrage, skipper?'

Chief Hintenberger, the boat's engineer, joining them at the table, squeezing himself in beside Stahl. Coastals weren't all that roomy

4

— although these UBIIs were a hell of a lot more so than the originals, the little UBIs. Hintenberger was a small man anyway — paper-white bony face, black beard and quick, hard eyes, in contrast to his captain's tallness and blondness, or Stahl's crumpled, flabby look. Otto told the engineer — answering his question about the Dover passage — 'By the same route we took coming south. A route which incidentally Franz Winter in U201 assured me was safe enough.'

'Safe enough *then*, no doubt. Things change, don't they. *Are* changing — aren't I right? For one thing the barrage is a lot deeper than it was — you'll agree you can't just paddle under it now, cocking snooks, like we used to do, eh? Remember, skipper, we discussed it in Bruges, you and I, and — '

'Are you suggesting I should take her back through the Irish Sea and round the Scottish islands?'

'No.' A shrug. 'Wouldn't presume so far. Although that *was* the intention, wasn't it, earlier on?'

'When we were expecting to be shifted up that way in any case. And who knows what's happening on *that* coast now — now the English have pulled their socks up . . . Anyway, since we're where we are, and have received immediate recall — and have a way through that's been checked out and found safe — '

'Found passable *then* — '

'Chief.' Otto's cold stare held the engineer's. 'Having known each other as long as we have, and you being as damned ancient as you are, one

5

has tended to allow a certain degree of — self-expression, you might call it — '

'I beg your pardon — sir.'

'It would be better to keep things in proportion.' His expression hadn't softened, although his tone was still quiet. 'For instance, d'you agree that this — er — reminder to you should not be necessary?'

'I do. And I beg your pardon, *mein kommandant.*'

'Good.' He asked Stahl, 'Battery right up, did you say?'

'Could have done with another half-hour's charging, sir.'

'Something else that can't be helped.' He leant back, stretching. 'Take a peek up top now, perhaps.' He turned his head, raising his voice: 'Happy in your work there, Hofbauer?'

Rudolf Hofbauer, Leutnant zu See, nineteen years of age, the boat's navigator and currently officer of the watch, was leaning over the chart-table, figuring out distances and dead-reckoning positions from UB81's present location to the Dover Strait and the dogleg from there to Wilhelmshaven. He said, straightening, scratching his lightly furred jaw with a pencil stub, 'Looks like three-and-a-half days, sir, into Schillig Roads. That's calling it twelve hours' daylight and twelve dark, nine knots surfaced and five dived.'

'Average seven, so about a hundred and sixty miles a day, and' — Otto muttering this, thinking in nautical miles as he walked dividers across the chart — 'allowing for diversions here and there

6

— including avoidance of reportedly new minefields.'

'Say four days?'

'More like it. As a rough estimate. And today's October twenty-second, so — arrival twenty-sixth.' Turning away, adding, 'Maybe. Let's have a gander up there now. Bring her to ten metres.'

'Ten, sir.' Hofbauer moved further into the control-room. 'Klein . . . '

The for'ard hydroplane operator, a leading seaman, muttered acknowledgement as he tilted the fore 'planes' control. The after 'planesman, Freimann, at the same time angling her stern-down, bow-up, while Hofbauer passed orders over the electric telegraph for a slight adjustment of the boat's trim, allowing for transition into less dense water closer to the surface. Von Mettendorff pausing and turning back to the chart, checking on how long the passage to Wilhelmshaven might have taken if he'd opted for the Irish Sea route. Well, at a glance, seven or eight days, say. Twice as long — and *that* would be cutting all the corners. Four days longer to get to Helena — while Franz Winter in U201, having by now left his patrol area — Biscay or thereabouts, Azores-Canaries — would be several days ahead of him; with that ocean-going boat's superior speed, even a week ahead.

Whereas now they'd be about neck and neck.

It was Winter, oddly enough, who'd introduced him to Helena, despite having a keen interest in her himself, apparently. Not that she took *him* very seriously. He was too old for her,

7

for one thing, too set in his ways. A dedicated, highly successful submarine commander, but in other respects — well, on dry land, you might say, a fish out of water. Certainly no ladies' man — more the crusty bachelor. Origins obscure at that — table manners appalling, for instance: one had known dogs one would sooner feed with. All right, so he'd done a lot for Otto von Mettendorff at one time and another — pushing him through for command at an unusually early stage had been the end result of it. Rough diamond selecting the aristo as protégé, getting some kind of satisfaction out of that?

Frowning, with his eyes on the chart — on the Dover Strait — but still with his mind on Helena. Reminding himself then, *All's fair in love and war* . . . Even if the war *was* on the point of petering out. Make the most of it while it lasts, is all . . . And now back to business: moving into the centre of the control-room as Hofbauer reported, 'Depth ten metres, sir.'

A grunt of acknowledgement and the customary signal: movement of both hands palms upward. Boese, mechanician of the watch, long-faced and already balding although not yet out of his twenties, stooped to the control levers of the periscopes and inched one of them upward. Thump of applied hydraulic pressure, then the scope hissing up out of its well, steel-wire hoist purring around deckhead sheaves. The larger of 81's two periscopes this was, bifocal and providing low- or high-power; the other, the 'attack' 'scope, unifocal and operated from up there in the conning-tower,

8

was as slim as a broomstick and gave one-and-a-half times magnification, non-adjustable. Otto was waiting for the big one, jerked its handles down as the eyepieces rose level with his face, murmured, 'All the way up, Boese.' With a fair suspicion that from this depth he wasn't going to see anything but the insides of waves in close-up — as now, indeed, a confusion of green and white, kaleidoscopic motion in the glittery light of this new day. He told Hofbauer without taking his eyes far off the lenses, 'Nine-and-a-half metres', and heard the order repeated by the fore 'planesman Klein, whose wife had given birth to a baby girl less than a month ago. It would most likely be necessary to come up to nearer eight or eight-and-a-half metres to get any decent all-round view, but on principle you didn't show more stick than you had to, especially when the sea-state made depth-keeping difficult. There was even the risk of breaking surface, exposing periscope standards — the structure that housed the periscopes — or even the bridge itself, in a great flurry of seething foam visible for miles, with the danger then of being spotted by one of the Royal Navy's dirigible airships that patrolled these inshore waters, and which if they weren't themselves in a position to drop bombs would whistle up destroyers.

At eight-and-a-half metres he had a good enough perspective, could even bring the 'scope down a little. Stooping, shuffling hunched around the well, while the men around him saw daylight reflected brightly in his eyes, his own view being of grey-green heaving sea ribbed and whorled with the broken white and backed by low, grey cloud. Circling first with the 'scope in low power, then again, more slowly, with four-power magnification. And — nothing anywhere. Which was fine, since in the present unexplained circumstances you weren't looking for targets anyway, only for dangers that might be threatening. He straightened, snapped the handles up, told Boese, 'Down periscope', and Hofbauer 'Fifteen metres.' The 'scope already hissing down, oil and droplets of salt water from the deckhead gland shimmering on its bright and greasy barrel. Otto telling both Hofbauer and Claus Stahl as he headed for the wardroom and his bunk, 'If I'm still asleep at noon, give me a shake.'

★   ★   ★

The Dover mine barrage *was* scary. Hintenberger — now snoring in his bunk — was right as far as that went. Otto had been in the game long enough to have his senses, instincts, tuned to the realities — including the plain fact that a U-boat man couldn't expect to live for ever, even if for his own comfort he had to believe he might. The engineer was several years older than himself, and conscious of it, not only in terms of submarine experience, but in plain maturity — and in his own view, probably, wisdom.

Comparative youth, for a commander, wasn't all beer and skittles. You saw the envy, resentment in contemporaries who hadn't got on so fast and asked themselves *why* they hadn't, what von Mettendorff had that they did not.

The professional and personal support of Franz Winter, who despite his rough manners was now well established as one of the 'Ace' COs, having at the last count 160,000 tons of British and Allied shipping under his belt, had certainly been a major factor in one's advancement. Otto had been Winter's first lieutenant in U53: had been appointed to her originally as navigator, been advanced by Winter to the position of second-in-command when that job had fallen vacant. U53 had been Hans Rose's boat earlier on — *the* Hans Rose — so that joining her as a junior lieutenant, with comparatively little submarine experience of his own at that stage, he'd had a sense of walking with the gods. And with that came determination to follow in their footsteps, an ambition that made for ruthlessness, which Franz Winter had duly noted and approved, and in due course — really very little time at all — had recommended him for command. For the command *course*, naturally — which he'd come through with flying colours and been rewarded with one of the original coastals, the little UBIs — single screw and only one periscope, no for'ard hydroplanes, top surface speed six knots, crew of fourteen, and designed to be deliverable by rail: five wagons per boat, assembly at Hoboken and Antwerp, then towed through the Scheldt and the Ghent-Bruges canal. So cramped that if you'd wanted to sign on a ship's cat you'd only have got it in with a shoehorn, and would *not* have tried to swing it round. But he'd been reasonably successful in her, operating from Bruges — had become a top-scorer, in fact — and after only a few months graduated from her to this UBII, taking her over from Reinhold Salzwedel, who'd moved to command of one of the minelayers, the UCs.

Franz Winter, who'd made a similar move when U53 had gone in for a major re-fit, had returned almost at once to an ocean-going boat — U201 — and his advice to Otto had been to stay clear of minelaying if he could; there was a lot of it going on, and the UCs' mines were sinking a lot of English ships in the approaches to their harbours, but it was more nerve-racking, he said, than anything in his previous experience.

More recently — *very* recently — he'd given him quite a different warning.

'You've been doing a good job, from as much as one hears. Regrettably, one also hears that you've been throwing your weight about. As you'll recall, in days gone by I've had occasion to caution you about that sort of thing?'

'Too big for my boots is the expression I recall, sir.' Taken by surprise, and trying to make light of it, but Winter hadn't been standing for that, had added, '*Arguing the toss with men greatly senior to yourself.* Eh?'

He'd sprung this on him on the fore-casing of U201, of which he, Winter, had just assumed command and would be taking out on patrol in a few days' time. Standing on her grey steel casing with booted legs apart and hands clasped behind his back, head up, peak of his cap jutting skyward, jaw out-thrust. He was a head shorter

12

than Otto: sturdy, gruffly self-confident, well aware of his own social disadvantages while still robustly certain of his value to — and future in — the U-boat arm, which in fact was all he cared about; and cautious in his personal relationships, typically would have given a lot of thought prior to issuing such a reprimand. While the last thing Otto had expected had been to be hauled over the coals like this. He'd been invited to a *party*, for God's sake, a small celebratory shindig that Winter had been throwing, the guests mostly fellow COs but a few others too — shore staff and some of their wives. Otto's feeling was that he'd been ambushed: was only thankful that no-one else was in range to hear any of it. Winter adding, having seen a group of late arrivals approaching his boat's gangplank, 'Point is, von Mettendorff, you don't need any of that. Gets you disliked, certainly wins no-one's admiration. You're a talented, capable young officer with a sound future ahead of you, maybe even a great one — as long as you keep your head screwed on. Don't ruin it for yourself — or for the Service, which is a hell of a lot more important, although — understand this — I'm drawing it to your attention in your own best interests.'

'I appreciate that, sir. I'm grateful.'

The hell he was. Could guess where that 'arguing the toss' bit had come from, too. A kapitan-leutnant in the Flanders flotilla who didn't know his arse from his bloody elbow . . . Winter now waving him away: 'Go on down. My first lieutenant, Neureuther, is looking forward to making your acquaintance. I have to greet these friends.'

Friends who included a sensationally attractive girl in an orange summer frock. Glossy chestnut hair, wide-set blue eyes, at this moment on *him*, Otto von Mettendorff. She was with an older woman and a grey-haired *Wehrmacht* captain, and was looking now in what might be mock trepidation at the narrow gangplank with its single rope handrail. Winter calling laughingly, 'The handrail's especially for you, Helena. We don't usually provide one, we simply run across. Frau Lukesch, Captain, how splendid that you could come . . .'

Otto had rattled down the ladder from the torpedo hatch and turned aft. In Wilhelmshaven, submarine crews were accommodated in barracks, and there were only a few duty-men on board. The party in the wardroom, spilling over into other accommodation space and the control-room, was already noisy, and there were several familiar faces, including those of one or two particularly good friends. Neureuther, who'd got him a brandy and soda from a sailor acting as barman, he hadn't met before; nor Kantelberg, Winter's young navigator. But Max Valentiner — very much an 'Ace' — was there, and greeted him pleasantly; also Otto Steinbrinck, another close friend of Winter's. Steinbrinck had built up his impressive score mainly in command of UBs, but was driving a minelayer now, and professed to be enjoying it. And Hans Dittrich of U42 with his wooden-looking countenance. There'd been plenty to talk about — other men's achievements as well as

14

their own — and Otto had made a point of being modestly reticent when questioned about his own successes — which he could see went down well, and was something to bear in mind. To thank old Dutch-uncle Franz Winter for, maybe. Speaking of whom — well, it must have been thirty or forty minutes and several brandies later that Otto found himself virtually alone in the crowd with Helena Becht, who'd been practically glued to Franz W. all that time, in a group which had included Valentiner and Steinbrinck. Otto had exchanged glances with her more than once, over the heads of others — but no more than that, and not sure what he could do about it, in all the circumstances, until to his surprise Winter had brought her to him, hauling her through the crowd with an arm around her and telling her as they reached him, 'Otto von Mettendorff here was once my first lieutenant. Now he has his own command and he's been knocking 'em down in heaps. Otto — Fraulein Helena Becht — a very special friend of mine. But Helena, if you'd excuse me . . . '

Face to face and very close, they had a sort of privacy by virtue of the crowd itself, having to duck down and speak close to her ear, then offer her one of his, and so forth. After a few minutes of this he'd taken her arm: 'More room next door. The central control-room, it's called.' She'd acquiesced, and they'd edged through, Otto getting a wink from Hans Graischer as he passed him. Telling her — as if conducting a tour — 'There is also the CO's control-room — up there in the conning-tower, up that ladder.

Above that, up a second ladder, is the bridge . . . ' She'd stopped and turned to face him, he guessed not all that rivetted by what he'd been saying. He smiled: 'End of lecture. So. If I heard you correctly, you're special assistant to a brigadier by name of Hartmann and you're based in Oldenburg. May I ask what it is you do?'

'Intelligence liaison. My section is concerned with links or — well, known contacts — between certain elements in the *Hochseeflotte* — High Seas Fleet — and individuals and groups in — oh, military units, primarily.' She shook her head. 'I'm not supposed to talk shop, though.'

'Something to do with last year's mutiny?'

A smile: 'Don't you mean last year's *strike*?'

'One of the few 'strikes' ever to have been settled by a firing-squad!'

They'd shot two men — a youngster by the name of Reichpietsch, and another — Kobis, Albin Kobis. *Pour encourager les autres*. Helena suggesting, 'Perhaps we should avoid that subject, anyway?'

'I only asked about your work because I'm interested in *you*, Fraulein. To be completely honest with you, I'm indifferent to what brings you here. All that matters is you *are* here — the most beautiful girl I ever met in my life — may I tell you this?'

'I hear you *say* it, Herr Oberleutnant zu See — '

'Say it *and* mean it. How did you meet Franz Winter?'

16

'Through Brigitte and her husband — Captain and Frau Lukesch — the couple with whom I arrived? — and he met *them* through the deputy to Kommodore Michelsen — Kapitan zu See Schwaeble. Hans Lukesch is in the same field that I am, you see.'

And Kommodore Michelsen was U-boat chief in Wilhelmshaven. Short title FdU, the 'F' standing for *Fuhrer*, 'U' for *Unterseeboote*. Otto had been introduced to him on one formal occasion, but he'd never met the deputy. He told her, ducking closer to that small ear again, 'I'd bet a lot of money you'd find no subversion amongst U-boat crews. Wasting your time — or his. We have the best, the crème de la crème. I'm sure Schwaeble would have told him so — it's a fact, always has been.' He touched her arm: 'I'm sorry — talking shop. When all I really want to talk about is you. You're by far the most beautiful girl I ever stood this close to, d'you know that?'

'I know when I hear that kind of thing to tell myself hey, watch out!'

'When you're paid a little compliment reflecting nothing but the truth? Tell me — Franz Winter — is it as he says a *very* special friendship?'

'Oh, he's — a character. And such a *lonely* man. Don't you think so?'

'I'm sure — if you say so . . . But — *not* all that special?'

'Well — it's conceivable that from *his* point of view . . . ' Looking for him in the throng around them and not seeing him. Eyes back on Otto: 'I don't know what you're asking, really. Did you

17

say your family's from Dresden?'

'Between Dresden and Leipzig. Hundred and fifty kilometres south of Berlin, say.'

'Brothers, sisters?'

'One sister. Listen — will you dine with me tomorrow night?'

'I'll be working until late in Oldenburg. But in any case I'm not sure — '

'We could meet at Rastede, perhaps?'

'No — thank you.' She began to laugh. 'Thanks very much, but — '

'What's wrong — or funny? They say the food's superb — huh?'

'It may be. But it's not called the Snake Pit for nothing, is it? Although to me I must say it's a new slant on snakes.' She thought *this* was funny. Laughing, shaking her head: 'Thank you again, but no.'

'Happens to be on the road between us, is why I suggested it. But if you have something against it — '

'As if in our innocence we didn't know. Simple sailorboy, uh?'

'Simply stunned, is what. You are absolutely lovely!'

'Not a complete idiot, anyway. What's *that*?'

'What?'

'That machine?'

'Oh, that. A calculator — for the aiming and firing of torpedoes. The navigating officer works it during an attack. Have you ever been to the Snake Pit?'

'Once, yes. Downstairs only. Someone told me — or hinted — what happens *upstairs*. You're not the first who's asked me, I may say. Although — well, never before on such very brief acquaintance. It's usually some time before they try it on.'

'I thought the dining-room was upstairs. Am I wrong? I've only been downstairs myself, stopped there for a drink — oh, an age ago.'

'We have restaurants in Oldenburg — in case that interests you. If all you wanted was for us to have a meal together. One place called Kramer's, for instance — if ever you should be passing through — '

'Dine with me at Kramer's tomorrow night? Would eight-thirty suit you?'

Gazing up at him. The tip of her tongue visible for a moment, as if taking a crumb from her lips. *Fascinating* lips — in memory *or* dream — shaping to ask him, 'How would you get there?'

'Why, borrow a motor. But the day after tomorrow, you see, I'm off again, so — *will* you?'

'You're very persistent, Herr Oberleutnant. But I'm not certain. I half-promised Brigitte Lukesch I'd make up a four. She and Hans will want to be on their way home at any minute now, incidentally.'

'You could ask to be excused. From tomorrow's arrangement, I mean. Tell her that since it'll be my last night in Wilhelmshaven — you're certain they'll understand — and that it might be tactful not to mention it to Franz Winter?'

'Perhaps it might be. Yes.'

' 'Yes' that you'll dine with me?'

'Would you collect me at my apartment?'

'If you'll give me the address — of course!'

'The house is owned by an elderly couple who never go out in the evenings. I just have two rooms, and live — well, cheek by jowl with them, you might say.'

'So?'

'So no Snake Pit business, is what I *think* I'm saying.'

'Still don't follow you on that. I must make enquiries, catch up on what you know and I don't. But at this Kramer's, would *you* book the table in my name? Since you know the place?'

'All right.' She nodded towards the ladder that led up into the tower. 'You were telling me what happens up there? Is it the conning-tower?'

He nodded. 'And in it, the CO's control-room. Above that, the bridge. Like to see it?'

'Well — '

'Lovely night, breath of fresh air after this fug?'

Small smile, and a second's hesitation: 'If it doesn't take too long. It *is* smoky, isn't it. Although as I said, Brigitte and — '

'We'll be quick.' They were under the hatch by this time, looking up. 'We'll go straight up into the bridge, I think. You don't have any great interest in periscopes and so forth, do you?'

'Not all that much.'

'Well, then.' Glancing round as he put a foot on the ladder and reached up, he found old Graischer's eye on him again. Or on *them*. Graischer had some medical problem, was on the Staff now. Otto nodded to him — letting him know that everything was normal, under control

— and smiled at the girl. 'Follow me?'

Through the tower, continuing up into the bridge and then crouching to more or less lift her out. The September evening was cool, already darkening but not cold. Helena gazing around, breathing deeply; the dress was close-fitting and distinctly *décolleté*.

'*Lovely* cool!'

'Why I thought to bring you up here. Helena — '

'*Oh* . . . '

'Meeting you has made this the night of my life. Truly, I swear it. Here I was just killing an evening — *thought* that was all — '

In his arms, first allowing and then returning his kiss — and more . . . Otto stooping to her, nuzzling, murmuring her name, kissing her throat, the hollow inside one shoulder, the swell of her breasts. On this side of the bridge the bulk of the periscope standards shielded them from anyone on the dockside, while from the basin's other side, across water reflecting the first stars — well, distance as well as fading light . . .

'Otto, pet, we mustn't — '

'Mustn't what?'

'Mess me up. Or — heavens, what they'll — '

'You are *exquisite*!'

And not unwilling. Making as it were a bit of a joke of it — as was natural enough in the circumstances and her innocence — well, the place, and the speed of it, her surprise — all that. *And* not wanting to be 'messed up'. Although given a few minutes, and if one had dared and *she'd* got over being scared —

21

'Otto — enough. Please. *Please?*'

Pushing at him: her elbows up between them, and twisting her head away. 'We must be sensible, now . . . '

An echo of that, a repetition of *sensible, now* . . . Dreamlike, or had become so — deliberately sought, provoked by memory — all right, self-indulgence, a dream *out of* memory. Lost in it now — in the warmth and the motors' hum — the dream losing both its own origins and his control, the focus on a different girl entirely. Taller, darker, hair not up as Helena's had been, but long and loose, she'd been naked but trying to cover herself with a négligée or nightdress, whatever. Hair so dark he remembered it as blue-black, silky blue-black, glorious . . . Pale, oval face, well-shaped nose, mouth rather wide and full for the narrowness of her face, magnificent breasts. Gasping, telling him — a long forefinger pointing — 'Otto, you are *shameless!*'

He'd got it suddenly. The *English* girl.

'Captain, sir!'

Male voice — urgent tone, loud — and a hand on his shoulder, shaking him, Claus Stahl telling him, 'Propeller noises ahead of us, sir — fast, reciprocating, more than one of them . . . '

★   ★   ★

Not easy to make out — even in high power. UB81 at eight metres, back in trim with her crew at torpedo action stations, motors at slow speed now he had the big 'scope up. Although in such a

22

disturbed sea there was no likelihood of being spotted; at this range in fact virtually none. Target fine on the bow to port, no more than five degrees off — own course being 087, which it had been since dawn — and making no more than — oh, three knots, say. UB81 must have been very slowly overhauling this lot, which consisted of — he said it aloud for the benefit of those around him, where he hung with his arms crooked over the spread handles of the periscope while making sense of the picture in its lenses — 'Large ship in tow of a small one — tug, most likely. Two destroyer escorts — one to starboard, other's ahead at times and out of my sight, otherwise out to port. Yep, one on each bow. Enemy course is within a degree or two of ours. Set it as 085 degrees.' This instruction was for Hofbauer at his plotting diagram and calculator. Continuing, 'Masthead height, say, thirty-five metres. Vertical angle is — *that*.'

The signalman, Wassmann, read figures off the little window displaying that angle, and after a few seconds Hofbauer interpreted it as: 'Range two thousand metres, sir.' Otto told him — circling, searching — 'Start your plot. Set enemy speed three knots . . . Down periscope.' Addressing that to the mechanician, Boese. To Stahl and others then, 'Fifteen metres. Full ahead both motors. Steer 090 degrees.'

All of it happening then, and all logged by Beyer, ginger-headed wardroom messman, diminutive on his stool beside the helmsman, mouth twisted in concentration as he scribbled. Such a grimace, it could have been

23

pain. Helmsman Riesterer, who was also the gunlayer, reporting, 'Course 090, sir.' For'ard hydroplanes with ten degrees of 'dive' on them; the coxswain, CPO Honeck, who apart from having short legs was built like a prize-fighter, had used his after 'planes to put angle on her but had them levelled now. Depthgauge needle circling as speeding propellers drove her deeper. In the motor-room, LTOs (electrical ratings) Schacht-schneider and Freimann would be watching gauges — volts, amps and revs — in the hot stink that electrics conjured up; while up for'ard in the tube space, Leading Seaman Bausch muttered, 'Thought we was ordered not to attack the swine?', and Stroebel, torpedo CPO, told him, 'Maybe won't, lad. Depends what we got there, don't it. Only merchantmen we was to leave alone — right?'

The question was in other minds as well, including Stahl's and Hofbauer's, Hofbauer having on the skipper's instruction got out the German-language edition of *Jane's Fighting Ships 1914* and opened it at the Royal Navy section; Otto telling him, 'Depot ship of some kind. Single funnel, I think. Can't be sure from this angle, but — *think* so.' Hearing Stahl's report of 'Depth fifteen metres, sir'; Hofbauer pushing the book's pages over hurriedly. 'Depot ships. Here, sir.' Depot ships could be motherships either for submarine or destroyer flotillas, those for destroyers being listed as 'Torpedo Depot Ships' for some reason. Pointing at the photos, with the skipper at his elbow:

'Here's some single funnels, if — '

'Neither of those. Nor these.' With a brush of fingers he'd dismissed *Tyne, Woolwich, Adamant, Maidstone* and *Electo*. Shake of the head: 'Bigger than them.'

'Here, maybe. Torpedo Depot Ship *St George*. Near eight thousand tons, length three hundred feet — hundred metres. No picture of her, though.' Thinking, *Could be any old steamer up there, skipper calling her a depot ship because he's been told to leave merchantmen alone, here's a sitting duck and he wants to build up his score. Don't blame him either, really . . .* Skipper peering at the book more closely now: 'What's *this*?'

In the dim lighting Hofbauer read her name as *Hecla*. And in smaller print, 'Six thousand six hundred tons, length three-ninety feet, sir.'

'Thirty metres. That's her. Does it give her draught?'

'Mean draught, twenty-three feet.'

'Torpedo settings five metres, then.' Beyer passed this over the telephone to the tube space, while also recording it in the log. Otto meanwhile checking the time — however many minutes he was giving it before going up for another look, by then obviously from much closer range.

Touch wood, it would be. Unless in this interval the little convoy had turned away. Its present course would take it past the Eddystone lighthouse and eventually to Start Point; and from Start Point — well, on a little north of east to — maybe Portsmouth, their destination?

25

Telling them mentally as he checked the time again, *Won't get as far as the Eddystone, boys, let alone your bloody Portsmouth.*

'Gasse — what now?'

'Sir.' The leading telegraphist, currently hydrophone operator, pulled one 'phone of the headset off that ear — although he'd have known what his skipper was asking — told him, 'One of 'em's gone out to starboard. Bearing now — 108. Revs for maybe ten, twelve knots . . . Oh — moving back again — 106 — 105 — '

'All right.' Destroyer doing a little sweep, he thought. Bored stiff with that snail-like progress — and hoping *his* hydrophones might pick something up. Otto asked Gasse — giving him a moment to move the earphone off — 'Hearing all three now?'

'Closer 'n they was, sir. Confused like, but — '

'All right.' 'All three' meaning two destroyers and one towing ship, say, but it probably was a tug. Not that it mattered. All that did was getting into position to attack, then wasting no time in doing so. He had a comfortable feeling, meanwhile, that once he got up there with the range and firing angle right he couldn't really miss, with a target so slow-moving and unmanoeuvrable.

As long as the fish ran straight. They usually did, nowadays. Earlier on there'd been a lot of duds. Like the British mines you could just about have played football with. Unfortunately *they'd* improved a great deal in the past year or two.

He looked from his watch to Claus Stahl.

26

'Ten metres. Half ahead both.'

Reducing revs in order to come up quietly, but also because high speed had been taking a lot out of the battery and he'd need power in reserve if after he'd sunk the target the destroyers gave him problems. Which you could bet they would. He'd reduce again from half to slow speed before he put the stick up. Asking Gasse, 'Bearing now, and a guess at the range?'

'Red two-oh to red two-five, sir. Range — I'd guess six to eight hundred metres. More than five hundred and less than a thousand, say.'

So he'd need another period of high speed on the motors before he'd be in anything like certain hitting range. Poor old battery. You wouldn't want a *third* expenditure of amps at that rate. Give up the bloody ghost, like as not. Best of reasons to make as sure as possible of coming up in the right place *next* time.

'Ten metres, sir.'

'Make it eight. And slow both.'

He made certain that Stahl had the trim under control at eight metres, before nodding to Boese and gesturing for the periscope. Familiar thump then hiss as the glistening, yellowish tube slid up; he grabbed its handles, jerking them out and down. Eyes at the lenses then: daylight was strong, the sea a brighter greenish-blue, and —

There. Twenty-plus degrees on the bow, a starboard-quarter view of a destroyer making heavy weather of it, scooping the stuff up and sending it flying back like snow. Leaving that, training left, stopping on the target, which (a) *was* the ship he'd found in *Jane's*, (b) was down by the bows — had rammed something or hit a mine, stopped a torpedo. Her forepart or some of it had to be flooded, her screws probably too high in the water to be useable — in present conditions anyway. Even right *out* of water, in that great pile of foam.

Aim to hit her abaft the foremast, second one no further aft than her bridge. With depth-settings as ordered, five metres. And keep to the big periscope. With the sea as lively as it is, he thought, *safe as houses* . . .

It *was* a tug, lugging her along. But as before, the second destroyer wasn't in sight at this moment. Up ahead somewhere: fine on the bow, he guessed, at about 1,000 metres, probably. Target range still too great, anyway, and the angle wasn't acceptable. Ideally you wanted your torpedoes to approach on a ninety-degree track, which meant firing from anything between say forty and seventy on her bow: and to overhaul her by that much meant a return to — well, say, twelve metres this time, for another longish spell of full power.

Nothing else for it. Sink the swine, *then* worry about evasion. He was about to snap the handles up and step back, telling Stahl to take her down, when he got his first indication of an impending alteration of course: a flag-hoist dropping from the target's mainmast yardarm, and the destroyer on this side cracking on speed. Must have increased a minute or two ago, although the flag signal would still have been flying: it was already far enough ahead soon to be crossing the target's bows.

Target about to alter to port therefore, he guessed. Training the 'scope left a bit now — and the other escort was in sight, pushing out northward . . .

He grunted, told Stahl and/or Hofbauer, 'May be in luck. They're going round to port.'

He'd guessed right: the depot ship was stern-on to him now. Still under helm, making a slow, wide turn, tug dragging her round, the cripple's raised stern acting like a sail with the northwester pretty well on her beam at this stage. Starboard-side escort somewhere out of sight, beyond her, and the other — he shifted the periscope back to the left — *there*. Steering something like northeast or north by east.

'Course of northeast, where'd it take 'em?'

Glancing towards Hofbauer, who came back promptly enough with, 'Steering to pass west of Eddystone, probably on course for Plymouth, sir.'

Confirming what had been his own guess *without* looking at the chart. He nodded. 'Down. Twelve metres, full ahead both. Steer 060.'

Would check that on the plotting diagram and adjust if necessary, but it had to be *about* right. Target and escorts on 045, UB81 cutting the corner. Own speed five-and-a-half-knots, target speed three — or maybe less now, with the weather on her beam — rate of overhauling therefore three knots or a little less.

'Both motors full ahead, sir, depth twelve metres, course 060.'

Whine of the motors speeding, boat angling downward. He'd been lucky to have had the periscope on them at just that moment, to have seen that change of course. At the plotting diagram now, juggling figures — bearings, distances, speeds, firing angles — in his head. Hofbauer suggesting, 'Should we give it sixteen minutes, sir?' He had his stopwatch running. Otto told him, 'Twelve.' And over his shoulder, 'Bring her to 065.' A better course on which to intercept — cutting the high-speed period to a minimum, for the battery's sake — and he'd run in and fire torpedoes from abaft the target's beam, to hit him on as much as a one-twenty track. At close enough range you'd hit all right, saving several minutes of full battery power and then starting your withdrawal about half a sea-mile further from where the destroyers were likely to be at the time of firing than you would be if you held on for a ninety-degree shot. Getting in as close as 350 or even 300 meters would compensate for the obtuse firing angle.

Waiting while the minutes crawled. Motors at full ahead, swallowing amps by the bucketful.

Close on ten minutes gone. Thinking, as a way of making himself relax, *Back with you in just a few days, my little darling* . . .

Kramer's had been great, an exciting evening, and at the end of it, when they'd been kissing goodbye and taking their time about it, she'd agreed breathlessly, 'All right, next time, Otto' — sending his spirits soaring. It was the Snake Pit she'd been agreeing to — although as things were then, or as he'd thought they were, there was no telling whether 'next time' would be in two months or three or — hell, *six*, since at the end of this patrol and the one after — *this* one — he'd expected to return to the base at Bruges, not Wilhelmshaven. Driving himself back from Oldenburg in the motor he'd borrowed from old Graischer, he'd warned himself, *If there does happen to be a next time . . .*

Would be now. In only four or five days, at that. Any fool can stay alive four or five bloody days!

Touch wood . . .

'Twelve minutes gone, sir.'

Hofbauer. Otto pushed himself off the panel of blows and vent levers where he'd been leaning, told them, 'Both motors half speed. Bring her to ten metres.' Then when she was in trim at ten — another minute gone — '*Slow* both motors.' And to Stahl, 'Bring her to eight.' Relief at the slowing down smoothing out some of the furrows in Stahl's dark-stubbled face as he acknowledged, 'Eight metres.' Otto glancing at Boese and lifting his hands — for the thump, then the long hiss, seconds later the light of day like an explosion in his eyes.

Sort *this* out now . . .

New bearings and ranges. 'I am — ninety-five degrees on his bow. Target's course 045, speed three knots. Starboard fifteen, steer one hundred degrees. Stand by both tubes.' He stepped back: 'Down periscope.'

At the chart table then, scanning Hofbauer's plot, Hofbauer setting figures on the calculator and muttering, 'Director angle at three hundred metres — fourteen degrees, sir.'

He nodded, moving back to the centre. 'Up.'

31

Grabbing the 'scope and making one fast preliminary circuit, checking all round. No change, no problem. Setting the 'scope therefore on green fourteen — there was a bearing-ring on the deckhead where the periscope pierced it, the starboard half of it green, port-side bearings red. When the target's bow crossed the hairline in the lenses he'd have a fourteen-degree aim-off and *could* send away the first torpedo, although his point of aim for the first one would be under the foremast, second under the leading edge of the bridge. The 'scope was set and he had his eyes at the lenses, waiting, seconds ticking by and range closing all the time: he'd told Beyer — the telephone link to the torpedo room and tube space — 'Stand by tubes', and the answer from Stroebel came back instantly as 'Tubes ready, sir.'

Target's sea-swamped bow crossing the hairline *now*. The length of the *Hecla*'s pitching, half-drowned foc'sl-head was the distance to the foremast-step. Slow intake of breath and — 'Number one tube, fire!'

You felt it, heard it, felt a rise of pressure in your ears from air venting back. Gulping to clear it, then, 'Number two — fire!'

Gasse reported a second later, 'Both torpedoes running, sir.'

'Down. Thirty metres. Starboard fifteen, steer 180.'

All of *that* happening — UB81 corkscrewing downward and the torpedoes running, in echelon and five metres below the waves. *Run straight, please* ... Gasse was removing the

32

headphones, to avoid having his eardrums damaged. As they might be before much longer anyway; depthcharges tended to be more damaging, if they were close enough, and the English *had* become rather better at it in the course of the past year or so. Hofbauer was frowning at the stopwatch, Otto seemingly studying *him*. UB81 angling down, depthgauge needle circling past the fifteen-metre mark, and the motors quiet, conserving amps. Up top, that old depot ship's crew still doing whatever they'd been doing before — eating, sleeping, playing cards or —

Explosion. *One* hit: the sound of it distinctive enough to be clearly recognisable. Faces lighting up, mouths opening to whoop or cheer, Stahl and CPO Honeck snarling for silence. Then — same again, second hit. Unquestionably a kill — and no stopping them now: all through the boat men were cheering, hitting each other on the back, laughing. What they were here for, and they'd done it — *again*. Well — their skipper had, but he couldn't have managed it on his own. UB81 had done it. Still on her way down — passing twenty-four metres, and with thirty degrees to go to get herself on the ordered course, due south. Chief Hintenberger was applauding clownishly from the entrance to his engine-room, ostentatiously clapping his hands above his head — big hands, arms as skinny and hairy as spiders' legs — while Claus Stahl turned briefly to offer congratulations to his skipper. Hofbauer the same. There was a smile even on Boese's long, usually gloomy face; Wassmann was beaming and chuckling; Gasse was putting his headset back on — knowing that a lot was going to depend on him and his hydrophone in the course of the next half-hour, hours, rest of the day, maybe through the night as well. You hoped for the best, prepared yourselves for the worst — at least for a bollocking. Otto telling Beyer at the telephone, 'My congratulations to Chief Stroebel.' The torpedo chief, whose fish *had* run straight. Otto heard that message passed, then called for silence: 'Pass the word for'ard and aft — settle down, sit, lie — no-one even fart, let alone drop a spanner.'

The big hope, as always, to sneak away, not to be detected at all, have no hunt even start. It was a possibility, *had* been known, although recently had become more rare. Stahl, glancing round to confirm that the boat was now at thirty metres and catching his skipper with closed eyes just at that moment, wondered as he turned back to watch and adjust the trim, *Long blink or quick prayer?*

2

Gasse, with his eyes shut, informed his skipper, 'Breaking up noises astern, sir. Tug's stopped engines.' Eyes open, on the dial: 'One destroyer on green 180 — moving right to left. Other's on red 165 — same. Both cut revs now.'

Searching, listening on *their* hydrophones. The tug would be picking up survivors — or looking for them. Breaking up noises — from the ship they'd torpedoed — bulkheads collapsing as she sank, gear smashing loose and so forth. In something like thirty fathoms, wouldn't be long before she was in the sand. While the destroyers — well, the one that had been on the target's port bow would have reversed course and cracked-on speed southward or southwestward, the sector from which torpedoes must have been fired and in which the submarine might still be. Having attacked from that quarter they'd guess you'd have turned back towards open water, deeper water — meaning any direction between southeast and southwest. And the other skipper would have figured it out in much the same way but would probably stay out of his colleague's way — colleague having got there first — and search to the east or southeast, where for all any of them knew he might strike lucky.

As soon as one of them detected you, of course, that would all change; they'd join up, work in tandem.

Might *not* detect you. Otto crossing fingers, thinking it might be possible to remain unheard until dark. Eight hours, say. With very good luck, it might. Another imponderable was that one didn't know how far this lot had come, how long the destroyers might already have been at sea, how soon they might need re-fuelling. But Plymouth being so close, if they needed to they could go in one at a time, or wait for others to be sent out to take over the hunt from them. Proximity to a major naval base being a considerable advantage to them; another was that since the Americans had joined in, their anti-submarine forces weren't stretched as thinly as they had been.

That was the picture, in rough outline. UB81 paddling south on only one motor now, starboard motor at dead slow — (a) to stay as near mouse-quiet as possible, (b) to take as little as possible out of the battery from now on — battery having been well and truly caned already.

Have Freimann take density reading some time. Not yet. Better to guess the worst than *know* it, when there wasn't a damn thing you could do about it anyway.

Gasse murmured quietly over the motor's purr, 'Second destroyer's crossed astern of us. On green 175 now, still moving left. No more'n a hundred revs.'

Five, six knots maybe. Prime listening-out-on-hydrophones speed, maybe. And moving right to left suggested a course roughly parallel to the other's. Otto visualising the scene up there: one of them say 1,000 metres away, the other maybe 1,500 or 2,000. If they *were* both concentrating on that southwestern sector — well, go right ahead, boys . . .

Not that you could count on it. On *anything*. Thinking about it, though: on the control-room deck with his back against the end of the chart table, arms folded on raised knees, looking patient, even slightly bored. He raised his head, said quietly, 'Port five, Riesterer.'

'Port five, sir.' Putting five degrees of rudder on her; Beyer recording the order and the time of it in his log, and Riesterer glancing Otto's way: 'Five of port wheel on, sir.'

'Steer 135.'

'One-three-five, sir.'

Southeast. Leaving the destroyers to hunt southwestward. On the new course he'd have his stern to them. He'd ordered this gentle turn — normally you'd use ten or fifteen degrees of wheel — in order to make only minimal disturbance, minimal movement of the rudder in its pintles, iron on iron.

'Course 135, sir.'

Bye-bye, Englanders . . .

Gasse cleared his throat: it was all he had to do to win everyone's attention. 'Nearer destroyer's altered to port, sir. Bearing red 150.'

As he'd recognised a minute ago; at this stage it made no odds to them which way they went. It only just *seemed* now that that one was following them around. Small shake of the head, thinking about this. Bastard might have decided that holding on in that direction was taking him too

37

close to his chum. Or had been told to clear off, search down this way. At thirty metres you didn't see winking signal lamps.

Any case, no immediate problem. Stay as we are, as we're going, let *him* think again.

'Gasse . . . '

The telegraphist held one earphone off, gazed across at him enquiringly. Otto asked him, 'Bearing now, the nearer one?'

A nod — meaning he'd check. Gasse was pale, with light-coloured eyes which when he was drunk were said to turn pink like an Angora rabbit's. Did look a bit rabbitty anyway. Good man for all that, knew his job, both as a telegraphist and hydrophone operator. Fiddling with the knob that turned a pointer in the dial in front of him, also trained the receiver in its housing on the after casing. Looking up from it now: 'Bearing's steady, sir.'

'Distance, at a guess?'

'Got louder. Closing still. Still about a hundred rpm, so — '

'Closing fast then.' Staring at Gasse, thinking critically, *Wouldn't have known if I hadn't asked, would I . . .* 'Bearing *what*, Gasse?'

More knob-twisting . . .

'Right astern of us, sir.'

'*Is* it.' Right astern and steering UB81's own course — so it must have altered again, which was a bit damn much of a coincidence. Unless — Otto's eyes on the deckhead as he thought this — *unless we're towing something or leaking oil or blowing bloody bubbles . . .*

Impossible. Depthcharges caused oil leaks on

38

occasion; and some of those a few days ago *had* been damn close, but —

Forget it. What's real is his bloody hydrophone.

He told Claus Stahl, 'Stop the starboard motor.'

'Stop starboard . . . '

Stahl had whispered it and Wassmann had passed the order aft. You didn't use the telegraphs, which were noisy, in circumstances like these. Stahl's upward glance showed that it was as clear to him as it was to Otto that within a minute or so the destroyer would be passing overhead. While stopping the one motor you'd had running meant there'd be no motive-power now, she'd hang pretty well as she was as long as she still had way on, then either rise or sink as she lost it — rising or sinking according to whether he, Stahl, had her trimmed slightly light or slightly heavy.

Gamble, really. There'd be nothing for the English to hear — that was the great thing. If the trim did hold her reasonably well, at least for the next few minutes, there was no reason they shouldn't pass over and carry on . . . If it didn't — if the trim was wonky and you had to restart a motor to hold her —

Avoid that. At all costs, avoid that.

'Starboard motor stopped, sir.'

Not even a hum now. In the silence you could hear — distinctly, getting more so all the time — the regular thrashing of the destroyer's screws. *All* hearing it. Glancing at each other, and at him. He — Otto — shrugging, pointing

39

upward and astern, hand movements then explaining his intentions — enemy passing over the top and continuing, thrashing on while 81 turned away to port, sneaked off *that* way. Some of them were catching on too, nodding as if they were buying it, at any rate only a few of them looking as if they might be seeing the snags, such as the fact that without motive-power the boat couldn't — wouldn't — (a) hang motionless for long, (b) alter course and depart eastward without going ahead again on at least one motor. 'At least', because if she lost trim now to any large extent she might need more power, not less, to return her to the depth she'd left; and as likely as not need to run a pump to shift internal ballast between trimming and/or compensating tanks. Pumps were noisy things — as Otto was of course keenly aware and had taken into account before deciding on this move; a subsidiary decision being to play it off the cuff, see how it went, and react suitably.

Stahl telling him now, 'We're a touch heavy, sir.'

She was at thirty-one metres, the gauge showed, and bow-down, heavy for'ard therefore. Thirty-one-and-a-half. Thirty-two . . . Otto looking upward as the destroyer's propeller noise still grew from astern, urging it, *Come on, come on . . .* Wanting it to pass on over and distance its bloody self. He was actually desperate for this, while showing only a modest degree of impatience. The boat now at thirty-three metres with something like a five-degree bow-down angle on her, and the destroyer's screws beating

40

drum-like but still not overhead, still bloody *coming* . . . Gasse making a show of counting the revs, and the coxswain glaring round at him — CPO Honeck as after 'planesman being impotent now, as was Klein on the for'ard ones, since without any way on, hydroplanes couldn't function.

Depthgauge showing thirty-five-and-a-half metres: angle still increasing. The depth did not pose any immediate danger in itself; these UBIIs were tested to fifty metres, and most, including this one, had been deeper than that when being hunted and driven deep by depthcharging — which admittedly was not the most pleasant of experiences.

Screws thrashing over *now*.

'Beyer.' Otto spoke with his eyes on the deckhead, as if he was watching that narrow, slicing hull and the pounding screws. 'Tell CPO Stroebel I want him to send Bausch and Socol on their bare feet to the after ends.'

'Aye, sir . . .'

Those two torpedomen weren't needed up for'ard now. All they might be wanted for at some later stage could easily be accomplished by Stroebel himself and the man Otto was letting him keep — Wernegger, who was a skinny little fellow — whereas the other two were on the heavy side; shifting their weight from right for'ard to right aft would have a positive effect on trim. He'd stipulated bare feet to drive home to them the need for total silence.

Beyer had passed the order. Otto called softly, 'Engineer Officer . . .'

'Sir?'

Hintenberger — instant appearance in the watertight doorway, currently latched open, between the control-room and the crew's accommodation spaces. Engine-room was abaft that, then came the motor-room and the after ends. At action stations as they were now, all that after part of the boat was the engineer's domain. Odd-looking creature that he was — monkey-sized, black-bearded, eyes like black holes in a face carved out of bone. Otto told him, 'Two torpedomen on their way aft, for purposes of trimming. Let 'em through quick and quiet, see how it goes and if necessary send some of *your* men aft.'

'Aye aye, sir.' She had something like a fifteen-degree angle on her now — which was a lot, and felt like it too — and the depthgauge was showing forty metres. Bausch and Socol arrived bare-footed from the fore ends, Hintenberger backing out of their way, beckoning them through. Otto told the signalman, 'Wassmann, we can spare you too.'

Propeller noise thrashing away southward was still audible but fading rapidly, leaving an impression — expressions of relief here and there — that the worst was over. As it might be — or might not. There was good news in any case in the coxswain's growl of 'Bubble's moving back, sir.' He'd addressed this to Stahl, who looked round to see that the skipper had heard it too. It meant the angle was beginning to come off her — effect of the shift of human ballast. It had been twelve degrees when the coxswain had spoken, was now ten. Stahl observed quietly to Otto, 'Trouble could've been the compensating gear again, sir. If you remember, we did wonder — '

A nod. 'Look into it when we get back.'

When, not *if* . . . But when you fired a torpedo, a system of automatically opening and closing valves admitted sea water to what was called the torpedo intermediate tank, to compensate for the loss of the torpedo's weight. They'd guessed it might have been out of order a few days ago when they'd sunk a Dutch collier off Castletown Berehaven in southwest Ireland. It and two smaller colliers had had an escort of American destroyers, who'd been on to 81 like a pack of hounds, several patterns of depthcharges coming uncomfortably close at one stage. There'd been no lying doggo as on this occasion, but the trim had needed a lot of adjustment afterwards.

Propeller noise fainter now. You could almost forget that fellow — for the moment. Could *not* live with a continuing bow-down angle of six degrees, however, nor the depth of forty-six metres. Would probably be safe enough using the motors now, from the audial point of view, but if you went ahead while there was still this angle on her you'd drive her deeper.

Otto — on his feet — told Stahl, 'Better pump some out of A.'

'Aye, sir.' Reaching up to the electric order-instrument on the curve of deckhead above and between the 'planesmen, telegraphing to stokers in their respective machinery spaces to

43

(a) open trimtank 'A's suction and inboard vent, then (b), pump from for'ard.

'Pumping on 'A', sir.'

You could hear it. He thought it was unlikely that either of the listening destroyers could. Depthgauge now showing fifty metres, but the angle *was* coming off her. Would have been disturbing if it hadn't. Pumping water out of that for'ard trimtank would be lightening her bodily as well.

'Bubble's amidships, sir.'

So you could move now. He said quietly, 'Slow ahead starboard.'

'Slow ahead starboard. Starboard motor slow ahead, sir. Bubble is one degree for'ard.'

'Thirty metres. Hands who went aft, return to their stations.'

'Bubble's degree-and-a-half for'ard, sir. Depth forty-seven metres.'

'All right. Stop the pump, shut off 'A'.'

Done it. Creep away southeastward now . . .

'Captain, sir?'

Gasse. Otto told him, 'Wait', and asked Riesterer, 'Ship's head now?'

'One nine five, sir. I've starboard wheel on.'

'Port your wheel, steer 160.' He looked at Gasse then, who burst out with, 'On green one hundred, sir, closing! Loud as — '

'Damn.' A whisper. Other murmurs too, and hard looks at Gasse, who should have been watching both of them — listening all round — and could not have been. Otto blaming himself for not having *asked* him 'Where's the other?' Re-assessing now: rising through forty

44

metres, starboard motor slow ahead, under port helm, ship's head passing through south towards SSE. Rising quite fast — *might* be a touch light now — and this swine somewhere on the quarter, close and getting closer.

Hearing them? Heard the pump running and the start-up of the motor maybe, started the run-in *then*?

To Gasse: 'Where now?'

'Green 120, sir. Closing. Down to one hundred revs.'

In touch, therefore, straining its damned ears. 'And the other?'

'Faded south, sir.' Checking that: and an alarmed look suddenly. 'Moving right to left now, sir. Revs increasing. Two hundred, could be . . .'

On the turn and hurrying to join the fun, not bothering for the moment about listening out. This other one having signalled him to come and help. He'll run over and drop charges, with number two by that time ready to take his turn.

Turn and turn about.

You could hear the one that was attacking now. About that same speed — six knots, maybe. *Thrash, thrash, thrash . . .*

'Course 160, sir.'

And depth thirty-four metres; slight bow-up angle. Thinking, *Going to have to splurge more bloody ampères. With the battery very low already and as they say in the song, a long, long way from home. This is the time to do it, though — get out from under before they cripple us; any later'd be too late.* He was in the centre now,

45

against the ladder with his arms up on it as high as they'd reach, leaning against the slant of it, hearing Gasse say thinly, 'Coming up astern like the other did, sir. That other one's — '

'Never mind him for the moment.' Anyone who wasn't stone deaf could hear this one closing in: and it was *not* like last time — for the simple and unwelcome reason that this one had a bead on them. Glancing to his right as Stahl cleared his throat, muttered, 'Depth thirty metres, sir'; he told them all, 'Depthcharges coming shortly. They've no way of telling what depth we're keeping, remember. Soon as they've stirred the muck up we'll see if we can't dodge away in it.'

Hardly original: in fact a standard tactic. But nods of acceptance, confidence, and the coxswain growling, 'Gotter let 'em 'ave their fun, sir . . .'

Coming over *now*: a rushing, roaring sound like the passage of a train surrounding the propellers' beat. You tended to look up, at the curve of white-enamelled deckhead, as if seeing as well as hearing. Reminding oneself that the English up there in the daylight and fresh salt air not only didn't know at what depth to set their charges to explode, but couldn't know the precise moment that they were overhead or for how many seconds then to run on, on what they reckoned to be the U-boat's track, before sending the barrel-shaped charges rolling out of the racks on their ship's stern and others lobbing out from the throwers. The noise of it passing over was like sandpaper scouring the brain:

46

charges would be on their way down now. Hofbauer leaning over the chart making pencil doodles on its margin, Otto with his hands in his pockets, his back against the ladder, expression once again showing nothing much more than impatience — to have this over, be in a position to make *his* move.

First explosion — ahead and to port. The crash of it like a roof falling in, metallic echo bouncing off the hull: they'd set it too shallow — from *their* point of view. Might also have misjudged, passing not quite directly over the top. Two more now, one right on the other's heels and both to port, one closer than the other, shaking her. There'd be two more coming — off the thing's stern, one in the centre of the pattern and the last of them completing the diamond shape. One — rather close, but wrong depth again. Otherwise — he checked that thought. No point in that kind of speculation — but also a mistake to relax too soon, even though it was a fact you'd had them a lot closer. Even those just the other day, when they'd sunk the collier. Another due now, though . . .

Hell, why wait for it?

'Full ahead both motors, hard a-port!'

In order to use the very considerable sub-surface disturbance from all that, the stirred-up ocean and — last of them now, ahead somewhere, last of the pattern of five. He told Riesterer, 'Steer north.'

'North, sir . . . '

Passing through east — turning fast, under the burst of power. Otto pushing himself off the

47

ladder, hands still in pockets, amending it to 'Stop port, slow starboard.' Which wouldn't slow the rate of turn by much, and should as it were clear the hydrophone's ears for it. Glancing questioningly at Gasse — who was adjusting his headset, having removed it during that explosive period. One hand back to the knob on the 'phone control, fiddling the pointer in the dial a little this way and that, round eyes blinking as he listened.

Might have worked. Just *might* . . .

Gasse had shaken his head. Getting nothing. Maybe they'd be getting nothing on theirs, either.

Stay like this anyway. They don't know which way I've turned.

'Course north, sir.'

Stahl whispered, 'Could've lost 'em, sir.'

A shrug: it was the hope, but too soon to think it — even though he himself just had — certainly much too soon to express it.

What one *could* say — murmur — was, 'She's light, isn't she?'

'She is, sir.' Coxswain, nodding. He had a small angle of 'rise' on his after 'planes, lifting the stern to hold her at one degree bow-down, countering the effect of that lightness. Which was all right. This was no time for tinkering with the trim.

Gasse had grunted, moved suddenly, reacting to — surprise, shock? Right hand jerking to that earphone, left hand's fingers on the training-knob.

'Well?'

'One's bearing green 170, other's' — pausing, shifting it some more, and back again — 'green nine-five. Both closing. Ah — one astern's also closing — bearing steady, and — other's right to left, cutting revs now . . .'

Dismay: the sound and look of it. Otto sighed, said, 'We're lucky there aren't *three* of them', and won some grins. Mind at work, though: telling Riesterer, 'Starboard fifteen, steer 120.'

'One-twenty. Fifteen of starboard wheel on, sir.'

Putting on helm gave her a tendency to rise and Klein was meeting that with dive-angle on the fore 'planes. Otto with the picture in his mind of one destroyer about to make a new attack from astern — present distance-off uncertain, but closing anyway — and the other coming in on roughly a ninety-degree track from starboard. Otto's aim being to turn short of that one, anticipating that the one astern would have to put on a similar amount of starboard wheel if he was going to stay with them and in a position to attack, but in doing so might well find himself in danger of ramming his colleague. Who'd presumably turn away. At least confusing the issue: and might not be in a position to pick you up on his hydrophones after the first had dropped charges, and *that* one might at least not be able to use his throwers.

Glancing at Gasse, as ship's head passed through northeast. Gasse looking strained, telling him, 'One from starboard's crossed ahead, turning away — on red three-five

. . . Other's on — green 110. Closing — green 120 now — '

'How close?'

'One on the quarter — *very* close. *Loud* — '

'Here we go again, then.'

And audible to them all by this time. UB81 continuing her turn to starboard and the Englishman coming in — over — on that quarter. Under helm, obviously; give it half a minute or less he'd be over you and dumping more explosive. *Not* so clever, Otto me lad . . . Riesterer easing his wheel as she approached the ordered course: whereas the destroyer had to be under a *lot* of wheel.

'Forty metres.'

'Forty metres, sir . . . '

Because that last lot had been set shallow and hadn't brought results, so they'd put a deeper setting on this batch, but probably not as deep as forty. Might guess they'd have set thirty — the depth one *had* been at. They of course measured depths in feet, not metres, so they'd be calling it ninety — between ninety and a hundred, say.

Propeller noise building: and the boat at thirty-five metres, nosing down, fore 'planes at hard a-dive. Could have driven her down faster by putting both motors half ahead, say, instead of only one at slow ahead, but you had to think of the battery and more high jinks of this kind, then more hours submerged before — touch wood — surfacing in the dark and —

Nice to envisage, but no time for it here and now. Enemy thrashing over, and Riesterer reporting matter-of-factly, 'Course 120, sir.'

Depth thirty-eight metres, and still bow-down.

Otto said, 'Hard a-starboard. Full ahead port.'

To get out from under before the bloody things got down this deep. The destroyer having come over in a curve, charges from her throwers might well be flung out farther to port than if she'd been steering a straight course: so a jink to starboard might be as good a bet as any. It *was* mostly a matter of placing bets, though. You used what skills you had, and beyond that could only tighten your gut, set your jaw, tell yourself it couldn't be worse than drowning in Flanders mud under heavy shellfire.

Less bad, in fact. Over sooner, and —

She'd convulsed. Like having driven into explosive rock. And more of it: the closest ever. Men had been sent flying, lights had failed, gyro alarm shrieking, trim gone to hell and two more bursting close — Christ Jesus, could have been right *in* the bridge. Stahl was back on his feet with a flashlight on the depthgauge showing forty-eight metres — bow-down, going down so fast she could have been heading for the bottom: like so much cement, except cement didn't crush, not like a tin tube could. He'd stopped both motors and put them half stern, emergency lights were glowing weakly, men were picking themselves up, coming to their senses. He — Otto — had got to the gyro controls and pulled its fuse, telling Stahl and Riesterer, 'Steer by magnetic.' Steer *where*, and what bloody difference could it make, might have been the question. She was still diving, all that the screws working astern were doing was shaking her, her downward momentum too much for them to check. Stahl shouting, 'Fifty-six metres, sir!'

'Blow diving tanks eight and ten!'

Boese was seeing to it: checking vents shut and kingstons open before opening the blows. Blowing those two forward main ballast tanks rather than just the bow tank because it was imperative to stop her dive, and if you blew only number ten and it wasn't enough to stop her quickly you might not have time to think again before it really was too late. And he preferred to spread the effort over eight and ten main ballast rather than nine and ten, not to put *all* the new buoyancy in her snout, although he'd just heard some panicky report of water forcing entry up for'ard somewhere, and she was getting near sixty metres, well below test depth; from here on down there was a real danger she'd implode. That old nightmare: and if there was damage for'ard, *why* hadn't — well, that question was answered now. Hofbauer, whom he'd sent for'ard to investigate, reporting that water was spurting in at high velocity via the fore 'planes' hull-glands, which were accessed from the torpedo-stowage compartment. Boese had got a pump running on that bilge, and Hintenberger and Mechanician Haverkamp had gone for'ard, more or less sliding downhill to get there.

Boese now reporting, 'Blowing eight and ten, sir.'

Already taking effect too. Needle in the gauge still close to sixty but seemingly hesitating there. Beginning to edge back. Angle coming off her, bubble sliding towards the centre.

'Stop both motors.'

'Stop both, sir . . . And — stop blowing?' Stahl worrying about his trim, adding, 'She *was* light — so if it was only the charges that sent her down — '

'Stop blowing eight and ten.'

Boese seeing to that, Stahl requesting permission to vent the tanks outboard — which would send up huge air bubbles. Couldn't vent them inboard, though — not tanks of that size, into the boat's atmosphere. Boat meanwhile at forty-five metres, rising fast and now with a steepish up-angle growing on her: Stahl had been right — employing drastic corrective measures could send you from one kind of emergency to another very suddenly.

New one coming now — unconnected, but both Stahl and Otto saw it coming a second before Klein gasped, 'Fore 'planes jammed, sir — '

'Fore 'planes in hand!'

To put them into hand control you had to by-pass the telemotor system at this end, and ship heavy steel bars up for'ard where they were already working on the leaking glands. Torpedo-men would jump to that now; and once the bars were rigged and in hand, orders in regard to putting on so many degrees of 'dive' or 'rise' would be passed verbally by men stationed between here and there. Boese flat on his face opening the by-pass, having first to remove a screwed-down deck-plate to get at it. He'd shut the blows to eight and ten main ballast, but the tanks still being full or half-full of air she was fairly rocketing up: thirty metres, twenty-five, coxswain struggling with the after 'planes which weren't as yet making any impression on the angle or rate of ascent. As the only way of checking it, Otto had told Stahl yes, vent eight and ten main ballast outboard. All these things had been happening in the last fifteen or twenty seconds, in conditions amounting to pandemonium, and since Boese was still on his knees, Hofbauer had jumped to the panel of vent levers, opened number ten then shifted to eight, jerking the short steel levers over, but with only limited result, no clang of eight's starboard vent dropping open as it should have done. It was an external tank, had vents in its top on both sides; it would vent completely through the one that *had* opened, but not as instantly as it should have done.

Twenty metres. Ten, nine, eight. *Surfacing*, for Christ's sake. Periscope standards showing above the waves by now. Five metres, four. The bridge would be exposed and streaming, the gun emerging, fore-casing awash. Rolling — feeling the sea now, and more than that too — what he'd been expecting and was half-ready for, ringing crash and impact of an explosion overhead as the first shell hit the standards or the bridge. Next one would hole the pressure-hull — if they knew what they were doing. No time to think about it, this was *it*, come-uppance, another ten seconds you'd be finished and bloody *deserve* to be. Air all gone from both tanks though, all main ballast full: he'd shouted ''Planes hard a-dive, full ahead both motors!'

Fore 'planes *in hand* and hard a-dive . . . To drive her under — as she began to wallow into it in any case, and another shell burst in the bridge — or the tower, could be, in which case it would fill now as she ploughed on down.

3

Anne Laurie got home to Chester Square just before six-thirty p.m. on this dark, wet Saturday, having hoofed it all the way from the Admiralty despite a steady, soaking rain. She'd given up waiting for her omnibus, left the queue as several others had done, then had the damn thing pass her before she'd covered more than 100 yards. Her route on foot wasn't all that far, though — the length of the Mall, then Buckingham Gate and through the last bit to the square. She'd have had to walk that part of it anyway. She shared the flat with Sue Pennington, sharing the rent too, but only after it had been quite heavily subsidised by Sue's father, who owned a brewery.

There were three letters on the doormat. She skirted around them, hung up her dripping mac and stood the umbrella in the stand, went into the bathroom and dried her hands before coming back and scooping them up. Two were for Sue and the other for her — Forces' Mail, from Harry St Clair, his handwriting clearly recognisable even if he hadn't filled in 'sender's name' on the back. He was a major now: on his last short leave he'd been a captain, and in 1916, when he and Charles had gone into the field, they'd both been subalterns.

Charles had been killed about six weeks after landing in France. He and Anne had married three weeks before that, and Harry St Clair had been best man at their wedding.

Read this later, she decided. To get warm and clean was the priority. Including removal of wet shoes. Good strong shoes, part of her kit as a 3rd officer in the Wrens, which she'd had to become in order to work in the Intelligence Division, although she contrived hardly ever to wear the uniform — except for the shoes, in this sort of weather. Item two now anyway — in slippers, riddle out the stove and feed it some coal. Sam Lance was coming for her at eight, taking her to the Ritz. If she gave the stove half an hour to itself after the riddling, might get about two inches of warm water which she'd leave in the bath in case Sue wanted it.

Sue was a cryptographer, and like Anne was employed by ID — Intelligence Division of the Royal Navy — but more specifically in that Holy of Holies Room 40, the ultra-efficient and ultra-secret organisation that intercepted, decoded and/or decyphered virtually every signal the German Navy sent. Others too — diplomatic stuff, on occasion. Including an extremely hush-hush item that was known to the few who'd heard of it as the Zimmermann telegram. Room 40 — which in fact was now known as ID 25 and occupied not only Room 40 but about a dozen others as well, in the Admiralty's Old Building — had broken that. Anne had assisted in the translation and her boss, 'Blinker' Hall — her *ultimate* boss — had kept it in his own quite extraordinarily capable hands, rather than allow it to become lost or simply wasted in those of senior admirals or politicians. He'd handled it to such good effect that it had been largely instrumental in coaxing America into the war. He'd been plain Captain Reggie Hall RN then, was now Rear-Admiral Hall, KCMG — a genius who when he thought it necessary worked twenty-three-and-a-half hours a day and was adored by everyone who worked under him.

Apart from Sue, the cryptographers were all male, all extremely brainy as well as interesting in themselves, drawn from many different backgrounds: academics, former diplomats, scientists, businessmen, two naval school-masters, a barrister, an historian, and so on. Most of the young civilians had by now been forced into naval uniform, which annoyed them.

Anne was no cryptographer. Couldn't even manage the *Times* crossword. At least, not often. Her contribution to the business was her fluency in the German language. French as well, but German was what the Division as a whole and ID 25 in particular had need of. Many of the cryptographers had some German and a few were bilingual, but a fair proportion were mathematicians, not linguists. In any case, decrypting was their trade.

Stove now filled, could be counted on to do its best. Somewhat limited best, admittedly. One put on gloves for the riddling process, otherwise had to wash off coaldust in very cold water, the stove not being up to much until it got into its stride. As Sam Lance had commented when she'd explained this to him, 'Do without the gloves, you have the makings of a vicious circle there.'

He was American, a lieutenant-commander in the US Navy, one of six assistant naval attachés working at and out of the American Embassy. His boss, *the* naval attaché, Captain Powers Symington USN, had become a close friend and admirer of Blinker Hall. As had Admiral Sims, the US Navy chief here. Blinker briefed Sims virtually every day, withholding no information that could be of use or interest to him, only giving him to understand that the intelligence came from agents in the field, not Room 40. The existence of Room 40 and its code-breakers was a closely-guarded secret, with which the powers in Washington were not to be trusted.

Sims, as it happened, agreed on that point. Not in relation to Room 40, which he'd never heard of, but on Washington's weak security.

No hurry now: the stove had to be given time. Get out a dress that was fit to wear — well, she knew which one — and a few other things, then read Harry's letter. She could visualise him as he'd have been when writing it: hunched in a dugout lit perhaps by a storm lantern, Harry in mud-stained khaki writing the letter maybe on a board or a book on his knee, and from outside the rumble or mutter of the guns. He was a very, very nice man, she thought, and was obviously a good soldier; he'd been a staunch friend of Charles's and had been stricken by his death. When she thought of him, she saw Charles too: Harry's face squarish with a blunt nose and a thick black moustache, Charles's longer and narrower with a slightly cleft chin and a brown moustache. And that quirky smile she'd loved.

To kill a man like *that*, she'd asked herself. Like squashing a bug. She'd thought about it, puzzled over it a thousand times. The futility and cruelty of it, the *stupidity*. And the numbing shock that *bloody* telegram had brought her.

Thousands — millions — of equally bloody telegrams, of course: and the same applying to every one of them. Obviously. It was just that one's own was the one that opened one's eyes to the irrevocability, the *lasting* remorse, the injury that no-one ever could 'kiss better'.

Returning to the sitting-room in dressing-gown and slippers, she picked up Harry's letter, slit it open with her thumb and dumped herself on the sofa. He'd written, *Dearest Anne. Just a few lines while I have the chance to let you know that all is as well as I suppose one could expect it to be. In fact things have been looking up, rather, as I imagine you know — with the bird's eye view of everything that you must have in your job — at least as I imagine it — you must in any case have a clearer view of events and probabilities than any of us here can, with our noses more or less literally in the mud. There is an awful lot of that stuff about. But there's hope too, now — which is amazing, wonderful. I must say this, Anne — if only Charles was around to see it and feel it! Of course, one mustn't count one's chickens. It may not be quite on its last legs yet. Personally I think it is, but — anyway, the one thing I do want to say, Anne, is that when it is over, if I'm still here and in one piece,*

*if I could muster the damn nerve and cheek to
— well, I've got to put it in plain words — not to
replace Charles, which no one ever could, but to
refill a little of the space he occupied in your
warm and lovely heart? Now I've gone further
than I've dared go before, but please, just give it
thought? What sort of future I'd be able to offer
you I can't say, but my uncle —*

She looked up, palming the letter, hearing
Sue's key in the door. Read the rest of it later:
there were only a few more lines.

She wouldn't marry him, though. Might well
marry Sam. Marrying Harry St Clair *would*
seem like trying to replace Charles. Stay friends
with him for life — please God — but not —

No. Harry as one might love a brother, Sam
— well, as a lover. Not that he *was* her lover, in
that sense.

Didn't want to be rushed into it, was all.
Wanted to be certain. Did *not* want to remarry
while still at war.

Was that only prevarication? Reluctance to
commit oneself to *any* second marriage —
replacement marriage as it might seem to be?

'Anne, you home?'

'Sure am!'

A groan. 'Talking American these days, are
we?'

'That was just slang, not necessarily American,
it's common parlance. Did you get a tram,
or — '

'A lift, from Danny Boy.'

'Oh, *did* you, then?'

Sue in the doorway, spotting her letters on the

61

Chinese table, darting in and snatching them up, inspecting both and dropping them. 'Nothing.' A sigh. Anne knew who it was Sue was hoping to hear from. She was shortish, fair-haired, rather stocky, in a tweed skirt and jacket. Freckles on her nose. When she could get away, she hunted with the Grafton; despite the brain power — which didn't stand out a mile but was there, all right — she was not by nature or inclination an indoor girl. Looking again at her letters: 'Correction — not 'nothing', by any means. I only meant they can wait, one doesn't exactly drool . . . Stove OK?'

'Pulling itself together, I hope. Thought I'd bath, then you could top it up, by which time — '

'Good wheeze. What time's Uncle Sam coming for you?'

'You're impossible. But — eight.'

'Remind me, he's — thirty-five, is it?'

'Thirty-two.'

'And you're twenty-four.'

'And a widow-woman. That ages one, you know.'

'In your mind it may, but no other way. I'd have guessed you were twenty-two at most. I've some news that should interest you, Anne.'

She'd got up, to go and try the water, but now paused. '*Good* news, I hope?'

'The German family you knew, the' — a second's hesitation as memory faltered — 'von Mettendorffs, the son a U-boat commander?'

'What about him — or them?'

Controlled alarm, and contrived lack of any

great interest, Sue noted. The same guarded manner Anne had affected when telling her about them — oh, eight or nine months ago, when amongst names in an intercept from U-boat Command listing new submarine appointments had been that of von Mettendorff, Otto, Oberleutnant zu See, appointed to UB81 in the Flanders flotilla, in command. In the course of a routine meeting at which Sue had been present, Anne had told a fleet paymaster by name of Thring, who'd set up the Operations Division's U-boat tracking-room, 'This one — von Mettendorff, first name Otto — must be the brother of a girl I knew at the Berlitz School in Frankfurt.' She'd added, 'I met him only briefly — but I'm pretty sure his name was Otto, and he was transferring to U-boats, doing some conversion course. For what that information's worth . . .'

She'd shrugged, making it clear that to her it wasn't worth a row of beans, she was only mentioning it — disclosing it — as a matter of form. It had also emerged — because Anne had later mentioned this too — that in her interview for the Intelligence Division job a year earlier, when she'd applied for transfer from the Foreign Office after Charles had been killed — she'd felt the need of a change, and Sue had told her there might be a job going for another fluent German-speaker — she'd put it on record that she'd had this friend Gerda with whom she'd shared student digs in Frankfurt where she'd been studying German at the Berlitz School. She'd also spent some of the summer holiday period as a guest of the family on their estate in

63

Saxony — summer of 1913, that had been — and in the course of it briefly met Gerda's brother Otto, then a junior naval lieutenant — or sub-lieutenant, he might have been, she wasn't certain; her stay on the estate near Dobeln had only overlapped with his few days' leave by — she *thought* — one day.

'Could have been two or even three. Honestly don't remember.'

Thring had told her, 'It's no great issue, anyway. Many of us have met dozens of 'em, here and there. The fleet review at Kiel, for instance — all hobnobbing like Billy-oh.' A second thought then, and he'd contradicted himself: 'Well, actually *not* all that much hobnobbery . . . Anyway, quite right of you to own up — eh?'

He'd chuckled at the concept of 'owning up'. Anne had been slow to react to what had been intended as a joke, and Sue had suspected then, as now, that she must have known Otto von M. rather better than she'd willingly have 'owned up' to. This seemed to Sue to be the only viable explanation. And so what? Had a bit of a fling with a Hun — pre-war, and when she'd have been not long out of school, for heaven's sake. No-one else's business; just interesting, that was all. He must have been a very *personable* young Hun, she thought. Anne was discriminating to a fairly high degree. Sam Lance, for instance, whom she'd been more or less fending off for quite some time now, was a most attractive as well as thoroughly decent man, and she was still barely encouraging him at all. Unless she was doing so on the sly, of course . . .

Telling Anne now, 'This wasn't an intercept — came by landline from C-in-C Plymouth. On the twenty-second. Torpedo Depot Ship *Hecla*, being towed towards Devonport — having hit a mine while being moved from Rosslare in County Wexford a week or so earlier, apparently — got herself torpedoed and sunk by UB81 — commanded by your friend Otto von Thingummy. Mettendorff.'

Silent for a moment, staring . . . Then: 'Hardly my *friend* . . . Anyway, what — '

'Destroyers depthcharged his submarine to the surface, then opened up with their guns, scored several hits before it went down, quote, leaking air and oil, unquote, and — then not a peep. As you might say, *kaput*. No doubt of identity either — the U-boat's, that is — broad daylight and on the surface, U81 on its conning-tower plain to see.' She shrugged. 'Cross *him* off your Christmas card list.'

Anne had subsided on to the sofa again while listening to this. Had seemed at first startled, but now — Sue thought — sort of deadpan. Maybe just not giving two hoots about it: after all, every U-boat destroyed *was* something to celebrate. Although it still did look as if she was finding it hard to — well, almost to comprehend, you'd think. Touching her back-swept, blue-black hair: 'I can't help feeling sorry for Gerda. We were really good friends — and she thought the world of him . . . She and I, though — imagine it — trying to convince ourselves there *couldn't* be a war — getting on as we did, being as like-minded as — well, as we *thought* we were. Although the country as a whole was fairly anti-British at that time. Well, anti-foreigner, say . . . '

Gabbling a bit, Sue thought. Quite unlike her. Highlighting the sister as a way of leaving him in the shadows?

★   ★   ★

Sam Lance was a large, brown-haired man, clean-shaven, with hawkish features in which it was still a surprise to her to find kind eyes. Brown ones, as it happened. He looked especially handsome tonight, in US Navy uniform with a wing collar and black bow-tie, providing what he referred to dismissively when she'd complimented him on it on some previous occasion as 'the tuxedo effect'. He'd lavished praise on her, though, claiming to be stunned speechless all over again by her 'sheer damn beauteousness' in a mid-green silk dress which was the newest evening-wear she owned and was well up with the fashion, full-skirted and lowish-cut with narrow shoulder-straps, hem-line a clear inch above her ankles. Sam had asked Sue, holding Anne's coat while she slid her arms into it, 'Isn't she really *something*?'

Sue had agreed, 'Something, all right.' Anne meeting her privately derisive look, knowing that in Sue's opinion both the décolleté and the hemline were going it a bit; Sue teasing her with: 'As long as they have heating in that place now. Did you read how many Londoners died of 'flu

66

just this past week?'

'Now, Sue — '

Anne told him, 'She's trying to embarrass me.'

'Only because I'm envious. Makes it a compliment, don't you think? Truth is you both look tremendous. I hope you have a really spiffing evening.'

In the hired car, Anne said, 'This Spanish flu really is terrifying. Death-roll for last week more than two thousand just in London!'

'Two thousand two hundred and twenty-five, as I read it. We have it on the rampage back home too. Heck — everywhere, isn't it. They say China and India are the worst. Anyway, let's not let it spoil our evening.'

'Absolutely not! Three cheers for us, and devil take the rest!'

'No, that's not *quite* — '

'I know, I know. Teasing you. What I was going to say, Sam — the Ritz, such extravagance . . . '

'Hah. Only live once. And I have an idea to put to you, so I need to have you in a complacent mood.'

'I'm already about as complacent as I could be, but if it's what I think it *might* be — '

'It's not. On that we have a deal.'

He'd asked her more than once to marry him, and she'd asked him to ask her again when the war was over. Telling her now, 'Reason I accept the delay is (a) I don't have any choice, and (b) it can't go on much longer, truly can't. This is no time or place for talking shop, but — well, OK, still hurdles to be crossed, but the truth is the Germans are finished, their Army's broken and

67

on the run, country's starving — thanks to your Navy's four-year blockade . . . '

He'd checked, leant forward: 'You getting all this, driver?'

No reply or reaction. There was a glass screen between the driver and his passengers, and seemingly it did its job. Sam flopped back beside her. 'They're out of Flanders, did you hear? Or as good as. Belgians have taken Ostend and Zeebrugge. Might guess at something like six weeks at most, I'll come knocking on your door again?'

She told him, 'Six weeks or however long it takes, *if* you still want to ask me then, Sam. Since you may think I'm behaving like a spoilt brat, meanwhile.'

'On the contrary, I understand entirely. After your Charles.' His large hand had covered one of hers. 'I said 'understand' — I mean that one appreciates it's — well, *beyond* understanding.'

Charles was most of the reason. She'd had doubts then of wartime marriage — not doubts of him or of her feelings for him, or of his for her, but marrying in war *at all*, and in this one in particular, at a time when the likely period of survival for a young officer in the trenches had been given variously as three or six weeks — which they'd both been well aware of and dismissed as not applying to *them*, and had been taught almost immediately that it certainly did — had . . . After which she'd thought *she* might as well stop living; with the other thing constantly in mind as well, brought back into her mind like some incurable and unmentionable

68

sickness — less the thing itself by that time than whether Charles had believed her — as he'd professed to — or whether he'd died in *dis*belief, or at least doubt.

In all other ways you might say it didn't matter now, had been to all intents and purposes expunged by those depthcharges and the gunfire. *Could* say that. If you were looking for a let-out, you could. Knowing very well that that was all it would amount to, that they could have burnt him at the stake and it wouldn't make a shade of difference to how Charles had felt about it, in his heart of hearts — being no kind of simpleton. It was how he'd felt *then* that mattered, the state of mind in which *he'd* died — not who'd died since, or how.

Sam was saying, ' — no time or place to talk shop, but on that subject — German government wanting to throw in the towel — you'd think it'd be easy, wouldn't you. But there are these complications — as you'd know, I dare say. After all, we get most of what we know from your department. Division, I should say. Long and short of it, however — well, my own guess would be five or six weeks. *Could* even be less.'

'Depending on which way various monkeys jump.'

'That's nicely put — if we're talking about the *same* monkeys.'

'We'd better not, though, had we.'

'Hah.' A pat on her arm. 'You're not only a beautiful woman, you're a very smart one.' The car was running up St James' Street towards Piccadilly, edging over for the left turn. 'Nearly there . . . Should one assume your work keeps you generally *au fait* with the broader strategic situation?'

'No. Not at all. Really, far from it. All I get to know is whatever happens to be dropped in my lap. Or said or argued in my hearing . . . Oh, here we are!'

Still raining, but well enough sheltered under the Ritz portico. Doorman with a very large midnight-blue umbrella; Sam helping her down and telling the hire-car driver, 'Eleven, all right?' Anne reflecting that it had been absolutely right of Harry to have written as he had: she'd guessed that he'd been getting round to it, and she'd be able to concoct an answer now that would disappoint him, obviously, but shouldn't too badly hurt his feelings or destroy their friendship.

The thing about Gerda von M's brother Otto, though: when Sue had started telling her about it she'd had a vision of his having survived, being fished out and taken prisoner, in which event it would have been on the cards that she might have had to sit in on his interrogation.

Which would have been — extraordinary. She'd had a dream about it once. Not all that far-fetched either; strangely realistic. She *had* taken part as interpreter in a few interrogations.

'Penny for those deep thoughts?'

She let the smile break through. 'Sorry.' Gaze wandering around the glittering foyer, and back to him. 'Gist of them is I really do love being out with you, Sam.'

* ★ *

The entrée she chose was a chicken and mushroom pâté with Melba toast, and they both ordered Dover sole, which the head waiter had assured them were the size of small whales; Sam had ordered champagne. Chatting then about this and that, including his family, who had what sounded like a biggish house on the coast a few miles from the naval base at Norfolk in Virginia. They had a commercial boat-yard there which by the sound of it had been a thriving concern and was now, with war contracts, a booming one. Sam wasn't regular Navy, but he'd been on the Reserve all his adult life.

'You said your father has a cousin or somesuch with him now, in your absence?'

'One of my two brothers-in-law, guy by the name of Tad Noakes, has joined him. My sister Jennie's husband. Younger sister Gina's in the fashion business in New York. Nice guy her husband, Colin.'

'You mean the other brother-in-law is less nice?'

'I'm just a little wary of him, tell you the truth. He's an accountant by training, sharp business-man I suppose, whereas Dad and I — well, we're boat-builders. I spent my first years out of college working right there in the yard.' He put his fork down, spread his hands: 'With these. I mean, *real* work. Then joined the old man in the office — had a stab at designing too. So there's a difference in approach and outlook between me and Tad, and I anticipate he won't be exactly

71

eager to move over. When the time comes, I mean.' One hand rested on one of hers for a moment. 'When this is over finally and — '

'He'll *have* to move over, won't he?'

'Sure. Only I may have to throw my weight around a little, and I'll be at a disadvantage, I guess, in that the business will have changed so much. Jennie'll be no help, I can see *that* coming. She has a keen eye for which side *her* bread's buttered.'

'And your father?'

'Getting old. Maybe a little hazed himself by all the changes.'

'But you're his son, spent most of your life working with him, know it from the ground up?'

A nod. 'Sure.'

'Well, doesn't that *entitle* you — '

'Could still have some fights on my hands.'

'And you'll win them. Point of fact — as you say, when this is over — war ends, war contracts end, you're back to where you were, except you may need new projects. Exit Tad, enter Sam — and if there *are* Navy contracts still going, won't your overseas service make you the man to get them?'

Smiling at her. 'You're what's called the bee's knees, you know. I'm nuts about you — love you, want you, can't take my eyes off you . . . We like this thing they're playing, don't we?'

'We adore it!'

After you've gone . . .

In his arms then on the crowded dance-floor. Most of the men in uniform, and all the women pretty. Well, a lot of them were . . . And this scent of victory — the certainty of it in men's eyes, joy of it in girls' voices. As well as each other's closeness. She *did* love him: or would get to. Not as she'd loved Charles, but that had been in another world: or it might be that she'd been a different person.

And left me crying . . .

Sam wouldn't do that, she thought. Sam was a rock. Music coming to an end, though.

'That was lovely.'

'Sure was. But listen to *me* now . . .'

Breaking the spell somewhat abruptly and surprisingly, in the lingering aftermath of that song, but still holding her. Straight from the shoulder then: 'I'll be gone in about a week, Anne. Just for a while. Be able to tolerate that, will you?'

'How long a while and going where?'

'Well, I'll tell you.' Back to their table first, though, to await the fish. He told her, leaning close, 'Orkney Islands, Scapa Flow. One of the assistant attachés has to visit our Sixth Battle Squadron every so often, and it's come round to my turn.'

'I thought the Fleet had moved down to the Forth.'

She'd glanced round to check on their closer neighbours first, then just murmured it, with the thought that most people probably knew it anyway. By 'the Fleet', referring to the Grand Fleet, now commanded by Beattie, who'd been Jellicoe's number two at Jutland, and comprising as well as that host of British dreadnoughts the US Sixth Battle Squadron under Rear-Admiral

Hugh Rodmer. Sam nodding, reaching to top up their glasses. 'It has. Our lot included, since they're part of it. But Scapa's still in use, off and on, and our battle squadron's due to call in there for a day or two — actually *half* the squadron, half at a time, that is, re-fuelling break from covering the Northern Barrage and Norwegian convoys, so forth. I'll be taking dispatches for Admiral Rodmer — by hand of officer stuff, you know?'

'I suppose I shouldn't have asked, and you shouldn't be telling me. Next question, though, how long will you be away?'

'Well — listen.' His hand covering hers again. 'You're thinking I'm telling you this kind of suddenly and maybe not too well. Sort of blurting it out. Reason for that is I suspect I may have a job persuading you — well, in a nutshell, persuading you to come with me. How d'you react to *that* now?'

Bewildered, frowning . . . 'What *is* this, Sam?'

'Not what you might think, there's no' — he smiled — 'no ulterior motive, as one might call it — '

'You're either mad or joking. I couldn't *possibly*. Even if there was any kind of reason that made sense, I wouldn't be allowed to. I actually do have work to do, and anyway they'd *never* — '

'Your mother lives in Argyll, right?'

Still frowning. 'How is that relevant? *Hundreds* of miles from Scapa Flow!'

Her mother lived at the head of a sea-loch not far from Oban, with her eccentric Scottish artist husband, Angus McCaig. Anne's father had died of heart failure when she'd been twelve and they'd been living in France, and her mother had re-married when she, Anne, had been at the Berlitz in Frankfurt, seven years later. Grandparents had more or less supported mother and daughter in the interim, and had made it possible to afford the Berlitz venture.

Sam was telling her, 'I hope you won't think I had a damn cheek raising this with him rather than talking to you first, but I've met recently with a Royal Navy commander whom you know — name of Hope, very nice fellow and an influential guy in your Division?'

'He's the big white chief, to all intents and purposes. Reports to Rear-Admiral Hall directly. Anyway, what — '

'Sir. Miss . . . '

Waiter, with the fish. In the next few minutes of comparative silence she was wondering what he'd have had to talk about with Bertie Hope, the salt-water boss of ID 25 whose considerable sea experience and expertise balanced the civilian geniuses' ignorance of naval matters. But why on earth Sam should want her with him in the Orkney Islands . . . Apart from the obvious — which was *too* obvious, and really not his style.

Any case, who'd pick the Orkneys for anything of that kind?

'Some fish, those!'

'Indeed they are, sir.' Grey-haired, as waiters tended to be, these days. She wondered whether they'd all lose their jobs when the young men

75

came back. She smiled at this one. 'Marvellous-looking fish!'

'Would've been swimming in the sea only this morning, Madam.'

'The poor things.'

She liked 'Miss' better than 'Madam'. Although of course she *was* Madam — wore a ring which he'd no doubt spotted. Mightn't he have guessed she was playing fast and loose — her husband at the front, maybe, and dining expensively with this Yank? No sign that he had, anyway: he'd gone off still smiling at her sympathy for the sole. Conceivably, she supposed, she and Sam could have been wife and husband; or the incidence of widowhood in this era was so great you didn't bother to question it — or the morality of dining with a man who was not one's husband.

Would she have, she wondered, if Charles had been alive? Might she *ever* have?

Sam relieved her of the need to answer that, breaking into her muddled thought sequences with 'In Commander Hope's view there's no reason you shouldn't visit Scapa, if you felt so inclined and had leave due to you and I was there to see you came to no harm, and — hang on now — *and* you were accompanied by a chaperone. He said he thought it mightn't be a bad idea at all — all of you cooped up there handling stuff about the Grand Fleet and Scapa for quite some while now and never getting a glimpse of anything outside the walls of Admiralty. He has a point, I'd say — although I have a better one, as I'll explain in a moment. As

76

for a chaperone, what chance do you think there might be of persuading that nice little Sue to come along?'

'She'd think what I'm thinking — that the idea's ridiculous!'

'Well, hold on — it may seem so at this juncture, but when you think it through — '

'She wouldn't *want* to think of it. Any time she's let out of London all she wants to do is hunt. And as we're at the start of the hunting season, Sam — '

'Someone else, then. Hope said you have three German interpreters in your outfit now, and the other two could handle your work between them easily enough for — well, a fortnight, maybe. But one of the other women — one of those you call typewriters, for instance — '

'A *fortnight* . . .'

'We'd go by rail to northeast Scotland, place called Thurso, embark in a destroyer at — oh, Scrabster, just across the bay from Thurso; land an hour or two later at Stromness — which is right on the edge of the Flow, on an island they call Mainland. You'd travel on first-class railway warrants — only condition being you'd have to wear uniform, being an officer in your women's naval service, even though you don't exactly advertise it?'

'Wrens — WRNS, Women's Royal Naval Service. And no, I don't. It was only that to work in ID I had to be given a commission and a rank — and 3rd officer, which is what I'm supposed to be, is the lowest. I never wear the uniform, if I can help it. Never even did what they call the basic training course — two weeks at the Crystal Palace learning to march and salute and all that. I'm an impostor, really — simply because the admirals prefer people to look as if they belong ... But you're bullying me, Sam, I don't want — '

'I'd never bully you. *Never*. Let me explain, though?'

'All right.'

'What *I'd* get out of it is I'd get to meet your mother — which I'd like very much, for reasons that must — well, how or when she and I would meet otherwise ... See, when they surrender or there's an armistice — if that's what it's to be called — well, heaven knows, but I could be sent off somewhere or other at no damn notice at all. To a sea-going job — which in other respects would be just dandy — or back to the USA, even. And if it so happened that you were giving me the answer I crave — well, if I *had* met your mother she'd know the sort of guy I am, might not *necessarily* throw a fit when you told her. Huh?'

'I dare say we *will* be all at sixes and sevens. But — I don't know, Sam — '

'*Oh!* D'you mean — '

'I mean about the rest of it. I don't want to be committed, or feel I am, and have you — or my mother, either — *assuming* — '

'Wouldn't be like that. I guarantee it wouldn't. And up there — in Argyll — I wouldn't hang around, I'd like to meet her, tell her of my hopes and then clear out. Where we'd get out of the train on our way south — having landed back at

Scrabster, see — is some small station called
— hold on, I have a note of it — '

'Crianlarich.'

'That sounds about right. You'd know your
way around up there, of course. There's a
branch-line from there to Oban, but — '

'Oban, Sam, not oh-ban.'

'Oban. Right. But it's no great distance, and if
the connections aren't all that frequent, I was
studying the map and I thought maybe I'd have
a car meet us. My personal contribution to the
expedition. Then depending on how it worked
out — time of day or night, whatever — I'd leave
you there, with or without your chaperone
— after coming so far you'd want at least a few
days with your mother, I guess — '

'Want but might not get. If we've been away a
fortnight — '

'I was including a stay in Oban in that
estimate. In the Orkneys I'd want no more than
a day or two days. Unless one had to wait, if they
weren't in harbour when we got there. But on
top of that, say two days' travel in each
direction?'

'Your fish is getting cold, Sam.'

'Ah . . . '

'It amazes me that Commander Hope should
even have listened to such a wild idea!'

Sam nodded. 'Because I'm one of these Yankee
fellows. Liable to have crazy notions. Best to
humour 'em, don't you know?'

'It's still extraordinary.'

'Then again — and your forgiveness, please
— I told him in the strictest confidence that I'm

79

desperate to marry you, you won't give me a yea or nay until it's over, and — the chance to meet your mother, only opportunity I might have. He kind of liked it, I believe. Bit of a romantic — uh?'

'I'd never have imagined so.'

'Thinks well of you, I might say. Mentioned that you're far from work-shy, and — well, I deduce that he has a soft spot for the beautiful young widow. Incidentally, I made it clear you did not have the least notion of this scheme, I wanted to know might it be feasible at all, and if I found it was I'd see how you might feel about it. As I now have done.' He sighed. 'I don't blame you for your hesitance — especially for your determination not to appear committed. But — '

'You're so patient, I'm ashamed of myself — taking such advantage . . . But — may I think about it — the Scapa thing — let you know tomorrow?'

Slow smile and a couple of blinks. Then: 'I'm patient because I know what I want. But you're saying you might agree to this crazy proposition?'

'I'd like to sleep on it, and — '

'Sunday, tomorrow. Sleep *late* on it, and — '

'It's my duty Sunday, and I have to go down to Portsmouth. So I'll have plenty of time in the train to ruminate. Call me in the evening, at the flat?'

4

He would have wirelessed his estimated time of arrival at Wilhelmshaven, giving it as noon 26 October — today, Saturday — when he'd surfaced on Thursday night after groping his way blind through the Dover Strait. Not sooner than that because he couldn't have been anything like certain of making it, for various sound reasons including blindness, ie having no periscope; and in point of fact he hadn't been able to transmit even then, for the additional good reason that the boat's wireless had been defunct. Explaining this to Kapitan zu See Schwaeble, in Kommodore Michelsen's office — Michelsen, the U-boat chief in Wilhelmshaven, being away in Kiel and Schwaeble being his deputy — Otto added that amongst other action damage the two wireless masts and the aerial they carried had been shot away — along with most of the after part of the bridge and the periscope standards. Schwaeble, a hard-faced man in his early forties, hair greying at the temples and a duelling scar on one cheek, had broken in with: 'As I saw. My first thought was how astonishing, the punishment a UBII can stand up to. Then, von Mettendorff, what about the punishment her captain and crew endured — and despite it brought her back!'

Otto blinking at him, as if he barely understood the interruption. Head swimming at

81

that moment. He got it together again, though, finished with 'and although my telegraphists had rigged a jury aerial during our first hours on the surface — Tuesday night — they were to discover later — Thursday, as I was explaining — that the set itself had packed up, was not repairable.'

Hence he'd been unable to send an ETA or other report. So this morning he'd called up the signal station on Borkum by light, identifying himself and adding, *Request inform FdU Wilhelmshaven that my ETA Schillig Roads is noon today 26th. Proceeding on surface with considerable damage from gunfire and depth-charging to bridge, conning-tower and after-casing, battery containers cracked and periscope will not rise. This followed the sinking by torpedo of British destroyer depot ship Hecla, six thousand six hundred tons, at 1258/22nd in position 50 degrees 05′ N, 4 degrees 40′ W. I also had five men killed and seven with broken bones and suspected skull fractures.*

In the same message he'd given the names of those killed — Leutnant zu See Hofbauer, Torpedo Chief Stroebel, Signalman Wassmann and Stoker Reihl. Stroebel had died only this last night, having never recovered consciousness. He, like the others, had been buried at sea, lashed in a weighted hammock and launched from the fore-casing. One prayer, and finish.

Schwaeble frowned at a copy of the message, which had been passed from Borkum by land-line. 'Your third officer amongst those killed. So you and your first lieutenant — Stahl — have been sharing watches these four days.'

'Together, mainly. Wasn't much chance of sleeping.' A shrug: 'None, for me.'

'You are very much to be congratulated, von Mettendorff, and I have no doubt your achievement will receive the recognition it deserves.'

'I had a great deal of luck, sir. But on the subject of — as you say, recognition — may I suggest that my entire crew, every man of them — and foremost among them I'd say my engineer, Hintenberger — '

'Include all relevant details and recommendations in your patrol report, and have it ready for the Kommodore first thing Monday morning. That gives you all of tomorrow to draw it up, the rest of today for catching up on sleep, no doubt. And a square meal or two — uh?'

In response to the message telephoned from Borkum they'd sent a minesweeper to meet him and escort him into the Jade — passing the buoyed western limit of Schillig Roads, in which he'd been interested to see battle squadrons of the High Seas Fleet at anchor — and finally he'd berthed his noticeably misshapen submarine, with new victory pennants flying from a makeshift flagstaff, in the inner *Ausrustungshafen* shortly before two p.m. Not bad, in the circumstances, in relation to the ETA he'd have sent two days ago if he'd been able to; but as far as he himself was concerned, there'd been one thought predominantly in mind, nothing to do with the crowd of cheering submariners and phalanx of senior officers including this Captain Schwaeble — whom Helena had said she'd met, or knew. *Helena*, whom he'd had in mind and had been looking for, scanning the crowd and the surroundings for, while a brass band blared and ambulances were parked with their rear doors open, medics and stretcher-bearers as well as the brass-hats waiting for a gangway to be thumped over by the shoreside berthing party.

They'd seemed awed by the extent of the damage — bridge with most of its after part shot away, periscope standards shattered, jagged shell-hole in the conning-tower, port side, and half the after-casing gone. To the repeated question from his distinguished visitors as to how on earth he'd managed to bring her back — with no periscopes and the conning-tower flooded, all that — he'd found himself almost tongue-tied, as surprised by the daftness of the question as they seemed to be by his achievement. His answer to them — if he could have put it in some way that might not have seemed rude — being simply that as the boat's commander, it had been his duty as well as natural inclination to bring her and her crew back, and — that was it, he *had*. Although one of them, a korvetten-kapitan who was an Ace and had recently been appointed to command one of the new U-Cruisers, had commented that many a commanding officer in a situation such as von Mettendorff had found himself in might well have not been able to confront the problems this young man had licked. So what *would* they have done, Otto had wondered — sat there on the bottom and bloody died? Oh, he'd had luck, for sure — on the heels of extremely *bad* luck

— bad management even, might have been arguable. But in terms of sheer achievement — actually, his own pressing *need*, all he was really thinking about once the wounded had been carted off and Claus Stahl had taken over other administrative details — was having managed to extricate himself from that circus by about two-thirty, aided and abetted by Hans Graischer, who'd shown him to a dockside office with a telephone in it so he could ring Helena. All Graischer or any of the others knew was that it was an extremely important private call he had to make — maybe to his family — so having showed him in there he'd left him alone to do it.

Fairly desperate by this time, having expected her to be on that quayside: he'd actually prayed for her to be, during the long but suddenly so much easier escorted passage up around the islands. After Borkum, Juist, then Norderney — where the minesweeper had met them, passing close alongside before taking station ahead, her men on deck cheering and waving — then Baltrum, Langeoog, Spiekeroog and Wangerooge, finally Minsener and Oog, around which they'd turned into the Jade. Hintenberger had come up into the bridge at that stage to ask for special weekend leave in order to visit his old father in Bremen — the old man being more or less bedridden and alone except for half a dozen cats. Otto had told him yes, of course, ask Claus Stahl to fill in an authorisation for a travel warrant and he'd sign it. But he was thinking of Helena every other minute, *knowing* she'd be there. She did after all have contacts in the base

— had mentioned Schwaeble, for instance, but knew Franz Winter too, must surely know others; and since they'd have had the news of him from Borkum by no later than say 0700, there'd have been plenty of time for her to have heard it and rushed to meet him.

It had taken him a while to get through, having first to get an outside line from the exchange, but eventually he was connected, and was informed by some male colleague of hers that she'd gone to Hamburg for the weekend, wouldn't be back until Sunday night or early Monday. No, they did not have a number at which she might be contacted in Hamburg. At least, this fellow — a soldier of some sort — didn't think so. He added that he was the only one there and would shortly be locking up.

It would have been surprising if she had not had an engagement of some kind on a Saturday night, but he'd counted on persuading her to get out of that and come with him to the Snake Pit. But — Hamburg, for God's sake: and the question in mind then, *Who with*? He'd hung up clumsily and leant across the table, folding his arms on it and resting his head on them. Lunch had been biscuits and hard cheese washed down with what passed for coffee — which was all right, was what they'd more or less lived on these last few days, but wasn't exactly strengthening, and he hadn't slept for more than seconds at a time.

In fact if she'd been there and *had* agreed to break her date, it might have been questionable how he'd have made out. Except that he'd have

86

had a few hours' rest. And if *anything* could have galvanised one . . . While definitely non-galvanising was having to submit himself to debriefing by Schwaeble — now, immediately, in advance of the usual patrol report which he'd be submitting when he'd had time to get it down on paper. One usually prepared it in rough form on one's way back from patrol, and this of course had not been possible. Apart from that — well, other priorities were to visit the men in hospital, and telephone the couple in whose house Helena had rooms. Might in fact do that right away: *they* might have a contact number for her.

Probably would not. Since even her office didn't. Which seemed odd.

A covering of tracks?

Graischer burst in, looking anxious. He knew about the Schwaeble meeting, had queried whether Otto shouldn't be getting that over before making private calls, however urgent . . .

'Get through all right?'

'Yes. Thanks.' Still sitting there, on this stool with the telephone in front of him. No time to ring those people. Made no difference: if she was in Hamburg, that was where she *was*. Out of reach. Schwaeble first, *then* call them. Hands flat on the table, pushing himself up. Graischer began, 'There's a room allocated to you in the Mess block, main building. Secretary'll give you the key. He's having your gear put up there — if it's amongst the load that's arrived. Most has, but some not. Coming by rail and road from Bruges.'

'Never thought of that.' Tapping his forehead.

87

'Christ, my brain . . . '

'Probably is there.' Graischer smiled: 'The gear, I mean, not your brain.' Otto thinking that whoever had organised all that so quickly — the recall signal 21 October, and one's stuff shipped from Bruges to Wilhelmshaven by today or maybe yesterday — had to be more on the ball than *he* was, at this juncture. The evacuation of Bruges and the surrounding area must have been ordered several days before the 21st, of course. But how might he have dressed for a date with Helena this evening, if he'd had one? Well — in the sea-going uniform he had on now. Shabby, but adequate. And he'd have borrowed what else he needed — including a razor, which with a few other items he'd left in the boat. Just hadn't bloody thought of it: thoughts had all been focused on Helena, not on himself. Abrupt release from the fairly considerable tensions of the past few days could have had that effect, he supposed, shutting out everything but her. Blinking at Graischer — who looked as if he was worrying about him, his state of health and/or the undesirability of keeping Schwaeble waiting. Both concerns were valid enough. Standing up suddenly, as he just had, had left him feeling dizzy for a moment. Telling Graischer, while adjusting the raked angle of his white U-boat CO's cap, 'Thanks for the help, Hans old man. I'll go see Schwaeble.'

'Know your way?'

'Kommodore's office. Well — know where it

is, sure. More or less.'

'I'll take you along. You look a bit groggy, to be honest.'

'Tell me, though — Franz Winter, U201 — he back yet?'

'Not as far as I know. No, he can't be.'

So she wasn't spending the weekend with old Franz, at least . . . Graischer was saying, as they clattered down an iron fire-escape-type staircase to the roadway, 'Boats have been flocking back, those from the nearer billets, and the first — oh, ten or twelve, I suppose, mostly your own flotilla mates — have already been fuelled, re-armed and re-victualled and pushed out again. Shouldn't talk about it, but the rumour is of impending action by the High Seas Fleet, so we'd be setting a trap for the British, presumably.'

★ ★ ★

Schwaeble was making notes from time to time in pencil on a signal-pad. He'd just scribbled *69½ metres*. Frowning at those figures: 'Less than forty fathoms, although you were to seaward of the forty-fathom line?'

'Unmarked shallow patch, it must have been. Can't swear to our position within a couple of thousand metres, I'd been dodging around quite a bit, but — colossal piece of luck, nothing short of hitting the bottom would have stopped us.'

Raising one hand open, then closing it as if crushing an egg in his palm, the by-now rather over-worked symbolism for a submarine imploding, squashed by sea-pressure well below her tested depth.

Schwaeble agreed. 'Rated to fifty metres and stopped at seventy, where there should have been no bottom much short of a hundred.'

'She struck hard, too. The tower was flooded, of course — result of the destroyers' gunnery — and short of blowing main ballast — maybe I should have, blown her to the surface and ordered abandon ship — but diving that fast and perhaps slightly concussed oneself — '

'Think you were?'

'Hard to be certain, sir. We were thrown around like ninepins — and head injuries, as I said — other breakages as well — legs, an arm or two, collar-bones — '

'On the bottom then, with all machinery stopped — were you hearing the enemy at all?'

'I thought I did, from time to time, but — ' He stopped, shook his head. 'Don't know. And we'd no hydrophone that worked by then.'

'No more depthcharging either, I take it?'

'Two isolated charges soon after we struck, but a long way off. They must have believed they'd sunk us, tried with those two to see if they could stir us up, maybe. We may have travelled further slant-wise than they'd have reckoned. Any case, long as we stayed absolutely quiet — and we had no option on that score — '

'Of course not. Although — '

'Oh, a very large 'although'.' Cutting in as if talking to himself, with his eyes shut for a moment, thoughts clouding. Recalling the

90

extreme anxieties, life-and-death quandaries. Pulling himself together then: 'I beg your pardon, sir. But — on the sea-bed, not knowing we'd ever get off it, and the worst of it that I daredn't lift a finger to find out. Except I did know the tower was flooded. Opening the vent in the lower hatch by just a crack we got a needle-jet at full sea-pressure, warning me that when the time came to try to get her off I'd have to start by pumping out some — well, the midships comp tank was the obvious choice.' A shrug that might have been a shiver: 'That is, if the pump would work. Another thing I couldn't ascertain was whether if we did get her up I'd have the use of a periscope. The main 'scope's gland had succumbed to blast or pressure, giving us a continuous intake — similar trickles into the TSC bilge via the for'ard hydroplanes' glands — but whether the big 'scope would eventually be useable or the topside damage might have jammed or even bent it — one realised this was at least quite probable. And the attack 'scope was of course inaccessible in the flooded tower.'

'UB81 being different in that respect from others in her class.'

He nodded. 'Most do have them the other way about.'

'Was she on an even keel?'

'List to starboard of about fifteen degrees, once she'd settled. And slightly bow-down. That was another possibility, that she'd have dug her snout in, and depending on the consistency of the sand or mud — '

'Time, when you hit the bottom?'

91

'Two-forty p.m., sir. Control-room clock stopped on impact. My own' — he tapped his top pocket — 'kept ticking. The impact was violent. As you can imagine. How she *didn't* break apart . . . ' Shake of the head. 'The men who died, incidentally — or did I say this already? — well, they were only three of about a dozen who eventually came round. Not Hofbauer, my navigator, his skull was actually crushed. But gas — chlorine — was another threat; battery containers had been cracked — hardly surprisingly — so there was electrolyte washing around in the tank. Obviously if salt-water had got in — '

'Quite.'

Schwaeble got up, moved to a window, stood gazing out. His shape and stance were similar to Franz Winter's — that fighting stance, assertion of virility, pugnacity. Head jerking round on a rather short, thick neck — which was also an attribute of Winter's — demanding, 'How long were you in this state of enforced inertia?'

'Four hours, sir. No — four-and-a-half. I had to wait for darkness — and give it longer than might be absolutely necessary, since I thought it was conceivable a destroyer might have hung around. If they'd guessed there might be life in us they'd know this was the way we'd play it. And if they *were* lurking up there, they'd hear our first stirrings, and — stayed quiet too, no doubt have stood by their guns.'

Remembering. To an extent, re-living. The lack of light, for one thing: not even the emergency lighting, after they'd hit the bottom, only a few flashlights of which he'd forbidden the use until they did start moving and might need them. Damaged and unconscious men having been taken care of first, of course, and the pressure-hull inspected for leaks by Hintenberger and his henchmen.

He added, 'Something of a dilemma, initially. If I found I could shift her, whether to accept the rather slim odds on making it back here — via the Dover Strait and other minefields, in the state we were already — or save at least some of our lives by surfacing and abandoning ship. That's — as I say — if surfacing were possible. But with the necessity of waiting for darkness — well, abandoning wouldn't necessarily have saved any lives at all — in a roughish sea and no rescue ships near. And if I'd tried it *before* dark, might have been blown to pieces the minute we broke surface. As to surfacing, incidentally, or even getting off the bottom, another possibility was that the exterior main ballast might have been holed — when the casing was shot away, could have happened then. In which case we might well not have had sufficient buoyancy, if we had only internal main ballast tanks that we could blow.'

'But you made the best possible decision, and succeeded.'

A shrug: 'Had the luck of the devil, sir.'

'Your crew stood up well to the four-hour wait?'

'Did indeed, sir. I explained the situation — that we had no option but to just sit tight, and what we'd do then — *try* to do — and they

93

settled down. Some slept — couldn't play cards or other games, having no light. So — dozing, chatting . . . '

He remembered Hintenberger growling — on his bunk, Otto and Stahl on theirs, only a few feet distant from each other in the darkness — the engineer musing philosophically, 'Had a fair run for my money, anyway. Lasted a lot longer than a good few of the fellows I started out with. But it's a fact that no-one's luck lasts for ever.'

Otto had cut in, 'Mine does, Chief. Therefore as far as this little *contretemps* is concerned, so will yours.'

'You reckon?'

'Definitely. With your assistance and experience contributing, naturally. Dare say there'll be a few bad moments, but — '

'Under the Dover mines — as we were saying earlier, eh?'

'Through them, more than under.'

'On the surface? A night-time passage?'

'Hardly. Along with the mine barrage goes a whole fleet of trawlers and drifters. I'm not mad, Chief. We'll go through dived, using the route we know and trusting in the continuance of my well-proved luck.'

'Well.' The engineer had reached over to rap on Hofbauer's bunk-board. They'd put the navigator in his own bunk, with his broken head wrapped in a towel that would by now be scarlet. 'Didn't help this lad here much, did it. Barely weaned, and — *phut!*'

'His own personal bad luck, that's all. But I

truly *am* a lucky swine, Chief, and it must be better to serve with a lucky skipper than the other kind — uh?'

'You're lucky as hell with girls, we all know *that*.'

'Well — since you mention it — '

'Pin your great bat ears back, Stahl, here comes the dirt!'

'No, it doesn't. What I was about to say is there's one waiting for me in Wilhelmshaven that's truly out of this world!'

'Saying there weren't half a dozen in Bruges?'

'This one's — frankly, she's exquisite. And keen as mustard. Honest truth, she's a corker, and she and I have — an understanding. So I have a powerful interest in getting there, and I damn well *will*, you can count on it!'

'Saying that if it wasn't for the expectation of a bit of nooky we could *not* count on it?'

It had gone on for a while, he remembered, that exchange. The engineer complaining that it must be great for Otto with his good looks and height, fine physique; but lacking any of those attributes he'd always had to rely on hypnotism or Mickey Finns.

'Don't suppose you ever had to trick one into it, Skipper, did you?'

'Trick . . . no. Not *trick*. Oh, except — '

'True confession time now, Stahl!'

'No.' Letting himself off on that one, shaking his head in the dark and the deep-water silence. He'd said something like, 'No, confessing nothing.'

Yawning, jerking upright on his chair, having

come close to falling asleep — Schwaeble was on his way back from the window, dumping himself behind the desk again.

'At six-thirty or thereabouts, then — managed to pump out that midships comp tank, did you?'

'Yes. Yes, sir. We did. The pump ran, all right. Might not have, but — thank God . . . Sounded *very* loud, after the long silence. Enormous relief initially, but I remember thinking then that if one or both of 'em *had* stayed up to listen for us, that's as far as we might get.' Suppressing another yawn. 'Another worry — should've mentioned — was the battery. Specific gravity frighteningly low, I *had* to lighten her enough to have her lifting-off before using motors — before *trying* to use 'em, wasting that effort of battery-power if she was actually immoveable. Using enough on the pumping effort meanwhile — and no certainty *that*'d last out. Although it did. Took a while — sweating blood second by second, to be honest. Must have been — no, *was* seven — seven o'clock — before she began to straighten up, lose the list she'd had on her. A sort of quiver — like she'd felt it suddenly — after pumping all that time and damn-all coming of it . . . '

Despair *had* been close to setting in. Using a torch several times during that period to focus on the depth-gauge and the bubble, its beam poking this way and that, he'd seen it in others' faces and — he hoped — had managed to keep the signs of it out of his own. Highly conscious though he had been that at any moment the ballast pump might just stop — overheat, seize up, or simply the battery giving up the ghost, therefore no hope of using motors either. Last resort then — HP air to blow main ballast, the *Tauchtanks*, of which some — externals — might have been holed, so that trying to blow them you'd only be venting high-pressure air out through them, expending your last resource to no purpose. Lose your reserves of HP air, you'd have nothing; obviously the compressor could only be run when you were on the surface with the hatch open.

But then: that quiver. Pump still running and she *was* shifting. Hardly daring to believe . . . Stahl, he remembered, suggesting rather vacuously, 'Try the emergency circuits, sir?'

Because the LTOs — electrical ratings — Freimann and Schachtschneider — had reckoned to have fixed them by something as simple as replacing blown fuses; so maybe you'd get some dim light if you wanted it that badly — which he didn't, hadn't allowed them to switch on, preferring to conserve what vestige of power they might still have. He said no again now to Stahl. Why waste power on bloody lighting? Weak flashlight beams were enough, that and working by feel, knowing as one did (or should) where every vent, valve and blow was to be found. Hintenberger certainly did: that little ape was a *real* tower of strength. But whether or not there was air remaining in the bottles and groups of bottles — and whether the externals would hold it if/when you gave it to them, which you'd do gently anyway, to reduce the chances of her reacting to it violently, suicidally . . . In the

97

first place because sea-pressure could have crushed her at any time in the last four-and-a-half hours — without anyone opening a blow or even sneezing — and in shifting her even to the very small extent that had been done, now you were already imposing new stresses. Also because the external tanks were constructed of thinner, lighter steel, were thus more vulnerable.

Better not use externals, he told himself. May well not need them anyway. Blow *internals*: and even those with caution.

'Stop the pump.'

'Stop the pump.' Stahl, thin-voiced, and the stoker crouched in a machinery-space a few metres for'ard didn't need to report it stopped, you heard it — or rather, *ceased* to hear it.

'Shut the comp's suction and inboard vent. Boese — you at the panel?'

'Am that, sir.'

'Check main vents shut.'

'They are, sir. Just checked 'em.'

'Check again numbers five and six — and check their kingstons open.'

Those were the midships internal main ballast (or 'diving') tanks. The extra weight in her, in the tower, was directly above this control-room; it made sense to put the lift as near as possible right below it. Kingstons were large valves in the bottoms of some main ballast tanks; water was expelled through them when high-pressure air was blasted in, as long as the vents on top were shut.

'Fore 'planes to five degrees of rise.'

Leading Torpedoman Bausch was in charge in

the TSC, where the 'planes were still in hand control. Acknowledgement came back by word of mouth: 'Fore 'planes at five degrees of rise, sir.'

In the hope that the motors *would* respond, by and by. A flashlight beam on the after 'planes' indicator dial showed that Honeck had them level.

'All right, cox'n?'

'Right enough, sir, considerin'.'

'Boese, listen. Put one two-second puff of HP air in *Tauchtank* five, and the same in six.'

'Aye, sir.'

In pitch darkness, using a wheelspanner to wrench number five's blow open, counting loudly, 'One — two!' and jerking it shut; then the same with six.

'Five and six blows shut, sir.'

You'd heard the blast of high pressure thump into each of the tanks and then cut off. Felt the boat's lurch — and heard from a distance Hintenberger's sharp, 'Ah, the darling!' A flashlight on the depthgauge simultaneously showing the needle jump from 69½ metres to 68, then continue sweeping shakily through 67, 66, 65 . . .

They were applauding quietly. He let it go on for about ten seconds, then called for quiet. Thought of reminding them that she was still a long way below her tested depth, and so forth, but decided they must all be aware of it, weren't idiots or children, actually were bloody heroes. He told Schwaeble, 'When I'd nursed her up to less than fifty metres I opened number six's vent because she was coming up too fast. Left the air in number five while we tried motors slow ahead — which was all right, but she was still too buoyant and I vented five. As well as the normal trim change when rising I guessed she'd have brought mud up with her, and as that fell off she'd have been getting lighter still, so I flooded the buoyancy tank again and that near-enough put us right. The empty comp tank alone was compensating for the flooded tower.'

'And you were able to surface.'

He nodded. 'Blind, though. Periscope wouldn't move; nothing I could do until the tower had drained down. Felt a bit — irresponsible, *asking* for it, tossing around waiting to be shot at or rammed or — well, couldn't be helped. And as it happened, we had the place to ourselves. Actually *did* . . . Anyway, I guessed the tower would empty itself as far as it could through the hole or holes they'd shot in it, so I gave it time for that before opening the drain.'

Schwaeble recalling, as if to himself, 'Which is there in case one might be so rash as to dive with the top hatch open.'

'If one were to be killed — stuck in that hatch maybe — having given the order to dive — those below *would* slam the lower hatch.'

A nod. 'Of course.'

'Both hatches were in working order, anyway. With the tower and standards shattered, the top one at least might not have been, could have been jammed solid. Yet another considerable relief.'

Actually, he remembered a near-screaming,

howling sense of relief as he'd unclipped the top one and sent it clanging back, aided by the pressure from inside, and climbed out into the wrecked bridge, found the voicepipe intact — the forefront of the bridge hadn't suffered — opened it and yelled down, 'Start main engines! Set standing charge one side! Steer east by south!' The sea had still been rough and there'd been a lot of movement on her, spray lashing over in night air like iced champagne — actually bloody *nectar* as the diesels grumbled into life and UB81 under helm and gathering way swung her fore-casing into the direction of east by south.

'You all right, von Mettendorff?'

Cheeks wet below the eyes, he realised. Using two or three fingertips of each hand to deal with it as unobtrusively as possible. Head and heart throbbing; heart actually thumping. Telling Schwaeble, 'I'm fine, sir, thank you.' He'd nodded, then wished he hadn't — his skull felt loose. Getting back to the sequence of events, however: 'Main problem facing us — looking ahead, I mean — was having no periscope. Obviously couldn't use the tower when dived, and the artificer couldn't do anything with the big one, it simply wouldn't budge.'

Schwaeble murmured sardonically, 'Certainly a *slight* problem . . . '

'Sheer luck got us through. Worked out a straight course for each day's dived run, went to twenty-five metres and hoped for the best, surfaced at night not knowing what company we might have — same slow business, of course,

101

surfacing, the draining-down of the tower each time. No eyes, no ears, and no other way, did provide several pretty awful minutes — Wednesday, Thursday and Friday nights. In the dark, of course, but still — not *comfortable*, exactly. While as to mines — couldn't wireless for information on new fields or recent clearances, just had to take our chances. Did have a charted track through the Dover Strait — courtesy of Korvetten Kapitan Franz Winter — and — well, as I say, sir, just damn lucky.'

'In my view, a good deal more skill and courage than luck. A degree of it, of course, but we all need that; if there weren't a certain amount of it about we'd all have been dead years ago. Go get some rest, and eat. Then you'd better have a check-up from the quack. I'll see that's arranged — for all of you. Sorry I had to put you through this, von Mettendorff.' On his feet, with his hand out across the desk: 'Once again, congratulations.'

Otto shook his hand. Then: 'May I ask, sir — is there likely to be a job for me now?'

'A job for you.' Eyebrows lifting. 'You mean while your boat's undergoing some major reconstruction?'

'Exactly, sir. Repairs'll take weeks, and — '

'And what?'

'I'm told a dozen or so boats have been turned round in something like record time and sent out again?'

'That is — ' He checked, staring at him, then nodded. 'Yes, they have. But as UB81 will be out

102

of commission — yes, perhaps two, three weeks — '

'Only wondered if there might be a new boat coming along, or if another CO happened to go sick?'

'A little holiday from sea won't do you any harm, von Mettendorff. In fact I'd say you need one.'

'But — can't help wondering why this general recall and re-deployment, sir. Unless something big's going on? I saw units of the *Hochseeflotte* at anchor in Schilling Roads on our way in — Third Battle Squadron, I think, but also — '

'Third Battle Squadron's coaling. What they may be up to after that, God knows. What makes you think — what you just said, something big?'

'Trying to understand it, sir. Guessing.' With his hands on the back of the chair he'd been using, letting it take some of his weight. 'Taking us off patrol then rushing us out again — and the *Hochseeflotte*, as you say — '

'The general recall of U-boats, von Mettendorff — I tell you this in confidence, now — follows a change in strategy. Policy, perhaps I should say. You've been out there to sink Allied ships — *any* Allied ships — and it has been decreed that this should not continue. The order came from the Chief of *Admiralstab*, Admiral Reinhard von Scheer himself. Effectively it returns us to the situation we were in prior to February of last year, when what they call 'unrestricted submarine warfare' was introduced.'

103

'Meaning we're now restricted to sinking warships?'

A shrug: 'That would seem to be a logical conclusion.'

He'd caught the note of sarcasm. Schwaeble also — and perhaps regretting it, having spoken out of his own weariness and maybe frustration, correcting himself with: 'But in theory, not entirely — as far as merchant vessels are concerned we'd be confined to the ridiculous procedures involved in 'stop and search'.'

'You say Admiral von Scheer has initiated this, sir?'

'The order emanates from him. I know nothing of its origins beyond that. But even the Chief of *Admiralstab* is accountable to Government — uh?'

Seemingly angry now, whether at Otto's persistence or at the situation itself, or both — the persistence more or less obliging him to discuss it. Natural inclination to play ostrich, for the head to remain buried in the sand. Otto apologised. 'It's only that one feels so much in the dark, sir. There were rumours in Bruges — weeks ago — of the new government seeking an armistice — which at the time seemed more like subversive propaganda than anything to take seriously. But with *this* now — '

'All right. All right.' A sigh. 'But again in the strictest confidence. There is reason to believe that armistice negotiations *are* in progress. My own understanding — on which I would prefer not to be quoted — is that the American President — Wilson — insisted on the suspension of attacks on merchant vessels — passenger vessels, anyway — as a condition of entering into such discussions. Which might explain the position in which Admiral Scheer now finds himself.'

'So the boats that have recently been sailed — '

'Are taking up whatever positions they've been ordered to. Others too — not necessarily returning here. Boats from the Mediterranean as well as the Atlantic and the North Sea. But, von Mettendorff, I have not said a word to you on this subject. Go and sleep.'

5

He woke on the Sunday morning feeling almost as good as new physically, but in a state of slight foreboding. Time — by the old silver watch that had survived a great deal one way and another, since he'd received it as a Christmas present when he'd been about knee-high to a Rottweiler — just past seven. Darkish out there, still. He'd slept-out his exhaustion — had had a few hours flat out yesterday afternoon and evening, then after dinner in the Mess had got his head down again by ten — having resisted urgings by a bunch of others to have one more brandy for the road and then see what was happening in the town.

Kurt Edeltraut, one of those who'd been trying to persuade him, had challenged him with 'Not scared, are you?'

'Scared? Of what?'

Deuker, a paymaster lieutenant, cut in with: 'There've been incidents in the town, of late. Mutinous swine from the battleships. They get drunk, lose their heads. Don't merely fail to salute their officers, damn well push 'em off the pavement!'

'I don't believe it!'

Walter Bohme, until recently of the Flanders flotilla, confirmed it. 'Happened more than once. That *sort* of incident.'

'And then what's ensued?'

106

'Depends who's involved. None of *us*'d stand for that kind of thing obviously, but the officers of our *Hochseeflotte* just huff and puff and damn-all else. Many of them are not of the same calibre as ourselves, I regret to say. But there are patrols in the streets, of course. And I can tell you, when the rebellious swine see we're U-boat officers they back off and shut up damn quick!'

'So what's behind it? Same as the so-called 'strike' a year ago?'

'Similar, yes. Complaints of bad food and not enough of it, while their officers guzzle away like hogs and drink like fish. Which is nothing but the truth. Get yourself invited to dine in any of the battle-wagons, you'll see it for yourself. Discipline's harsh, I may say — aimed at keeping the hotheads in line, but tending to have the opposite effect.'

'Open and shut case of rotten officers, then.'

'Well, it is. Most of 'em either too young or too old. Very few sound, experienced men of middling rank — of *our* rank, for instance. Simple reason that the best of us infinitely prefer an active life in submarines or destroyers to swinging eternally round moorings in protected anchorages. They're left with youngsters who're scared to make 'emselves unpopular and deadbeats who've lost heart.'

Otto had glanced at Edeltraut, who nodded. 'Same with the ships' companies, mind you. We've got the pick of the bunch.'

'Of course we have. In the nature of the business, isn't it. But what about political influences?'

107

'Plenty.' Franz Stolzenburg, with whom Otto had an appointment for a medical check-up this Sunday morning. Blue cloth between the gold stripes of a kapitan-leutnant marked him as a doctor. He added, 'Ashore *and* in the ships. Although the barracks are stuffed full of some of the worst of them. It's got worse of course since the revolution in Russia, and the USPD has a lot to answer for. Independent Social Democratic Party they may call themselves, but there are a lot of ultra-lefties in their ranks. Going by a lot that I've seen and heard — we medicos do get around, you know, and of course we all know each other — well, there've been numerous points of contact — political, I mean — and the mood's not getting any better.' A shrug: 'The prognosis, eh? To be frank, I don't see how we could expect it to do anything but get worse, in present circumstances. There's a strong tide of opinion to the effect that we've lost the war — which I believe *is* the case — little doubt anyway that the Army's shot its bolt. So the talk of armistice — well, much more like defeat, isn't it, surrender? Our apology for a government humbly requesting armistice — meaning they want to chuck their hands in — and the enemy dictating the terms on which they might start talking — but our lot calling it 'armistice' because defeat, which is the reality of it, historically leads to revolution?'

'Hence' — Kurt Edeltraut again — 'the talk of *Flottenvorstoss*.' Meaning fleet action. 'The concept being — I'd guess — that with a major naval victory — even Pyrric — armistice terms

108

must swing in our favour to some degree — and at least the *Navy's* honour's not sold down the river.'

'A naval victory is considered achievable, is it?'

The doctor looked around before he answered, saw that they were alone — no stewards in earshot — and nodded. 'Whether achievable or not, it's being planned. Orders from von Scheer, plans being laid by von Hipper, doubtless with the enthusiastic assistance of von Trotha. Nickname for it in the wardrooms is 'The Death Ride'.'

'Hardly suggests confidence in the outcome?'

'Smacks of bravado, doesn't it. Coined by the kind of young brats of officers we were talking about.'

'But' — Otto put his last question facetiously — 'Do we know when this Death Ride is scheduled to take place?'

The doctor shook his head. 'Only that it can't be long delayed. I'd guess a day or two, no more. And you see, it's much more than the honour of the Navy at stake, although that's the great issue that motivates our *Chef der Seekriegsleitung.*' The reference was to von Scheer. 'Way beyond that, it's to avert revolution — meaning amongst other things the loss of privilege and advantage enjoyed by — well, by *him*, and his friends — admirals, generals, rich industrialists, right-wing politicians, landed families such as' — shrugging — 'well, not to put too fine a point on it, such as yours, von Mettendorff.'

'And the government — '

'Aren't being told about it, or asked. *Nobody's*

being asked, and no signals are being sent that might give the game away.'

★ ★ ★

He'd got through to the house in Oldenburg before dinner last night, introducing himself as a friend of Fraulein Becht. 'I had the pleasure of meeting you, Frau Mueller, not so long ago, when I called for her at your house.'

'She's not here this weekend, however.'

'No. I spoke to someone at her place of work. She's in Hamburg, I was told. I only wondered — '

'She'll be back tomorrow night, possibly quite late. If you like, I'll tell her that you called. Your name — I didn't catch — '

'Von Mettendorff, Oberleutnant zu See. But I thought you might know of a number in Hamburg at which I could contact her.'

'I'm sorry, Herr Oberleutnant, but we do not.'

Firmly, as if protecting her lodger's privacy: the tone implying that she wouldn't tell him even if they did have a number for her.

Maybe had been snooping around in the dark when he'd brought her back from Kramer's?

'I'll call tomorrow evening, then.'

'On Monday at her office might be better. My husband and I retire early, and she may not be here until quite late. I'll leave a note that you called, in any case. Goodnight, Herr Oberleutnant.'

Probably got a lot of calls for her, he guessed. When he'd brought her home from Kramer's

110

that evening the whole place had been in darkness; he felt sure they *had* retired.

Last night would *not* have been so good, he realised now. But today — well, telephone the parents — or try to — and also Gerda, give *her* a buzz. She was in Berlin now, working at the Foreign Office on the Wilhelmstrasse and renting an apartment close by. Only a few hundred metres, in fact, from the apartment Leo Schneider had had the use of and had lent to Otto at the time of the English girl. Not that Schneider, who was a bit of a prig — or *had* been — had known anything about her. He remembered telling him in the Mess when he came back from that leave — with no more than an hour to spare, as it happened, since he'd had to stay over to the Monday in Berlin in order to buy some new sheets, expensive ones that had left him on his uppers until next pay day — 'You're my maiden aunt, would you believe it?'

Schneider had glanced up from the newspaper he'd been reading; aware that he was having his leg pulled in some way, and cautiously delaying reaction. This had been at the U-boat officers' training establishment at Kiel, in the summer of '13. Otto had explained the reference to a maiden aunt: 'Aunty as owner of that very nice apartment. If I'd said it belonged to a brother officer, she might have smelt a rat.'

Schneider had shrugged. 'She was *listening* to one, anyway. And by now I dare say she knows it. But for your information, the apartment doesn't belong to any brother officer, it belongs to my

111

mother, who would be extremely angry if she got to know that it had been used for immoral purposes.'

'Meaning that although you have the use of it whenever you want, you *don't*?'

'Meaning that not everyone is like you, von Mettendorff, and that I shan't lend you the flat again.' One hand out and a snap of the fingers: 'The key, please.'

'In my cabin. I'll put it in yours when I'm up there.'

'Well — see that you do. Anyway — was it worth the effort?'

'*Worth* it?' He'd rested a hand on his friend's shoulder for a moment. 'It was the best *ever*!'

He'd thought so at the time. Then, there, in those moments. And *she* . . .

He remembered Schneider's facial expression — or expressions — when he'd told him that: the conflict of disapproval and prurient interest, even envy.

Dead now, poor Leo. He'd been Otto Steinkamp's first lieutenant in a minelayer and they'd not returned from an operation in the Thames estuary a year ago. Several UCs had been lost in those waters in the past year or eighteen months. And Leo had as like as not died a virgin. Sitting up there polishing his halo now, wishing he'd taken his chances when he'd had them.

Otto had never told anyone about the English girl. Not at any rate about her being English. Even in '13, England had been the enemy. Although to him she'd only been Gerda's friend,

112

who spoke perfect German, was extremely attractive and a lot of fun. Gerda had told him all that before he'd ever set eyes on her, had insisted that he and she would get on like nobody's business. No doubt telling her English friend how she'd love *him*.

'Otto, do please come?'

Over the telephone, this had been, when he'd been staying with other friends and she'd wanted him to spend the last few days of his leave at home. Before this she'd mentioned the girl in a letter from the Berlitz school at Frankfurt, but he'd had no reason to take notice. He'd asked her over the 'phone, though, on this later occasion, 'How do the parents take to her?'

'Papa *certainly* does. And you know how he can be about the English! Mama tends to fix her with the famous steely glare, but I *think* approves of her — or would if Papa wouldn't keep twirling his moustache at her, and that's not *her* fault. She and I giggle about it like mad things when we're on our own. We've been riding a lot — all over the countryside — and bathing in the lakes. It's so *warm* . . . Otto, listen, she'll be here all this next week — until Saturday, when she leaves for Scotland. If you meet her just on her last day or two you'll kick yourself you didn't get here sooner!'

He'd dozed off — almost — returning to full consciousness asking himself why he was thinking about that girl so much after five long years. First dreaming of her at sea, then *almost* telling Hintenberger about her the other day.

Because he was so desperate for Helena, he

113

supposed. Shutting his eyes again, filling his mind with *her*.

★ ★ ★

He'd had his check-up from Franz Stolzenburg soon after breakfast, Franz summing up by telling him that despite the bruising he was as strong as a horse, but that if he liked he'd prescribe a week off duty.

'Not much point. My boat's laid-up, and there's no other job for me.' Second thoughts, then: 'Except — no. Please *do* put that in.'

'To avoid a big-ship appointment, by any chance?'

It had come up last evening, after talk about the shortage of competent middle-rank officers in the battle fleet, a conjecture that with all U-boats withdrawn from patrol there'd be a number of officers of the kind they so badly needed available for transfer to the surface fleet. In fact it didn't seem to be turning out that way, since returning boats were being sent out again as soon as they'd embarked stores, water and torpedoes, but in his own case — well, that was a truly horrible prospect, which one should certainly take any possible steps to avoid.

Stuffing shirt-tails into his trousers, he'd asked Stolzenburg, 'Make it ten days, rather than a week?'

'Well, why not . . . '

The Sunday church parade was taking place — guard and band, drilling and inspection of base personnel and crews of ships that were still

114

in harbour as distinct from those out in the Roads, a march-past then *en route* to church, with the salute taken by some admiral. Several of the big ships were still in harbour, he noted, identifying from a distance the battle cruisers *Derfflinger* and *Von der Tann*, and beyond them battleships *Markgraf* and *Konig Albert*. And another he wasn't sure of . . . Oh, *Baden*, Hipper's flagship. They'd be moving out to the Schillig Roads soon, presumably. He gave the drill area a wide berth in making his way down to the basin where UB81 was still lying. She'd be shifted in a day or so, Schwaeble had said, when the dockyard people were ready for her, but for the time being they had their hands full, and here she was — with Torpedoman Wernegger on sentry duty at the gangway and Claus Stahl at the wardroom table struggling with paperwork.

Otto told him, 'Don't move. You all right, though?'

'I'm fine. Supposed to report for a medical check at noon, but — nothing wrong with me, so — '

'Don't tell 'em that. Be tired, Claus. Unless you want to accompany the *Hochseeflotte* on its death-ride.'

'Did hear something about that. But why on earth should I — '

'Once this boat's in dockyard hands — or maybe even sooner — there's a danger you and I might be appointed to some battle-wagon. They're blaming the crews' indiscipline on a shortage of capable middle-rank officers — meaning chaps like you and me, who are not by

115

nature or inclination big-ship types. I've had *my* check-up, and the report's going to say I need ten days' rest. Just sag a bit and look tired out, you'll get the same if you ask nicely.'

'That's a good tip.'

'Ten days from now, heaven knows how things may be. Here and now, I need the control-room log and Hofbauer's navigational notebook — for the patrol report.'

'In the safe. I'll get 'em.'

Otto got out a couple of charts that he'd also need. He had the shape of the thing in mind, based on his oral report yesterday to Schwaeble; only in order not to bore them all to tears he'd pare it down to short paragraphs of bare facts, times, positions, actions and reasons for decisions taken. He'd expand only on his crew's exemplary conduct under difficult and hazardous conditions. And stress the part played by old Hintenberger. He told Stahl when he came back with the logs, 'I intend recommending all hands for gallantry awards. Including you, naturally.'

'Very decent of you, sir. *Krieger Verdienstredaille* for *you*, if there's any justice.'

'Never know, do you. But I shan't be counting on it.'

'First Class in gold, I'd say.'

'Now that's not likely!'

He was looking forward to Monday evening more than anything else. Sunday night or Monday morning, even, to hearing her voice and — he hoped — her pleasure at hearing his. Trying not to envisage disappointment — change of mind or heart or whatever you might call it.

That degree of disappointment would be positively shattering, the possibility needed to be kept right out of mind . . . Snake Pit, though — didn't have to be only Monday night. If Monday came up to scratch — and one would make sure it did — make it all the evenings she could spare. Funds were adequate — it was a long time since he'd spent a penny, except on Mess bills — and *anything* could be happening by next weekend. *Flottenvorstoss* might have been a victory, defeat or non-event, the war itself — well, armistice, surrender . . .

Sickening — almost literally so. Unbelievable, hard to convince oneself this was how things were, what they'd come down to; but all of it was either happening or imminent. *Anything* on the cards. What on earth one would do thereafter . . .

Think about that when the time came. At least one had a home to go to. Even land to work. Might do something of that sort, at least for a while.

If the family were able to retain their land?

Glancing round at Stahl — he himself working at the chart table — 'Thought I'd visit our lads in the hospital this afternoon. Like to come along?'

'Yes. I would, sir.'

'Start from the Mess after lunch, then. Two-ish. The walk'll do us good.'

Back to his report: winding up detail of his sinking of the Dutch collier off southwest Ireland and the depthcharge attack by Yank destroyers. Two torpedoes expended on the Dutchman, leaving the two re-loads for the depot ship near Eddystone.

'Oberleutnant von Mettendorff — sir?'

'Uh?' Looking to his left — at a sailor, messenger, whom he recognised as the leading writer from Schwaeble's, or rather Michelsen's outer office: smart, intelligent-looking, he'd recognised *him* too.

'Kapitan zu See Schwaeble's compliments, sir, he'd be glad if you'd join him in the bar of the officer's Mess at twelve forty-five.'

A nod. 'Thank him, say I'll be there.'

Better get a move on, get this done with. Still hadn't telephoned Gerda or the parents. He'd muttered, 'Wonder what *that*'s in aid of.'

'Wants to buy you a drink, I'd say.'

'Or invite me to volunteer for the death-ride. Listen — on the subject of recommendations, I'm putting you up for the command course. Although whether or not there'll ever *be* another one . . .'

'I'm immensely grateful, sir.'

She wouldn't have belted off to Hamburg on her own, he thought. On the other hand, having only met her twice and taken her to dinner once, he could hardly claim exclusivity. Would like to — would give his right arm to, but —

Best of all would be to discover she hadn't gone there with anyone at all. But, he warned himself, *Don't count on it* . . .

* * *

He finished the report in time to make his telephone calls before the lunchtime meeting with Schwaeble. Went up to the Mess to find a

118

telephone he might use, ran into Paul Deuker, the paymaster, who'd very kindly unlocked the staff office from which he'd rung Helena's landlady last evening.

'Service call, is it?'

'Not really. Long-distance to my people.'

'Well, if you're asked, give 'em your name. But they don't usually bother.'

There was no reply from Gerda's flat in Berlin. No reason there should be, of course, on a Sunday. She might even be at work, but she didn't like to receive private calls there. He got back to the exchange and gave them his home number — longer-distance still, but the operator obviously didn't give a damn.

Ringing. Longish silence then. Another ring . . . Then a rattling sound, harsh breathing, and old Drendel, Papa's long-time butler, piping up with: 'The Mettendorff residence, who is it that's calling?'

'Otto von Mettendorff, Sergeant — calling long-distance. Still fighting fit, are you?'

'Why, Herr Otto! Yes, I'm in good health. And you?'

Wheezy chuckle: 'Still sending the swine to the bottom in short order, I hope?'

'Doing my best to, Sergeant. But is my mother — '

'Yes. Please hold, I'll — '

'Either of them, if — '

He'd gone.

Papa commanded a remount depot and riding-school near Halle, in the rank of lieutenant-colonel. In his mid-sixties, it wasn't bad to have got a war job of any kind, and he was good at it; as Gerda had remarked not long ago, he got on better with horses than he did with people. While old Drendel, known to the household as *Sergeant* Drendel, was close to seventy. He'd lost a leg at St Quentin only a week before the French surrender in 1871, had stumped around on a wooden one ever since.

'Otto?'

Slightly quavery high tone, and an impression of astonishment, as if she'd thought he might be dead. As indeed he might have been. And it *was* a long time since he'd been in touch with them; communications out of Bruges hadn't been all that good. Telling her now, 'Splendid to hear your voice, Mama — and sounding strong, you're obviously in good health and heart. Listen — in case we're cut off — this is long-distance — I'm only calling to ask how you both are, and let you know I'm in good shape. Happen to be on dry land and near a telephone that works, for once . . . You *are* well, are you?'

'I am — *quite* well, thank you, Otto. Your father too. He's at his depot, of course. Have you sunk more English since we last heard from you?'

'Two in this last week, as it happens. Got slightly dented in the course of it, so for a while I'm land-bound. I'm so glad you're bearing up, Mama — and the Sergeant sounds his usual self — '

'We're fortunate, of course, in that we have our own produce — eggs, poultry, cereals and — you know . . . The ice-house is well stocked.

But the country as a whole, in the towns especially — '

'Turnips as the staple diet, so I heard.'

'Thanks to the damned English! And we hear now our so-called government's begging for an armistice! Going on bended knees to the Americans!'

'I don't know about bended knees, but — yes, I gather . . . Mama, is Gerda all right?'

'You didn't hear, then.'

'Hear what?'

'Heinrich — the week before last — '

'What? Shot down?'

'Killed, anyway. He used just to laugh when I told him how *frightfully* dangerous — '

'Poor old Heinrich.' Gerda's husband, Heinrich Hesse, when Otto had last heard of him, had been leading a squadron of Albatross fighters. 'Or rather, poor Gerda. *Damn* it all. I tried to call her a few minutes ago. Oh, really, that's too bad!'

'She's devastated. *Devastated.* Otto, you look after yourself now. We want you home safe and sound. And soon. Isn't it time you had leave? Look, *take* some, go to Berlin, give her a shoulder to cry on and then bring her home. Those things you go about in — *submarines* — why, they're worse than — '

He cut in with an assurance that the modern submarines were as safe as houses. Safer, in fact. But that if the armistice negotiations got anywhere he'd be home the first minute he could in any case. And yes, *would* see poor Gerda. But he had to run now. He'd try to get through to her this afternoon. If by chance *she* spoke to her before he did, please give her his love and deepest commiserations. And love and respects to Papa, of course.

He hung up. Glad to have heard about Heinrich *before* speaking to Gerda, who'd be lost without that fellow.

★ ★ ★

'Ah — von Mettendorff.'

The group around Schwaeble opened up to let Otto through. There were a dozen or fifteen officers in the bar, all with glasses in their hands — a few had beers but it was mostly schnapps. Schwaeble said, 'I'm in the chair, what'll you have?'

'Well — thank you, sir. Schnapps, I think.'

He'd gestured to the steward, now looked back at Otto. 'Any particular reason to look so damn miserable?'

Smiles and chuckles all round. Glasses all full but no-one actually drinking yet. He nodded to Schwaeble. 'Heard only a minute ago that my brother-in-law was shot down — killed — week before last. I don't know where. He was commanding a fighter squadron.'

'I'm extremely sorry, von Mettendorff.' The steward came with Otto's drink on a silver-plated tray. There'd been a general murmuring of sympathy. Schwaeble held up his glass: 'Our first toast then, to that brave man. What was his name?'

'Hesse. Heinrich Hesse.'

122

'To his memory and honour!'

They drank to him, Otto restraining a sudden and unexpected urge to weep. The schnapps' fire in his throat might have served as cover for such a lapse, but in fact the excuse of it wasn't needed: he'd regained control and Schwaeble was raising his glass again.

'Gentlemen! We drink to Kapitan-Leutnant Otto von Mettendorff!'

Shouts of applause, before the glasses were emptied. Otto hearing it all, of course, but with Gerda's misery still in his mind needing a second or two to catch on to what Schwaeble had just told him, that he'd been promoted from senior lieutenant to lieutenant-commander. Schwaeble booming now, 'Well deserved, at that.' Signalling to the steward, this time indicating only his own glass and Otto's. 'Your promotion comes with Kommodore Michelsen's personal congratulations. I had him on the telephone this morning. Incidentally, what about your patrol report?'

Otto took the wad of foolscap from an inside pocket. 'Haven't access to a typewriting machine, unfortunately.'

'I'll get it done. Drop by the Kommodore's office tomorrow forenoon to sign the copies.'

'Aye, sir. Your health. With your permission, the next round's mine.'

Helena would be entertained at the Snake Pit by a kapitan-leutnant, he was thinking, not a mere oberleutnant. *That* shouldn't exactly spoil one's chances.

6

Helena called Otto at the Mess on Sunday evening. He'd had a few brandies by then, with a bunch of brother officers intent on celebrating his promotion. Wanting *some* damn thing to celebrate. These included Stahl, with whom he'd spent an hour or so at the hospital during the afternoon, chatting with crewmen who'd had bones broken — ribs, legs, arms and collar-bones, one fractured skull, other less serious head-injuries — and in the early evening he'd managed to get through to Gerda.

Contrary to what his mother had said, she seemed to him to be taking the loss of her husband very well, phlegmatically acknowledging that she was only one of thousands in that situation. 'And you can't have half the female population sitting round moaning and wailing.' It was a situation which simply had to be accepted and coped with; one had also to remember that Heinrich had been doing a job he'd enormously enjoyed, that he'd have *chosen* to be killed in the course of it rather than to have survived in some less hazardous occupation.

'So who am *I* to pity myself, disgrace him?'

'I don't see any disgrace in natural grief — or any advantage in suppressing it. Better for you to shed tears, Gerda.'

'Oh, I have done. A lot of them, and I expect I'll shed more. No-one else will see them, that's the point. I'm deeply saddened, I mourn him and miss him, I dare say always will. Well, my whole life is changed. Like roots pulled up is how it feels. But it goes on — as he'd have expected it to — even if it's privately miserable for a while — or for ever.'

'Mama said you were distraite. No — 'devastated' was the word.'

'I was. *Am.* Taking myself in hand now, that's all. As I think most of us do, after the first shock. What's your news?'

'I've been promoted. This morning, actually. I'm now a kapitan-leutnant.'

'You should have started off by telling me that!'

'No I shouldn't. But certainly, it's good.'

'It's wonderful! I'm so glad for you!'

'Although the way things are shaping — '

'Not to be spoken of, I think. Best to talk and think of *now* — and yesterday — maybe tomorrow at a pinch, but not much further. Beyond that, blind eyes and deaf ears, and — *hope?*'

'You're a great girl, Gerda.'

'Always was. Didn't you notice? How's the love-life these days?'

'Exciting. At least, very promising. In fact — '

'Wedding bells in prospect?'

He'd snorted. 'Not on the cards at all. Not even thought of it. At this of all times one would be crazy to. Even if *she* — '

'Bet you she *is* thinking of it. So watch out. Pretty, is she?'

'How many guesses d'you need?'

A laugh. 'Never a spiritual exercise exactly, was it!'

'Oh, I don't know. Always was a degree of — spirit . . . Believe me, there certainly is now!'

'Spirit like a stallion has, you mean. That's hardly what . . . ' She'd checked that. 'Anyway, who or what is she?'

'I'll tell you when I see you — which I look forward to very much. For the time being I'll only say that she's irresistibly attractive and absolutely charming. Intelligent, amusing — this amuses you?'

'Otto — those very words and identical tone of voice about a certain other young lady — to whom *I* had introduced you a few years ago?'

'Really. Well — it's possible. Only a certain number of words to choose from, eh? Similar emotions involved, too . . . But — as I say, let's save it till we meet. It's amazing we've talked this long already without being cut off. Gerda — however things turn out, take care of yourself and let's see each other soon. Before long we may all be at loose ends — you realise that?'

'Of course I realise it. So we'd meet *chez nous*. There are worse fates . . . Where does she live, this paragon?'

'Actually, I'm not sure.'

'Don't know where she *lives*?'

'I know where she's living and working at the moment, but — '

Click, and a dead line. He swore, put the receiver up on its hook, thought of trying to get through again but decided against it. It had been a satisfactory call: he was fond of his sister,

126

always had been, and now was proud of her as well.

Might write her a note, tell her so.

A lot of the talk in the Mess later on was about the projected fleet action or *Flottenvorstoss*. Schwaeble with a loosened tongue at lunch this morning had divulged that the *Hochseeflotte*'s battle squadrons that weren't there already would be assembling in Schillig Roads on Tuesday, and that at some time or other there was to be a conference of admirals and captains on board Hipper's flagship, the *Baden*. Michelsen as FdU had been summoned to attend. So it seemed it *was* going to take place, the so-called 'Death Ride'.

Louis Farber was saying — speculating — 'Sailing at dusk on Tuesday, say — having by then raised steam for full speed — this is really most likely, from what you say Schwaeble told you — then action would follow in the early hours of Wednesday, maybe. Or in the course of Wednesday. If the British have taken the bait and come storming out as they're supposed to — eh?'

Farber's boat was currently in dry dock getting a new propeller-shaft fitted. He was a korvettenkapitan and had recently got married.

Walter Bohme asked him, 'Excuse me, but — if they take the bait and come out where?'

'Well, nice question, and I can propound my theory. Simple, but logical enough. There was a large-scale fleet operation planned two years ago, latter part of '16, after the Skaggerak imbroglio. Von Scheer's plan — he was still C-in-C, of course, and Hipper had the battle cruisers. The scheme was dropped, for some reason that I forget — if I ever knew it — and all we heard thereafter was how splendid it *would* have been. The entire fleet was to have been at sea — battle squadrons, battle cruisers, cruisers and destroyers — and ourselves, of course. Attacks by light surface forces, cruisers and destroyers would have been made on the Flanders coast and in the mouth of the Thames; this would have provoked a sortie by the Grand Fleet into the southern part of the North Sea, into newly-laid minefields and — all of *us*, of course, we'd have been sitting there waiting to greet them with our torpedoes, the *Hochseeflotte* then only having the trouble of finishing a few off. Well, it's odds-on, *I* reckon, that this must be what Hipper's planning now. Having a ready-made plan, so to speak, in his bottom drawer — some detail requiring alteration here and there, no doubt . . . '

'Excuse me, sir.' A steward, low-voiced at Otto's elbow. 'Telephone call for you.'

'Oh. Good.'

Thinking as he put down his brandy glass, *Helena*. Then warning himself against disappointment: might be Gerda ringing back; or their father, if she'd called him with the news of the promotion. But no — couldn't be, for the simple reason he hadn't told Gerda — or his mother — where he was. Before the door clashed shut behind him he'd heard the steward call after him, 'Telephone in the Mess secretary's office, sir!'

No Mess secretary in it, anyway. Door

standing open and the 'phone with its receiver lying on the desk beside it. He went round the desk to a swivel chair and pulled the thing closer, back-handing a basket of paperwork out of the way.

Taking a breath: heartbeat quickening.

'Von Mettendorff.'

'Otto! It's Helena! Just got in and I had your message. Such a *lovely* surprise! How long have you been in Wilhelmshaven, for heaven's sake?'

'When I first tried to call you — at your place of work — I'd been here about five minutes. That was yesterday. Oh, *Helena* — you beautiful, sweet-sounding — '

'If I'd had the least idea, I wouldn't have gone home.'

'Home?'

'My parents like to see me now and then. Matter of fact I quite like to see them, occasionally.'

Maybe she *had* told him she lived in Hamburg. He'd thought about that, after the chat with Gerda, recognising that in the course of the long evening at Kramer's he surely would have asked her — or she'd have volunteered the information — as part of the usual getting-to-know-each-other process. In which case he couldn't have been listening very hard; mind on other things, maybe. Well, it *would* have been. One might rather hope hers might have been too. She asked him now, 'How long are you going to be with us this time?'

'Can't say. Weeks, perhaps. *This* week anyway. My boat's had a knock or two, out of action for a while. But things are so uncertain anyway — in general, I mean — '

'Great God, aren't they!'

'We can discuss all that when we're together, though. Monday, for a start — Monday evening? Matter of fact I'm off duty for ten days, so whatever time you have free — '

'Have you been hurt?'

'No. Only dazed — reeling just at this moment, hearing your voice and picturing you . . . I've been living with you constantly in my mind, Helena, days and nights on end, *longing* for you and — '

'Definitely not hurt — telling the truth now?'

'Definitely. I was feeling a bit played-out yesterday, but — anyway, the sawbones is a friend of mine. Tell you about it when I see you. Helena — Monday evening, all right with you?'

'That's — tomorrow — not far short of *today* . . . '

'Is it all right for you? *Please* say yes it is. I'll book at Rastede, all right? What time should I come for you?'

'Rastede . . . '

'We did agree — '

'I know we did. Only it's — out of the blue like this, a little — well, unnerving . . . '

'Don't let it be. I'll take good care of you, I promise. And listen — the rest of the week as well — to kick off with, say Tuesday to Saturday? There or wherever else you like, I don't care as long as we're together — and with at least *some* privacy.'

She'd breathed a laugh. 'Talk tomorrow. Must

130

hush and creep upstairs now. You know, under cover of the snoring. Come about eight?'

★ ★ ★

The train from Portsmouth was an hour late chuffing into Waterloo, and following what had been a long day's work at C-in-C Portsmouth's headquarters on Portsdown Hill, Anne was tired enough to have dropped off once or twice. Third Officer Anne Laurie in her long-skirted sailor's outfit, head back and mouth open — snoring, as like as not.

Having to wear uniform was enough to make one feel tired. No real reason for that, just that she felt out of place and character in it. Drab, unglamorous. Uniforms, it seemed to her, were for men. She wasn't truly a Wren in any case, she was an interpreter First Class in German and in French, *disguised* as a Wren. And if she was going on this jaunt to Scapa Flow she'd be attired like this for the whole darn trip, at least until she — they — came back down to Argyll and her mother's house.

If her mother, incidentally, could stand the idea — and her husband tolerate it. Send Mama a telegram in the morning, she thought — if it's still on, Sam can put a date on it and Sue can fit in with that. The big surprise, and influence on her own thinking, had been Sue's jumping at the prospect of accompanying her as chaperone. Not last night, when Sam had brought her back to Chester Square in his hired car, escorted her to the door of the flat and kissed her goodnight,

131

accepting the fact she couldn't have brought him in. As it turned out, Sue had been asleep and hadn't woken, but bet your life if they'd risked it she would have.

Discussion of Sam's proposal had had to be left to this morning, anyway, when the alarm had gone off at five-thirty and she'd made tea and taken some in to Sue; Sue waking and asking grumpily what was going on — middle of the damn night . . .

She'd begun, 'It's a quarter to six, and — '

'And you're *dressed*.' Then remembering: 'Of course. All got up like I don't know what. Portsmouth, isn't it?'

'It is, but — Sue, tell me one thing. When does your hunting season start?'

'Huh?' Blinking at her. 'Fortnight's time. Lots of hunts have started, but the Grafton are late this year for some reason. Why?'

'How would you like a free trip to the Orkney Islands?'

'When?'

'A few days' time, probably.'

'Well — yes, I think I'd love it. Only thing is, they'd never let me go. But — hang on, the grey matter's stirring — Orkneys alias Scapa Flow deriving from some plot or scheme of Uncle Sam's, intuition tells me?'

'Not bad, either, at this time of day. He wants *me* to go because it's a chance for him to meet my mother. Stopping off in Argyll on the way south, to get her blessing — or not, as the case may be. That's a contingency which he seems to discount. But as the lid's going to blow off any

132

day now, he thinks it might be the only chance he'll get.'

'Makes sense. If parental approval's necessary — and if you're going to marry him, in any case. Romantic evening, was it?'

'*Lovely* evening. Indoors, that is. It's still drizzling now, by the way. Don't you envy me, setting out for blooming Portsmouth? But listen — Sam's talked to Bertie Hope about it. Damn cheek really, before inviting me — he admits that. But Bertie apparently wasn't at all against it, except for stipulating that I should have a chaperone with me. And I'm putting this to you at Sam's suggestion. He said something like, 'What about taking that nice little Sue along?'' She saw Sue's grimace, and added, 'Whether Bertie'd agree to letting you off for a fortnight is something else, of course.'

'Fortnight?'

'Two days getting there, two more coming back, about two on Orkney. It's a routine thing, the assistant attachés take it in turn, taking secret stuff up to their battle squadron, Rear-Admiral what's his name.'

'Rodmer.'

'Right. So say a week doing all that, and a second one to allow for the stop-off in Argyll. Which might be fun. Once he's met my mother, Sam would take himself off, and we could have a relaxed few days.'

'With your mother and mad stepfather?'

'Eccentric, let's say.'

'And you've agreed to all this, have you?'

'Not by any means. At first I thought it was

133

plain daft, no question of taking it seriously, then I said I'd think about it — and he's going to telephone this evening, by which time I'm supposed to have made my mind up. My inclination from the start's been to say no, not on your life, then I weakened slightly. But — for instance, he could do it all on his own, call on old Mum and introduce himself, couldn't he? Shy of that, I suppose. He *is* a shy man, you know. Doesn't seem to be, on the surface, but he is. Anyway — it *is* barmy this time of year, freezing cold, sea probably very rough — '

'God, yes. Sea to be crossed. How'd we do that?'

'In a destroyer, he said. Only an hour or two, but — Sue, that bit of sea is the Pentland Firth, it's notorious for being rough!'

'Still, it's something *different*. Heavens, a ride in a *destroyer*! And I'd like to meet your mother and her artist. Him especially. Angus McCaig, I've always liked his stuff — as much as I've seen of it. The one big doubt is whether Bertie'd let me go, isn't it. In fact — unless you're absolutely set on going, no point even asking him.'

'Sam suggested that if you wouldn't or couldn't I might recruit one of the typewriters.'

'Blinker's Beauty Chorus?'

'All terribly nice, I know, but there isn't one I'd want to have with me for a fortnight.'

'Don't take La Bailey, anyway. She'd have Uncle Sam off of you in two shakes.'

'From what one hears, she has more than enough on her plate already. He'd run a mile, anyway. Sue — do me a favour, stop calling him

Uncle Sam? Amusing once, faintly boring the second time, thereafter *very* boring. I doubt if he'd like it even once.'

'You *are* going to marry him, are you? Are you sure this isn't just him getting up to a bit of hokey-pokey?'

'He assured me it isn't. But marrying him — God knows . . . This Scapa thing, though — he'll be 'phoning me this evening, so if by then you haven't changed your mind — subject to Bertie Hope's approval, obviously — '

'If it's not forthcoming you surely *could* find someone else.'

'Don't think I'd try. Frankly, I'm surprised you're interested. I told Sam I was sure you wouldn't be — on account of the hunting. But if you did come along — well, it really *might* be fun . . . Sue, I must run now. God, look at the time . . . '

That had been this morning, cock-crow time. An age ago, it felt like — an age of cold trains and wet streets. She took a taxi from Charing Cross to Chester Square. Feeling extravagant in doing so, but tired enough to justify it. Besides which there was the same cold drizzle that had persisted all day, she felt some obligation to be there when Sam called, and last but by no means least she could claim reimbursement from ID funds.

Shivering at a bit of drizzle, she chided herself as the taxi trundled out of the station precincts, while actively considering a visit to Scapa Flow in the depths of winter?

Have to be nuts.

As well as shamingly indecisive — on the Scapa issue, but more importantly the much larger, life-shaping one. How long before Sam's patience snapped?

Well — if it did — *when* it did, *tant pis*. Maybe it *ought* to. All right, so she was setting the terms, and he wanted her enough to accept them; you might think of that as determination, single-mindedness, might even be flattered by it. Maybe she was, a little. Although she doubted whether Charles would have put up with her as she was now.

Delaying tactics hadn't arisen with him, anyway. By the time he'd popped the question they'd both known the answer to it — she'd been *longing* to be his wife, and he'd felt the same, with a shared desire — anxiety — to have as long as possible together before they sent him off to France.

In fact they'd had a few weeks, which in the basic, physical sense had been sadly disappointing. First night as marvellous as they'd both known it was going to be, but from there on, from that morning —

Forget it. She'd still loved him. Had been reminding herself ever since how *much* she'd loved him.

Sue met her in the hall. Comfortably warm hall, stove obviously doing its stuff, and Sue in her woolly dressing-gown and slippers, telling her, 'He telephoned an hour ago — your not-to-be-called-uncle Sam did — expressed *chagrin* that you weren't back, said he'd be in touch tomorrow. He was just leaving to dine with some other Americans, he said. We didn't discuss the Orkneys project. Had a hard day in Pompey, did you?'

'Not all that bad. Even if I do look like death warmed up. Lovely and warm in here, anyway.' Reverting to Sam and the Orkneys, then: 'Gives us more time, at least.' Sue had retreated into the sitting-room, while Anne had been shucking off her long Navy raincoat and hideous but rain-stopping Wren hat, and now followed, asking her whether she'd had any further thoughts on the subject.

Sue nodded, swinging her legs up on the sofa. 'No change of mind, however, not in the least. It'd be silly not to go. You anyway, me too if Bertie permits. I think it might be tremendous fun — and not the sort of chance we'd get again. Don't you agree? Oh, but listen — a rather pleasant-sounding man telephoned earlier on, first asking for you and then probing in would-be devious ways which actually wouldn't have fooled an infant, wanting to know whether you were still in widow's weeds and unengaged, etcetera. His name is — or was — I've got it here somewhere . . . '

Anne had removed her black uniform shoes and was massaging her toes. The shoes kept the wet out, all right, but became heavier as the day wore on. Probably come back from the Orkneys lame, she thought. Sue meanwhile finding an envelope on the back of which she'd scribbled 'Wing Commander Bunny Farqhuar, RAF, formerly Flight Commander Farqhuar RNAS.'

She'd read that out. Anne gazing at her in surprise.

'Well, I'll be . . . '

'Good or bad?'

'Well — you know . . . Old friend — quite close at one time. Forgotten all about him!'

'Get him along here anyway, I rather liked the sound of him.'

'Might have him here when you *aren't*, then. Hunting weekends, for instance. He must be back from — oh, wherever it was they sent him. Italy, I think. Yes, Italy. I last heard from him when he saw Charles listed as missing believed killed. He flew seaplanes — I mean Bunny did.'

'And?'

'I knew him before I met Charles. At least, before I married . . . He tried to dissuade me, I remember. Fat hope he had, but — yes, *nice* man. I wonder how he got my number here?'

'Hm. He didn't say. Some mutual acquaintance, probably. Certainly couldn't have got it from *us*. Foreign Office, perhaps?'

'That's it. Where I was working when I knew him. Frightening how the brain slows down when one's tired. But — yes, of course, his letter was forwarded from the OF, I remember.'

'I wish *I* had hair the colour of Indian ink.'

'Silly. Your hair's lovely. Think we might open a tin of sardines?'

'Go ahead. I've eaten. Welsh rarebit. Yum-yum . . . Your Wing Commander said he'd ring again, probably tomorrow. You going to bath?'

'If the water's hot. I'll get my snack first, though.'

'Then I'll bath and leave the water in for you.'

★ ★ ★

Monday morning, the 'phone rang when they were having their breakfast of coffee and toast. Sue asked her quickly, 'If it's Himself, what'll you say?'

'That I'll go along if they'll let you come as chaperone. Otherwise, not.'

She was on her feet. Sue nodding. 'He might get on to Bertie himself. Might be best if he did, in fact. But Anne — do ask him *when*?'

'Yes.' She picked it up, thinking as she did so that it might be Bunny Farquhar: seeing *his* face, not Sam's, in that moment. 'Hello?'

'Anne. Sam here. We missed each other last night. You must have had a long day, eh?'

'*And* the train was late. Anyway, Sam — the answer's yes — yes please — as long as they'll let Sue come with us. Think you can fix that — with Bertie Hope?'

'I don't know. I'll try, sure. And as far as that goes — well, wonderful. Great to have her along as well. But — definitely *no* if they can't spare her?'

'Yes. I'm sorry, Sam — forgive me, but I don't want to be stuck for a fortnight with someone I don't get on with. Sue and I are good friends, it'd be fun for both of us — and when we're on Orkney and you're busy with whatever you'll be doing . . . In any case, it's Bertie Hope who's insisting on the chaperoning, so — '

'I'll have a word with him. If I can get him. But meantime you and Sue might — exert persuasive charm?'

'If we get a chance, we'll try. But Sam, I was thinking — if the answer's a lemon, you *could* visit my mother on your own. I'd send her a wire introducing you, and — '

'I'd much, *much* prefer to have you with me. In fact the both of you. Please tell Sue that. But listen, departure's set for tomorrow, Tuesday, the night train.'

'*Tomorrow!*'

'First-class sleepers from Euston to Glasgow, slow train to Thurso — a night there, probably — land at Stromness Thursday. Gives me the rest of that day and Friday, and we'd travel south over the weekend, get to Oban late Sunday or Monday — if that could be left a *little* vague, in case of hold-ups?'

'I won't wire until we know for sure, anyway.'

'No. Better not. Listen, does Sue have a uniform of any kind?'

'Oh, yes, she does.' Looking at her across the room. 'She's a Fanny. No — seriously — FANY, stands for First Aid Nursing Yeomanry. Actually nothing to do with nursing — not in her case anyway; her sort mostly drive generals about in motor cars, that kind of thing.' She told Sue, 'Have to wear uniform, worst luck, both of us.' Then to Sam, 'She's pulling a face. But actually she looks very nice in her get-up, which is more than I do in mine. Sam, here I am seeming to lay down conditions, but we both really do hope we can go with you, and it's a very good idea — the Argyll bit, meeting my mother, all that.'

'Well, I'm glad. Very glad.'

'So let's keep our fingers crossed.'

'I'll ring Hope, or try to. Meantime, do whatever you can. Soon as we know, I'll book the sleepers and your own people should issue you both with railway warrants. All you'd need do is pack your bags — and allow for the weather not being exactly tropical, huh?'

★ ★ ★

Hope was closeted with Blinker Hall. Sue left a message with Miss Tribe, Hope's secretary, to the effect that she and Anne would be grateful for a minute of his time when he could spare one, and went off to her Room 40 work. Anne in the ID general office had a sheaf of intercepted and decoded signals with their German texts rather hastily translated into scrawled English by the night-watch people, who'd now gone off to their breakfasts, leaving the corridor at this end of the Old Building slightly steamy and soap-scented, where an office which in days of yore might have housed some hoary old admiral — 'solid ivory from the jaw up' — had been converted into a wash-room for their use.

Although the signals were of a routine, unexciting kind, the translations still had to be checked minutely in case one of them might be something more than that. A word or two inaccurately translated had been known to lead to quite drastic misunderstanding of the message as a whole. Tedious work therefore, but essential. She was about halfway through when Sue came back to tell her there'd been a signal from U-boat HQ Wilhelmshaven addressed to three different U-boats demanding *Report forthwith your ETA Wilhelmshaven*, and UB81 had not been one of them.

'So?'

Sue looked, surprised at having to explain the obvious. 'They're chasing up boats that haven't responded to the general recall. Knowing they might have come to grief. Logically, shouldn't that have applied to what's his name, von Munchhausen? They can't know he was sunk — can they?'

Anne shook her head. 'You tell me.'

'Two possible solutions. One is that his patrol area was so close to home he'd have made it back several days ago if he *hadn't* been, and the alternative is that he *did* get back.'

'You mean wasn't sunk?'

'That's conceivable.'

'But with the detail in that report you quoted to me — seemed to me fairly certain. Didn't you think so?'

'*Seemed* so.'

'What about those that *are* mentioned?'

'In the past week, two others have been sunk — both as it happens by British submarines. One in the Skaggerak approaches, the other off Cape Wrath. One might assume those are — were — two of the three. No way of telling which, though, they weren't identifiable.' She shrugged. 'Question for Bertie perhaps, whether in his seaman's-eye view the destroyers could have been mistaken. The *big* issue of the day, though — well, it connects peripherally with this, the fact they're still trying to round up their strays — is they're being turned around and sent back out. To God knows where. Unusual dearth of signals now, coinciding with it.' She'd dropped her voice. 'Distinctly fishy, lots of head-scratching in progress. Almost certainly what our lords and masters are conferring about — needing to tell Operations Division what's happening, and not much more than guesswork to go on. Meanwhile, all telephone calls for either of them are being held — ie they're in purdah.'

'Let's hope it doesn't last too long, then.'

'What it amounts to, in a nutshell — the *guess* is U-boats are being deployed to lie in ambush for Beatty's ships. Reason to suspect this being that we know the *Hochseeflotte* have been ordered by von Scheer to 'strike at the English fleet', and that a new, very extensive minefield's been laid during the past forty-eight hours. We know *this* for absolutely sure because our chaps have already swept it up. One way and another it does look very much as if they're going to try to lure Beatty out — which means they'll send out their battle squadrons: what Beatty's been praying for ever since Jutland.' A smile, and a hand on Anne's shoulder: 'At least *as* important as our jaunt to Orkney.'

7

He'd booked at the Snake Pit — Grueninger's Restaurant and Weinstube, as it called itself and was listed in the directory — as soon as he and Helena had hung up. At the Pit one booked not a table but a room, and he'd told the woman, might have been Frau or Frl. Grueninger, that he and the young lady would be there at about eight-thirty. Mentioning the 'young lady' so they'd know the table should be laid for two and that it wasn't a stag party, for which they'd usually offer to get waitresses in, instead of the old waiters who tended to be blind, or at least unseeing.

Monday now: 28 October, and the whole day to pass. On his back on the iron-framed bed, hands linked behind his head, listing what he did have to do, despite being on the sick-list. Down to the boat first, check that Claus Stahl had everything in hand. There'd be leave granted to those who had it due to them and wanted it now — wouldn't get it until the boat had been taken into dockyard hands — but Stahl needed to have the paperwork ready for Otto to initial, then for FdU's rubber stamp, and a copy for the paymaster's office for the issue of railway warrants as well as pay. Ship's stores, then — muster and accounting, always a pain in the bloody neck. Torpedo and ammunition expenditure was simple enough — about the only thing

144

that was. Engine-room stores were for Hinten-berger to deal with, of course; he'd gone on his weekend leave to Bremen but should be back by 0800.

Had better be, in fact — he'd gone in Graischer's motor. Which was another thing — see Graischer and beg for the loan of it this evening. Also, as instructed by Schwaeble, call in at FdU's office, sign typed copies of the patrol report.

What else . . .

Well — various things to discuss with Hintenberger, who surely *would* be back. Oh, and visit the naval tailor to get an extra gold stripe sewn on the sleeves of three uniform jackets, and epaulettes changed on his full dress uniform and greatcoat. One jacket to be attended to immediately, rest at the tailor's early convenience.

Not a word to Helena about that. See how long it takes her to notice.

Turning his head to gaze out at steel-grey sky and fast-moving clouds, thinking, *This very evening* . . .

Might she be thinking of it at this moment? On the 'phone she'd sounded scared, sort of breathless. Right from the start therefore, calm her, reassure her, give her time to recognise her own need and warm to it, relax to it. She *might* even be a virgin. As the English girl had been: not that that had particularly surprised him, hadn't really given it much thought, but she *had* had that school-girlish look and manner, as he'd recalled in later musings. Manner, for sure: she

145

and Gerda very much alike then in their giggly ways; the English friend she'd raved about being in fact prettier than her. Enormously attractive, with a stunning figure — he'd found it difficult to take his eyes off her, after a while hadn't bothered to. And *she* hadn't been scared of anything — not visibly, in any case, had sort of revelled in it. Schoolgirl playing tricks on teacher, out for all the fun she could get.

He had, he supposed, thought about her quite often over the years. In some ways, regretfully. Not that they'd have got together or even tried to, even if there'd been no war. Not even with Gerda as a go-between — which might not have been on the cards in any case; relations between those two had cooled considerably just at that time — he didn't think they'd continued to share digs from then on.

Blamed Gerda for the way it had turned out, maybe?

Helena was a different proposition entirely: not in the least schoolgirlish, but seriously, consciously sexy. *Might* be a virgin — hence the nervousness, which that breathlessness had seemed to indicate — but despite that, knowing exactly what she was about, wanting it and *intending* it.

Could *not* be a virgin. And even if she was, might be utterly fantastic. If the breathlessness was for *him*, her word 'unnerving' applicable more to the venue than to the rendezvous itself?

Possible. The place did have a reputation, and when at their first meeting on board Franz Winter's boat he'd proposed taking her there, her reaction had been sharply negative, dismissive even. In fact — recognising this for the first time, oddly enough — he'd have deserved a *total* brush-off, having been so brash as to have made such a proposal — blatantly, right off the cuff.

A measure of (a) his own condition, (b) her effect on him. The life one led as commander of a U-boat, the strain one was used to and lived with, took for granted but none the less *was* strain, considerable and in some ways constant. There'd been no such element in 1913, obviously; to match what one remembered as her girlishness, one's own approach must have been fairly juvenile. Exceptionally attractive girl — no lack of *physical* development — and that glorious summer; a kiss or two — or 200, more like: she'd been *extremely* tactile.

Out of sheer innocence?

She and Gerda must have discussed such things, though; she must have known what she was getting into. When he'd grabbed her that day in the tack-room and she'd responded so keenly to his kiss and touch, and after a few minutes whispered, 'Oh, if only you weren't leaving and I didn't have to either.' He'd kissed her some more, then murmured close to her ear, 'Why don't we spend an evening together in Berlin?'

'How? When? You're off to Kiel, and — '

'Kiel by way of Berlin. My aunt has an apartment there which she rarely uses and to which I have a key. You're leaving the day after tomorrow — I could explain to you how to find it, and be there to greet you, then move into a hotel nearby so you'd have the apartment to

147

yourself. How might that be?'

'My mother's expecting me, though, and she knows when I'm leaving, so — '

'So send a telegram. Say you're spending a day and a night in Berlin with Gerda in her aunt's flat. We'd have a splendid evening on the town. Go on a Bummel — Berliners' word for a promenade — window-shopping along the grander streets — the Linden, Ku'damm, Leipzigerstrasse — find some cabaret we like the look of, dine and dance. The tango, huh?'

'I adore the tango!'

'We've been forbidden to dance it. The Kaiser has decreed that it's an immoral dance, unsuitable for officers to indulge in. I ask you — *immoral!* Nuts to the old clown anyway — I'll be in civvies, we'll tango till the cows come home!'

'Sounds absolutely *ripping*, Otto!'

'Shall we do it, then?'

Her answer had been to hug him. In her own language, he'd thought afterwards, in the excitement then possessing her, 'glee' would vie with 'spree', and kisses were a fun thing, *naughty* thing, they'd go along thrillingly with playing hooky. Her head back, greenish eyes glowing into his. A whisper then: 'Draw me a little map?'

★　★　★

He suggested to Helena that Monday evening, 'We might take a few days off together — if you'd like to and they'd grant you leave. Somewhere not too far, but far enough not to

148

bump into acquaintances round every corner?'

'I'd *like* to, certainly. Hanover, perhaps? If one *could*. Trouble is, with everything so unpredictable — '

'Might moot it, though? Grounds of some relation sick or bereaved?'

What had led to this had been her querying whether he truly *was* all right to have been excused duty for ten days: she'd asked him this in the presence of the Muellers, in whose living-room he'd spent an awkward few minutes waiting for her to come down. When she'd appeared he'd kissed her hand, murmured to her that she was even more beautiful than he'd remembered, and how kind to spare him an evening so soon after his return. While every natural instinct was to take her in his arms, kiss her more deeply and for longer than she'd ever been kissed before. She was utterly sensational. Despite the hip-length fur jacket she'd already put on and had buttoned as high as her throat. He'd been on the point of dropping some reference to Kramer's, the restaurant there in Oldenburg, had desisted because it was conceivable that it was shut on Mondays, which as locals they'd have known. Might have checked, he thought, telephoned the place, if he'd had his wits about him. He did at any rate have the nous to warn them that he might bring her home rather later than one would normally, since the people with whom they were dining tended to drag things out, rather, and the host being very much senior to him — well, one would simply have to sit it out.

She'd commented as he'd helped her into Graischer's motor, 'Nothing wrong with your imagination, Otto.'

'It's you I've been imagining.' Kissing her while arranging a rug around her. Her dress, black and lacy, wouldn't have kept her warm, exactly. Telling her, 'You'd be amazed, the hours you've spent in my arms. And at some of the things we've said to each other. Said and *done* . . . But wasn't I good in there, with your Muellers?'

'So don't spoil it now.' Evading him, turning away. 'They've eyes like buzzards. And when one's on the telephone I'm sure they listen — whatever's been happening, it all goes dead quiet!'

That was when he'd suggested going away together. Since he had nothing to keep him in Wilhelmshaven, or wouldn't as soon as his boat went into the shipyard for repairs.

'Had that bad a time of it, did you?'

'Well. Hang on a minute.' He'd set the choke and the timer, now went to the front to use the crank. Back inside then, switching on weak headlights and squeaky wipers to clear the screen, telling her, 'Your scent's exciting. So are you. Everything about you. Honestly, I've thought about you so much you wouldn't believe it. Sorry — repeating myself . . . But yes — answering your question — we did have quite a hard time. Sank one of them — two actually, there was one earlier on and we didn't get off exactly Scot-free from *that* one. Then the second time, *really* got it in the neck.' He had the car

150

moving: tried doing without the noisy wipers, but one needed them to clear the glass of a fog that had thickened in the quarter-hour he'd been in the house. Into third gear, reaching to her then with that hand. 'Tell you the truth, there was a stretch of hours when it looked as if we were done for. It was the thought of not getting back to you that really made one desperate. I'm not saying that made me sit it out, do the things that eventually did save us — that's my job, I have a submarine and twenty-five men besides myself — '

'As few as that?'

'Perhaps you're thinking of Franz Winter's boat. Mine's smaller, what's called a Coastal. Franz's is bigger and in some respects quite different in layout. He's due in tomorrow, by the way.'

'*Is* he . . . '

'But they'll send him out again pretty well immediately — unless like me he's in need of repairs. Anyway, what I was saying — I'll get this over, because I do want to tell you, and that'll be the end of 'shop' talk — in the worst of it we were lying on the sea-bed, waiting for it to be dark up top so I could try to surface — couldn't before that, the enemy destroyers who'd smashed us up would surely have been waiting to finish us off. Several hours, therefore, nothing to be done except lie quiet. Well, I made it bearable by concentrating on *you*. Visualising you, daydreaming of getting back here to you — of this exact situation in fact, only as a fantasy, a *dream*!'

'Are you saying you're in love with me?'

'Since the moment I first set eyes on you. I was with old Franz on the casing of his boat when you came along the jetty with those friends of yours — you in that orange dress which you also wore the night we went to Kramer's. It's in that dress I've seen you and loved you ever since.'

'Would have been much too cold tonight. So you'll be getting quite a different picture.'

'Well, I already glimpsed — black, and — '

'I was going to say — if I may, please — that speaking of love — '

'*Please* do. Oh — damn it . . . ' Rounding a sharpish bend, and a heavy truck coming the other way, taking up more than half the road's width, Hans Graischer's weak lights washing at close range over regimental markings on its mudguards, and *its* lights which hadn't been visible from around the corner, for a moment blinding . . . 'Damn. Sorry, Helena.' Then: 'You were about to say?'

'That I feel the same. It's — I suppose — why I'm here.'

That hand to her again: 'I can't wait to kiss you.'

'Might be safer if you did. Wait, I mean. Is it going to be all right, at this place?'

'Going to be fine. Don't worry about a thing. I stopped on my way out to you, saw our room and — '

'Our room.'

'Our dining-room — which we have to ourselves, yes. It'll be cosy enough — they'd only just lit the fire but it'll be going great guns by now. I took the liberty of ordering the meal and wine. A main course of roast venison — I hope you can stand that?'

'Why surely.'

'Soup to start with, later a cheese they smuggle in from France, and for our pudding, profiteroles *au chocolat* with cream. For the wine, a Gewurztraminer from Alsace and then a Burgundy. And if we call for it, cognac with the coffee.'

'All of that, in this starving country?'

'I think it's the same all over — there are places where you can get what you want.'

'At a certain price, no doubt.'

'Of course. But at sea one spends nothing — and I've never felt more like celebrating. I *don't* just mean the fact I've been promoted, am now, my darling, as you've failed to observe, a kapitan-leutnant.'

'Otto, *congratulations!* I admit I didn't see, but — '

'No reason you should have. Anyway, what we're celebrating is simply *us*.'

'Even against a background of disaster or near-disaster — '

'Not necessarily *that* disastrous. Turmoil, for sure, but I'm sure there are moves that can still be made. As for the revolutionary attitudes in the country generally — and closer to home, of course, the indiscipline in the Fleet — about which you may know more than I do, since it's a part of your own unit's particular interest?'

'Nothing's good, I can tell you that. In fact — '

'Tell me when we're upstairs. If you must. Here we are — Grueninger's . . . '

Slowing and shifting gear, having to look hard to see the vehicle entrance. Fog still thicker than it had been. Telling her, 'There's a covered shelter at the back. But listen — having been here earlier, I know the way to our room, we don't have to hang around downstairs, we just go straight through and up. Here we are now . . . ' Negotiating a narrow alley down the side of the old building and into a cobbled yard, crossing that and nosing into — well, a carriage-shed, might once have been a cowshed, two other motor cars already in it. He braked, switched off the lights, took her in his arms: 'Oh, that perfume! Helena, darling — ' Her lips opening to his for one long minute. Then: 'It wouldn't do for you to be seen on our way up — at any rate to be recognised. Stay close beside me, turn this up' — the collar of her fur jacket — 'and this' — silk scarf inside it — 'to hide some of your lovely face — d'you think?'

'I'll fix it when we're out.'

'We go in at that doorway.' He kissed her again gently. 'Best almost to make a run for it, not stop for anything. Not scared now, are you?'

'Should I be?'

'You said on the telephone — unnerved.'

'Oh — one minute not knowing you were within a hundred kilometres, or alive or dead, and then hey presto — and one has *heard* of this place — '

'We have a private dining-room, that's all. Talk as we like — even kiss, if the spirit moves us. It'll

154

move *me*, I admit.' They were out of the car, arms around each other. He assured her, 'Nothing you don't want, take my word for that.'

'Waiters coming and going?'

'Bringing the courses, naturally. One waiter only, though — old, discreet. And when we don't want him — '

'You'd send him away.'

'Exactly. But come on, the fire's waiting. Incidentally — '

'Uh?'

'There's a lock on the door.'

She sighed. 'I thought there might be. I spent half the night wondering. One's heard — you know, gossip — '

'But again, I wouldn't turn the key if you didn't want me to.' They stopped on the edge of a pool of light escaping from under the door. 'I'm not forcing you into this, Helena. If you feel nervous at any time — '

'You've been here before, obviously.'

'Not upstairs — never. Never had anyone I'd have wanted to bring here anyway.'

'But you know all about it . . . '

'I've *heard* all about it. First-hand accounts from friends who *have* been here. What I was saying — speaking frankly, openly — if at any point you think I'm going too far, if it worries you — '

'I'd say stop. Or please stop.'

'If it came to that we could just eat the meal and drink the wine — leave the door open, even. Pretend we're at Kramer's — uh?'

'Then I'd lose you, wouldn't I?'

'*Lose* me?'

'I want you as much as you want me, Otto. And I *don't* want a plaster saint. I'd have no use for one. You couldn't look as you do and be one, anyway, I'm aware of that. But I want to feel safe — that it's not just some casual affair, another conquest for you — and for me the conse- quences, maybe.'

'There's no question of a conquest, and there'll be no consequences. I'm equipped to make sure of that. I love you, it's nothing casual. As I told you — '

'In that case I'm more likely to say please *don't* stop. Let's get to the fire?'

★ ★ ★

It was a good fire, bright enough to provide some of the soft lighting in the room, the rest of it coming from candles and an oil-lamp. The table, set for two, with candles in glass holders, was at the door-end of the room, and nearer the fire were two dark-green velvet-covered chaise- longues, one each side of it. Paintings on the walls were of ladies in elaborate but revealing dresses. The carpet was of Middle Eastern origin, predominantly amber, and in front of the fire was a sheepskin rug. Helena, still in her jacket and with the scarf around her neck and ears, had walked straight in and stopped in the middle, looking around as if making up her mind whether to accept it as she saw it; moving towards the fire now, hearing the white-haired waiter asking Otto whether he'd like him to serve the soup immediately, or wait until the Herr Kapitan-Leutnant and the lady had got the night's chill out of their bones — and should he take the lady's coat, or —

She turned slowly, toasting herself in the fire's warmth, at the same time opening her jacket and pulling off the scarf. The black dress hugged her figure, revealed more than a hint of upthrust white bosom. An enquiring look at Otto, who stared at her for a moment like a man half-stunned, before telling the waiter, 'You can serve the soup in fifteen minutes. Don't bother with our coats. Open this, please, leave it for me to pour.'

The Gewurztraminer he wanted opened. The Burgundy was already uncorked — as it should have been. Otto took off his greatcoat with its shiny new epaulettes and threw it down beside Helena's coat. Taking her hand then: looking down into her wide blue eyes, luxuriant mane of chestnut hair, exposed crescents of her breasts.

'The most beautiful ever. I told you so the first time we met, but it's an understatement, you're *sensationally* lovely. You must know it too, huh?'

'I know you *think* it.'

'You take my breath away. I — '

A movement of her eyes and head: he looked round to find the old waiter killing time, studying that long-necked bottle's label before replacing it slowly in its ice-bucket.

'Thank you. Fifteen minutes now?'

'*Jawohl*, Herr Kapitan-Leutnant.'

Otto's lips on hers then, as the door closed. Remembering that he'd dreamt of this, in a pitch-dark iron coffin on the sea-bed with hunters overhead and the English coast less than fifteen miles away. This as the start of the sporadic, rambling, thrilling dream: her hands behind his neck and his own tentatively on the move. Telling her, 'We've twelve minutes.'

'Let's sit?'

'Don't want wine?'

'In a minute. Or say twelve.'

Curtain-raiser, threshold of paradise. The wide straps of her dress sliding easily from her shoulders, his hands moving then to a small catch between her shoulder-blades. *She* pulled all that away then, let it drop. Firelight flickering on her breasts, and her whisper into his mouth: '*Love* you, Otto . . .'

*   *   *

By the time the waiter knocked on the door and Otto called him in, she was sitting upright and had her dress pulled up, its straps in place again on her shoulders. He'd done that, without replacing the brassière. He raised his glass to her: 'You, Helena. *Only* you.'

'Make it to *us*, so I can drink to it as well.'

'All right. Us.' He glanced at the old man. 'That smells good.'

'Does indeed, sir.' Having set it all down, he was adjusting the positions of their chairs. Stooped, deferential, eyes never approaching Helena; Otto thinking, *Poor old devil* . . . Except he was no doubt well paid — and the tip would have to be on the lavish side. On his way now, but pausing to ask, 'Should I attend to the fire, sir?'

'No. Leave that to me.'

'As the Herr Kapitan-Leutnant wishes.'

'Ready for soup, my darling?'

Door closing — clicking shut. Helena joining him at the table. 'Should you be calling me your darling in his hearing?'

'Better than using your name, don't you think?'

'Well. Perhaps you're right . . . This wine's delicious, by the way.'

'And you're a dream I'm having. Can't be anything else.' Her nipples clearly visible through the material of her dress: more clearly still as they reacted to his appreciation of them. Remarking as he started on his bowl of soup, 'You know, as far as the old boy's concerned, I think you could be naked. He doesn't look anywhere in your direction. Did when we arrived, but now he's not taking chances.'

'Bet you he would if I were naked.'

'Bare to the waist, then.'

A sigh. Looking down at herself for a moment. Then: 'After he's brought the last course, why not?'

Gazing at her: 'Helena . . . '

'I never felt quite like this before. So — wanton. It's *you*, of course. *You*, Otto!'

'And what d'you think you do to *me*?'

A laugh. 'I *know*, don't I?'

'If you don't, I guarantee you will. But listen — while I think of it — as I said, Franz Winter's due back tomorrow. Will he get in touch with you, d'you think?'

159

'Quite likely would, but if they're sending him straight out again, who knows . . . You're asking will I mention that I've been seeing you. Well — if he *asked* me, I think I'd say yes. Say you took me to Kramer's, maybe.'

'If he asked *me*, I'd tell him I'm crazy about you, and express gratitude to him for having introduced us. As it happens I've often asked myself why he did.'

'All I remember is that he said to come and meet a young protégé of his. That you'd been his second in command, now had your own boat and were very successful, might even be approaching the status of an Ace.'

He'd nodded. 'Said some of that in my hearing, when he brought you to me. But the best theory I've come up with is that rather than leave you with certain others, he thought he was putting you in safe hands.'

She laughed. He went on, 'Might have thought I wouldn't dare pinch his girl. If that's how he thinks of you. And it's a fact I'm rather in his debt — I wouldn't personally describe myself as his protégé, but he did push me along when he was my CO. On top of that, when I was on the casing with him just before you arrived he was warning me against getting above myself. Does rather think he's God, you know — despite the fact he eats like a pig — but actually I think he'd had some yarn from a friend of his in the Flanders flotilla, who might have been stricken with pangs of jealousy or — oh, resentment, I don't know. He's a friend of Winter's and also a damn fool. Telling me what to do when I knew it

160

better than he did, that kind of thing. So, old Franz having clubbed me into line, feeling confident that I'd behave myself?'

'As distinct from dragging me up into that — what d'you call it — conning-tower.'

'Dirty trick, wasn't it?'

Watching her nipples.

'Playing dirty now, too. You know what that does to me.'

'Certainly I do. I *love* to see it. Love *you*.'

'Happens to be mutual. Aren't we lucky?'

'I know *I* am. The worst of times, and I'm happier than I've ever been. Isn't that extraordinary?'

'Have you made love to hundreds of girls?'

'Certainly have *not!*'

'Dozens, then?'

'Believe me, no. A few, certainly — '

'*Quite* a few, huh?'

'Nothing like this, Helena. Nothing to compare for one split second with what I feel for you. I've never even dreamt it *could* be anything like this. Never been in love, I suppose. Oh, way back, puppy-love maybe . . . '

A double rap on the door. He cocked an eyebrow at her, she nodded vaguely, her thoughts still on what he'd been saying. This was the venison arriving: main course, if not main event. Otto making this allusion while the waiter was taking their soup bowls, replacing them with dinner plates decorated with hunting scenes. She murmured, 'Can't think what you mean', and he told her, '*I'm* thinking of little else.'

'May I pour the wine, sir?'

The Burgundy. Otto told him no, he'd attend to it himself, and did so when the old man had shuffled off again: getting up, half-filling her glass and his own and replacing the bottle, then pausing behind her to slide the wide black straps off her shoulders.

'You don't object?'

'My mind is concentrated entirely on the meal before us.'

'Of course — it would be. But so *lovely*, my darling!'

Looking down. 'Quite ordinary, really.'

'On the contrary. Entrancing — irresistible.' Stooping — almost to his knees, brushing a shoulder with his lips on the way down, Helena half-turning and one of her hands moving to stroke his head and neck. She said, 'Venison was a brilliant choice.'

Still down there, kissing. She murmured, 'You're driving me quietly frantic, you know.'

'Myself, too.' Kissing her lips now. Then, straightening: 'The choice was venison because the only alternative was rabbit.' Back at his own side of the table, he sniffed at his glass. 'Not bad . . . To us, again.'

'And to the main event.' She sipped at hers. 'You're right, it's delicious. But — let's distract ourselves a little? Forget about main events, ask me about my work and the trouble that's brewing.'

'Looking like *that*, you expect me to ask you about your *work*?'

'Well, I'll cover up, if — '

'No, please — '

162

'Did you know sailors were rioting today in Kiel?'

'I did not.' Looking her in the eyes now. 'Is it true?'

'I'm sorry to say it is. Malcontents from the barracks there, apparently — but hundreds of them. Officers were stopped in the streets and disarmed of their dirks, and the epaulettes torn off their uniforms. My department's chief concern is to prevent it spreading to Army units and other towns. *Your* fear must be that it might spread all through the Fleet, turn into actual mutiny afloat.'

'It won't happen in U-boats. Or I think in destroyers. The battleships are a different matter. One's heard of recent disaffection here in Wilhelmshaven. As I understand it, created and steadily worsened by political agitation, third-rate officers, inadequate rations and sheer boredom. But now — Helena — this truly is neither the place nor situation for such utterly depressing observations, so please, let's — '

Slow smile, and a nod towards him: '*Depressing*, Otto?'

'As a matter of fact, no, but might become so if it continued. Despite the visual stimulation. Your shoulders are entrancing, too, Helena. And your hair, eyes, lips — *all* of you, darling — '

'You haven't seen all of me yet.'

'*Would* you come away with me for a few days — if they'd allow it?'

'I'd like to. Love to.' Quick smile: 'Wearing a ring, perhaps. But whether there's a hope they'd give me leave — at this time especially — '

'If everything *is* going up in smoke, though — '

'Mightn't it be best — I mean *wiser* — to stay put, in touch with our own people and authorities, at least until we know what's happening?'

'Might be the *sensible* thing. But then later — '

'Later might mean a long, long time. Could extend to years.'

'I suppose it might. From where we are now, we're blind, aren't we.'

'If you're thinking on the same lines that I am, it's rather a fundamental issue, isn't it?'

'*Could* be. If we made it so. Yes.' Surprising himself with that agreement and its implications, and re-hearing Gerda's, *So watch out* . . . 'So at this stage, when things might be expected to go from bad to worse, and perhaps very suddenly — '

'I'd probably join my parents in Hamburg. And your people would want you with them, wouldn't they?'

'I suppose — if one no longer had naval duty. It's an extraordinary thought. But — what we're both saying — it need only be a stage, a temporary suspension, separation, a sorting-out period one might call it. Things couldn't remain chaotic for ever. One way or another, chaos has eventually to subside. Although on the personal level, exactly what one would do — whether for me there'd even be a Navy to stay in, for instance — '

'I rather doubt there will be. Nothing like the one you're used to, anyway. Or an Army, or anything much else . . . Have I *completely*

164

ruined this lovely evening now?'

'Certainly not. You may have done your best to, but — '

'I've eaten as much venison as I want, anyway. No room for cheese, either. I'll watch *you*, if you're still hungry, but — '

'Profiteroles, then. Red wine goes well with chocolate. I'd better just dress you a little before I summon the old man.'

'Might even manage to dress *myself*, but — '

'I'd like to do it — if you'd permit — '

'D'you know, I *would*?'

★ ★ ★

'Fire's so nice. Like sunbathing. Except nine times as good.'

Exposed to its glow and warmth together, on the chaise longue they'd used before. He'd built up the fire after they'd eaten the profiteroles, drunk most of the wine and summoned the old man to clear the decks, then locked the door, turned to find her already half-undressed and taken over the rest of it.

'Now you, my darling.' She'd interrupted his ravings. 'Why do they give us *two* chaise-longues, d'you think? Oh, my God . . . '

He told her — ignoring that muttered exclamation, watching what she was doing now — 'I suppose because we might be dining with friends, a foursome, and we'd *need* two.'

'I don't think I'd like that — would you?'

'Much better on our own.'

That had been half an hour ago. After the

165

second love-making he'd fallen asleep, was woken by her sleepy remark about the fire. Tracing outlines on her with his fingertips until she squirmed around, had her hands on him again, asking him then, 'Would we ever tire of this?'

'If we did we'd be fit only to be put down, so what the hell.'

'People do tire though, don't they. Married people. When the newness wears off, I suppose?'

'By that time I think that if they belonged together in the first place a new dimension comes into it. Sort of *deep* love more than *in* love.'

'I'm in *deep* love with you now, though.'

'Same here. Put it any way you like, though — '

'*Here*, I'm putting it. If you don't object.'

'By far the best place for it. Brilliant, the ideas you have. And this way up — see, my hands are free and — '

'I like that. Otto, Otto — '

'Yes, you lovely creature . . . '

After some more lazy time he agreed with her that they should be making their way home. Even the sort of dinner party he'd invented for the Muellers would have packed up by now; and the fog that had been worsening earlier might be really dense.

'One thing I forgot to say — on the subject of Franz Winter, when or if he gets in touch with you — at least, if he asks you out, to dine with him or — '

'He'd never suggest coming *here*, I can tell you that much!'

'If he asks you anywhere, tell him you're busy every night this week?'

'What if he asks me who I'm busy with?'

'Well — two options.' Watching her step into her knickers while he buttoned his shirt. 'One, tell him it's none of his damn business, or two, tell him the truth.'

'He may not ask. May not even try to get in touch. In any case I won't mention you if I don't have to.'

'But you can. I honestly don't care.'

'Wouldn't it make for trouble between you?'

'No reason it should. He has no proprietory right to you that I'm aware of. Nor have I, come to that — although I'd like to have . . . Anyway, there's no need for you to tell fibs, I'll handle anything that comes of it.'

'You handle everything so beautifully, Otto.'

'You're not exactly fumble-fisted yourself. Maybe I said this before — or something like it — but I'm — I've completely fallen for you, Helena. I want every minute of you that I can get. Minutes, weeks, months, years — '

'I want the same. You can have any proprietory rights you want.' Arms round his neck, breasts against his shirt-front. 'Think we might even marry, one day?'

'Yes. I do. I'm not proposing it here and now because with things in such a mess and no idea what position I'd be in to support you — support *us* — but yes, *please* let's pray to have it turn out like that?'

'We should drink to it.'

'Regrettably the bottles have become empty. I

167

could go down and get another, of course — if the Weinstube's still in operation, which I think it may be — '

'Metaphorically drink to it, I meant. Having never proposed to a man before. But in any case — '

'I'm deeply honoured. Should have been quicker off the mark myself. Although — for those reasons . . . Anyway, you want to be taken home now. Get your beauty sleep. How about tomorrow — collect you at eight again?'

'To come here again?'

'I don't know where else. Kramer's is a little dull, and — '

'It's not so bad. We could eat there, then take a little drive, find somewhere, you know, quiet, and — '

'Could do that. Put some blankets in the motor — or some other one if necessary. Two nights in a row in this place *might* be overdoing it, rather.'

'The *expense* of it. Kramer's is quite reasonable, isn't it?'

'The main thing is the risk of being seen here, if we came too often. Your reputation, so forth. But how about I book this room again for Wednesday?'

There *were* still customers in the Weinstube, you could hear them. Earlier they'd been singing to the music of an accordion. Otto left Helena in the ladies' powder room, went down and paid his bill to the woman — who it turned out *was* Frl. Grueninger — and booked the same room and dinner for two on Wednesday. He'd telephone or call in before that to arrange the menu. Yes, it had been an excellent meal, and the service had been more than adequate. He'd already tipped the old waiter. He went back up to collect Helena and escort her down; she was ready, had her fur jacket's collar turned up and the silk scarf arranged as before. He told her, 'All fixed for Wednesday. I asked for the same waiter if he's available.'

'Another week of it, you'll be bankrupt.'

'Well, not quite . . . '

They went down together side by side, her arm crooked inside his and holding it tightly. It was, he realised, an ordeal for her, a running of the gauntlet. Off the bottom of the stairs, starting across the tile-floored public area that was an anteroom to the Weinstube premises and off which was the office where he'd paid the bill. This was the back way out, of course, to the yard where the car was. He'd just tried to encourage her by muttering, 'In the clear, almost . . . ' when one of the Weinstube's swing doors was flung back, and glancing that way in quick reaction he was virtually face to face with a rather bulky naval officer, a U-boat CO by name of Willi Ahrens — Korvetten-Kapitan, friend of Winter's — and emerging behind him two others, one of them an Oberleutnant by the name of Hahn who'd been in the Mess last night or the night before and whom he thought was Ahrens' first lieutenant. They'd seen and obviously recognised Otto, Ahrens raising a hand and calling his name — jocular, tipsy — while Otto kept going, manoeuvring Helena as it were on to his

169

starboard bow, at least partially hidden: if Ahrens had got a clear sight of her, as he might have done, he'd have known her — he'd been at Winter's party on board 201 that evening, one of the group of COs who'd been with her and Winter. Otto shouted, 'Can't stop, motor's waiting!', and pushed on out, heeling the yard door shut behind them.

No idea whether Ahrens *had* had any clear sight of her. If he had, it would be the first thing Franz would hear about when he got in tomorrow. Or rather today — midnight having come and gone.

Helena said, 'That's really torn it. Friend of Franz's, name of Willi something?'

'Willi Ahrens. D'you think he saw you?'

'Certainly he did! For a second we were looking straight at each other! Before you nearly yanked me off my feet. Christ, it's so dark . . .'

'Fog's still with us, is why. Come on.' The door had opened behind them, sending a shaft of light across the cobbles. Otto bundling Helena into Graischer's motor and reaching across her to pull out the choke, shutting that door then and moving to the crank-handle, hoping to God as he stooped to it that (a) it would start easily, and (b) that he hadn't left it in gear. Taking a chance on that anyway and — OK, on the second swing the engine fired, and it was not in gear, *didn't* run him down . . . On round to his own side, into a reek of petrol. Too much choke. Helena saying as he got them moving, 'He'll tell Franz, won't he?'

'Certain to.'

Down the alley, having switched the lights on while backing out of the shed — not looking for those others, preferring not to see them — then to the left into the road. Headlights behind them brightening the yard end of the alley as he turned out of it. He'd known they must have a motor, otherwise the three of them wouldn't have been leaving by the yard door. Anyway, they'd be heading north, back to Wilhelmshaven.

Shifting into third. Seeing the answer, or beginning to — at least *an* answer — to Helena's reputation being shot to ribbons, Helena herself in any social sense virtually destroyed. To have been caught leaving an upstairs rendezvous in the Snake Pit — well, for a woman, a young girl of anything like decent background . . .

And who'd taken the chance of having this happen to her?

'Helena, darling, listen now — '

'It's actually quite dreadful . . . '

'No. Seems so, but actually it's not.' Noting as he spoke that she should have been crying and was not. Explaining then what he'd just said: 'What we were saying earlier — how we feel about each other, but having to wait and see what comes out of any so-called armistice and all the rest of it . . . Well, slight change of plan, that's all. Marry me, will you?'

'You mean, not wait? Just like *that*?'

'So I can tell Franz Winter — or Ahrens — anyone — that you're my fiancée. Believe me, I'd be very proud to. It's what we both want, isn't it — an adjustment of timing, nothing else. And you see, our engagement explains your

171

presence at the Pit. Which we'd better refer to as Grueninger's, henceforth. Where else could I have taken you where we'd be completely on our own? Man to man, as an explanation this is perfectly understandable. Your mother mightn't like it — if she got wind of it — but one, with any luck she won't, and two, I'd swear to her I took you there only to have you to myself while begging you to become my wife. A little unconventional, I know, but that's the plain truth of it, there's no other — and naturally there was the devil of a lot to say, we talked for *hours* — huh?'

'We did, didn't we. I mean, *would* have. But do you mean this, Otto — you'll stick to it?'

'Of course I'll stick to it, it's what I *want*! If you'll accept me, that is. Damn it, I *love* you!'

'And I love you. Respect you, too. Of *course* I accept. I'm — well, *reeling* . . . But — in practical terms — no way we could set a date, or — exactly as we were saying before, as things are at present — '

'When they've settled, I meet your parents and you meet mine. Meanwhile, we're engaged to marry, and in the immediate future — '

'Kramer's, etcetera?'

He reached to find her hand. 'Etcetera.'

8

Tuesday 29 October, one a.m. Otto had dropped Helena at the Muellers' house in Oldenburg and was on his way back to Wilhelmshaven, a distance of less than fifty kilometres via Rastede and Varel; while Franz Winter in U201 was in position 50 degs 40′ N, 7 degs 20′ E, steering SSE, making-good ten knots with a running battery-charge from both diesels and ETA Wilhelmshaven 0930.

Winter lowered his binoculars, used a scrap of absorbent paper to clean their front lenses. Hohler, officer of the watch, had just queried whether they'd make it into the Jade by that time and at this speed; he told him, 'You'd have found it in my night orders, if you'd taken the trouble to read them, that at five o'clock the charge is to be broken and speed increased to fifteen knots.'

'*Jawohl, mein Kapitan.*'

One didn't argue with one's skipper — certainly not with this one — but he thought it hadn't been in the night order book when he'd come on watch; in any case he'd be out for the count at five a.m. They were working two-hour watches — he, Neureuther the first lieutenant and Kantelberg the navigating officer — thus had two hours on watch and four hours off, round the clock. With occasional interruptions in the form of alarms or sightings, leading sometimes to action, they'd been doing this for

173

the past three weeks, and it was a magnificent thought that one would be getting the whole of this next night in the sack. An early one, at that, please God. Knowing damn well that in practice you never did and that it had damn-all to do with any God. On the last day of every patrol you swore you would, but midnight of the 'first night in' invariably saw you still celebrating in the bar.

Celebrating what? The fact of having returned — survived yet another patrol? Being now nineteen years of age, at sea in submarines since clocking-up seventeen, having maybe a decent chance of reaching twenty?

Winter had his glasses up again: swivelling slowly as he swept across the bow then down the port side as far as the beam or a little farther. The seascape, nightscape abaft the beam could be left to the two seamen look-outs in the after end of the bridge. The looking-out primarily for enemy submarines, which tended to be active in these waters, between the mine-belts: the boat that spotted the other first was the one that got home.

New minefields permitting, of course.

Not that one took such a fatalistic view of it. Although aware that according to the statistics one's chances were roughly fifty-fifty every time. Better than that maybe in this boat, with a skipper as experienced and competent as Franz Winter. A rock of a man, was Franz. So thoroughly committed to his duty and the service of his country — and in particular to the submarine service — that there were jokes made and circulated about him, as the automaton with the one-track mind, also as 'the bison'. In fact he was as highly respected as any U-boat CO you'd ever heard of — by his own officers and crew, at any rate, those who knew him and served under him. Do the job as it should be done, according to his precepts, and he'd support you through thick and thin; fail in it or shirk it, you didn't stay long with 'old Franzi'.

His subordinates wouldn't want you to, either.

Emil Hohler was maintaining a bare-eyed lookout while wiping his own glasses. You needed to quite often in this salt sea-mist, as well as occasional bursts of spray as she dipped her stem lance-like into the long, low swells, tossing a few bathfuls of it back over her grey length, the solid white flood rushing over and inside the casing to burst against the base of the tower and stream away over her flanks.

Glasses up again: sweeping steadily across the bow. The wind was of the boat's own making, a ten-knot wind from right ahead therefore, and the motion regular, the grumble of her 1200-HP diesels seemingly in rhythm with it. He'd often thought how he'd miss all this, when he left it — as he'd have to one day, obviously. But years and years ahead, as an old man, whatever he might have done with his life between now and then, he guessed he'd hear in his sleep the thump and flood of sea over the hull and through the casing, only a few metres below your feet at any time, and in the rougher stuff a lot less than that, the noise and the power of it, rearing whiteness pounding aft from her

175

plunging stem, swirling around the gun down there and bursting over, while solid green ones mounted to drop on you in ton weights. Old man waking and telling himself, *That was how it was, was my life, was me, one time . . .*

'Going down.' Skipper lowering his glasses. 'Shake me for anything at all.'

Meaning he'd sooner be woken and/or have the boat dived for a seagull or a Flying Dutchman than be left to sleep and the boat continue on the surface when it *might* turn out to be an enemy. It was entirely possible, all too easy, to see things and dismiss them as figments of the imagination — which they often *were* — but the truth was that a few seconds' delay in reacting to that 'figment' might prove to be the last seconds of existence for the boat and her crew of thirty-two seamen and stokers and four officers. It was one of the themes on which old Franzi tended to hold forth.

★　★　★

The five o'clock dead reckoning position put them twenty-five nautical miles NNW of Heligoland, sixty-five miles from Wilhelmshaven. The ETA could be amended or confirmed when Heligoland was abeam; meanwhile the charge was broken and revs increased to bring her up to fifteen knots. Kantelberg — navigator, Oberleutnant — had the watch at this time, having taken over from Neureuther at four a.m. Franz Winter, who'd been at the chart table checking speeds, distances and tidal streams, joined his first lieutenant now at the wardroom table, where A.B. Thoemer, wardroom messman, had just set down mugs of a coffee-like liquid and a plate of biscuits. Winter had had three hours' uninterrupted sleep, which for him was a lot: he told Neureuther, as he dumped himself into the canvas chair in which no-one else ever sat, reached for a biscuit and crammed it into his mouth with the flat of his hand, that it looked as if the DR position would turn out to be spot-on, which after a run of about 600 nautical miles from the Pentland Firth was not at all bad.

He took a swig of coffee, then went on munching the biscuit. The cement-mixer routine, Neureuther had heard it called. Cement well in evidence as Winter added, 'That is, if the log's behaving itself.'

'One might reasonably assume so, sir.'

'A log of the same type made monkeys of us off Liverpool on one occasion, if you remember. That one had had all my trust until it decided to chuck its hand in — eh?'

A smile on his first lieutenant's long, narrow face. 'Remember the occasion well, sir.'

During Winter's time in command of a 'C', a mine-layer, that had been. Neureuther had been his first lieutenant then; Winter had brought him with him to U201 when he'd transferred to her. While not exactly outstanding — as von Mettendorff had been, for instance — he was competent, hard-working and loyal, the ship's company respected him and Winter trusted him.

'How long d'you guess we'll stay in, sir?'

'No idea at all. What the devil they're playing

at . . . Recalling boats from patrol and not relieving them with others suggests some change of strategy. One possibility for instance would be transferring us to work with the *Hochseeflotte* — conceivably therefore some kind of fleet action.' Pausing to light a cigarette, expelling smoke, which the diesels' powerful suction instantly snatched away. 'Talk of an armistice — which some were doing before we left, if you remember — well, sending most of us back out, whatever it's for, at least it's not bloody surrender.'

'But fleet action — if that's what's in the wind — a submarine trap, they'd most likely want us for — we might be too late for it now?'

Winter shifted in his chair; glancing to his left past the chart table into the central control-room, then the other way. Back to Neureuther: leaning forward, forearms on the table, staring at him fixedly under shaggy greying brows — the legendary 'bison's stare'. Growling, 'Wouldn't mind if we were, Neureuther. Two reasons — no, three, if one includes the usual one that we're overdue for docking. Bigger reason is — how to put this . . . See — if there's to be an armistice, rendering all we've done in the past five years plain damn futile, I'd as soon call it a day, be done with it. May surprise you that I should say this, but — we've not dishonoured *ourselves*, you know!'

What surprised Neureuther was that he was hearing this at all. Right out of bisonic character as well as custom, principle . . .

Bison stubbing out his cigarette. Shoulders

hunched. 'Thank God we haven't.' A scowl: 'So who *has*?' Another glance left and right, shake of the wide head, cutting himself short, thinking better of it. Neureuther watching him curiously — knowing his man, who was most certainly not given to baring his soul; had never been known to do so. At least, not to an inferior. Therefore, guessing that he had to be seeing this as a moment of crisis for him personally as well as for the Navy and for Germany. Continuing, 'Is the *Hochseeflotte* up to it, I wonder. Intelligence informs us that the British and Americans are in fine fettle and eager for a fight. British learnt some lessons they needed to learn at the Skaggerak confrontation — and now they have this fellow Beatty at their head. Thinks he's a latter-day Nelson, apparently. Doesn't matter whether he is or not, *he* thinks he is and it seems he's sold the notion to others. The word is that the Grand Fleet is on its toes and exceptionally well trained. You know me, Neureuther — or you *should* by this time — you know I'm not disposed to run from any fight — '

A shake of the head. Eyes startled . . .

'Or to blather as I'm doing now, eh? Well, don't quote me, not a word of it. But to take on a first-class, well-led fighting force with a bunch of demoralised near-incompetents — '

'As bad as that?'

Winter drained his mug. He was both smoking and eating now, having pushed another biscuit in. You'd have thought he'd choke. But a shrug was the only answer he was giving. Neureuther tried after a pause: 'You said three reasons, sir?'

179

'The third is personal.' Jaw up again, as in meeting a challenge, disbelief or censure . . . 'Yes. I'd sooner have a few weeks in harbour than — whatever's contemplated. For the private reason — telling *you* this, but no-one else at this stage.' Neureuther gesturing his assent to secrecy, leaning closer, Winter muttering, '*Extremely* private and personal. Concerns a young lady whom I've been seeing in recent months. You've met her, I think. Yes, you have. Well — I believe the time has come to — shall I say, formalise our relationship. If she'll have me, of course.' The bison stare again, but a hint of mockery in it: 'Surprised you, have I? Well, I'm a human being, Neureuther. Never occurred to you, I dare say. Wish me luck, eh?'

★ ★ ★

Off Heligoland between 0630 and 0640, after calling up the signal station by light, establishing U201's identity and amending the Wilhelmshaven ETA to 0920. Dead reckoning *had* been spot-on, and tides in the next few hours would be favourable. Having passed this message, Signalman Kendermann began taking in one from FdU at Wilhelmshaven to the effect that on her arrival U201 was to berth on *Sudwestkai* in the *Verbindungshafen*, and requesting information as to the boat's fuel state, torpedoes remaining, major defects if any, men sick or injured if any. In effect Winter was being asked whether there was anything that might prevent or delay him from sailing as soon as he'd re-fuelled, taken on fresh water and stores and embarked torpedoes.

Kendermann lowered the lamp with which he'd been acknowledging the message word by word, at the same time calling it out for Boy Telegraphist Rehkliger, below them in the tower, to scribble down. Winter — and Hohler, who had this six-to-eight watch — had both been reading it as it came stuttering in, and as the station signed off Winter shouted down to the boy, 'Take it to the first lieutenant, ask him to draft an answer.'

Fog still thickened the darkness. Without certain lights on shore, the island itself wouldn't yet have been visible, although a lit and identifiable buoy which they'd passed within fifty metres of had given them their exact position. And still the long, low swell, 201 rocking over it, diesels rumbling, the stink of their exhaust obnoxious on what was now a light following wind. But definitely no happy home-coming, this. Those questions apart, the *Verbindungshafen* was plainly the most convenient temporary accommodation for a boat that wasn't expected to remain in port for more than a few hours. You wouldn't even be getting ashore for a hot bath, by the looks of it.

Neureuther came up and offered the skipper his draft reply. He'd have had to have gone down into the tower's light to check it, though; he shook his head, growled, 'Send it.' Kendermann with the lamp's sighting-tube already at his eye, beginning to call the station, give them the answers that would be passed to FdU in

181

Wilhelmshaven by sea-bed land-line. Neu-reuther, on the starboard side of the bridge, said quietly to Winter, 'Not the best of prospects, sir.'

A grunt. Bison with one shoulder jammed against the for'ard periscope standard for support against the boat's rhythmic pitching, while the lamp leaked its long and short flashes blindingly, drawing pinpoints of acknowledge-ment from shore. Winter told Neureuther, 'Pass the word — after berthing, all hands are to remain on board until we know what's wanted of us.'

★ ★ ★

Schillig Roads, the extensive fleet anchorage in the broad entrance to the Jade river, this top end of it about midway between Schillighorn and Alte Mellum, was crowded with ships of the High Seas Fleet. Adding to the impression of massive, concentrated power, when Neureuther came up to take over the watch at 0800, two Zeppelins were passing low over the lines of anchored battleships and battle cruisers. Light cruisers too — notably the 4th Scouting Group, their flagship *Regensburg* lying closer than any other to 201's track inshore of them — inshore on the western, Schillig side. The Zeppelins were flying seaward — a scouting mission, Neureuther guessed. Checking all round and especially ahead, then switching back to what he could see of the battle squadrons, shifting his binoculars' focus from ship to ship and identifying most of those whose profiles showed up well enough,

182

with no overlap and reasonably hard-edged in the growing but still fog-laden early light. Hipper's flagship *Baden*; and the 3rd Battle Squadron, including the modern — well, five-year-old — *Konig* and *Markgraf*. Beyond them — view changing rapidly as 201's diesels drove her southward still at fifteen knots — *Derfflinger* and *Von der Tann*, battle cruisers, *Derfflinger* the more modern of the two and the larger, 28,000 tons as compared to *Von der Tann's* less than 20,000, but both with the long, low look that made them easy to identify. And there now, the 1st Battle Squadron — *Thuringen*, *Ostfriesland*, *Helgoland* — and two others overlapping. One of those would be the *Oldenburg*. All of them as static as models set in putty, which in this light was the colour of the surface anyway, surface with virtually no movement on it except for 201's wash rolling out on her quarters. The dreadnoughts *Friedrich der Grosse* and *Kaiserin* there; beyond them, the *Konig Albert* — and those were only the fringe of it, those to which one was passing closest and with open lines of sight. Neureuther lowered his glasses, remarked to Hohler: 'All raising steam, you'll have noticed. What for, one might ask.'

Dark columns of funnel-smoke from the big ships were rising vertically, that pre-dawn breeze having dropped away. The smoke would be visible a long way offshore, he thought, once the light improved. He nodded to Hohler: 'All right, I've got her.'

'I'll get my breakfast, then.'

'*May* have left some for you.' Running a hand

183

around his jaw: he'd shaved for the first time in three weeks, and his face felt naked in the cold, salt-damp air. Glasses up again, examining the river ahead, picking up the buoys that marked the channel at approximately 1,000-metre intervals and were identifiable by their flashing lights. Schillig Roads falling back on the quarter now, and 201's course of 195 degrees due to be altered by fifteen degrees to port after — checking again — two more pairs of lit buoys.

Winter came up, stood with his arms akimbo, staring round. As bare-faced as his first lieutenant; he'd been up here until about half an hour ago, had gone below for breakfast and a shave. A hand up to the new sensitivity of *his* jaw too; binoculars up then, checking ahead initially — buoy-spotting — then astern at the now distant, indistinct mass of battle-wagons — only the smoke columns seemingly solid from this distance and line of sight, massive supports to the ceiling of cloud.

He turned back, checked the time.

'Come down to three hundred revs. We're well up to schedule.'

'Aye, sir.' Neureuther stooping to the voicepipe, passing the order while thinking about the skipper and that strikingly pretty girl. Had to be all of fifteen years younger than him. Extraordinary, really: year upon year of never showing the least interest in any female, then — *crunch*, falling for a kid like that one. Even contemplating marriage, going by those few words he'd uttered. But that was Franz Winter, Neureuther supposed — doing nothing by halves: he either went for it flat-out or he bloody didn't.

Like the way he ate, come to think of it.

Putting his glasses up again, he wondered how the girl would react: whether maybe she'd be expecting it, might have her answer ready for him.

Extraordinary, anyway, that burst of loquaciousness. Criticism of — well, un-named persons — one might guess, political — as well as the private revelation.

Iron crust crumbling, suddenly? What the end of a war did to a certain kind of man, when for years on end it had possessed him absolutely?

The girl, though: he wondered again — with her looks, get just about any man she wanted. How'd Franzi take it if she turned him down?

Voicepipe: engineer officer requesting permission to come up on the bridge. He was a warrant officer, name of Muhbauer, tall and bald, with hands the size of shovels. Winter had nodded, and Neureuther called down, 'Permission granted.' Muhbauer, Neureuther guessed, would be bringing with him a list of engine defects, reasons 201 definitely needed at least a few days in harbour for repairs and maintenance; he'd been working at it on and off for days.

★ ★ ★

The gathering on this basin's *Sudwestkai* included Kapitan zu See Schwaeble, Winter noticed, as well as a few fellow COs including Waldo Rucker and the tubby Willi Ahrens. He'd expected to be met by Michelsen himself: if U201 was being denied any stand-off at all, as all the indications suggested, you'd think the head man would make himself available to explain it.

Heaving-lines had arced across and were being hauled in, dragging hemp breasts over at the bow and stern. Springs were coiled ready on the stone jetty, would be passed over and secured as soon as the breasts were made fast. Hardly worth bothering with springs, maybe, if the boat was only to be here for an hour or two.

He stooped to the voicepipe, called down, 'Finished with main engines and motors. Open fore hatch.' Glancing up to the wireless mast, from which victory pendants for this patrol's four sinkings flew — or rather dangled, like stockings on a washing-line, in the near-windless air. He turned back to where a gangplank was about to be swung over. Reflecting that this should have been a happy, satisfying moment, as returns from successful patrols always had been: but it wasn't, nobody *looked* happy, and he, Franz Winter, certainly didn't feel it.

He'd get a call through to her anyway. Have a brief word, explain . . .

The springs — steel wire rope — were being hauled over. Hohler, amongst whose jobs was that of casing officer, was supervising all that, with Leading Seaman Lehner, second coxswain, in charge aft. U201 at rest, for the time being. Winter told Neureuther as the gangway thumped down, bridging the four-metre gap between casing and dockside, 'I'll go down and shake it out of him.'

Shake it out of Schwaeble, he meant. The boat wasn't in any state for entertaining senior officers, and he, Winter, wasn't in a mood for it either.

Von Mettendorff, he saw then: tall figure at the rear of the throng, tall enough to see over others' heads, tossing him a salute. *Two stripes on that sleeve.* Well, good for him. His Coastal must be in need of repairs, or they'd have turned him round and sent him out again. Winter climbed over the side of the bridge on that starboard side and down iron rungs to the catwalk, edging around it to the fore-casing. Schwaeble was already halfway across the plank; Winter saluted, then accepted the offered handshake as he stepped on board.

'As always, glad to have you back, Winter. Another — what, twelve thousand tons, was it?'

'About that. May I ask how long we have in port now?'

'You read the signs, eh?'

'Would have had to be pig-stupid not to.'

'Yes. Well — FdU will brief you. He was taking a call from Berlin, couldn't leave the office, I'm to take you to him right away.'

'May I give my first lieutenant at least some idea of what our programme is?'

'Oh.' A glance at his watch; a sigh, then. 'If you'll tell him quietly and briefly, we don't have time to waste. But a vanload of fresh provisions is on its way — in case you need to stay out there longer than we expect. That's all: you've enough fuel remaining, and four torpedoes — right? More than you'll need. Rather hope you won't

187

need any. Shouldn't take more than a couple of hours at most — thing is, you're the only boat we have that's currently fit to do the job, the timing of your return's thus highly fortuitous. FdU will explain it all, so — '

'What is the job, sir?'

Schwaeble sighed, lowered his voice. 'In a word, mutiny, in the *Hochseeflotte*. It's a shameful and dangerous situation — as FdU will explain. All right?'

'A word to Neureuther, if I may, sir.' Turning, beckoning to him, he gave him the gist of it. 'Means we can expect to be back alongside in a couple of hours, apparently. Exactly what we'll be doing I can't say. Some kind of police action, by the sound of it. Oh, there's a vanload of fresh provisions on its way, and I'm to be briefed now by FdU.' He was breaking off, but then remembered: 'Look here — Muhbauer's asked me for compassionate leave — I said yes — his wife was giving birth just when we sailed. But as this is only a few hours' work there's no time to find a replacement, tell him he must hang on.'

He followed Schwaeble across the plank. On the stone quay, Ahrens' bulky frame approached. 'Franz — '

'Sorry, Willi. See you later, if — '

'Must speak to you, Franz. It's most urgent.'

Schwaeble waved him off. 'Later, Ahrens.'

* * *

Kommodore Andreas Michelsen, FdU — Fuhrer of U-boats — was a head taller than either

Schwaeble or Franz Winter; also slimmer and greyer, with piercing blue eyes under jutting brows. He came around his desk to shake hands with Winter, asking Schwaeble, 'Have you explained the position to him?'

'Only in outline, sir.'

'Very well. Sit down, Winter. I should have opened this with my congratulations on yet another successful patrol — and apologies for the fact we can't *quite* let you rest on your laurels yet.' He'd resumed his seat behind the desk. 'Schwaeble — I'll brief him. Perhaps you'd get through to Henniger, suggest he embarks his men and makes a start.' To Franz Winter then, 'From the time you leave this office, can I assume you'll have 201 on her way within, say, thirty minutes?'

'If no special preparations are required, sir. And bearing in mind we've been three weeks at sea, my crew *are* overdue for stand-off and the boat for docking.'

'That prompts an important question. Can you rely on your crew absolutely?'

Winter felt and showed surprise. 'If I couldn't, I'd say I was unfit for command.'

'Good answer.' FdU looked at Schwaeble. 'Captain, go ahead, tell Henniger to mark time outside, he'll be joined by U201 in about forty-five minutes. Winter — listen. It's a sad and sorry tale, and I'll make it brief.' The door closed behind Schwaeble; Michelsen pushed a wooden box across the desk. 'Smoke?'

'No thank you, sir.'

The Kommodore helped himself to a cigar,

put a match to it and told him with the smoke wreathing from his lips, 'We have mutiny in the *Hochseeflotte*. In several of the battleships, but the trouble at the moment seems to be centred on the *Thuringen*. I should explain: the purpose of the fleet's assembly here in the Schillig Roads is that Vice-Admiral von Hipper is intending to launch a fleet action against the British. A briefing of admirals and ships' captains was held on board the *Baden* last night, finalising details. Essentially, there are to be attacks by cruiser squadrons with destroyer escorts on the Flanders coast and in the Thames estuary — shore bombardments as well as dealing with whatever shipping's encountered. This will have the effect of drawing the British out: *their* aim will be to cut the *Hochseeflotte* off and force a fleet action. Hipper will sustain losses, obviously, but I've deployed U-boats across the southern North Sea and especially in the Terschelling area, and a sizeable new minefield has been laid. The importance of all this, the basis of it, is that armistice terms are being discussed between Berlin, Washington, London and Paris, and by demonstrating that our Navy at least is still very much to be reckoned with, the terms of any agreement should be much less to our disadvantage than would be the case if we just sat around and allowed the damn government to sell us out. Even if victory is not achieved, even if our losses are severe, we'll have shown them that we're a nation to be bargained with, rather than dictated to.'

Winter nodded. 'Sound thinking, sir.'

'I've explained it to that extent so you'll understand the importance of crushing this damn mutiny. Which I'll also describe to you. First — well, signs of trouble have been growing in recent weeks; yesterday sailors were rioting in the streets of Kiel, and here in Wilhelmshaven, when preparing to move the big ships out into the Roads, several hundred men from *Derfflinger* and *Von der Tann* simply walked ashore. Shore patrols soon rounded them up and returned them to their ships — they're mostly sheep, you've only to arrest the ringleaders and the rest cave in — so those two and the rest of 'em moved out, they're at anchor out there now. But — for instance — I mentioned Hipper's conference last night, on board *Baden*; when the captain's boat was called away in *Thuringen*, to take him to the flagship, the boat's crew hid themselves, ignored the pipe. Of course he got himself over there, but that's the mood, and apparently it's spreading, heightened now by rumour of the impending *Flottenvorstoss*, to which they're referring as 'The Death Ride'. The swine are waving red flags, crowding their ships' upper decks, cheering President Woodrow Wilson and the Russian revolution and whatever else they can think of — and in *Thuringen* they're preventing access to machinery spaces, shutting-off steam to the capstan to prevent her weighing anchor, venting steam-pressure from her boilers, and so forth. Oh, and a message was flashed from *Thuringen* to *Ostfriesland*, flagship of the First Squadron, stating that her captain was no longer in control.'

191

'Well . . .'

A nod as he dropped ash from his cigar into a brass ashtray. 'There's trouble also in the *Konig, Oldenburg, Markgraf* and *Friedrich der Grosse.* Probably others too, but those we know of. Anyway, it's hoped that breaking the mutiny in one ship should break it or avert it in the others, and for this *Thuringen* is to be the target. Marines are being embarked in two harbour tenders, steam transports. Escorted by you, they'll board her and arrest the leaders, while you stand off with your tubes trained on her to ensure compliance. When they see we mean business to that extent, we very much hope it may bring them to their senses.'

'If by chance it doesn't, am I to fire on her?'

The Kommodore tapped off more cigar ash. 'When they see that you're prepared to, they'll give in, and you return to harbour, escorting the tenders, in which the ringleaders will be brought ashore under Marine guard and locked up. Better have your gun manned, incidentally.'

'But I must be prepared to fire — fire a torpedo, say — if they don't give in?'

'You must act in a manner that makes it plain you *will* do so if necessary.'

'So in actuality, I'll be bluffing?'

'Nothing of the sort! You'll assess the situation and its likely outcome, use your own savvy and act accordingly.'

'Then I *am* authorised to open fire if they don't surrender. May I have it in writing?'

'I can't see how that would help. To be bound by explicit orders in a situation of such an

192

unprecedented kind could only limit your options. Whereas leaving it to your judgement — as a senior U-boat commander of considerable experience — '

'Sir, I've no experience at all of firing on my own countrymen or sinking a major unit of our own fleet. If I *am* required to do so — '

'Mutineers, Winter, are customarily shot or hanged. Whatever in your assessment may seem necessary, you are empowered to proceed with. But time's short now, so . . . '

A gesture, indicating that he'd now said as much as needed to be said. Winter thinking about it, Michelsen holding the bison's glare through a drift of cheroot smoke. Winter tried, 'With respect, sir, may I discuss this with Vice-Admiral von Hipper?'

'I would have suggested it myself, but he'd be difficult to find. He *had* transferred his flag from *Baden* to the *Kaiser Wilhelm II* — alongside here. So we were informed — by Chief of Staff von Trotha, I believe.' *Kaiser Wilhelm II* was a disarmed pre-dreadnought battleship, vintage 1897, relegated to service as a headquarters and accommodation ship. Michelsen continuing, 'An attempt at contacting him an hour ago, however, drew blank. He had been on board *Kaiser Wilhelm*, but, well, seems he may be touring the fleet, assessing the situation for himself. In any case, action has to be taken, the mutiny has to be nipped in the bud, you're the man to do it and the time for it is *now*!'

Winter got to his feet. If he'd held out longer

he'd have begun to look like a mutineer himself. 'Very well, sir.'

'Good. And good luck. An enormous amount hangs on it. Remember that whatever you do, you do for the sake of Germany.'

★ ★ ★

Thuringen lay beam-on to her sister-ship *Helgoland*, which was a cable's length away to starboard. Three-funnelled, displacing just over 20,000 tons, 550 feet long, crew of about 1,000, main armament of a dozen twelve-inch guns and fourteen six-inch. Actually, five-point-nines, same calibre as the gun on U201's fore-casing: which was manned now, to the extent that its seven-man crew were crouching immediately abaft it and had the ready-use ammunition lockers open.

But those were handsome, powerful-looking ships. Neureuther had commented to that effect, and Winter, with his binoculars trained on *Thuringen* as 201 came up abeam of her, growled, 'Fine ship, certainly. Only a pity about the rabble on her decks.'

Low grey sky, grey-brown river, misty haze of distant greenish seascape to the north. Still no wind, the columns of funnel-smoke from the anchored battle-fleet rising vertically, black against the surrounding murk.

Winter lowered his glasses, told the coxswain — at the wheel in the bridge here with him — 'Starboard ten, Muller.'

To circle widely around *Thuringen*'s bow,

194

having on the way past her seen a considerable proportion of her crew milling around on her decks — even on the quarter-deck, where off-duty seamen weren't ever allowed. They were all over her: and slovenly-looking, dressed like tramps, a few waving red flags.

The ship herself looked filthy too, Neureuther saw. Others they'd passed had been in similar condition.

'Ten of starboard wheel on, sir.'

'Ease to five.'

The end of the reversal of course would bring her nosing into the 200-metre gap between *Thuringen* and *Helgoland*, about midway between the two — between their anchor cables, say, which at this stage of the tide were growing northward. His intention being to aim her and her bow torpedo tubes directly at *Thuringen*. The steamboats bringing the Marines being still some way back, on *Thuringen*'s quarter, half a mile away; he'd lie there in full view of the mutineers with his tubes trained on them, during the boarding vessels' approach on her other side.

'Stop both. Out engine clutches.'

Neureuther passed the order down, heard it acknowledged a couple of seconds before the diesels ceased their pounding.

Silence, but for the swish of water along her sides, and distant shouting.

'Engine clutches out, sir.'

'Slow ahead port.'

On her motors now, for the sake of manoeuvrability — the diesels couldn't be put astern, for instance — and using the port screw

195

only at this stage to assist the rate of turning, the submarine's long forepart at this moment pointing at *Helgoland*'s foc'sl, swinging on past her for'ard twelve-inch turret — bridge upperworks then, the portside turrets and casemates, triple funnels at the midway point between her masts, then the after control position, stern twelve-inch turret and length of quarterdeck. Lounging spectators were moving to the ship's side to gawp at the submarine as she swung. Still turning: open water ahead for half a minute, the southward gap of open river with small craft moving on it, and the two battle cruisers hazy at a distance of a couple of miles or so. Now *Thuringen* was in her sights as the swing slowed.

'Stop port. Midships and meet her.'

'Stop port, sir. Meet her.' Meaning, put on port helm to check the turn, hold her on her present heading, point of aim for any torpedo or torpedoes that might be fired, halfway between the for'ard twelve-inch turret and her stem — in other words the foc'sl, crew's accommodation. Winter with his glasses up again, watching the drift of mutineers across her decks.

'Slow astern together.'

'Slow astern together, sir. Ship's head two-one-five.'

Motors running astern to take the way off her, hold her in this clearly threatening position while the tenders brought their Marines up on *Thuringen*'s port side. Shouldn't be long now, getting there.

Neureuther reported loudly, sharply, '*Helgoland*'s six-inch training on us, sir!'

Winter took a look at her — bare-eyed, no need for glasses — they were in fact closer to *Helgoland* than to *Thuringen*. By the same token, the threat directed at 201 was point-blank

'Signalman!'

Kendermann — diminutive, red-haired — in his customary position on the port side, within reach of the signal lamp in its bracket, whipped round, and Winter told him — turning away again to continue watching events on *Thuringen* — 'Make to *Helgoland*, train all guns fore and aft.'

'Aye, sir . . . '

Lamp already clacking, calling, and getting an answering flash almost immediately from the battleship's signal deck, after end of her bridge. It should work out all right, Neureuther was telling himself, *if* her officers and/or loyal crew members, especially NCOs, could re-assert their control of her armament. They might not even have known they'd lost it, or been in the process of losing it. Winter had to be banking on that, he supposed. Couldn't do more than hope, though: could be blown out of the water in split seconds if mutineers were in even partial control — as well as prepared to escalate the situation to such a degree of enormity.

Clashes ceasing, as the brief message was received and acknowledged. *Now*, proof of that pudding . . . Winter, Neureuther noted, not having ordered his own gun's crew to man, load and train it on *Helgoland* — as he might have done, and Neureuther thought *he* probably would have, despite the risk of considerably worsening the confrontation.

Winter hadn't even glanced again at the *Helgoland*.

But — Christ . . .

Glasses up, and actually holding his breath. *Helgoland*'s port-side turrets moving — training fore and aft. He told Winter, who was still concentrating on *Thuringen*, '*Helgoland*'s complying, sir!'

A shrug of the heavy shoulders. As if he'd known she would. He was, Neureuther thought, not by any means for the first time, a quite exceptional man. He had his glasses up again, focused on the masthead of the first tender bringing its load of Marines up on *Thuringen*'s port side aft, masthead momentarily visible above the stern turret, hidden now behind a taller superstructure, the after control and searchlight position. Also, a sudden rush of action on the battleship's decks: officers and others clearing the quarterdeck of mutineers, sending them scurrying for'ard and following-up determinedly, officers with pistols in their hands and others — chief and POs, seamen too — with dirks and cutlasses. Mutineers were vacating even the fo'csl deck, diving for the hatchways; and some, who initially might have thought they'd stand their ground, were being arrested or knocked down and sat on. And the Marines whose arrival had triggered this had got aboard: helmeted and with bayonets fixed, making a clean sweep of it.

'Didn't need *us* here.' Winter lowered his glasses. 'FdU called 'em sheep. I say they're bloody vermin.'

9

Having spent some time in UB81, also visited the hospital to see two men who were still confined there, finding that he still had an hour before lunch, he'd visited the tailor and collected the rest of his gear with its second stripes and new epaulettes. The second stripes were noticeably brighter than the older ones and the gilt crowns above them, but it would have been a waste of money to have had the whole lot renewed.

Sooner spend it on Helena. Especially as one mightn't be wearing uniform much longer. Extraordinary thought, that: never having considered any possibility of not wearing it for life. Barely imaginable, in fact — overnight to become a civilian, *former* kapitan-leutnant — and maybe to be seeking employment with adequate renumeration for the support of a *wife*, for heaven's sake. This thought occurring when on his way out of the base he'd been passed by a platoon of young trainees moving at the double under the command of a PO who, seeing Otto, had ordered 'Eyes right!' and saluted him as they trotted past. Training as *what*, he'd wondered. Street-sweepers, beggars? Well, like everything else, training obviously had to go on until it stopped, so to speak — but when it did, how many millions of unemployed would there be on German streets?

Better telephone Helena. Not now: after lunch. Let her know he'd booked a table and arranged to borrow Hans Graischer's motor again. And tell her about Ahrens' attempt to buttonhole Franz Winter. As well that she should be forewarned. Ahrens might or might not have got hold of Winter between his briefing by FdU and 201's departure for the Schillig Roads. Maybe not, since the departure had been a rushed one; in which case you could bet fat Willi would be on the quayside when Franz brought her back in.

Get my word in first, maybe, spike the bastard's guns . . .

He'd brought his re-vamped kit up to his room, shoved things on hangers and was at the window now, with a view over the various basins and dry docks and swing-bridges to the Jade's sliding, barely rumpled surface. No sight of U201, no submarine movements at all in progress. A minesweeper just entering, lighters in tow of a tug moving up-river, gulls wheeling, screeching . . . Thinking of Helena again, and making himself face the question he'd woken with — whether he was a lucky man, as he'd thought when turning in, or an idiot; whether he shouldn't have kept his damn mouth shut. Drink, high blood-pressure, afterglow of the best sex he'd ever had: on top of that the jolt of running into those people — Ahrens of *all* people — a jolt to *him*, near-lethal body-blow to *her*; her tone of despair, his shocked recognition that it had been entirely *his* doing, having assured her he'd look after her . . .

In fact, seduced her. Although she hadn't been a virgin, and had been fairly keen on being seduced.

Well — girls were. Always had been. From way back. At least, since the English girl. Maybe since the dawn of history, but the English girl — well. Different kettle of fish, that one. Different circumstances entirely, as well as different people. Oneself so young, she even younger.

Remember to put a couple of blankets in Graischer's motor. The rug that was in it already was of course softer, silkier; rug next to her skin, therefore . . .

★　★　★

Claus Stahl was in the Mess; Otto bought two glasses of schnapps and joined him, gave him an update on the two still in hospital. Three others had been sent home on sick-leave. And there'd been a rumour floating around, Stahl told him, that they'd be wanting 81 moved into a repair dock tomorrow, Wednesday.

'No doubt someone will be good enough to let *me* know about it, if it's true.'

'I'm sure they will, sir.'

'But how far they'll get with mending her before the whole show grinds to a halt . . . '

Stahl wagging his head: gloomy look on the pale, creased face. 'Never dreamt it might come to anything like this, did we. Saw ourselves entering British ports in triumph. Our ensign above theirs on every mast. Eh?'

'I suppose that's true. But *we* haven't lost,

201

Claus. As well for morale to bear that in mind.'

'Absolutely right. Result's the same, though — ground cut from under one's feet, nothing to do but jag in. Then we *are* beaten. Oh, hello, Kurt.'

Kurt Hahn, Ahrens' first lieutenant, who'd been with Fatty at the Snake Pit last night. Scrawny, dark, weasel-faced. He'd raised a glass to Stahl, glanced nervously at Otto and turned away, resuming a conversation with the paymaster, Hans Deuker. And beyond them — just arriving — Schwaeble's sturdy figure trailed by Ahrens' tubby one. Schwaeble calling an order to the bar steward, then looking round, seeing Otto and beckoning him.

'Excuse me, Claus, I'm summoned.'

'Of course.' Stahl moved to join Hahn and Deuker. And now Hintenberger had sloped in, was joining them. He still looked like something out of a hole in the ground, but it looked as if he'd at least trimmed his beard. He'd found his father in reasonably good shape, and the cats now eight in number instead of six, apparently. No explanation given, that was simply how it was. Otto, edging through to Schwaeble, saw Ahrens' moon-face freeze. Had already been telling tales, maybe? Walter Bohme was joining them too: Bohme's Coastal still languishing in dock, presumably. Otto heard him offer, 'Buy anyone a drink, can I?'

Schwaeble told him, 'You can come in on this round. Timed it just right.' Nodding to the steward: 'Add another, Hartje'. Then to Otto,

'They'll be starting on 81 tomorrow, von Mettendorff. Best be ready to shift her first thing in the morning. Enough juice in the battery to move on your motors, or will you need a tug?'

'Battery should just about manage it, sir.'

'Cracked containers and all. You were *very* lucky not to have had a chlorine problem.' He told Ahrens, 'Took quite a bashing. Getting her back was a remarkable achievement.'

Otto said, 'Quite a bashing, but luck as well.' From the normality of Schwaeble's manner he didn't think Ahrens *had* as yet spilled the beans. Saving it for Winter, no doubt . . . 'Any news of 201 yet, sir?'

'Not as yet.' Raising his glass: 'Here's to her. And to Winter.'

'Winter.' Ahrens gulped some schnapps and added, 'Couldn't have a better man on the job, in any case.' A hostile glance at Otto, then to Schwaeble, 'He's the best we've got, in my opinion.'

'One of the best, certainly.'

'Remember U3's accident?'

Schwaeble frowning, remembering . . . 'Long time ago, that. His first boat, wasn't she?'

'First and damn near his last!'

Bohme shook his head. 'I know U3 came to grief, but — '

'Before your time. *I* was still in training. At Kiel, naturally, which was also where U3 completed her fitting-out — *had* completed, was making her first trip to sea, and — yes, Franzi's first submarine appointment. Leutnant zu See, green as grass. There was to be a trial dive in harbour, and they'd left an engine-room ventilation outlet open. In fact it was the builders' doing — KW — the indicator showed it as shut when it was open, and vice-versa. Soon as the dive started she took in enough dirty harbour water to make her stern-heavy, and down she went. Her captain was in the upper control-room with an officer of the watch and helmsman, passed the order down for all hands to shut themselves into the for'ard compartment — which they did, twenty-nine of 'em. Well, two floating cranes were towed over from KW, and it took the best part of twelve hours for divers to rig cables around the boat's forepart. Cranes were then to drag her bow up and the lads'd crawl out through the torpedo tubes. But as the bow broke surface the cables parted, and down she went again. Second attempt took not twelve hours, but fourteen — thirty hours altogether before they had her up, and they all crawled out — the twenty-nine, including young Franz — but the three in the tower had been dead some while by then. Chlorine gas up the voicepipes, apparently.'

Schwaeble nodded. 'Hence airtight cocks on all voicepipes now. The chaps for'ard were saved by the Drager filtration system, weren't they. Caustic potash filters. Couldn't see *you* crawling through a torpedo tube, Ahrens.'

'Very amusing — sir. But as I was saying, Franz Winter was one of them, and that was his first outing!'

'Did him no great harm, anyway.'

'That's rather my point. Going through that ordeal, then coming out of it declaring, 'Hey, this is the life for me!' He *did*, though. So impressed by the way they'd all behaved throughout those thirty hours, he told me not long afterwards.'

Bohme nodded. 'I can see that. One would be. But he's a good 'un, is Franzi.'

Otto agreed. 'Is indeed. A brilliant CO.'

'Certainly gave *you* a helping hand in the early stages, von Mettendorff?'

A nod to Ahrens. 'I owe him a great deal.'

'Repaying the debt now, in your own inimitable manner?'

Tone and look of contempt. Otto saw surprise in the others' faces, and shrugged. 'I'm afraid I'm not with you.'

'With no-one but yourself, I'd say.' He tossed his drink back, bowed slightly with a click of his heels to Schwaeble. 'If you'd excuse me, sir.'

Gone. Schwaeble and Bohme staring after him. Schwaeble fingering the duelling scar on his cheek; asking Otto after a moment, 'What was that about?'

'Well.' Shake of the head. 'I'd deduce that he's taken a dislike to me.'

'Reasonable deduction.' Bohme and Otto both smiled. Schwaeble didn't; he asked Otto, 'What have you done to offend him?'

'Really can't say. Saw him ashore last night, as it happens, but we didn't speak. He was half-seas over, by the look and sound of him.'

'Where was this?'

'At the Weinstube in Rastede. Grueninger's. I

was just leaving and so was he. I'd been in the restaurant upstairs, but — '

'The Snake Pit.' Bohme grinning at him. 'Well, well . . . '

'I'd been dining with my fiancée, as it happens.'

'Fiancée?' Schwaeble's eyebrows hooped. 'In the Snake Pit? And since when have you aspired to possession of a fiancée?'

'Since last night, sir. I took her there to have her to myself, talk her into accepting me. You know, you get a room to yourselves — and when they put themselves out they can still lay on a lavish meal. And the strategem worked.' He nodded. 'Proof of the pudding — which incidentally was profiteroles *au chocolat.*'

'And who is she?'

'If you don't mind, sir, even our parents don't know about it yet. And with things as uncertain as they are at present, one can't — well, set a date, for instance.'

Looking at their glasses, and his own. Schwaeble murmuring congratulations, Bohme echoing them, then asking, 'Why should running into you in that place have upset Willi?'

'Heaven knows.' Otto had signalled to the steward for another round. 'Might be something else entirely. Except — well, he shouted to me and I kept going. It's not a place to keep a decent girl hanging around, and he and his pals had obviously been making an evening of it.' He shrugged: 'But if his skin's *that* thin — as well as grossly inflated . . . '

★ ★ ★

206

He got through to Helena's place of work in Oldenburg at about two-thirty, and when he asked for Frl. Becht was required first to identify himself and then to state the nature of his business. He told the man, who sounded young and not over-educated, 'Personal matter', and was then asked not to occupy the line for longer than was essential, as they were exceptionally busy. Then he was put through to her.

'Helena. Me.'

'Otto — darling . . .'

Low-toned, that 'darling', so evidently not alone, or not sound-proof anyway. He told her, 'They're guarding you closely. I had to state my business to some office boy. I said it was personal. Might have said, 'I wish to speak with my fiancée', but I didn't know whether you'd have liked that.'

'No-one here knows about it yet. Might just as well, mind you. But — '

'I'd have thought it might lead to mass suicides.'

'Ha ha. But we're frantically busy. Well, you can imagine — the way things are, and our concerns being what they are?'

'Of course. But here our engagement is now known to certain individuals. The man we ran into last night — '

'Ahrens?'

'Right. He became rather insulting in the Mess, before lunch, then waddled off in a huff, so I told the others who were present — one of them Kapitan zu See Gunther Schwaeble, whom you know — he's second in command,

Kommodore Michelsen's deputy — I told them the circumstances of our presence at Grueninger's, and — here's the point — they swallowed it hook, line and sinker, neither of 'em doubting you were with me for the purpose as stated — privacy, for the proposal of marriage. I excused myself from naming you — on the grounds that our parents didn't know yet. And that's it.'

'I'd have no objection to being named. Rather looking forward to changing it, that's all. I was trying out what'll be my new signature — takes up about half a line!'

'Don't put it on any bank cheques yet, that's all. I've got to be quick, though, so — essentials now. I've booked at Kramer's for eight-fifteen and I have the loan of the car. Eight, at the Muellers'?'

'Dying for it. For *you* . . . Is Franz Winter back?'

'He's been back, but had to take a cruise up into the Schillig Roads for purposes I can't go into, should be back again any time now. Ahrens, I may say, is waiting to pounce on him.'

'You'll tell him about us anyway, won't you?'

'Yes. When he raises the subject. Or I suppose even if he doesn't.'

'If by any chance he should telephone me, *I'll* tell him. Have to, obviously. Oh, I'm so *happy*, Otto!'

'Good. Me too. Ecstatic. Transforms — well, *everything!* Extraordinary . . .'

'Soon as I get a minute I'm going to tell my parents. Maybe I'll call them from the Muellers', so *they'll* know too. I've been thinking about how I'll describe you to them — tall, fair and — '

'Ugly, overweight, foul-mannered, lecherous — '

'*That*, for sure. They'll love it, be dying to meet you! Better stop this now, though — our lines are madly busy, it's a wonder you got through. Are you telling *your* parents?'

'I will soon. Evenings are the best time to ring them. I might tell Gerda — my sister — for a start. She'll be a great help. You'll like her — and she'll be thrilled. Which will be good for her, incidentally: she lost her husband very recently, poor — '

'Otto, I've been told I must clear this line. Sorry, but — '

'See you at eight.'

He hung up, on a line that had already gone dead, thinking that Gerda really *would* be thrilled, and if the parents were sticky about it, which they might well be to start with, her enthusiasm would help a lot. In fact the parents *would* be difficult; they'd be aghast, to start with. He'd recognised this from the start and tried to keep it out of mind, telling himself, cross *that* bridge when we come to it. He was in the office that Hans Graischer used and had led him to when he'd docked 81, last — oh, Saturday. Only three days ago, although it felt more like a month. So much happening, both personal and professional. Well, more political than professional: although all one got of it were dribs and drabs, rumours and speculation, mounting awareness of general confusion, which according to some of the papers presaged revolution, or at the very least drastic change.

Which would be likely to include one's career going up in smoke.

So thank God for Helena, he thought. For love as well as lust. Permanence. In all the mess, the rising flood of it — revolution, even — something really thrilling, combining happiness and excitement and — and which was largely in one's own control. Remember that, next time one started having second thoughts.

★ ★ ★

Land and sea were darkening when 201 re-entered and Franz Winter conned her through to the berth she'd occupied before, in the *Verbindungshafen*. Lights glowed along the quay where the berthing party were standing ready, some of the light glittering on Gunther Schwaeble's and Willi Ahrens' greatcoats' epaulettes — four stripes on Schwaeble's, three on Ahrens'.

'Slow astern together. Midships the wheel.'

Scummy water sluicing up her sides. He stopped the starboard screw first, and put on starboard helm, waited while the astern-running port screw brought her stern in: her bow was already in; this was largely a matter of taking the angle off her. Now — 'Stop port.'

U201 drifting in alongside, Coxswain Muller's voice grating, 'Wheel's amidships, port motor stopped, sir.' Heaving lines were tossed over, bringing fore and after breasts over from the quay; Winter passed down the voicepipe,

210

'Finished with motors, open fore hatch.'

Find out what they have in store for us *next*, he thought. Asking Neureuther, 'Who has the duty tonight?'

'Regrettably, sir, *I* have.'

'So have one of the others cover for you while you get a bath and a meal first.'

'But I've paperwork to catch up on, sir. Make a start on it, at least.'

The plank crashed over; almost simultaneously the fore hatch swung open and thumped back, light from the torpedo stowage compartment streaming up. Breasts had been secured by this time, springs were being hauled over — fore spring running from her stem to a bollard well aft on the quay, back spring from her stern to well for'ard. Neureuther asked, 'Fall out from harbour stations, sir?' and Winter nodded, told both him and Muller as he climbed down through the tower, 'Tell you what's what as soon as *I* know it.'

'Aye, sir. But about Muhbauer's compassionate leave — '

'Yes. Let him go.'

Lucky bugger. Probably wasn't one man on board who wouldn't leap at the chance of being 'let go'. Oneself included. Tired, and fed up to the back teeth. Had had to lie out there in the Schillig Roads while mutineers had been hunted out from every corner of the *Thuringen* and transferred to the tenders under guard; the second tender had had to be seen to finish and cast off before 201 could start back. While during those hours there'd been cat-calling and occasionally the sight of a red flag — on *Helgoland* — and whether the mutiny had been affected in the least, let alone nipped in the bud . . .

Telephone *her*, though. Stiff drink first, then call her, forget all this — for five or ten blessed minutes anyway.

On the casing, Schwaeble shook his hand.

'Well done. The first of the tenders has already landed its prisoners, I'm told.'

'Think it'll have done any good, sir?'

'That, I'm not sure of. Kommodore'll have a better idea of it than I have. He's been in communication with the Chief of Staff. And he's in his office now, expecting you.'

'Can we count on at least a week's stand-off, sir?'

'Ask *him*. But I'd imagine so. Pretty sure of it, in fact.'

'Then we won't be taking part in the fleet action plan that's — '

'No. Far too late. But FdU *is* waiting, so — '

'I'll go along.'

'And Ahrens is still after you for something or other. On the quay there. Don't let him hold you up — Kommodore has the devil of a lot on his plate at this juncture.'

'Right.' He looked round for Neureuther, found him sort of hovering, told him, 'Duty-part of the watch to remain on board, rest carry on ashore. Seems we'll be in at least a week. I'm on my way to see FdU. If I don't come back you can take it for granted that's how it is.'

★ ★ ★

212

Willi Ahrens, bulky in his greatcoat, was waiting near the plank, stamping his feet to warm them.

'Franz . . . '

'Hello, Willi. You want to talk. I'm on my way to FdU, why not come along?'

'I will. You did the job out there, I gather?'

'Did what I was told, that's all. Whether it'll get any of us anywhere, I rather doubt. What's on *your* mind?'

'Nothing pleasant. Not by any means.' Falling in beside him, matching his steps to Winter's. 'Important that you should know, however — and before you get in touch with — I'm sorry, Franz, as an old friend I do have to tell you this — *before* you speak to Fraulein Becht . . . '

★   ★   ★

In his room, Otto put studs and links into a clean shirt and collar, and brushed down his better uniform jacket and trousers. The steward who attended to the rooms on this floor had cleaned his boots for him: and that was about all the preparations necessary. Oh — clean socks, and a handkerchief . . . Six o'clock now, by the old watch that had been a paternal gift almost before he'd learnt to tell the time; he needed to be on the road by seven, or even a little before that, so —

Blankets. He peeled them off the spare bed, rolled them and took the bundle down to Graischer's motor, which was in the yard behind the Mess. Hoping not to encounter friends or acquaintances on the way down there. To run

213

into Willi Ahrens, for instance, might have been *slightly* embarrassing, with these.

He stowed them on the floor at the back. It was going to be a cold night, hard frost was a certainty, but — the rug as a wrap-around, plus blankets, greatcoat on oneself . . .

Won't be like *last* night. Wednesday, for that. Had the reservation, in any case. Discuss it with her tonight: might be wiser not to risk another incident like last night's. Wouldn't put anything past bloody Ahrens . . . On the other hand, how about the jaunt to Hanover which they'd discussed earlier? Depending on the dust having settled here, of course . . .

Ring Gerda?

Six-ten now. Ten minutes, say, to make the call, then half an hour for a bath and change, be on one's way by about six-fifty.

The Mess secretary was just leaving his office: didn't mind Otto using the telephone, only asked him to lock the door when he'd finished, leave the key on the board in the hallway. Local call, was it? Otto nodded, thanked him, asked the exchange to get Gerda's number in Berlin, and again, surprisingly, got through in only a few minutes.

'Gerda — how are you?'

'Better for hearing your voice, my dear Kapitan-Leutnant. Seriously, *is* a nice surprise. Everything's going from foul to stinking, whichever way you look, isn't it?'

'The general outlook's not good, but — '

'You haven't seen the evening papers, then. If you had, you'd know it was a lot worse than just 'not good'.'

214

'Well. Afraid I haven't time for you to expand on that, either. Sorry, but — '

'You'll sleep better for not knowing. What's new with you?'

'That is absolutely the right question, and I'm only too happy to give you the answer to it. Gerda — I've become engaged.'

He heard her intake of breath. Then the beginnings of a laugh, and — 'Trapped at last?'

'Congratulations would be in order. She's absolutely lovely — also charming, intelligent, enormous fun and — and you'll adore her. Don't tell me I've used some of those words before — if I have, put it down to my limited vocabulary. I'm not exaggerating, she's *all* those things. Enthuse now, please. You asked me last time we spoke, how about wedding bells — or something of that kind — '

'That was ironic. A joke!'

'Well, this is *not*. I assure you — '

'A reaction to the hard time you had at sea, perhaps? Crazed stallion desperate for a regular supply of oats?'

'Gerda — please stop that. I've known Helena for several months, I love her and she loves me. It's the happiest, most wonderful thing, and I'd expect *you* to be happy for us, with us.'

'Is she German?'

'Of *course* she's German!'

'Have you told the parents yet?'

'Haven't had time. On my way to take her to dinner now. She's based about half an hour away — an Intelligence outfit, military. Her parents live in Hamburg.'

'Otto!'

'What?'

'What sort of people live in *Hamburg*?'

Silence, for a moment. Then: 'I have to go. We'll talk again when I hope you'll be in a better frame of mind.'

Damn her!

But — could be very much a matter of her state of mind. The loss of her husband — despite her apparent bravery last time they'd spoken — and some kind of awful news this evening . . .

He locked the door of the office, took the key to the board in the hallway, started back up to his room. Gerda, he thought — really *very* disappointing. Call her again, offer sympathy . . .

Might make it worse, though. And without her backup, the parents really *were* going to take some handling . . .

'Kapitan-Leutnant von Mettendorff, sir?'

On the first landing — he recognised the man from FdU's outer office, the leading writer who'd made copies of the patrol report. He'd been descending the stairs at speed, now skidded to a halt.

'Yes?'

'Kommodore Michelsen's compliments, sir, would you report to him at once, please!'

★ ★ ★

Andreas Michelsen had told Winter, 'You couldn't have done it better. Unfortunately we were over-optimistic in thinking that a mutiny which is now widespread in the fleet could have been snuffed out so easily. The Commander-in-Chief has been conducting his own investigations; his Chief of Staff Admiral von Trotha instructs me to thank you for your efforts, but the trouble's too deep-rooted. In fact it's become necessary to cancel the plan for fleet action. Battle squadrons are being dispersed — to Kiel, Cuxhaven, and so forth.'

'That's hellish news.'

He'd actually flinched from it. Had arrived grim-faced, now looked even grimmer. Sitting bolt upright, glaring across the desk at the FdU. Scowling — shaking . . . *Had* been, anyway, was struggling to control it. An abrupt shake of the head: 'What we're left with then — forced to — is *surrender*?'

Grimacing, as if the word had a bitter taste.

Michelsen said, 'Armistice negotiations are in progress, is what I'm told.'

'Politicians' negotiations . . . '

'Terms of an armistice would cover detail of naval and military cease-fire as well as political agreement — yes — though presumably the *Admiralstab* will have their say in it. That means Reinhardt von Scheer, on whom we can certainly count *not* to let us down. But political wrangling first, yes, I suppose, *then* detail as to how it's to affect us.'

'Such as surrendering our ships, including U-boats.'

Michelsen obviously didn't like that prospect any more than Winter did. It would be his unpleasant duty to preside over the implementation of whatever was agreed, that was all. Closing

217

his eyes, thinking, that's *all*, indeed . . . Winter grating, 'When we've not been beaten — nowhere *near* beaten — in fact we were winning hands-down until we were ordered to suspend operations against merchantmen!'

'True. Because our government were requesting an armistice, and that was a pre-condition imposed by the American president. You and I are on the same side, Winter, our views are I'm sure identical. Fact of it is, the Army *has* been beaten. Came near to sweeping all before them in von Ludendorff's spring offensive, lost it to the British, Canadians, Americans and French between the eighth and twenty-first of August, east and southeast of Amiens. The Kaiser said then, 'We are at the end of our resources', and Ludendorff declared that the war would have to be ended. You're right in saying *we* have not been beaten, but — '

'Dishonoured. This mutiny on top of everything else is an *appalling* thing!'

Michelsen nodded. 'I agree, of course. And obviously my immediate concern is for the U-boat arm. To start with, while recalling some and re-deploying others, I'm stipulating that any ship flying a red flag is to be treated as an enemy. We can preserve *our* honour — '

'May I suggest another way we might do that, sir?' Shake of the bison's head. 'My apologies — interrupting — but — '

'Go on.'

'Action by the High Seas Fleet was to have saved the Navy's honour, and influenced the terms of armistice. Since it's not now to take place, we might replace it with action of our own. *You* might, sir — by authorising the targeting of the British fleet in Scapa Flow. I request the privilege of doing so, sir. It hasn't been attempted since von Hennig's attempt in U18 in November of '14 — and this is not the first time I've thought of it — '

'The Grand Fleet is now based in the Firth of Forth, Winter.'

'But Scapa Flow's still being used. As mentioned in an Intelligence summary only a few weeks ago.'

'Detachments of the Grand Fleet deploying in support of the North Sea Barrage and Norwegian convoys, etcetera.' A nod. 'Quite so. But although we've probed up that way quite recently — '

'Valentiner and Forstmann both drew blank. I know that, sir. But what I'm proposing — '

'You'd try to get inside.' Gazing at him, thinking about it — or about *him*, Franz Winter. Both, maybe. Motives, chances . . . Asking him then, 'By the Hoxa entrance, as von Hennig tried it?'

Hans von Hennig in U18 *had* got inside, but finding the great anchorage empty — Grand Fleet out on a sweep of the North Sea — had turned to make his way out, given himself away by showing too much periscope, and been rammed first by an armed trawler and then by a destroyer. Damaged and out of control, he'd got U18 out of the Flow but had been swept on to the Skerries, where he'd scuttled her. He and others were picked up and taken prisoner. Winter was saying, 'Hoxa's the obvious entry point. Von Hennig followed some small supply vessel in. But I wouldn't just poke my nose in and if the Flow's empty come right out again. If the targets are there, I'd go for them, but if not, *wait* for them. I'd bottom, lie quiet and wait. Knowing they do periodically use the place, and being inside — well, one's *there*, in position.' He raised one hand with thick fingers crossed: showed his teeth. 'I think I'd stand a good chance, sir.'

'The risks would be enormous.'

'So would the triumph be. What the *Hochseeflotte* can't do — '

'Of course.'

'And since the Flow's only in occasional use, no longer the fleet base it has been, don't you think its defences might have become less efficient?'

'Conceivable.' Michelsen leaning back in his chair, eyes slitted, staring at Winter down his nose. 'Perhaps especially now, when they're thinking the war's as good as finished, that *we're* finished.' He nodded. 'Very well. But — *when* would you — '

'Sooner the better. Immediately. If a so-called armistice is truly imminent — '

'Yes. I agree. We'd be bound by its terms from the minute it's announced. You're right, sooner the better. Your requirements therefore — tonight, immediately — fuel, fresh water, stores, torpedoes — '

'I have four in the bow tubes, none aft. Need four reloads for'ard therefore, and — '

'You'd hardly have opportunity to re-load, surely!'

'Perhaps not.' Thinking about it. Having fired those four, would *not* be left in peace to lie on the bottom for the couple of hours it took to re-load. He nodded. 'Just need two in the stern tubes, then. And as you say, bunkers, fresh water, provisions — '

'Ammunition?'

Shake of the head. 'Didn't use the gun, this last patrol. Can't imagine I would on this task, either.'

'No.' Michelsen checked the time. Getting on for six-thirty. 'I suppose not. But — all right. I'll have the departments concerned alerted. Say an hour before any of it gets under way — you've got to get your crew back on board, for a start — but then with most of it happening simultaneously, and allowing let's say another hour for unexpected hold-ups, might sail you at 2300, say. Important question, though — how will your crew react to this?'

'They'll be astonished, furious, despondent. But they'll respond to my explanation of it. One other thought, sir — I'd like to take with me a — call him an alternate commanding officer. Then if I should crack up — I'm not expecting to, no such thing, but I could use some sleep on the way up there, to be on top form when I need to be — '

'Anyone in mind?'

'Yes.' A brisk nod. 'Von Mettendorff. His boat's out of action, isn't she; he's a first-class man — professionally — he was my first

221

lieutenant in U53, we know each other well enough. If he were invited to — *volunteer*, I suppose — '

'I'd guess he'll consider it an honour.' Michelsen looked towards his outer office, called, 'Hillebrand! Here a minute!'

10

The LMS night express from Euston rocking
northward towards Glasgow, from time to time
shrieking into the sleet-laden dark, and in its
first-class dining car, Sue remarking to Anne
— while Sam Lance was scribbling in his little
notebook or diary — 'Fairly conclusive, what
Bertie had to say about von Whatsit's U-boat, in
any case. Good idea to ask him, wasn't it?'

They'd asked Bertie Hope yesterday whether
the destroyers' claim to have sunk von
Mettendorff's UB81 could have been erroneous,
and he'd said he'd look into it. This had been an
extension of Sue's request to be allowed to make
the Orkneys trip as chaperone to Anne. He'd
said yes to that immediately, even snappily;
there'd been a lot going on and he'd been
closeted with Blinker Hall all forenoon, obviously hadn't thought Sue's temporary absence
would bring the Department to a halt or affect
the outcome of the war, exactly. In fact Sam
Lance might already have cleared it with him
— which would have accounted for the rather
testy manner. But the UB81 question did
interest him; he'd made a note of it, later
telephoned someone on the staff at Devonport,
had a reply from there this morning, Tuesday
29th, and had conveyed his own view of it to
them before they'd left the Old Building this
afternoon. Overall conclusion being that UB81

had been sunk. He'd told them, 'Ninety-nine percent certain. And if by some extraordinary fluke she was *not* sent to the bottom there and then, she couldn't have got away; she'd have had to have surfaced — if she'd been capable of it — for her crew to abandon ship. And as she didn't, you can take it she couldn't, she was finished. Well, look — unequivocal statement here — at least one shell penetrated the conning-tower, several others exploding in the bridge and on the periscope standards — as well as scoring hits aft — blasting off half the after-casing — and as likely as not puncturing the pressure-hull. No *certainty* of that, but — hell, *I* definitely wouldn't have wanted to have been inside her at that stage! And a four-inch shell — shells, plural — exploding on the standards — well, her periscopes would have been smashed and/or jammed. They're delicate instruments, for one thing; for another they're a very close fit in the tubes that house them. Have to be — obviously, uh?'

Anne had nodded. If Bertie said that something in the naval technical field was obvious, you could assume it was.

'The lower end of one periscope, anyway, in that class of U-boat — a UBII, or Coastal — is in the flooded tower. Manned from there by the skipper or officer of the watch, presumably. Inaccessible, even if it hadn't been wrecked by hits on the standards — because the tower was holed, so it'd have filled as soon as she dipped under. The whole boat would have filled, unless they'd evacuated the tower and shut the lower hatch. And as I say, the pressure-hull may well have been cracked open abaft the bridge in any case. Conclusion, therefore: they sent her down with holes in her, dead duck absolutely.'

His telephone had buzzed, and he'd put his hand on it, telling them, 'You can take that as read, anyway. Enjoy your Scapa trip.' Lifting the 'phone: 'Hope . . .'

Sue had made a rhyme of it on their way back to Chester Square: 'Take it as read, Mutton-dorff's dead.' Repeating it now in the train and adding a new thought: 'Couldn't have got a signal off, I suppose, in the minute or two they were on the surface? That'd solve the mystery, wouldn't it.'

'Doubt they could have. Saying what, anyway — *Nos morituri te salutamus?*'

'I rather doubt if Huns talk Latin.'

'Of course they do. Properly educated ones. But if they'd made any signal at all, it would have been intercepted, we'd *know.*'

Sam asked, in the train's lurching, yellowish-lit dining car — which earlier had been packed, but during the last half-hour had been emptying, grey-faced stewards relaying tables for breakfast — 'What mystery is this?'

He'd put the question to Sue, who'd glanced sharply at Anne, reproving her for having mentioned wireless interception. She told him, 'Pre-war friend of Anne's — a Hun, no less, and now a U-boat captain — or rather ex U-boat captain, as it seems he's now feeding the fishes.'

'You having me on?'

'Well — perhaps more likely crabs than fishes, at this stage — '

Anne cut in with: 'All true, Sam, except he wasn't a *friend* of mine. Acquaintance, yes — brother of a girl I shared digs with when I was at the Berlitz at Frankfurt, the year before the war. She was studying French. He was on some U-boat training course at the time, I think transferring to them from surface craft. I remember she was very full of it, thought he was frightfully brave. Well, a year or so ago that name — von Mettendorff, not a very common one — cropped up in an Intelligence report identifying the captains of various U-boats, including von Mettendorff and UB81 — which according to C-in-C Plymouth was quite recently sunk by destroyers somewhere in that area.' She shrugged. 'But then ID cross-referencing raised a doubt as to whether that one actually *had* been sunk — and as a matter of interest we asked Bertie Hope, who looked into it and came up with an answer just this afternoon.'

'That the guy *is* feeding the crabs.'

She nodded. 'Seems fairly certain.'

'Well, we all want as many U-boats sunk as possible, but — heck — when it's a *friend* — which is somewhat unusual, least I certainly never heard of anyone actually *knowing* one of them!'

'Hardly did, either. Gerda and I were quite good friends, though. As I said, we shared digs, and the summer of that year — 1913 — I spent — oh, I suppose a week or ten days at her family's place in Saxony. Big old house, oodles of land. And her brother turned up for — again I don't remember exactly, but maybe a couple of days, and his name was Otto, which matched him more or less unquestionably to that ID report. Might have come from an interrogation, I think — it listed quite a number of boats and their COs' names.'

Sue put in, 'Would have been passed on to your people anyway.' Glancing at Anne again. Room 40 — or 'OB 40', standing for Old Building, room 40 — still didn't exist, as far as Americans were concerned; they received summaries of all Intelligence received, but items were attributed to agents' reports and 'reliable sources', never to wireless intercepts. Sam had just muttered, poking at his half-empty cup, 'Not the finest coffee I ever had. Not a bad meal, though.' This being the 'second service', the selection had been limited, all three of them making the best of soup followed by liver-and-bacon and apple tart. Sam continuing, 'But I suppose, seeing the number of U-boats that've been sunk in recent months, any individual commander'd have had something like an even chance of what you call feeding the fishes, by this time.'

'Crabs.'

'Fishes and/or crabs.'

Sue told him, 'When I saw that sinking report, my words to Anne were 'Cross *him* off your Christmas card list!''

'But from what you say — the slightness of your acquaintance with him — '

'He wouldn't have been on any such list.' A shrug. Sam did tend to take quite inconsequential remarks or statements for serious consideration: obviously hadn't had all that much to do with girls, Anne thought. Adding, 'If I had one anyway — which I don't. No, my only feeling of — well, slight sadness — was for Gerda.'

'The sister.'

'Right. She adored him.'

'Tell me, honey.' His eyes wandering over her face and the back-swept blue-black hair, the length and slimness of her neck. 'I don't think I asked you this before — what persuaded you to make a study of the German language?'

'Well — I felt I should do something or other that might help me to earn a living — and I already spoke French adequately. I thought the combination of French plus German might be useful. Not for any cut-and-dried purpose, but — you know, wanting to be able to earn my keep. One obvious possibility was the Foreign Office, which as it happened was where I ended up.'

'French just happened because your people went to live there?'

'Well, it did, really. Although I *worked* at it. Went to school there — French school, in France. But I think once you get in the way of picking up other lingos — well, you know you can, so — '

'Like falling off a log.' The train had shrieked. Sue added, 'So what's next? Chinese?' She was edging back the window blind, but seeing only

228

blackness laced with smoke and stinking of soot: and the noise had changed; she guessed they might be in a tunnel. Sam had just asked Anne, 'What attracted your parents to France?'

'To save on tax. He had an inheritance — not much, actually not enough, so he gambled — well, to supplement it, but as my mother puts it, without conspicuous success. There was a lot of gambling — this was at and around Dinard, in Brittany; there was a whole colony of English — and Americans, by the way — and — well, what you might call the *social* game was Mahjong, and plenty of heavy gambling in that, but Papa also went in for poker and backgammon, and bridge, of course. And he had a heart attack and died. That's it, in a nutshell.'

'Did you leave France then?'

She nodded. 'Grandparents — Mama's, the Verities, not Garniers — more or less looked after us. Then she met Angus McCaig, and they married — well, she'd known him before, slightly, he was a friend of friends; anyway, they fell in love, etcetera, and married, and I finished school in England — I'd taken German and done passably well in it, and went to Frankfurt.' She opened her hands: 'Which is where we came in, as they say.'

'Might your determination to become self-supporting' — Sam, continuing the interrogation — 'might it have sprung from the years in France, your father's lack of — ah — conspicuous success?'

'Might well.' She nodded, smiling at him. 'In fact — yes, I'm sure it did. Although my mother

229

poo-pooed it, rather. In her book, marriage was the thing. A 'good' marriage, of course.'

'I kind of like the sound of that.'

'You're certainly a good man, Sam, we know that. Anne mentions it quite frequently.'

'*Does* she, though!'

Anne asked him, 'If eventually we did marry, and went to live in Virginia, would I find any use for French and/or German?'

Brown eyes on hers, serious and thoughtful. Small shake of the head then. 'Can't see it, tell you the awkward truth. Could be, I suppose, but . . . ' He brightened: 'Teaching, maybe?'

'I don't think I'm cut out for that.'

'Well — we'll see. I could do a little research by mail, maybe. Although you'd have no *need* to earn a living, honey.'

'From *my* angle I think I would.'

'Like a lifebelt you're clinging to, daren't let go of?'

'Oh, *Sam* — '

Sue cut in with: 'Would you two mind if I left you to it? Been a long day, one way and another — and early starts tomorrow, I imagine. Also chaperones shouldn't have to sit in on pre-marital disputes.' To Anne then, as Sam moved to let her out, muttering that there was no dispute he was aware of, but that he enjoyed her company and knew Anne did too, 'Give me fifteen or twenty minutes and I'll be out of your way. What time should we meet for breakfast, Sam?'

★ ★ ★

It was half an hour before Anne arrived back in their two-berth compartment, entering very quietly in order not to wake Sue if she'd happened to be asleep already: which of course she wasn't, had her bunk-head light on and a copy of Mary Webb's *Gone to Earth* propped on her chest.

'Hello. Settle our little tiff, did we?'

'Tiff?'

'The tone of that 'Oh, *Sam*' is what stampeded me. And I admit, his lifebelt analogy had a bit of an edge to it. Prelude to calling it all off, I thought to meself.'

Anne hung her navy-blue WRNS jacket with its single light-blue stripe on each sleeve in the little closet beside Sue's khaki-coloured FANY suit, then sat on the lower bunk to remove her shoes. Shaking her head: 'You can't 'call off' something that's never been called 'on'.'

'And *won't* be — right? I mean, with a difference as unbridgeable as that seems to me to be. Sam wanting Memsahib *chez soi*, Memsahib with notions of pursuing a career of some sort — as well as being as obstinate as a mule?'

'Well. Apart from that difference in general outlook — which on its own might I dare say be negotiable — there's a more specific problem. The night we went to the Ritz, he let me in on this. His father has a boat-building business; Sam's worked in it with the old man all his life, and now in his absence there's a brother-in-law who's horned in and Sam thinks may try to keep him out of it — or at any rate keep him somehow

231

subordinate to him when the Navy finally releases him.'

'But the father, surely — '

'Old man's slightly ga-ga, I gather. Reading between the lines. Hence the brother-in-law getting his foot in the door. He's an accountant, obviously fairly sharp and with an eye to the main chance, while war contracts have greatly expanded and substantially changed the business. Sam's worried he'll be such a stranger to it, and the brother-in-law — who rejoices in the name of 'Tad' — '

'Ye Gods!'

'Just see him, can't you?' She'd removed her stockings and her blouse, had to stand now. 'Any case — cuckoo in the nest situation. Sam imagines he'll find Tad running the show and holding all the cards.'

'He should have set things up so his position was assured. Or made sure his ga-ga father did.'

'He should have. Yes. But Sam's so straight himself, he wouldn't expect to be done down, especially have 'em take advantage of his having gone to war. I say 'they' because Tad's wife, Sam's sister, I forget her name, sounds like a bitch too. So imagine it — me as little English wifey, far from home and relying entirely on old Sam — who might by the sound of it be slightly out of his depth in that *milieu* — father might even have kicked the bucket by that time — '

'You're *not* going to marry him, are you?'

'I don't know. As I've already stated about ninety times.'

'But he thinks you *will*. Must think you're just

playing hard to get. Otherwise why bother with all this, aimed simply at his getting to meet Mummy?'

'I suppose because (a) hope springs eternal, (b) it would make things easier when the time came if he *had* met her, and (c), last but not least, laying on such a jaunt might predispose me in his favour.' She was in her nightie, folding things. 'Going to clean my teeth now. I'll put this light on so you can switch yours off, if you've finished reading.'

'Right . . . It's quite fun anyway — don't you think?'

'*Will* be, I hope. At least makes a change.'

'Incidentally, he didn't bat an eyelid when you told him about von Muttondorff, did he.'

'Why should he have?'

'Oh, I don't know . . . '

'Why should he have, Sue?'

'Oh, dear.' Eyes shut. 'Should have thought before I spoke, shouldn't I. And — well, you might put it down to my over-fertile imagination, but — fact is, I've thought more than once there might have been some element of romance in that relationship.'

'Between me and Gerda's brother? Are you insane?'

'Perhaps I am. But you make such a point of telling us all how little he meant to you, how little you saw of him, that it was his sister who was your friend, not him, you didn't know *him* from a bar of Wright's coal tar soap, etcetera.'

'But that's the simple truth!'

She'd managed to laugh at the absurdity of the

233

notion. Sue taking note of a slight falsity of tone as she pushed her book into the netting rack and switched off the light. Nestling down . . . 'I do have a fertile imagination.'

★ ★ ★

Rocking, rumbling north. By way of Watford, Hemel Hempstead, Rugby, Stafford. Seeing none of them, of course, and certainly not stopping at any of them, giving none of them anything more than a passing howl. And in the small hours of the morning — well, Preston, Carlisle and Glasgow: changing there after breakfast to a much slower train to Thurso via Stirling, Perth, Inverness, its more measured rhythm repeating over and over, *en route to Scapa, en route to Scapa* — where oddly enough one had no particular wish to go, but which Sam Lance wanted one to visit.

Alternately half-awake and half-asleep now, having slept soundly for about the first hour and then woken into dozing memory, prompted perhaps by Sue's voicing of her suspicions. That, and/or earlier mention of him. Sue *was* perspicacious. As she'd put it herself once, 'If there's a rat there, I tend to get a sniff of it.'

Tended to smell or sense *something*, anyway, even if it wasn't always what she thought it was. 'Rat', however, in recent years having been apposite enough as a description of Otto von M., although it would certainly not have been in those few pre-Berlin days. Then he'd been quite strikingly *unratlike* — in fact quite outstandingly

234

handsome — all right, *beautiful*, which wasn't an adjective one would oneself have used, although his sister had done so more than once before Anne had ever set eyes on him. She recalled having taken it with a pinch of salt, even disinterest. But — *handsome*, for sure, as well as amusing, charming — like no-one she'd ever met or known to exist. She'd thought of him *then* — looking back on it now almost in bewilderment — as the playmate who'd proposed that thrillingly exciting rendezvous — proposing it in one of the stables — no, the tack-room. In each other's arms, speaking in urgent undertones, Gerda's *fantastic* brother murmuring to her that his aunt had an apartment there which she rarely used and to which he had a key.

I'll explain to you where it's located and I'll be there to meet you, then move into an hotel nearby and you'll have the place to yourself!

'But my mother's expecting me — '

'So send a telegram. Say 'spending a day and night in Berlin with Gerda'. Everything else therefore put back by twenty-four hours. Huh? We'll have the *grandest* time, you lovely, *lovely* creature! Evening on the town, find a cabaret we like — there are *hundreds* of them — dance the tango?'

She'd told him, 'I *adore* the tango!'

Having never danced it, except on her own . . . Otto telling her, 'It's forbidden to us, by Kaiser Wilhelm himself. An immoral dance, unsuitable for German officers to indulge in. Imagine *that*?'

Most thrilling moment of her life, she

remembered thinking. Just a few years ago, but
— a different world. Logically, an *old* world, but
to her at the time absolutely brand-new.
Recalling even now though the amalgam of
odours — leather and saddle-soap, stable-
sweepings, the tweed of Otto's jacket — and
hearing her own whisper of 'Draw me a map?'
Then his insistence that Gerda wasn't to know
anything about it, which she'd found frustrating:
she'd have liked to have shared with her the
excitement and thrill of this adventure, which
after all Gerda had effectively brought about.
He'd still insisted, though. 'She'd want to join
us, and it might be difficult to stop her. I want
you to myself, Anne — that's the whole point.
Selfish, maybe, but — look, I can't tango with
two of you, can I?' He'd hugged her again:
'Swear to me you won't give her even a hint?'

The train had shrieked again — waking her to
fresh immersion in its night-long drumming
rhythm. Had been just about dropping off: *had*
dropped off, more or less. Back into a positive
effort of remembering, which often enough she'd
used as a remedy for sleeplessness, the effort of it
sending one into dreamland. With an early call
for breakfast before getting into Glasgow, one
did need more sleep than one had had this far.
So — Berlin . . . Recalling very little of *that* rail
journey: only studying his pencilled sketch of the
route across town to the aunt's apartment, the
memorised address, and that she'd had the
telegram to her mother already written out, so as
to send it from the station as soon as she arrived
— to have that done with and tracks covered,

236

while feeling some twinges of guilt over the deception; she and her mother had always been open and straightforward with each other. But — what the heck, no harm in it . . .

She'd taken a cab — horse-drawn, not motor, although there'd been plenty of those around too — because it was a hot afternoon and she'd preferred to have her head in the open air. It had been stifling in the train. Taking the cab was an extravagance, of course, but she wanted to get to the apartment in reasonably good shape, not like some waif or stray, lugging her heavy suitcase with her along the crowded pavements — and maybe losing her way, at that: the map hadn't been all that easy to follow. Extravagance, for sure, but she'd *felt* extravagant — as well as wild and wicked — and an unexpected dividend was that the cabby had taken her for a German, which was excellent for morale at a somewhat deeper level.

'Here is the building, Fraulein.' Pointing with his whip; Anne fumbling in her purse and giving him a tip that evidently satisfied him. 'The Fraulein is generous.' He'd climbed down, lifted the suitcase down. His mare wore a hat, she remembered, a fez-shaped thing with holes for its ears to stick out of, and Anne had asked him, 'Feels the heat, does she?'

'Something terrible, she does. They all do, in these hot streets, and with the traffic worse with every day that passes. Mind you, us lot'll be off the streets afore much longer . . . '

'Anne!'

Otto. He'd seen her from a window and come

rushing down — coatless, hatless, reckless. 'You're actually *here*!'

'Thanks to the good efforts of my friend here — and this poor suffering animal.' In his arms, in her swirly green skirt and pale yellow shirt, darker green jacket, straw hat with an upright peacock's feather in it. The feather had been Gerda's notion, and she loved it, laughed when it caught on Otto's nose, almost penetrating a nostril. 'How long have you been looking out for me?'

'Oh — a few hours.' Picking up her suitcase, he'd added, 'If not all my life.'

'Oh, *you* . . . '

'Anyway, the last ten years of it. Come on. Only one floor up.'

It was a nice apartment, stylishly furnished. A good-sized entrance hall, quite large L-shaped sitting-room, with the short end of the L furnished as a dining area and connecting to the kitchen. A rather sumptuously feminine bed-room — the bed wider than an ordinary single — with a door into the bathroom, which again was lavishly appointed.

'It's lovely, Otto. How far do you have to come from your hotel?'

'Ah. Ah, yes. Fact is, I've run into a bit of a snag there. The town's absolutely packed, not a room to be had. The kind of small hotel I'd hoped to find invariably gets booked-up first, of course, because the big, modern ones are so frightfully expensive; but I've tried them all — even the Adlon and the Kaiserhof, which I may say would have cost me a small fortune

— well, there are about ten of that kind and I tried them all, and not a hope, not even an attic!'

'Is there some special reason they're so busy?'

'Several. For instance, I hadn't realised, but it's been explained to me umpteen times by hotel receptionists in the last couple of hours — the population's doubled in the past three years. In 1910 it was two million, now it's four. And Saturday's *the* day here. Or rather *the* night. And this year's the twenty-fifth in the reign of Kaiser Wilhelm II, his quarter-century, people feel bound to celebrate, and it seems most of them can afford to. On top of which it's midsummer, the avenues are beautiful and the nights are long — so you see, one way and another — '

'What will you do?'

'The only thing I can do, really, is use the little spare bedroom. If you'd permit me to. It's a poky little room off the hall there, but — at least it'll cost me nothing, leave more to spend on our champagne. Here, I'll show you. Fortunately there's a lavatory also off the hall, so I'll be self-contained, as it were.' He led her back to the hall, pushed a door open. It was poky, all right, with an iron-framed bed. But that wouldn't do him any harm, she thought. She guessed it was probably used as a servant's room — for the aunt's maid, perhaps.

He pointed: 'Lavatory in there.'

'Hm. Well, I suppose . . . '

'There *is* a key in your bedroom door. If you had any worries of that kind. You needn't have, of course.' That heart-stopping smile of his. 'On my honour, you need not. But otherwise, you see

239

— short of my walking the streets all night or sleeping in a park — '

Actually, she'd thought, quite fun. Breakfast together, for instance. As long as no-one ever heard a single word about it . . .

11

Eleven-forty p.m. — still Tuesday 29 October — Otto leaning over the chart table in U201, noting courses and times from the Jade exit by way of swept channels to pass west of Heligoland, thence northwest on the surface at fifteen knots. Taking on the navigational chore unasked, for want of other useful employment and because they were leaving behind the boat's own navigator, a youngster by name of Kantelberg who'd gone down with stomach pains and diarrhoea during the hours 201 had spent in Schillig Roads, and had reported to Franz Stolzenberg in sick-bay as soon as she'd docked, Stolzenberg promptly ordering him to hospital. His absence helped in one way, namely in the provision of a spare berth, thus obviating the need to work a 'hot bunk' routine — man coming off watch taking the one vacated by the officer who'd relieved him. One small, practical consideration in a situation that was bizarre in the extreme.

As well as disturbing. Winter might in fact have gone off his head. With the angry bison's glare, monosyllabic responses to essential questions, but otherwise total lack of communication, and as yet no response to the question everyone on board desperately wanted answering. Everyone except Otto, who of course knew the answer but wasn't admitting to it — beyond having told

Hintenberger, who'd also joined 201 for this excursion, in place of a warrant engineer officer by name of Muhbauer, who'd been granted special leave and had actually left the base before Winter had had a chance to cancel it. Schwaeble had suggested Hintenberger as Muhbauer's replacement, and Otto had seen it as his own duty to let him know what he might be in for if he did. He'd also pointed out to him that if he declined the honour of moving over, which he could do, he'd qualify like the rest of UB81's crew for a fortnight's leave while she was in dockyard hands. On FdU's orders Otto had in fact handed over temporary command to Claus Stahl, who'd already finalised the leave documents and travel warrants.

Old Hintenberger had shrugged. 'Scapa, eh. No-one's dared try it since '14 — eh? Anyway — sure, just for the hell of it . . . '

Crazy. Looked crazy, sometimes acted crazy. Making *two* lunatics on board. The other one was in the bridge, conning the boat out of her berth and into the river; he had his first lieutenant, Neureuther, up there with him. U201 running on her starboard motor only, at this moment, ropes and wires all gone except for the fore spring on which he was turning her. His only communication with Otto, since leaving FdU's office earlier in the evening, had been put in the form of a request a quarter of an hour ago: 'Being short one officer, I'd be glad if you'd stand watches. All right? Start with the midnight to two then.'

Asking him — levelly and in fact quite

properly, in view of his having joined 201 as back-up CO, certainly not as a watchkeeper. But speaking as if they barely knew each other, might have met for the first time a few hours earlier in FdU's office. Icy politeness had been the tone of it. *Might* actually be deranged? Brain-damaged by what bloody Ahrens must have told him?

Obviously *had* told him. And seemingly it had pushed him over the edge. Must have meant more to him than she'd known or anyone else had guessed. Behind the bisonic glare, privately besotted?

When he'd reached Michelsen's office — just after six-thirty — he'd found Winter seated — immobile, not even glancing in his direction as he entered — while the Kommodore came around the desk with a hand out and a look of approbation on his face.

'Von Mettendorff. Congratulations. Your *Krieger Verdienstredaille* First Class in Silver has been confirmed.'

'First Class in Silver. *Well.*' Shaking hands: and still not a peep out of Winter. 'Thank you, sir. May I ask whether my engineer and first lieutenant — '

'*U-boot-Kriegsabzeichen*, both of them. And the rest as you proposed. It's a substantial list.'

'I'm grateful, sir.'

'You and they have earned it, no doubt of that at all.'

He'd come fast, answering this summons, to get it over and then have time to change and be on his way to Oldenburg. Taking it for granted that he was being sent for on account of Helena,

Ahrens, all that. A dressing-down for frequenting unsavoury establishments, bringing the Navy or its U-boat arm into disrepute — something of that kind. The name of Helena Brecht would not have been mentioned, he'd guessed — not until *he* mentioned it, explaining what had been his purpose in taking her there, the fact that they'd become engaged. Which should settle it, he'd thought. FdU must have a host of very much larger problems, surely wouldn't give this one more than about thirty seconds, at most. And actually the summons had nothing to do with any of that, he'd realised. Ahrens certainly *would* have told Winter, but Winter wouldn't have been so idiotic as to waste his Kommodore's time on such a private matter. He'd been sent for only to be told about these decorations. Winter's presence just coincidental — which in a way legitimised his detachment, refusal to acknowledge Otto's presence — which in truth had to be because he wanted nothing to do with the so-called protégé who'd pinched his girl. If he'd ever thought of her as 'his'. Anyway, in a couple of minutes one would be dismissed, and these two would get on with whatever they'd been discussing — events in the Schillig Roads this afternoon, maybe.

'Sit down, von Mettendorff.' Michelsen returning to his own chair behind the desk: glancing at Winter as if *he* found the man's detached manner and continuing silence peculiar. Back to Otto, though. 'I have to tell you that we're discussing a project of great significance, and that the time at our disposal is extremely limited. That's to say, we hope to get U201 out of here before midnight: and before that she has to fuel, embark fresh water, stores, torpedoes, so on.'

'Out again this soon?'

'As I said. My messenger, having found you, will have gone on to alert others, including those of her crew who've moved ashore. Can't expect 'em to be overjoyed, but — '

'They'll be happy enough when I've explained it to them.'

Winter had growled this, without looking at either him or FdU, only glaring down at the backs of his thick hands. 'Which I'll do when we're at sea, no sooner.'

'A matter for your own judgement, naturally.' Michelsen turned back to Otto. 'This damned mutiny — our efforts today have not borne fruit, unfortunately. The latest development is that in several of the battleships, stokers have let the fires die down, so they don't even have steam. In any event it's impossible in the present state of things for Admiral von Hipper to contemplate fleet action — the purposes of which would have been to show our enemies that we are still a formidable fighting force, to uphold the honour of Germany, and to some extent influence the detail of armistice negotiations.'

Pausing, he flipped open a cigar-box, peered into it, flipped it shut again. Resuming, then: 'Here's the point, now. Korvetten-Kapitan Winter has offered to take on his own shoulders what the rabble of mutineers has rendered impossible for the *Hochseeflotte*. His intention is to penetrate Scapa Flow in the Orkney Islands — which although it's used only sporadically by the British now — '

'Having shifted to the Firth of Forth.'

' — *is* made use of at intervals, by a few ships at a time, at most one battle squadron, say. They come and go. If there are ships in the Flow when he gets there, he'll do his best to sink them, and if there are not his plan is to bottom and lie in wait. What's your view of that?'

Winter was staring at him now. Morose, unblinking . . .

Otto began, 'I'd say that if he finds he *can* get in — '

'You can take it for granted that I shall.'

Another growl from Winter. Otto noted the senselessness of the statement, paused a moment before continuing — to Michelsen — 'If a boat *could* get itself in there — unsuspected — in advance of a visit by big ships — easy targets lying by then at anchor — quietly off the mud, then shove the stick up, one torpedo at each maybe, or more if you had more torpedoes than targets — why, yes . . . ' He shrugged. 'Getting *out* might have its problems. But having sunk one or more — maybe *several* major units of the Grand Fleet — well — '

A grunt from Winter: could have been either agreement or disdain. Observing then: 'Withdrawal is a secondary consideration.'

'Von Mettendorff has a point, though. Having accomplished that much, you could save your ship's company's lives by surfacing and scuttling. But — von Mettendorff. The three of us are of

246

like mind on the potential of this: that a successful outcome could be of enormous advantage to us. To *Germany*. At the same time, the element of hazard is — well, proportionate to that potential advantage. And the reason I'm putting this to you — Korvetten-Kapitan Winter would like to take along with him a back-up or alternate commanding officer. Primarily in order that he himself should be at the top of his form when he gets there, also to have an undoubtedly highly competent and reliable alternate commander to whom he can hand over from time to time — when inside the Flow and bottomed, for instance, duration of which is of course quite unpredictable.'

Otto suggested, 'Duration being — if necessary — as long as one's air lasts.'

'Never mind about *that*.' Winter's heavy shoulders shrugging. 'But in reply to Kommodore Michelsen asking me' — bison's eyes on Otto now, and addressing him directly for the first time — 'whether I had anyone particular in mind — '

'You're offering *me* the job.'

Michelsen put in, 'One might say, the *honour*.'

Winter's eyes on his still, mouth a hard line. 'Having no doubts as to your professional competence, and since your own boat's out of service — what d'you say?'

★   ★   ★

This track now. Course up the Jade of — oh, 350, 355. Keeping well clear of the Schillig

Roads and its litter of bloody battle-wagons, pitch dark unless they were showing lights — which they should not be, but with mutineers running riot, might be. Might be drunk as well. Historically, mutineers' first thoughts had always been to break into wine and spirits stores. There'd certainly be no moon or stars showing through what was now a heavy overcast. So take careful note of the light-buoys' characteristics. And then from Minsenen, with the Mellumplate light simultaneously abeam to starboard, alter to 290, into the Wangerooger swept and buoyed channel for seven-and-a-quarter nautical miles. Back to 350, then, and — near as dammit *twenty* miles, you'd have the Heligoland-W light-buoy abeam, and from there, going by memory, 315 degrees. Best to check it: running the parallel rule over again, and — 315 it was.

They had her running on both motors now, heading for the exit. One heard the few brief orders echoing in voicepipes, the coxswain's and telegraphman's acknowledgements of them, and the motors' whine, vibration through her frames . . . Otto turning his back on the chart, leaning against the short transverse section of bulkhead that screened the table off from the wardroom; he'd fumbled a cigarette out, and Hintenberger, passing at that moment, paused and clicked a lighter into flame. Otto stooped to it, grunted thanks, asked him, 'Settling in?'

A shrug of the narrow shoulders. 'Palatial, isn't it. After *our* little tub.' A nod towards the chart. 'When do we get there?'

'Get where?'

'Sorry. Not supposed to know, am I.' Moving on aft towards his engine-room, puffing at his own A. Batchari, bought no doubt in Bremen. Otto looking after him, inhaling deeply, his thoughts drifting back to Helena, rehearing her shocked but quiet tones — quiet because she'd have had the Muellers within earshot, he'd realised — but effectively — brain to brain as it were — *howling* at him.

'I don't *believe* it. Can't be true. It's a nightmare I'm having . . . Otto — be kind, admit it's not true? Or — look' — note of rising panic — 'doesn't *have* to be, does it, you could get out of it somehow, say you've changed your mind? For *my* sake, tell him? He can't *force* you into — whatever it is, this — '

'There's no force involved.' He'd spoken with deliberate calm, to counter the imminence of — well, breakdown, actual hysteria. He'd hated having to make this call, dreaded it. Explaining, 'I was in a position where I couldn't do anything but volunteer. Kommodore's eyes on me, expecting nothing less, and I'm sure knowing nothing at all of Winter's real motive — well, I didn't either, I *don't*, but — God knows, hatred, revenge? He's at least half out of his damn mind!'

'Hasn't mentioned me, or — '

'Not a word. Maybe when we're at sea — '

'Couldn't you go back to Michelsen, tell him about that business?'

'Not really. Wouldn't make any odds anyway, he's not concerned with personal issues. *His* manner, you see, was that of conferring an honour on me. I'm getting one, incidentally, for having brought UB81 home. He informed me of that, then brought up this other business — my being the one and only alternate CO Korvetten-Kapitan Winter felt he could rely on, wanted to have with him in this mission to restore the honour of the Navy. You see, if I'd refused, I'd have gone down as — '

'Is *that* what — '

' — at best a coward, at worst a traitor. Yes, that's the purpose of it — as *he* sees it, I imagine. But darling — listen. Try to think of it this way. I know it's shockingly disappointing — heart-breaking — but it's only for a few days we won't see each other, and we went through a couple of months of separation, didn't we — survived that. All right, it's different now — we've become so much more to each other, we're going to marry — in fact when you think about it we've only to get over *this* damn separation — very short one, at that — '

'Bring yourself back — *please?*'

'Why, of course I'll — '

'No — there's no 'of course', I'm sure you *know* there isn't. And so as not to go shrieking mad, *I* need to know for certain — '

'You *can* be certain. I'd guess I'll be away from here about a week. Can't be much more than that. And when I *am* back — '

'Yes?'

'My darling, you know what!'

'Announce our engagement in the papers?'

'Yes, why not. Except better tell parents first. I'll tell Winter in any case — when we're at sea.

Darling — while I think of it — be an angel, telephone Kramer's, cancel the reservation?'

'All right.'

'Can take time getting through, and I've got to do various things — like handing over the command of — you know, *my* boat — and signing things, and — oh, put some gear together then get down there and help out, or — see, it was only ten minutes ago this was sprung on me — '

'Swear you'll come back, *convince* me?'

'I do swear it. Thanking my lucky stars that I've *got* you to come back to. Darling, you don't have to consider any other possibility. There's no especial danger involved, only a certain urgency and — well, importance, if they're right. I mean the retrieval of honour, all that . . . '

'Isn't that all pie in the sky?'

'Not really. No, there's sense in it. Anyway, it's a fact that I've been on much more dangerous trips than this, time and time again, so — '

'But what you just said — and said before, the Kommodore's stuff about you being the only one who'd measure up — '

'That's just his way. And more implied than said — in any case *inspired* by Franz Winter . . . My darling, I do swear to you — '

'What *about* Franz Winter, then — you spoke of hate, revenge — '

'My guess, that's all. His manner's one of outrage. Taking me away from *you*, maybe — can't bear to leave me here, seeing you? That could be all it is, you know, he's a simple soul, and — still waters run deep, all that: you may have meant more to him than you realised? All right — simple and somewhat brutish, but — darling, listen — if time passes and you don't hear from me as soon as you expect to — a week, say — you've met Gunther Schwaeble, haven't you — Kapitan zu See? Call and ask him, don't just mope and bite your fingernails. He knows of our engagement, incidentally, and he's a very decent sort, so — '

He'd checked. There'd been a click, and he'd realised the line had been disconnected. He started again — tried to, joggling the hook, but — no good. He hung up. Having said it all, given her all the reassurance he had to offer — and she was no fool, no weakling either. In shock at this moment — as *he'd* been — but she'd calm down, rationalise, make herself accept, believe . . .

Did *he*?

Well, of course. Had to. How it was, had always been.

* * *

Michelsen and Schwaeble had both been on the quayside to see them off, and Otto had managed to have a minute alone with Schwaeble.

'Between ourselves, sir — the young lady to whom I've become engaged — I've told her that if a week or more passes without news from me, she might get in touch with you. She mentioned once that she'd met you.'

'We have met, yes. And I've guessed who she is. Fraulein Helena Becht?'

'Yes — '

'She's a friend of some people called Lukesch. But also of' — a glance in the direction of Franz Winter, then in conversation with Michelsen — 'Inclines me to ask whether you're wise to be taking part in this.'

Otto had shrugged. 'Little option, sir. Thing is, though — she's extremely upset. We'd made arrangements for this evening. If I'd left the base half an hour earlier than intended, I'd have been with her now. But if you do hear from her, sir, or have news to pass to her — '

'I'll do whatever I can to help.'

'Thank you, sir. Thank you very much.'

'Good luck . . . '

* * *

While Otto was on watch, Winter mustered his crew in the control-room, told them what they'd be doing and the purpose and background of it. What targets they'd find, he couldn't say; if there were none in the Flow when they got in there, they'd lie doggo on the mud and wait for some. There still *were* visits by units and squadrons of the Grand Fleet, and he believed that since the great anchorage was no longer in use as a permanent base, its defences might not be as effective as they had been in recent years. That, he said, was about all he had to tell them: except to explain that for reasons of security, especially with the current state of things ashore and in the *Hochseeflotte*, he'd decided to keep his trap shut until they were on their way. After all, they'd

253

never been given details of destinations and/or intentions, so why should this departure have been any exception? The one big difference, which he regretted but had not been in a position to do anything about, was this sailing at such extremely short notice, when they'd had every right to expect a good, long interval of shore-time and home leave. But that would come — later than expected, sure, but they could take his word for it — and by that time they'd be entitled to just about every honour in the book, and he'd see they got them too. All right — carry on . . .

Neureuther told Otto, when he was taking over the watch at 0200, 'There was some muttering, but very little. We all like to have our grouse, don't we. Fact is, sir, they respect him tremendously.'

'He's a first-class CO. As I know from my own experience.'

'It was gratifying to him that you agreed to come with us. He told me so, when explaining why he needed you. He added to that, 'Mind you, I'd have expected nothing less.''

'Did he, indeed.'

'He has a high regard for you; he's mentioned you often enough before this, in glowing terms. I'm sorry you've been called on to do this watchkeeping, though, sir. Gregor Kantelberg certainly picked his time to get the runs.'

'It doesn't worry me, Neureuther. Since I'm here — and more rested than any of you. But now — course 350 degrees, four hundred revs, in about forty minutes you'll have Heligoland-W light-buoy coming up to starboard within spitting distance. Alter when it's abeam — '

'To 345, sir. I've studied the night order book.'

'Right.' Otto handed him the binoculars he'd borrowed. 'You've got her, then.'

★   ★   ★

Wednesday 30 October: Otto came off watch at 8 a.m. It was still half-dark, under low cloud as well as intermittent sleet showers, wind force four from the northwest, right on her nose as she ploughed and pitched her way at fifteen knots through a moderate sea, waves fringed and flying white as she broke through them. Pretty well in the middle of the North Sea at this stage, despite which Winter had expressed the intention of remaining on the surface until about 10 am. Otto would have dived before that — would have got down into safety *now*, in fact. By nine, even in these conditions you'd have near-enough full daylight, so from then on if not sooner you'd be highly vulnerable to attack by any patrolling British submarine; and in staying up for that hour the only gain would be one hour's difference between surfaced speed and dived speed — a difference of ten knots, say, ten nautical miles therefore, very little gain indeed, reckoned against the Wilhelmshaven-Orkney transit of more than 500 miles. He checked it out on the chart, and over breakfast of bread and honey and enamel mugs of what passed for coffee, asked Winter whether he didn't think it might be as well to dive a lot sooner than ten o'clock.

Winter stared at him, still chewing. Emil Hohler, the affable young torpedo and gunnery officer, had had his breakfast and turned in again, and Hintenberger had finished his and shuffled off aft; Otto and Winter were thus on their own.

He'd slurped coffee, then asked Otto, 'Why?'

'Because although visibility's still poor, it could clear in minutes, and these are waters in which enemy submarines have been known to operate.' He shrugged. 'If it was up to me, I'd dive now. But you're the skipper, sir. Only a suggestion.'

'It would be, naturally.' Cramming more bread and honey in, and setting the heavy jaw working again, adding while continuing to masticate, 'Enemy boats are more likely to be patrolling off that coast than out here in the middle. To catch us as we come round the corner, you might say. The Firth up there gets a lot of traffic through it . . . Well, normally I'd dive earlier, yes.' Grunting, nodding, swallowing. 'But tomorrow at this time I want bearings on Peterhead or Rattray Head, and then Kinnaird's Head. A good fix before the run to Duncansby Head. That means being on the surface at first light if it's good enough, otherwise staying up until it is.'

'Because after five hundred miles you wouldn't want to approach Duncansby Head on nothing more than dead reckoning.'

A nod. Still chomping. Stuffing more in. Helena would *not* have enjoyed either the spectacle or the sound-effects. Maybe she'd never shared a meal with him: or at any rate sat opposite him. Sitting *beside* him, might not have noticed. Otto had forgotten what an ordeal it could be. He tried, 'But the saving of, say, fifteen sea-miles, no more — '

'Equivalent to an hour on the surface in fair conditions. On its own, could make the difference between getting into the Flow tomorrow night and having to mark time until the night after. An enemy squadron could have left in that space of time, and armistice terms might have been agreed. It's vital we strike our blow *before* the politicians sell us out. Hadn't you understood that?'

He gave up. Even to visualise, *think* about exposure to attack in daylight on the surface, in an area where there might be enemy submarines patrolling, and in sea conditions in which you'd be unlikely to spot a periscope, gave him the shivers. It always had, and he'd never taken such a risk, wouldn't have now if it had been his decision, was astounded at Franz Winter doing so — with his greater experience, and even a tendency in the past to hold forth on such themes. In earlier days he certainly would not have: chances were that neither of them would have been alive now if he had.

Winter had finished his bread and honey, drained his mug. Cigarette-stub between finger-tip and thumb — soggy, discoloured by food and coffee. He dropped it into the mug, heaved himself out of the canvas chair, belching as he moved to the chart.

'Near daylight now, you say.'

Otto got up, joined him. 'Light enough to scare me, sir.'

'You've made your point.'

In other words, shut up. But reaching for a pencil and the parallel rule, laying-off a slightly different course and walking dividers along it to measure the distance saved. A grunt then, and straightening. 'We'll alter to 320. Forget Rattray Head. Make for Duncansby Head and trust the DR.'

Cutting out the small diversion aimed at getting a fix from shore bearings would save several hours.

'And we'll dive now.'

Leaving Otto startled, as well as relieved. Pushing through into the control-room, starting up the ladder to the bridge. Maybe *had* taken leave of his senses, was returning to normal now? Or simply obsessed with getting into Scapa Flow at the earliest possible moment, and under that pressure ignoring first principles. So much damn risk ahead of them that taking just one more was something to shrug off? There was plenty to be said for making certain of one's position in approaching Duncansby Head. Entering the Pentland Firth at that point, sea conditions likely to be atrocious and tides treacherous, destroyer patrols not infrequent, and in the six- or seven-mile gap between Duncansby and Brough Ness on the southern end of South Ronaldsay — well, first the Pentland Skerries, on which von Hennig in U18 had been wrecked in '14 — then Stroma, Swona, and quite likely other hazards

— the tides, for one thing . . .

Lookouts came tumbling down the ladder. Then Neureuther, looking frozen. Diving hooter blaring, vents dropping open, diesels falling silent, thud of the upper hatch crashing shut. Bison at work, up there, jamming on the clips; Otto standing back out of the way as men who'd been off-watch moved swiftly to their stations: he was conscious of being no more than a spectator, passenger, outsider — knowing hardly any of their names or functions. The helmsman meanwhile had shifted down to the lowest of the three steering positions, Winter calling to him as he came down the ladder through the CO's control-room, 'Steer 320 degrees.'

'Three-two-oh, sir — '

'Twenty metres, Neureuther.'

'Twenty, sir . . . '

Sudden end of the night-long, battering motion: U201 gliding smoothly down into deepwater calm and safety. Time, 0835. Twenty metres was well below periscope depth, one could look forward to a quiet day.

★ ★ ★

He slept from about nine to eleven or just after, and being due to take over the watch at noon had Thoemer, wardroom messman, bring him his lunch of bread and cheese at half-eleven. Winter was in his bunk and snoring, as were Neureuther and Hintenberger, off and on. Dived conditions being highly conducive to repose, Hohler having the watch — with nothing to do

259

except watch the boat's trim and from time to time adjust it.

'Thank you, Thoemer.' The messman's was one name he did know. A lad of about eighteen — fair-haired, skinny, with a tattoo of an eagle on one forearm. He'd muttered, 'Glad to serve you, sir.' Whether it was his standard response to expressions of thanks, or like some of the others he'd heard of Otto von Mettendorff and felt inclined to show respect, one didn't know. Otto asked him where he came from.

'Berlin. Haven't seen it in a while, though. D'you know it, sir?'

'Been there a few times, but I wouldn't say I knew it. Were you born there?'

'No, sir. Parents moved from Stuttgart when I was ten.'

'Funny thing, that — ask any Berliner, he never started life there. What does your father do?'

'Butcher, sir.'

'Making sausage out of cats and dogs, I suppose.' Hintenberger had either not been asleep or had been woken by their quiet exchange; peering from the lower ship's-side bunk, dark eyes quick-moving, monkey-like. Thoemer laughed. 'About it, sir. Not so many of 'em about now, though.'

Hinterberger told him, 'I know where he could pick up no less than eight — cats, that is — if he wanted.'

'Where's that, sir?'

'Bremen. My father's house.'

'That fond of cats, is he, sir?'

'Not particularly. More that they like *him*.'

Thoemer went back to the galley, and the engineer asked Otto, 'See that girl over the weekend?'

'Girl?'

'One you were on about during our bit of trouble in UB81?'

'Oh. Yes. Yes, I did.'

'And got a bit, I dare say?'

He'd glanced at the mound of blanket on Winter's bunk. Still comatose. Back to the engineer: 'You'd be surprised.'

'Be surprised if you hadn't!'

'Well, stand by for a *real* surprise.'

'So?'

'I got engaged.'

'You're having me on, of course.'

'Within a day or two of getting back, you'll see it in the papers. And before you make some further coarse remark, let me tell you it's the best thing ever happened to me.' He reached for more cheese, adding, 'Invite you to the wedding, shall I?'

'Taking place when?'

'At this moment, hard to say. With so much that's uncertain — armistice, mutinies, God knows what next — '

'In Bremen there's talk of revolution.'

'Here too. In Wilhelmshaven and Kiel, I mean. The newspapers aren't much help, are they? I dare say it *is* on the cards. Historically, as you know, defeat brings political upheaval, nine times out of ten. And with the Russian example — '

'Revolution doesn't worry me.' Hintenberger

shrugged. 'Having damn-all to lose. But defeat — *that* I hate!'

A nod. 'Especially as we haven't *been* defeated. But I've had the same conversation two or three times in the last few days.'

'So in reference to this marriage — well, might one guess that in your position — family background, all that — it doesn't worry you that like me you could be out of a job before much longer?'

'Your prospects can't be so bad. As a fully-trained grease-monkey, you've a lot to offer; there'll be businesses falling over themselves to employ you. Whereas I've no qualifications whatsoever, except to drive one of these things around. But — no, I've been thinking about it recently, and the answer is I'll just have to find something I *can* do.'

'The girl's aware of this situation, I suppose?'

'Of course she is!'

'Doesn't worry her?'

'Not unduly. *My* lookout, isn't it.'

'And how does she feel about you ducking out on her again this soon?'

'That of course is something else.'

'What's her name?'

He glanced at the recumbent Winter, saw no indication of change, murmured, 'Helena.'

'*Nice* name. You said she's pretty.'

'More than just 'pretty', she's — '

Oberleutnant Emil Hohler came through from the control-room. Otto looked at his silver time-piece, saw it was still only eight minutes to the hour. Hohler's visit had nothing to do with him anyway, he'd come on more urgent business.

'Captain, sir?'

Instant upheaval on that bunk — Winter rolling over and rising on one elbow: 'Well?'

'Multiple propeller sounds, port quarter, overhauling, sir. Lange reckons three of them, probably destroyers, making eighteen or twenty knots.'

'Slow both motors.' Otto shifted to give Winter more space as he came thumping down from the bunk. Hohler had gone back into the control-room, ordering, 'Slow ahead both.' The motors had been at half ahead. Winter, bare-footed, in a collarless shirt and old serge trousers, but with his white cap crammed on his head, took it a step further with: 'Stop port.' One motor only now — for minimal hydrophone effect. Asking Hohler, 'Trim as it should be?'

'Near-perfect, sir.'

'Port motor stopped, sir.'

'Pass the word for'ard and aft, I don't want to hear a pin drop.' Otto sat down again, told Helena in his mind, *It's all right, don't worry, doing twenty knots they won't hear us, probably aren't even listening . . .*

12

In Glasgow at breakfast time it had been snowing, but from Perth northward there was bright sunshine, although the tops were gleaming white. Sam Lance ecstatic at the beauty of the scenery, asking Anne whether Argyll was as lovely. She'd said she thought it was: different, of course, its own kind of beauty, especially the littoral and the sea lochs — where her mother lived for instance, vicinity of Portnacroish, Loch Linnhe, the crazy artist's stamping-ground. Sam was boyishly delighted with it all; at Glasgow had been looking out for a poster he'd seen at King's Cross and made a note about, in order to try to get a copy of it for himself — 'to send home, they'll just love it!' It was an advertisement for Buick motor cars, an illustration of a uniformed and goggled chauffeur with the exhortation SEND YOUR CHAUFFEUR TO THE FRONT AND BUY A SELF-STARTING BUICK CAR. He'd noted the Buick agents' address in London in order to get in touch with them on his return, but in Glasgow had still hoped for another sight of it, although Sue had pointed out, 'Must have been on that wall for ages. Had conscription since the beginning of '16, haven't we.'

After lunch, the girls reckoned on taking siestas — not having sleepers now, but the first-class carriages were comfortable enough. It would be late when they got to Thurso, where

264

rooms had been booked at the Station Hotel, and from where they'd be making an early start next morning, a short car journey to the fishing port of Scrabster, from which a destroyer would be taking them to Stromness. Sam had said, 'They call it the milk run. Some fairly antique craft, destroyer down-rated to 'despatch vessel', poor dumb critter. Anyway, we'll only be on board an hour or two.'

'And on the island a day and a bit?'

'Tomorrow and Friday, yeah. I'd like to get away before the weekend. Long as I can get to see the Admiral. An hour of his time's all I'll get or need. Half-hour even.'

'Admiral Rodmer, that would be?'

Sue's memory, not Anne's. Sam confirmed, 'Hugh Rodmer. Flagship's the *New York*, and in company with her will be the *Wyoming* and the *Arkansas*. Received that detail shortly before we left. I'm glad I'll get to meet Rodmer — otherwise might never have. This visit could have been by any of the battle squadron.'

Pointing at Sue, further testing her grasp of things: 'The others being?'

Screwing her face up, concentrating . . . Then: '*Florida, Delaware* and *Texas*.'

'Well done you! But I should mention while we're at it, girls, on the island — Mainland, they call it, where Stromness is, also Kirkwall — I shan't be seeing much of you. I'll be on board the flagship mostly, and I'm expected to visit the others as well, give my chief's best wishes to their captains, and so forth. In any case, you'll find plenty to interest you. Did you have time to

265

study that little guide-book yet?'

'Only very briefly. Thought when we get there'd be soon enough.'

Anne cut in, 'Same here. Stone circles — as at Stonehenge, but of earlier date, is what I've noted so far.' She'd exchanged glances with Sue, before nodding to Sam. 'I'll peruse it again this afternoon. We'll have it with us when we're there, in any case.'

The truth being that she and Sue had discussed the matter and agreed that stone circles didn't greatly thrill either of them, although having come all this way at the government's expense they might just as well take a look — if there was some way of getting about on that island. In point of fact, she'd been thinking that she *could* have taken a train from Glasgow directly to Oban, let Sam do this part of it on his own; but that might not have been fair to him, when he'd gone to so much trouble — and wanted to have her with him anyway. Obviously liking Sue, and taking care to include her in all their conversations, but most of the time his eyes and attention being on Anne.

As it happened, she was enjoying being with him, too. This was the longest they'd ever spent together. In the long run, it might prove to have been well worthwhile.

He was on about this 6th Battle Squadron again now, how it was an integral part of the Grand Fleet under Commander-in-Chief Sir David Beatty, getting its orders directly from him just as any British squadron did, not from

266

Washington or even from Admiral Sims in London.

Chit-chat becoming desultory then, while the train pounded over the River Findhorn and soon after hurtled through a small station calling itself Tomatin: Sue proposing finally, 'What about our siestas now? You staying here, Sam?'

'I guess I will. Smoke a cigar, maybe.' Cigar as compensation for their deserting him, Anne wondered? Looking at *her*, although it had been Sue's suggestion, and she — Anne — looking back at him in much the same way, wondering whether something might be happening to them both.

* * *

When they got back to their carriage, Sue said, 'That stuff about the American squadron being under Beatty — I was tempted to ask him did he know who *else* was under the illustrious Sir David, much of the time.'

Anne stared at her, then caught on. 'You mean the delectable Eugénie?'

'Right you are. He might not have liked it, though. D'you think? Coming from what he might call 'a young female person' — who maybe shouldn't know anything about such goings-on, let alone refer to them out loud?'

Anne agreed. 'He is a bit — 'proper'. Or seems so. Could be at least partly my fault. I dare say it is. But don't you think most men are rather prim?'

'In regard to what we should or shouldn't

267

know — or should *pretend* not to know about or have interest in? Yes . . . Except when it comes down to — how should one put it — accommodating *their* interest.'

'Well.' Anne smiled at her. 'Should I take it you're speaking from experience?'

'Certainly not. More from — observation. As it happens, never *have* — for what that information's worth. And you said the other day that Sam's never made any sort of an advance?'

'Not seriously. None that I couldn't quite easily deflect.'

'Doesn't worry you?'

'Worry me . . . ' She shook her head. 'He's perfectly normal, if that's what you mean.'

'So he *has* tried.'

'If he has, it hasn't got him anywhere. Think that's mean of me? Well — maybe . . . But we haven't known each other all that long, you know. And he knows how I feel — or *think* I feel — and he respects that. Two factors — one, he wants to marry me — for some reason — and two, he's a gentleman. *Real* one. Unlike' — half-changing the subject — 'our friend Beatty, for instance, who one imagines wouldn't hesitate to try his luck, if he felt so inclined. Colossal damn nerve, when you think about it, Eugénie's husband being a captain in the Royal Navy and Equerry in Ordinary to King George. Although — one doesn't know, of course, but perhaps he didn't *have* to force himself, maybe *she* . . . But when you take into account that Beatty's only been able to afford his grand style of living through having married that rich

American divorcee — to whom of course he's *still* married — and she must know all about Eugénie, since everyone else does?'

'Stinks a bit, I agree.' Sue had grimaced.

Anne asked her — again turning the subject off herself and Sam — 'You say you haven't ever. Do you mean to stay that way until you marry?'

A small shrug. 'Don't see why I shouldn't.'

'I would, if I were you.' She added — without thinking, addressing herself more than Sue — 'Wish to God *I* had.'

'*What?*'

Anne turned quickly to the window: peered out at fields lying under snow. Shaking her head, feeling crass — and still in a way thinking about Sam. Turning back then: 'I didn't mean to say that. Do me a favour, forget I did?'

'Saying that Charles wasn't the first man in your life?'

'He was the first man I loved.'

'So how — I mean — '

'Things can happen that you don't *want* to happen, you know.'

'But *what*, and — '

'If I answer that, will you leave it then, forget it?'

'I'll try, if you insist, but — '

'I was raped. *Raped*. And that's all I'm telling you — now or ever, so — look, d'you want to read Sam's Orkney guide? Otherwise — '

'A subject such as that one can't be changed *quite* so — '

'Not changed. Discarded, Sue. Please, forget it?'

269

It lingered in one's own mind and memory, though. Had been in it either in the background or more pertinently in the foreground — depending on situation, mood, state of health or tiredness — for years now. The last time she'd said it — uttered those three words, *I was raped* — had been to Charles on the first morning of their marriage, by which time he'd become aware of the fact she'd not been a virgin, had looked at her with the question in his eyes and she'd shut hers, whispered that explanation which there and then she'd thought of as a lie. In the years since then — since his death, she supposed — she'd come to see it differently, that effectively it *had* been rape: that Gerda's damn brother had both intended and contrived to have their Berlin tryst turn out as it had; that she'd not wanted anything of the sort nor connived in it — or for that matter been able to prevent it. Therefore, the appropriate word for it *was* 'raped'.

In that flat just off Lothringer Strasse — on its narrower link with Griefswalder. Surprising that she'd recalled both those street names, when hundreds of times she hadn't managed either of them. Poor memory, psychological blockage, or the fact that most of the time she'd been more or less drunk?

As well as naive in the extreme. Trusting — *silly* . . .

There *had* been a key in her bedroom door, and she'd locked it before she'd taken off her

270

clothes. Had only the one suitcase, having sent her trunk ahead of her to Scotland. Anyway, she'd had a bath: he'd do without one, he'd said, so as to leave it clear for her. 'Might have one in the morning . . . ' *And*, she remembered, he'd opened a bottle of champagne and poured her a glass to sip while she was bathing. Bubbly in the bath: height of luxury, she'd thought. Or depravity. But one had said or thought that with a smile, a giggle; he'd been behaving himself at that stage — she'd had no doubts of him or of his intentions — it was all just the most tremendous *fun*. Including what he'd called this Berlin tradition, the Bummel — which meant promenading along the Linden and other great shopping streets — this in the evening when most of the shops were shut, one simply enjoyed the window displays, stopping now and then at pavement cafés or Weinstuben — at several of which Otto had ordered German sparkling wine, telling her, 'Champagne again with the tango and our supper. This is only the prelude, huh?'

'It's lovely, Otto!'

'*You* are lovely. You truly are. The most beautiful girl I ever went out with. As well as all the enthusiasm you display, your so charming personality. It shines out of you, my dear . . . And what a glorious evening they've laid on for us!'

She'd been wearing a cream-coloured cotton dress, she remembered, with its hem an inch above her ankles, and a striped jacket, and carrying a sequinned evening bag that went well with it. Rather nice French shoes on her small

271

feet. Oh, and the hat she'd travelled in, but without its feather. He kept telling her how attractive she was, and actually she could distinctly remember *feeling* that she was, catching sight of herself in shop windows and not at all disliking what she saw. The wine must have helped, of course. She was being looked at by other young men as well, once or twice actually smiled at, Otto noticing this and keeping her close to him, most of the time arm-in-arm, and chatting twenty-four to the dozen, making her laugh and taking no notice of pretty girls giving *him* the eye.

Part of the technique, she'd guessed afterwards. As if he'd been advised, *Don't waste your time. Concentrate on the one you've got* . . .

Guessing this through having concluded that he'd worked it all out carefully in advance, although it *might* have been a symptom of how he'd genuinely felt. Came down to much the same thing, anyway. And the truth was, they *had* been flirting, she as much as he; the difference being that as far as she was concerned, flirting and having fun was as far as it would have gone. Dancing on air was a phrase that came to mind: he'd tried to convince her that they were both under the influence of the famed Berliner Luft, the magically heady air that was supposed to affect everyone, making them feel quite tipsy. Which they were — or she was anyway, by the time they'd begun prospecting for a restaurant with a dance-floor, a cabaret, something better than a café or Weinstube, but not one of your stuffy restaurants, stuffed shirts and ridiculously

272

high prices. They'd looked into two or three places before settling on one that suited them. Suited *him*; she'd probably have settled for any of them. In each of them he'd scanned the menu and enquired as to whether the band was up to playing tangos — which they all were, it was currently the rage — finally settling on this small, darkish basement café-restaurant with banquette seating and a quartet playing a tango even as they arrived.

They'd drunk champagne — the real stuff now, not the local fizz — but she'd forgotten what they'd had to eat. She'd been left with the notion that his choices were based mainly on price, presumably to offset the cost of the wine, and she'd been in sympathy with that. His father did make him a small allowance, he'd told her at some time, but on a leutnant zu see's pay — that rank being the equivalent of an RN sub-lieutenant — well, it helped, but didn't go very far. They'd tango'd like mad, also danced the foxtrot: she didn't remember much of it in any detail, only that it was all hilarious and that she must have been fairly reeling by the time they left. It wasn't a tremendously long walk, fortunately, back to his aunt's apartment; he'd have needed to have supported her even on the flat, let alone when it came to climbing stairs. What she *did* remember was his offering her what he called a 'sleeping draft' of Cognac — his aunt's Cognac, presumably — which she hadn't wanted, and then telling her that he was going to take a bath. 'But I'll be quiet, don't worry. *Never* sing in my bath, never, *never*.' She was alone in

273

the bedroom then, humming 'La Cumparsita' and actually falling down while tangoing around with a pillow in her arms as partner; he'd gone off to what he called his kennel to undress. She'd been about to disrobe too, but went back to the bedroom door first, to lock it, and — no key. There'd definitely been one in the door earlier. Fallen out, maybe. She searched for it — on hands and knees — then gave up, thinking, Oh, why bother? Get undressed quickly and into bed, covered up, before he puts his head in to say goodnight. *Which he may well do — knowing him* . . . Oh, except that he'd be assuming the door was locked. Be fast asleep by then, in any case. It really had been an absolutely spiffing evening. She was naked and shaking out her nightie when she heard the door open, whipped round and saw him also naked except for a towel round his waist, exclaiming something like, 'Oh, my darling Anne, forgive the intrusion but you're even more beautiful than I'd dared *dream*!' He'd come on into the room — dropping the towel, for God's sake, stark naked, and that *thing* . . .

'Otto, you are *shameless*!'

How much actual memory in the years of reconstruction, analysis and shame? For instance, *had* he bathed, or only expressed that intention so she'd think she had so much time? To what end, though — seeing that he must have removed the key, could as easily have found her in the bed as on her feet? The efforts at reconstruction — recollection — had stemmed from her need to know to what extent she might have co-operated, or whether it actually had

274

been rape — not just the trickery but actually overpowering, forcing. She *had* been drunk. And had slept heavily, woken in the quiet of the Sunday morning to hear his heavy breathing within inches of her face, taken a few frightful moments to remember, realise, her sudden movement — to escape — then rousing him. She guessed this had been the sequence of it, did know for sure she'd had to fight him off, fight free of him and of the bed, while he'd protested, 'My darling, *why*? Anne, darling — please — '

'Don't 'darling' me, you foul *pig*!'

The blood on the sheets then: she remembered that well enough, and his moan of 'What'll I *do*, heaven's sake? Never *thought* of — '

'Of my being a virgin? Bet you didn't! Thought of every other damn thing, though!'

'Can we wash them, or — '

'Maybe *you* can. Or tell your damned aunt you had some girl here who was so inconsiderate as to bleed all over them!'

She'd felt ill. Recalled locking herself in the bathroom and being sick, and that when eventually she'd come out he'd gone back to bed and was asleep again. She'd taken her clothes into the sitting-room and dressed in there, then made herself tea, which was all she could face — as it turned out, had been more than she could face, she'd had to be sick yet again; worse, had somehow to drag herself across Berlin to that other station.

'Anne, are you asleep?'

Sue's voice, effectively telling her, *wake up*. Opening her eyes, for a moment not sure where she was, then focusing on Sue standing at the window and thanking God that she *wasn't* in Berlin, facing that ghastly journey and feeling like something it would have been kinder *not* to have dug up . . .

Telling Sue as relief flooded her, 'I was. Almost. I mean — '

'Ought to see this, anyway. We're somewhere past Inverness. Moray Firth, or Cromarty, snow on the ground but the sun's filtering through, it's really beautiful!'

'Hang on.'

She was right, it was beautiful. Ruggedly so: although in duller weather one might have called it bleakly so. Cromarty Firth, with Cromarty at its entrance and Invergordon on this side where it widened. The Grand Fleet, or parts of it, used Invergordon quite a lot, of course. And to the north of here, after a while you'd have Dornoch Firth, quite a long stretch along that coast-line. Sue was saying, 'It's not going to last long, though, the picture-postcard look of it. Black as your hat there where it's coming from. North or northwest, I'd guess. *Orkneys* weather coming up, one might say. Sorry I woke you.'

'I wasn't really asleep. Sort of — daydreaming . . . '

He'd insisted, she remembered, in a tone that made it plain — or would have done, if one hadn't by then known him to be a twister — that he actually did think she was treating him unjustly. 'You wanted it as much as I did, Anne. Allowing me to spend the night here with you in the first place, in the second leaving the door unlocked, and most of all, my darling, the way you — hell, how you *were*! Like some — I don't know — wildcat, or — '

'You set out to get me drunk — and you'd taken the key, damn you, I *went* to lock it and — '

'No, that's too much! Wait, I'll . . . ' He had the towel round his waist again: shot into the bedroom, returning immediately with the key, holding it up as if in triumph. 'Lying there plain to see! And accusing *me* — '

'I searched for it and it wasn't — was obviously wherever you'd hidden it.' She'd shut her suitcase and managed to lock it — with some difficulty, her hands shaking so much — dropped that little key into her bag, hefted the damn case. 'Out of my way, please.'

'Can't I take you to the station? That thing's much too heavy for you. Give me a few minutes — please, and — '

'Out of my *way*!'

★   ★   ★

She'd pushed past him, he remembered, using the case as a threat and looking as if she hated him. In defending himself, he'd felt very much the injured party. All right, so it had been the first time for her: maybe he should have given thought to that possibility — probability, even, when one remembered that she'd been a very young nineteen. Not physically, but every other way. One *should* have. None the less, it had been a riotous evening: the lake trout in cheese sauce

277

had been delicious, the bubbly had been first class, and as to the dancing — well, Kaiser Wilhelm *might* have found the tango somewhat lubricious — and it was — but she'd fairly revelled in it. Well, they both had. And certainly they'd had a lot to drink, but — *got her drunk?*

When one's guest kept emptying her glass, and one wanted to keep the party spirit going, one kept the glass topped up, did one not?

Hadn't needed to get her drunk, for God's sake!

Besides which, a wildcat was what she *had* been. Truly sensational.

After which — condemnation. Contempt, even. To assuage her own conscience, he supposed.

Nodding to himself as he straightened. This quite lengthy reminiscence had been prompted by Hintenberger asking him — here in the wardroom, only the two of them, Franz Winter being at the chart table studying Scapa Flow and/or its southern approaches, and Neureuther sleeping — which was something he did a lot of — 'In our musings in those dark hours in UB81, you were on the point of confessing how you once tricked some dolly into opening her legs. Then you back-tracked, or we were interrupted — '

'I thought better of it.'

He'd been semi-snoozing, forehead resting on his forearms on the table. Checking the time now — three-twenty. Had come off watch at two p.m., having had only an hour-and-three-quarters of it, after a period of silent running

278

while destroyers had been coming up on the quarter and overtaking, eventually to everyone's relief fading ahead — in the direction of Scapa Flow, incidentally, which might be indicative of big-ship movements being imminent. Might not, too: they could have been heading to pass through the Pentland Firth *en route* to Scotland's west coast or Ireland; alternatively to leave the Orkneys to port, heading for Shetland or Norway.

No telling where, or what for. All that mattered was they'd gone thrashing on.

He focused on the engineer again.

'We were in what looked like a somewhat hopeless situation, if you remember. Jabbering as one does at such times, to keep spirits up. That reference was to something that happened years ago — when I was very young and — you know, on the lookout for experience of that kind.'

'Are you telling me you've *stopped* looking for experiences of that kind?'

He nodded. 'I did tell you I'm getting married.'

'Oh — so you did . . . '

Tone and expression still vaguely disbelieving. Otto ignored it, told him, 'That other business — I was not only young, I was also — well, on the wild side. Irresponsible. Drinking more than I should have, too — consequently don't recall much of it. Actually prefer not to, although rather oddly it's come back to mind a couple of times in recent days. Stirrings of guilt, maybe — what one might in the course of time be answerable for — eh? Did think we might be

279

coming up hard against the buffers, in those hours, didn't we — only a fool would not have . . . But' — wide-eyed suddenly, and pointing at him across the table — 'Great heavens, man — I'll tell you something else instead. Should have told you sooner, but I forgot. You're to receive the *U-boot-Kriegsabzeichen* for making yourself as useful as you did on that occasion.'

The chimp's small, round eyes had begun a rapid blinking. 'You serious?'

'FdU told me, last evening. In all that rush, I clean forgot. They're giving *me* a *Krieger Verdienstredaille* First Class in Silver. Much more than I deserve, but since by some fluke or misjudgement I already have the *Kriegsabzeichen*, they probably felt obliged to cough up something grander.'

'I'd say every *bit* deserved.' Monkey's narrow, hairy paw extended: 'Congratulations!'

'Same to you.'

'Result of *your* recommendation, I suppose?'

'Well.' A shrug. 'One gives 'em the gist of what went on and who did what, that's all.'

'Anyway, I'm very much obliged.'

'Please your old father, won't it?'

'*I'll* say it will. My God, the *Kriegsabzeichen*! I've always hoped for it, begun to think too damn late now, missed the bus!'

Neureuther rolled to the edge of his bunk, reached to shake first Otto's hand then the engineer's. 'My heartiest congratulations. Mind you, after *this* trip — why, heavens above — '

'*Krieger Verdienstredaille* First Class in Gold, no less — for all of us!'

Laughing. Otto thinking that Franz Winter might get something of that kind. If anyone got anything, except dead.

But — not necessarily. Winter, when sane, did know his onions, and had an experienced, well-trained crew — whom incidentally he wouldn't be taking into this if he didn't think he had a reasonably good chance of bringing them back out of it.

At least, one might sincerely hope he wouldn't.

'Von Mettendorff.'

Speak of the devil: Winter, looking around and summoning him from the chart table. A jerk of the head: 'Take a look at this.'

Chart of the North Sea, its upper western edge showing the east coast of Scotland from Berwick to Duncansby Head and the Orkneys, with U201's track pencilled on it, transferred to it from the point at which she'd dived this morning at 0830 — by dead reckoning fifty-five-and-a-half degrees north, four degrees forty minutes east — and extended northwesterly at the dived speed of six knots to a new DR for 1600, four p.m.

'We'll surface then, or perhaps as early as three-thirty. Up to periscope depth three forty-five, say, surface by four. Your watch then — right? So — 420 revs and a running charge one side, say fourteen knots average over sixteen hours and diving at 0800 — here. Full day's run at six knots, again 0800 to 1600, call that another fifty miles. This time tomorrow, therefore, we should be ten or twenty miles short of Duncansby Head, but I'll take a squint up top at about two, for shore bearings, a good fix, and adjust course here — between the Head and the Skerries — in order to pass between Swona and Barth Head. Fixes by periscope then — we'll be close enough and still have daylight.'

'Into the Flow well before midnight, then.'

'Well — sooner, but not rushing it, exercising economy with the battery, since it'll be lower than I'd choose by then. Can't be helped, there's no way we can get in there with the battery well up, as I'd very much prefer. Ideally, to have it *right* up. But look here, now . . . '

He'd transferred the last DR position from the North Sea chart to the Scapa one, which he'd had underneath and now pulled out and spread on top.

'See. Skerries to starboard, then Brough Ness, and inside Swona here — '

'Gap of about two sea miles.'

'If that. And tide rips to watch out for. Very careful periscope fixing therefore, and passing closer to Swona than to Barth Head on a course of about 345. But — well, from that point midway between Duncansby Head and the Skerries to — here, Hoxa Head — that's less than ten miles. So we can come down to as little as, say, three knots, if the tides permit — in the interest of saving amps. It'll be good and dark by then, of course, but at such close ranges' — Winter glanced at Otto — 'given weather conditions no worse or not much worse than they are now — huh?'

'You wouldn't think of breaking through on

the surface — if it's that dark and did blow up to a gale?'

'No. The Sound of Hoxa here' — his pencil-tip touched it — 'which is our true point of entry — see, only a mile wide, and they have searchlights and gun emplacements both sides — on Hoxa and Stanger Heads. And logically, along this coast. One thing to be glad of is we don't have to concern ourselves with mines — the British are using this entrance pretty well every day, FdU's Intelligence reports show — and *he* impressed on me that dived entry's our best chance.'

'Settles it, then.'

'In point of fact, there was a boom — buoys supporting anti-submarine nets — here, between Flotta and Hoxa. But that's been removed. That's positive information derived from recent Zeppelin reconnaissance. Guns and searchlights only now.'

'And after Hoxa Head?'

'Off that headland we'll come round from 345 to 040 — here — two-and-a-half miles on that, then 020. Half a mile of that, and we're damn well *in*. Huh?'

'That'll be the moment.'

'It will, won't it. I'll come round from 020 to — well, 340, say. Another two-and-a-half miles — by log, playing safe as far as periscopes are concerned — we're in the middle and — see this sounding — forty metres? As good as we'll get. Bottom, and wait for daylight.' Throwing down the pencil, turning to stare at him: 'Any reservations, or alternatives to propose?'

Shake of the head. 'None, sir.'

'Good.' A glance the other way, checking privacy. Then, quietly, 'Is it a fact that you've become engaged?'

Complete surprise. He nodded. 'Yes. I'd have mentioned it, but — '

'I was not in a receptive frame of mind.'

One way of describing it . . . Otto added, 'And earlier, in FdU's presence, it might have seemed I was looking for an excuse not to join you.'

'Might indeed.' Bisonic nod. 'Especially as I had been given an incorrect impression of your relationship with a young lady of whom I am fond and would not like to see harmed in any way.'

'Nor I, sir. And she won't be. Incidentally, since it was you who introduced me to her in the first place — '

'Von Mettendorff — if I'd had the facts of it straight, I would not have brought you along. That's all I have to say on this.' He turned away, called through to Hohler, 'Bring her up to ten metres!'

In order to put the search periscope up and check on the approach of twilight. Moving to the ladder up to the CO's control-room for that purpose, and Otto returning to the wardroom, Neureuther asking him, 'About to surface, are we?'

'Maybe. In the next half-hour anyway. Checking how the light is.'

Hintenberger then — with a gesture towards the chart table — 'All right, d'you reckon?'

'Looks all right.' Nodding and crossing fingers. 'Looks fine.'

13

Thursday 31 October, still dark. They'd been called at seven by the hotel's boot-boy, and the car Sam had ordered was at the front door at eight, by which time they'd breakfasted on porridge followed by eggs and bacon. All three of them in the back of it now, as the driver turned it first south and then west, Sam in the middle with an arm round each of them, smelling of shaving-soap. The driver had thrown a rug over their knees, but it was very cold, despite bulky greatcoats, and the bodily proximity made it seem less so. Anne murmuring, '*Isn't* this cosy . . .'

They'd arrived at Thurso's station hotel after dark last evening, Sam going to his single room on the second floor and the girls to their shared double on the first, having about an hour and a half before supper in which to have baths and get ready. The bathroom was somewhat austere and at the end of a freezing-cold corridor; having checked that the water in the pipes was at least warm, Sue had been finding a coin to spin, to decide which of them would bath first, when there was a knock on the door. Anne called, 'Who is it?', and Sam's voice answered, 'Thought I'd let you know I'm going for a stroll. Case you found me gone, and worried.'

Anne opened the door. 'Might I come too?'

'Why, sure! Nothing I'd like better!' Then,

with barely any diminution of enthusiasm, 'How about our chaperone?'

Sue had snorted. 'Count her out. Strong as your unbridled passion for each other may be, on a wet and windy night, even in romantic Thurso — '

They'd laughed. Hadn't seen much of the place in the growing dark, but had been less than overwhelmed by the little they had seen: and the wind had been gusting quite strongly, with sleet in it, boding ill for the next day's crossing. (Today's, in fact.) Anne struggling into her Wren greatcoat; Sam advancing into the room to lend a hand, and Sue protesting, 'Oh, I don't know about *this*, now — '

'We're the sort you give an inch to, we take a mile.' She had the coat on, was tightening its belt. 'Isn't that so, Sam?'

'Would be. Far as *I'm* concerned.' He'd been at the door by this time, ushering Anne out ahead of him. Suggesting then, 'Hey, like to see the room they've put me in?'

'Hear that, chaperone?'

'Most certainly did!'

He'd pulled the door shut; Anne saying quietly, 'Yes, I would.'

'Huh?'

'Like to see your room.'

'Mean that?'

'No. Not literally.' Turning up the stairs, though; glancing round at him. 'Actually, don't give a hoot about the room, what I want is — '

She'd checked that. Above her on the stairs a rather stout maidservant was trying to flatten

286

herself against the wall to let them by. Didn't flatten all that easily. Anne smiled at her, squeezing by, murmured, 'Good evening.'

'Evening, ma'am.' A small knees-bend, ostensibly a curtsy. 'Evening, sir.'

'Very good evening to you, my dear!'

He'd got past her, and she'd continued downwards, murmuring to herself. He told Anne, '*That*'s ruined your reputation in the north of Scotland!'

'Better not stay up here too long, then. I was saying — or about to — all I want is to have you kiss me. After sitting staring at each other all day, or most of it . . .'

'Door on your right here. Oh, I have a key.' Passing her, opening the door and standing back while she walked in and turned to face him, commenting without having looked anywhere except at *him* — 'What a nice little room. Oh, Sam . . .'

'This actually *you*?'

'Me on holiday. Letting my hair down — having given our dear chaperone the slip. I love her but it's nice to be on our own for a moment. I'd like you to know I'm *very* much enjoying being with you, Sam. It was a good idea you had.'

On her toes, arms round his neck, kissing.

'Oh, my dear — '

'You're *my* dear.'

Beginning again — for a while . . . Then remembering that maid, and easing off, Sam telling her various flattering things about herself, she cutting in with: 'When we get back to

London, I think we should — well, pursue this, get to know each other really well?'

'If I'm understanding you correctly — '

'I'm sure you are.'

★ ★ ★

Their limousine forked off from the coast road on to one that slanted downhill towards the western end of Thurso Bay, where Scrabster was. Quite soon there were little houses up on the left, most with lights in their windows, then some on the right as well, and after a mile or two an iron gateway with guards — and a guardhouse — soldiers with slung rifles, braziers glowing to keep them warm. The driver slowed to a crawl and a corporal peered in, waved them through.

'There she is now.' Driver pointing to a lit section of quayside. Lights on a gangway, and the dark profile of a destroyer. HMS *Brecon*, she turned out to be. Sailors carried their luggage up the gangway, after Sam had identified himself to a petty officer and then returned to the car to pay its driver. By that time a lieutenant had appeared — exchanging salutes with Sam, telling them his name was Cholmondely and that they'd have the wardroom to themselves. There was an Army contingent already embarked, in one of the Messdecks.

'Pushing off in about a quarter of an hour, sir.'

'Timed it about right, then.'

Sue asked whether it was going to be rough, and he said they might find it a bit lively — as they probably knew, the Pentland Firth had a reputation to live up to — but in fact the sea had gone down during the night, it shouldn't be too bad — wouldn't last long, anyway. Sam asking him then, 'Is *Brecon* what I've heard referred to as a thirty-knotter?'

'Is indeed, sir. Also known as an oily-wad. Vintage 1894. She's done more than her bit in the last few years, though, I can tell you.'

'I'll bet she has.' Sam and the lieutenant were following the girls up the timber gangway. 'But if you're sailing in fifteen minutes you don't want to waste your time on us. Only thing is, at some point I should say how-do to your skipper.'

'Good thinking, sir. His name's Morton. Two-striper like myself. If you'd like to make your number with him right away, I'll take you along.'

'And where do *you* fit into the scheme of things?'

'Second in command, sir. First lieutenant — in other words, chief cook and bottle-washer. Now in this tin doorway, ladies — minding your heads and also the steps — ladder downward, right in front of you.'

There was light inside, anyway. The ladder — a short steel stairway — led down to what he called the wardroom flat, off which were the wardroom, several cabins and the wardroom heads, or WC and washplace. Wardroom about the size of that single room of Sam's, with a hatch through to what was called the pantry, in which lurked a steward who'd look after them, name of Smithers. Anything they wanted, within reason — coffee, lemonade, for instance. Anne asked Lieutenant Cholmondely, 'Best to avoid liquids, isn't it, in rough weather?'

'Well — yes, you're right . . .'

He took Sam away to meet the ship's captain, leaving them to settle down. Sue muttering to Anne, 'I've a feeling this is going to be what's known as a harrowing experience. I rather like that Cholmondely boy, though.'

★   ★   ★

Surprisingly, neither of them was sick, although Anne felt close to it at one stage and jumped at Sam's suggestion that they might see how it was on deck. He'd been looking a bit pale himself, she'd noticed. They were something like halfway, it was fully daylight and blowing hard, there was a lot of movement on the ship, and the land in sight to starboard was the island of Hoy, according to the steward, Smithers. He'd probably been told to keep an eye on them, and appeared from time to time, although Sam told him there was no need to. It was cold on deck, and the ship was rolling hard enough that one needed something solid to hold on to; but she was feeling better within minutes, Sam manoeuvring them into the shelter of the bridge superstructure, starboard side — their backs against it, him in the middle again with an arm around each of them; there was also a rail that ran around the superstructure at about waist-height, which they could hang on to behind their backs, as an additional precaution. Wind being from the northwest — the ship's otherside

— was giving her a corkscrew-like motion, combination of pitch and roll. But it was better up here than down below. The land — west coast of Hoy — was coming closer all the time: before long, Sam informed them, they'd see the Old Man of Hoy. Some kind of rock, apparently — either he'd mugged-up this stuff from the guidebook, or the skipper had been showing him their route on the chart up there. Before the Old Man of Hoy, though, there was a westward extension of the coastline to a headland of which he'd forgotten the name: it was half-buried in white foam, the sea sounding like distant thunder, flinging itself against the high, rocky coast. Dramatic — invigorating — and wonderful to be feeling *well* now. The Old Man when they came to him turned out to be a tall pinnacle of rock, a giant's thumb stuck up on the cliff about a mile away. Coastline receding then, the ship gradually altering to starboard, following it round. Cliffs taller than ever. She yelled to Sam — in the wind and noise you had to scream to be heard — 'Steam round the top of this island, do we?'

He'd nodded. 'Next island to the north is Mainland, we turn east between the two of them — through what they call Hoy Sound. Then north into Stromness.'

'How far?'

'I'd guess five, six miles.'

'And how fast are we going?'

'Don't they teach you *anything* in the Wrens?'

'Never taught *me* a thing!'

'Well — say fifteen knots.'

'Not much longer, then.'

'Sticking my neck out, say twenty or thirty minutes.'

'Then what?'

'Oh — we go ashore — to the Stromness Hotel, which is very close to where we berth — and I make a couple of telephone calls.'

'You still don't know whether or not we stay at the hotel, I suppose.'

'No, that's one of the things I'll discover. As I mentioned, there's a Wren establishment in Kirkwall — '

Sue shouted, 'Much sooner stay in a hotel!'

'Day or two ago they didn't have a room. All taken for military and naval personnel in transit, apparently.'

'So what are *we*?'

'Take your point, but — anyway, something will have been fixed up. Have to take what we're offered, I'm afraid. But you'll be looked after all right.'

'Slowed down, haven't we?'

'Sure have. That's why I said, sticking my neck out . . . '

'This far it's been top-hole, anyway. Really has.' She asked Sue, as the pitching eased but the roll became heavier, 'Don't you think?'

Sam's left arm tightened round her. Other one tightening around Sue, no doubt. Or maybe not. The motion had become more violent in the last few minutes, and he had one foot up, jammed against what he'd referred to earlier as a ventilator. She howled, 'I'm frankly amazed at not having been sick!' and caught Sue's reply,

'Probably still time, if you're keen to. What's *that* island?'

'Oh — that is . . . ' A pause while memory stirred. 'Graemsay, I think it's called. We pass in through the channel that's ahead now — see? Ten knot tide, apparently. Then hard a-port, and — lo and behold . . . '

★   ★   ★

The hotel looked down on the harbour and was quite large and rambling, but at the desk the clerk confirmed that there were no rooms vacant. Sam thought it was probably just as well, being jam-packed with various soldiery — also dockyard technicians from Invergordon, the clerk had mentioned — and having no less than three bars in it, he guessed maybe not all that suitable for young ladies on their own.

He went to make his telephone calls, which included one to the Wren hostel in Kirkwall, where a Wren 2nd officer who'd been contacted two days ago from London told him that since the hostel itself, which was in the course of being re-roofed, was fully occupied, she'd arranged for the girls to be put up in a guesthouse at Swanbister — proprietress a Mrs McGregor — which they'd used before as overflow accommodation. It wasn't far from Stromness, on high ground behind Houton and Orphir Bay, had wide views over the Flow, including the anchorage where the American battleships were at present anchored. And if they were to be taken out on a tour of the Flow, as had been mooted,

293

Houton would be conveniently near for embarkation.

Anne looked at him in surprise. 'Tour the Flow — by boat?'

'Doesn't seem likely now. I raised it as a possibility, thinking that if we had good weather — anyway, the lady's point was that trawlers work out of Houton, which is handy to Swanbister. But despite your having proved to be such first-rate sailors, a problem is you'd need to be escorted, and I'm not going to have the time for it. Even to set it up. On the other hand, this guesthouse — Swanbister's on the road between here and Kirkwall, and there's a regular two-way service by omnibus, so you'll have both towns in easy reach — '

'*And* the Standing Stones.' Sue had studied the guidebook last evening. Telling Anne now, 'Standing Stones of Stennes and what's called the Ring of Brodegar, also what sounds rather creepy, some 'chambered tomb'. All quite near, though. We could ask Mrs McGregor — if it's fine, borrow or hire bicycles?'

'Well' — Sam again — 'seeing as you have luggage, I was thinking I'd do something about a car — to get you out there, anyway. It's not so far, ten or twelve miles by the look of it.'

'Very kind, Sam, but we'll take the bus.' Glancing at Sue, who nodded. 'Find out when and where from, and fill in any waiting time by looking around this place. We'll manage, anyway. I think you should get on with your own business now. How will you get out to the flagship?'

'In her steam picket-boat, from right here in

294

this harbour.' Checking the time. 'Yeah, well — '

'There you are, you see. But when you know the weekend plans — '

'You did telegraph your mother?'

'Did indeed. Told her I would again when we know more.'

'Capital. I'll be in touch in any case. Be as well if you'd let Mrs McGregor know where you're going, what time to expect you back, so forth.'

★　★　★

Sue bought a sweater, Anne bought a map. The shops were all in the cobbled main street that wound its way between terraces of small houses along the shoreline and higher ground on which the hotel and other stone buildings, some quite large, were ranged. Looking down through gaps between houses one saw slipways and jetties, fishing-boats moored close inshore. In summer it would be pretty, now it was all in varying shades of grey. But pleasant enough, and not as cold as they'd thought it would be; sheltered, of course, by the buildings crowding in on the narrow street. Anne's map, which they studied while lunching in the hotel — herrings with bread and butter, followed by plum pudding — showed them why from here there was no view of the American battleships: the projection southward of the Mainland coastline, with the land rising inland into hills, hid that northeast part of the Flow where Sam had said they were lying.

But there'd be a view of them from Swanbister, he'd said.

'Or from down near the water's edge along here. Peculiar names — Smoogro, Roo Point, Greenigo . . . '

The bus left Stromness at about two-thirty, and a porter from the hotel brought their luggage down to it. Then, after grinding out of the village — or town, as it called itself — and over a narrow causeway with an inland loch on one side and the Flow's choppy surface on the other, they were passing turn-off signs for the Standing Stones and the Ring of Brodegar. High ground to the left, inland, and on the right grassland sloping down to the water's edge. Here and there, farmsteads; and all of it stone-walled. The island of Graemsay, its end with a lighthouse on it, was about a mile offshore. Driving south now — to the place called Houton, which Sam had mentioned, after which they'd be only two or three miles short of Swanbister.

Houton was an inlet, with jetties, cranes and fishing-boats, but the bus having stopped to set down a woman and her children now turned steeply uphill, away from the water, speed reducing to no more than walking-pace near the top, engine then near-convulsing as the driver forcefully changed gear and swung right. An old woman in a long black coat and woollen hat, with whom they'd exchanged a few polite words before departure from Stromness, told them that Swanbister was the next stop and they'd find the guesthouse up on their left.

'*There*, see?'

Grey stone house, greyish tiled roof. Way up

above the road. The bus stopped at a crossroads and the driver handed their bags down to them. He looked like a trawlerman, maybe had been. Craggy, grey-stubbled face, thick white hair, piercingly blue eyes under heavy brows.

'Enjoy your visit, ladies.'

Nice man, they agreed, heaving their suitcases up a narrow lane with that house at the top of it. There was a wooden sign saying GUESTHOUSE, and Mrs McGregor, who must have been watching out for the bus, came to meet them. She was a tall, stern-looking woman, with iron-grey hair and the beginnings of a moustache, but with a smile that made her almost pretty — which she must have been, Anne thought, twenty years ago. The garden-front of the house was of shingle, behind an iron gate which she'd pushed open. They dumped their bags while identifying themselves and shaking hands, then turned to look downhill and across this top end of the Flow: and there were the three battleships. Massive, dark-grey on the gleam of white-flecked sea. Maybe three miles away; a boat just leaving one of them, heading to where it would shortly disappear behind intervening hillside. Sue told Mrs McGregor, 'We were wondering whether you'd have a view of those.'

'Is it in some fashion on account of them you're here, then?'

'Not directly, but' — a nod towards Anne — 'my friend's fiancé's an American naval officer who has to visit the admiral, and kindly brought us with him. I'm their chaperone, you see.'

'Right and proper too.' She laughed, for some reason. 'Best come into the house now, the pair of you. This wind'd have the hide off you, else.'

'What a marvellous view!'

'Aye. Ye can as well enjoy it from inside, however.' Glancing up at the front of the house. 'From your own rooms' windows. Please, come in . . .'

Windows, plural — separate rooms for a change. Through a wide hall to the foot of the stairs, conscious of warmth emanating from an open fire in an inner room — livingroom, whatever — and then up the stairs. The low-ceilinged bedrooms she showed them both faced south. Sue was depositing her case in one of them while Mrs McGregor showed Anne where there was a bathroom just across the landing. Anne said, 'It's perfect. Lovely place to be, Mrs McGregor.'

'Well, just see *this* now.' Leading her into the other room: the outlook from its window was superb. Sue joined them, Mrs McG including her in the audience as she pointed southwestward across the Flow. 'Before Hoy, yon wee island's Cava. Hoy's the highest of them all, of course. And to the south there — och, Fara, but ye'd hardly see it — and Flotta there. And now *this* side' — eastward — 'over beyond your Yankee ships there's Scapa Bay. The northeast corner of the Flow, that is, Kirkwall town no more than a stone's throw from it.' Shifting to point south, then: 'Yon's Burray — there's blockships sunk in the Sounds both ends of it. To keep the U-boats from gettin' in, that is. Then

298

South Ronaldsay, and the Sound of Hoxa, that's the way in an' out for the big ships such as them lying there. Hoxa, see, is a headland that hooks out, like, from South Ronaldsay. From as much as you see from where we stand you might think t'was all one, but the Sound lies between 'em — twixt Ronaldsay and Flotta, that's to say. Ten miles from here to Hoxa Head, though ye might not guess it was as much, and wi' the light fading as it is — why I'm being quick to show it to you, half an hour an' ye'll not see much at all.' She'd turned her back on it. 'Tell *me* now — the lady said ye might be making a tour by water?'

Anne shook her head. 'Bicycle, more likely. If we could hire or borrow some — might that be possible?'

It might, she said. She'd see to it first thing in the morning, be glad to. Alternatively, there was Mr McGillivray, who often took visitors in his motor car to see the sights. And come to think of it, he might be the man for cycles too. She'd ask him. It was not a request she'd had before. But now she'd leave them to settle in: when they were ready for it she'd have a pot of tea and oatcakes for them beside the fire.

She left them still at the window. Anne commenting, 'What we've come five hundred miles to see. Stupendous, isn't it?'

'Forbidding, *I'd* call it.'

'Well. Yes. That too.'

★ ★ ★

299

'Up.'

Neureuther's quiet order, then the hiss of the big 'scope on its way up. In the almost total silence it was clearly audible to them in the wardroom. Neureuther having the watch, in the CO's control-room in the tower, and the time being a few minutes short of four p.m., you could assume he'd be trying for an updated fix before handing over to Hohler. Who in two hours' time would be handing over to Otto — less as to a fellow officer of the watch than to the boat's alternate CO, as she closed in towards her target.

They'd had fixes from shore bearings since early afternoon; were now a couple of miles south of Skirza Head, which itself was three miles south of Duncansby Head, and had reduced speed to three knots. Otto at the wardroom table, with a novel open in front of him which he'd borrowed from Neureuther but wasn't anywhere near holding his attention.

Navigationally, things looked all right. He'd told Hintenberger yesterday that prospects were good — 'fine' was the word he'd used — mainly because (a) Hintenberger had asked him, and (b) there'd been no point in telling him anything else. Same applying now: you were *here*, going *there*, couldn't get out and bloody walk . . . Navigationally speaking, you could count on it that maintaining three knots, while watching various other points carefully and closely, you'd be bringing U201 into the Sound of Hoxa at near enough 2100, nine p.m. Three knots, or slow ahead on both motors, was a quiet-running speed, and the periscope when you put it up made very little 'feather' as it sliced through a broken, tumbling surface. Conditions therefore might be described as favourable. Although a snag he'd have mentioned if there'd been any point in doing so was that they'd be entering the Flow with the battery three-quarters flat. Winter was well aware of this, had mentioned it himself. The battery had been brought well up by having a running charge during the last period of darkness, four p.m. yesterday to eight a.m. this morning, but you'd been running on it most of the time since then at a steady six knots, which would have taken a lot out of it; and whereas in the normal course of things — ordinary passage or patrol routine — you'd be surfacing now and putting on a charge, tonight of course you couldn't, had no option but to stay dived, would finish up entering the Flow — touch wood, as far as *that* was concerned — with the box near flat and no possibility of replenishing it until you were out again.

Which itself was looking a long way ahead.

A second reason for not feeling exactly optimistic on chances of success — of getting *in* — was that when you gave really serious thought to it, you couldn't help wondering whether the British could be so reckless as to leave the great anchorage as open to penetration as Franz Winter seemed to be assuming it was. He — Winter — was tackling it as primarily a navigational exercise; he'd noted the removal of a floating boom and anti-submarine nets between Hoxa and Flotta, for instance, and from that appeared confident that as long as he stayed dived he'd have nothing to worry about.

A conclusion with which FdU had apparently agreed. Although neither Michelsen nor Winter, judging by their careers to date, could be thought of as stupid.

Wishful thinking? A desperate situation justifying the acceptance of enormous risk?

Neureuther, relieved from his watch, edged in on the bench seat beside Hintenberger. Up top there, keeping watch at the big 'search' periscope, skipper or OOW had a sort of motor-bicycle seat, which after a while tended to become uncomfortable. Neureuther telling Otto, 'Couldn't get any new fix, too bloody dark already. Enjoying that yarn, are you?'

'Haven't really got into it. Save it for when we're inside, maybe.'

Hintenberger enquired, of either him or Otto, 'If it's so dark, why don't we surface and put a charge on? Standing charge one side, say. Even a few hours would be *something*. If all we need is three knots, for God's sake?'

'Because' — Neureuther had given Otto a chance to answer the question, but Otto was leaving it to him — 'because this close to Scapa Flow, also to the Scottish coast, and in waters that are invariably patrolled — with the Pentland bottleneck coming up very shortly now, what's more — as the skipper's pointed out, any sight or sound of us would alert them and scupper our chances altogether.' Glancing at Otto: 'Am I not right, sir?'

'It's your captain's view, in any case.'

He might be right, too. Although if one were running the show oneself — well, would *not* be attempting it with an already low battery. Would — yes, definitely *would* — postpone the attempt for twenty-four hours, move away from the coast and spend the night charging, start in again about this time tomorrow. Might miss out by such delay — targets in there now, gone by then — but the presence or absence of targets was a toss-up anyway. Improving one's chances very considerably, he thought.

Chances of *survival*, at that.

Dozing on his bunk — from not long after four — he dreamt of Helena crying in his arms on the chaise longue in the Snake Pit. Sobbing on and on, nothing that he could think of saying to her in any way alleviating her misery; he woke with the taste of her tears on his lips instead of kisses, waking to Winter telling him — and Hintenberger and Neureuther — that Duncansby Head was two miles abeam to port, visible by the sea's white-washing effect, although the night was as black as pitch.

Some *night* — five-twenty now, still early evening. But the visibility from close range of breaking seas was a factor they'd been counting on.

At half-past, young Thoemer served up supper of sardines and canned peaches. Otto was due to take over the watch at six; from then on either he or Winter would be at the big periscope pretty well continually, he guessed. They'd be up there together all the time, anyway, the two of them and the coxswain, PO Muller. He — Otto

303

— taking what would normally have been a navigator's place. To which end, although there was of course a chart table up there, he had the chart virtually photographed in his memory, with 201's north-north-westerly track on it, her progress by dead reckoning marked along it at fifteen-minute intervals. One would be able continually to check the distance covered — by log readings — and however black the night might be you'd have seas breaking white on headlands, which you'd be passing sometimes within a mile or so.

A *small* snag, in terms of navigational accuracy at a rather crucial stage, was that the tide would be on the turn when you were approaching the Sound of Hoxa — somewhere between Herston Head and Hoxa Head, a distance of about a mile-and-a-half; in that half-hour the stream would be at first on her port quarter, then when altering course off Hoxa Head, right on her snout. In those narrows, surprisingly enough, it would be running at only about one knot, but as you'd only be making three knots on the motors, the change — a *two* — knot difference — would have a greater effect than the figures suggested at first sight.

Winter broke into his reflections with: 'Something worrying you?'

He looked at him, thinking, *By and large, a damn-fool question* . . . Looked away again on account of mashed-up sardines spilling from the corners of his mouth. He told him, 'Thinking about the change of tidal stream off Hoxa. Once through that hole — altering to starboard

304

— you'll counter it by increasing to half ahead, I suppose.'

'Once through that gap, von Mettendorff, we'll be thanking God!'

So he *did* know in his heart that the business wasn't exactly cut and dried.

★　★　★

When he took over in the tower at six, the Pentland Skerries were abaft the beam to starboard at a distance of about two miles. Visible — with the search 'scope well up and its quadruple magnification engaged — as a flickering patch of white, seas breaking and spouting over and around what was effectively a mass of half-tide rocks. U201's course 350 degrees, motors providing three knots, distance covered as shown by log-readings matching the DR position closely enough to feel good about. The next sighting should be of Brough Ness on South Ronaldsay — which in the event he picked up, again as a flare of flickering white, when it was forty-five on the bow, range (going by DR) just under two miles. He suggested to Winter — who'd been prowling, dividing his time between this control-room with its small chart table and the one below — 'Be inclined to alter a few degrees to port, sir. So as to pass closer to North Head on Swona than to Barth Head on Ronaldsay.'

Hunched over the chart, nodding without looking up. 'Come to 346.'

'Steer 346, cox'n.'

Muller repeated the order. Below, Neureuther was issuing some of his own, making an adjustment to the trim. Otto thinking, *Shouldn't need to alter again until we're off Stanger Head.* Stanger being the southeastern extremity of Flotta: opposite Hoxa Head. Ideally you'd wind up midway between those two headlands at a little before nine p.m., and from there set course pretty well due north, into the broad expanses of the Flow.

Very wishful thinking . . .

'Course 346, sir.'

Muller was a tall man, about Otto's height, with arms that looked disproportionately long, giving rise to his nickname of Spider. He came from Bremen, was the son of a merchant navy man and had chatted with Hintenberger about the town and its surroundings. One was getting to know some of 201's leading characters now. Brohm, the torpedo chief, who was a gloomy-looking fellow, came from Hanover, signalman Kendermann — little shrimp of a man with bright red hair — telegraphists/hydrophone operators Lange and Siebertz, the burly Chief Mechanician Kopp, Stoker PO Wienands — and lesser fry . . . You felt you knew them well enough, even on such short acquaintance, in that they conformed to type, and having completed numerous patrols in U-boats shared the same or similar experiences, tended to treat each other virtually as brothers. Thirty-two of them — seamen, stokers, technicians and NCOs — plus five officers, including himself in place of Kantelberg.

Who'd be sorry he was missing this, Neureuther had said. He was well liked and a very reliable navigator, despite his youth. Same age as Emil Hohler — nineteen, apparently.

From seven onwards the salt-washed coast of South Ronaldsay was visible in high-power as a wavery whiteness about a mile to starboard. After Barth Head that distance would roughly double itself, the coastline receding sharply; and Swona's North Head would be abeam to port by seven-thirty. There'd be no land really close after that for about an hour, when Herston Head would be coming up to starboard — the last projection of land before Stanger Head and Hoxa.

Where they *had* had the boom, and nets, now allegedly relied on searchlights and gun batteries. Kantelberg could reckon himself damn lucky not to be here, he thought.

He'd been giving the periscope a rest during these last few minutes. Keeping the surroundings and the boat's progress none the less continually in mind; in his imagination *seeing* Barth Head gradually vanishing as it fell back abaft the beam — and to port, Swona swallowed up in the darkness by this time.

'Up.'

For another careful all-round search. One didn't know what patrols there might be, or vessels arriving or departing. Commercial traffic would favour daylight hours, he imagined: might be confined to those hours, even. Thinking of this as the 'scope's handles rose into his waiting hands and he jerked them down. Twisting the

307

left-hand one clockwise brought in the magnification. There'd be colliers and oil-tankers in and out of here, he guessed, to supply the re-fuelling station at Lyness on the northwest coast of Flotta, which according to FdU's intelligence files the British had completed about a year ago. Storeships too. But perhaps only in daylight.

With his eyes at the rubber eyepieces, he'd begun to sweep slowly across the bow when he heard Winter's growl of, 'I'll take her for a while. Until eight-thirty, say.'

Quite civilised now, the bison. Except when feeding. The bison feeding was still an awesome sight. Otto raised a thumb, completed his sweep round, finding nothing but the boil of sea up close and beyond that the empty dark. He'd expected to be left up here until just short of nine, when Winter would surely claim the privilege of conning her through the narrows; but he had no objection to relaxing for a while. Time now — seven-forty. He trained the 'scope fore and aft, pushed the handles up and sent it down, got off the seat suggesting, 'Cox'n might do with a break too, sir.'

'Cox'n?'

'Wouldn't mind, sir.'

'All right.' Sliding his broad rear-end on to the seat, telling Otto, 'Send up Leading Seaman Lehner.'

★ ★ ★

He went back up at eight-thirty, having rested his mind by thinking about Helena. Better than

308

leaving it to dreams: you could control your thinking, dreams took their own senseless course, which illogically continued to disturb one. She'd be all right, and so would he: for the simple reason they both *had* to be.

He was glad he'd asked Gunther Schwaeble to stand by her.

'Eight-thirty, sir.'

A nod. 'Herston Head's sixty on the bow to starboard, Switha's about eighty to port. I've altered by two degrees to 348.'

Otto checked those bearings on the chart, found that their intersection matched the eight-thirty DR well enough.

Log-reading from the repeater — ditto.

'On track and on DR, sir.'

Changing places. Otto then checking those nearer points of land. Herston Head not difficult to see, Switha less so, indistinct although actually closer. Because that was a lee shore, of course, and lower. Sweeping slowly round . . . Steady ticking of the log, low purr of the motors a reminder that the battery was still leaking amps. Winter's problem: or would be. Not that any problem of Winter's could be *only* his. Time now — eight-thirty-seven. Commencing another circuit, initially finding Herston Head as its starting-point — the centre of that smear of breaking sea. Near enough sixty-three on the bow. Head back while checking the bearing-ring, and — yes, sixty-three precisely. Aware of Muller coming up, taking over again from Lehner.

Swivelling slowly left now: Hoxa Head would be one's next landmark to starboard.

309

He checked, trained back again. Slight lurch of the heart, and now shifting the 'scope a degree or two this way and that — since either through a periscope or binoculars one picked up a barely visible object better that way than by trying to focus directly on it.

Trawler. Emerging from the bay beyond Herston's left edge. Showing lights, for Christ's sake . . .

'Down.' To dip it, no more than that: and into the voicepipe, 'Captain to CO's control-room. Stop starboard. Close-up hydrophones.'

Stopping the 'scope on its way down, bringing it slithering up again, having dipped it as a precaution against being spotted — which in fact was highly improbable, virtually impossible, at such a range in darkness and broken water. Hearing the report 'Starboard motor stopped' — for the sake of running more quietly, on only one screw — and telling Winter as he came panting up, 'Trawler coming out of the bay inside Herston Head — green six-four, range about a mile and showing lights.' He was off the seat, Winter taking over at the 'scope, grunting to himself: examining the trawler for about a second-and-a-half, then swinging anti-clockwise — towards Switha and Stanger Head, Switha Sound. 'Port fifteen. Stop port, slow ahead starboard. Steer' — checking the bearing-ring and giving this a split second's thought — 'Steer two-nine-zero.'

He'd sent the 'scope down. Acknowledgements and action meanwhile, by Muller here and others below. Otto at the chart, appreciating that on emergence from that bay — which was called Widewall, the chart reminded him — the trawler might continue straight over into Switha Sound, or turn to starboard up-channel or to port down-channel. His own inclination had been to turn away, which was what Winter was doing — to keep his distance from it while remaining at periscope depth because you needed to see which way it was going, in order to *continue* to stay clear of it. In fact *he'd* have had the 'scope up again by this time. And in case one needed to go deep, stay quiet and listen on hydrophones for instance — well, depth here was — upwards of fifty metres. Except for one shallow patch, where — oh, still minimally *thirty* metres. While if one continued on the course of 290 degrees, in less than a mile you'd be into Switha Sound — between Switha and Flotta — where there was considerably less water: *not* so good.

'What depths in Switha Sound, Mettendorff?'

Great minds thinking alike. Otto told him, 'Down to as little as fifteen metres. But also, sir, on your course of 290, if the trawler's holding on as it might be — '

Neureuther's voice then in the voicepipe: 'Lange reports hydrophone effect green one hundred drawing left, range closing, sir!'

'Stay on it. Frequent bearings, please.' Calm old bison. Always at his best in action or emergencies, one recalled. He had the 'scope on its way up again at last. Knowing he had still to be about half a mile clear. And needing to know *now* which way the thing was going, and whether it was hunting for U-boats in general or this one in particular. Handles clicking down, training around to the quarter, searching. Otto reminding him, 'Tide will be on the turn in about fifteen minutes.'

A grunt — not to that, but because he'd found his target. Holding it for a moment: then leaving it, swinging to forward bearings — Switha, presumably, and probably looking for Stanger Head. He pushed the handles up: 'Down. Port fifteen.'

'Port fifteen, sir . . . '

'Steer' — working it out, then — 'steer one-six-five.'

Muller repeating, 'One-six-five, sir.'

Reversing course. Telling Otto, 'Seems to be making for Switha Sound. Nothing to do with us, therefore. When he's out of the way we'll start in again.'

14

Mrs McGregor had given them a fish supper at seven-thirty, and now an hour later was telling them about the loss of the battleship *Vanguard* in July of last year. It was a story she'd obviously recounted several times: she knew the names of all the Grand Fleet ships that had been in the Flow that night — four battle squadrons, in all twenty-eight capital ships, as well as two cruiser squadrons, near sixty destroyers and numerous submarines. 'Five what they call flotillas o' them things . . . ' Among the battleships, the *Vanguard*, one of the 4th Battle Squadron, with a crew of 1,000 men. 'She were here, just below us here, on the eighth day of July. They'd brought her over from close off Flotta, and spent the night here — on what we call the Ophir coast. I remember admiring the looks of her, on a summer evening that was as beautiful as I've known, and 'twas next evening, the ninth, she returned to where she'd come from, wi' the others of her squadron — two miles to the north of Flotta there. Well, I tell you, I was in bed and asleep when it happened. Folk such as gunners on the islands or sailors on the other ships, likewise farmers as happened to be up an' doing, all told how they seen a great shoot of flames light the Flow, and islands with it, a sound like the crack of doom, and then another. I was woken *then*, all right — and at the window, and

I swear to you I pray never to see the like — burning objects flying through the air, and the heather on shore set alight — the very sky you'd think was burning! Then the smoke — black as hell, and when it cleared — oh, my Lord, she'd gone!'

'Were any of them saved?'

'Aye. Out of a thousand men, three. An officer, a stoker and a Royal Marine, but the officer died next day. To this day 'tis not known what caused it. 'Internal explosion', they said. Oh, 'twas a *dreadful* thing!'

Her telephone rang. It was fixed to the wall in the hallway: had just rung again. Anne said, 'Mr McGillivray calling back, perhaps.' He and Mrs McGregor had the only telephones in this area, and she'd called him earlier to ask whether he could lay his hands on two ladies' bicycles in good condition; he'd said he thought he'd be able to and would let her know in the morning.

She was saying, on her way to answer it, 'He'd never, though — at this time of night . . . '

Sue said quietly, 'Could be Sam.'

'Could indeed.'

'Hello?'

Silence . . . Then: 'I will enquire whether she is disposed to take your call. It's late, you know.'

'Likes to put 'em in their place, doesn't she?'

'Mrs Laurie — '

'*Is* Sam, anyway.' She went through and took the receiver from her. 'That you, Sam?'

'Did I wake you all, or something?'

'No, of course not. How are things?'

'May not have woken you, but I'm about to

shock you. Do you have transport that might get you down to the quay at Houton?'

'When?'

'*Now*. I'm about to leave the flagship in her picket-boat, making for some landing-place on Flotta, but if you two could face it we'd pick you up at Houton in half an hour. Seems a U-boat's trying to get into the Flow — they have hydrophones and suchlike — '

'What's it to do with *us*?'

'Well, not much, but — having dragged you up here, and now leaving you on your own, I thought the chance of having a ringside seat, so to speak — '

'To see it being sunk or depthcharged, or — '

'Well, let's hope so, *that'd* justify the whole trip, wouldn't it? Are you game? *I* want to see it and I'm tagging along with the flagship's torpedo officer. I've asked might we take you two along and the duty commanding officer said why not — he's never heard of you of course, but on my personal responsibility — '

'You're an extraordinary man, you know?'

'Right now, man in a hurry. Will you come? If so, wrap up well. Can't hang around though, because — '

'There's a Mr McGillivray near here who has both a motor and a telephone. If he'll turn out for us — '

'*Make* him. Bribe him. I'll foot the bill. Double his usual price, if that'd do it. But if you're not at Houton when we get there we can't wait, so — '

'I'll do my best. See you there, I *hope*. Bye.'

Hanging up, and turning to meet Mrs McGregor's shocked stare. In the doorway, Sue was looking excited. 'Mrs McGregor — '

'He'll no turn out this time o' night! An' what for, is it? Houton, I heard mention of?'

'What's Mr McGillivray's number, please?'

★ ★ ★

Houton Bay was a base for seaplanes as well as for trawlers and that, Mr McGillivray told them. But he was more intent on asking questions than imparting information. Curiosity, even veiled suspicions, as to how and for what purpose two young ladies should come to be embarking in an American battleship's picket-boat at such an hour seemed to have been a factor in his consenting to turn out.

Anne answered all his questions as the car jounced west and south. It was a Star, 15.9 horsepower, he'd told Sue. A big, heavy thing with very large, solid tyres and a flapping roof, canvas or somesuch. Its headlights weren't up to much. Were masked, maybe, as cars' lights were down south. But she gave him Sam's name and rank and said as Sue had earlier that he was her fiancé, Miss Pennington here her chaperone who'd come all the way up from London with them, and told him that apparently a U-boat had been detected trying to get into the Flow, and Lieutenant-Commander Lance had had permission from the *New York*'s duty commanding officer, whatever *that* meant, to take them with him to

316

some island down there. 'Flotta, would it be?'

It might be, he said. Which case — aye, the Sound of Hoxa, mebbe, was where they'd try it, like as not. 'But to be sanctioning the pair o'ye afloat — och, if ye'd excuse me sayin' so — '

'I agree, it's extraordinary. But my fiancé's an extraordinary man. Also conscientious — and having brought us all this way from London, he feels that if anything as exciting as *that*'s going on — '

'It's no' back to the ship they'd be taking ye, then?'

'I told you — that island — '

'Aye. Flotta. Aye.' Hauling left into that rather steep descent now. He was not a big man, although on the tubby side, and it took most of his strength to drag the wheel around. Sue meanwhile nudging Anne, muttering, 'Your fiancé, indeed . . . '

'Wasn't that *your* idea?'

'Seems to have become yours now. Method in his madness, maybe?'

McGillivray shouted, 'D'ye ken how long ye'll be detained on Flotta, then?'

'Not the least idea. I see what you mean, though. We'll ask him — if you get us down there in time, that is.'

'If I do not, then I'd return ye to the guesthouse, eh?'

'But I *very* much hope — '

'*There's* your boat!' Jabbing at the rather tall windscreen. 'If they've the eyes and sense tae see *us* — '

'Mr McGillivray — would they have a

317

telephone on that island?'

'The Navy, on Flotta? Aye — '

'If I telephone to you when we were starting back — could mean waking you up, disturbing Mrs McGillivray again — '

'Could'nae help that, however. In for a penny — eh? Would ye have my number wi' ye?'

'No, but — '

'I'll gi'e it tae ye, then . . . '

★ ★ ★

The car grated to a halt on the quayside; the picket-boat had bumped alongside the jetty that stood out from it at right-angles. Mr McGillivray had thrust a square of pasteboard into Anne's gloved hand — his telephone number, she assumed — and she and Sue were hurrying towards the boat with its thumping engine and gushing steam. Men were on the jetty — crewmen handling ropes, and Sam striding this way, yelling, 'You made it, then!'

Anne grabbed Sue as she stumbled. The quay was wet — by the smell of it, fish-wet — which tallied with the shapes of trawlers berthed on the jetty's other side — thumping against fenders, mooring-ropes thwacking in the surge. Fish, wet night air, seaweed, coal-smoke, steam . . . It was going to be a roughish trip, she guessed, the wind evidently having risen while they'd been lazing beside Mrs McG's fire. Crewmen from the boat had thrown lines around bollards and were backing them up, not securing them, looking at herself and Sue as Sam guided

318

them towards the stern where there was a shelter — cabin, if that was what they'd call it. Forward of that roofed section was deck-space and other crewmen — one in a cap with a shiny peak on it — petty officer, coxswain, whatever — and forward of that another raised section with the funnel slanting up out of it. They reached the stern, and a tall officer with a beaky nose put his arms up to receive Anne: 'Easy, now, easy!' Addressing her as if she was a horse, she thought: ought to let out a loud neigh. But she was on board, let go of him, and he was looking to give Sue a hand, but Sam had come thumping down like a ton of bricks and turned to bring her aboard with him.

'OK there, sir?'

'Sure, all aboard!'

'Let go — shove off for'ard . . . '

The one with the nose was ushering them into shelter. Sam grinning at them: 'Cut it fine, but — '

'Came as fast as we could, that's all. Could say *you* cut it fine.'

'You're really *something*, I'll tell you that!'

'Not so bad yourself, Sam.'

Sue said, 'I'm afraid you've done it now, she's gone on you.'

'Sue, really . . . '

The boat was off the jetty, engine pounding, rolling hard as they turned it across wind and sea. Sam had said, 'I'm gone on both of you. But listen, this is Lieutenant-Commander Jack Ray, of the USS *New York*. Mrs Laurie, Jack, and Miss Pennington.'

'Strange way to meet, but it's a pleasure . . . '

'How soon'll we be there?'

'Less'n half an hour. It's about five miles, five-and-a-half, and the boat makes twelve knots flat out. *Is* a little rough, I admit — could take thirty-five minutes, say.'

'Then what?'

'I'll tell you. Move further in, though?'

'Rough, all right!'

'Why it's better to be inside.' Sam added, 'Irregular motion, and — heck, when she really hits one — whoops, hang on . . . Jack, *you* blind 'em with science?'

'Sure.' Ray was red in the face and had a moustache under his beaky nose. 'See, there's listening-out equipment — submerged hydrophones, and other detection gear — off Stanger Head, Quoy Ness and Roan Head — those are headlands on Flotta — and over to Hoxa Head the other side — all across Hoxa Sound, in fact. Know where I mean?'

'More or less.'

'We'll be landing on a small pier — Vincent Pier they call it — just short of Roan Head and in shelter of a little island called Calf of Flotta. Fifty-yard walk from there to the control shack on Roan. Situation is that something like an hour ago, sea-bed indicator loops southeast of Stanger were activated by what must have been a U-boat. At the same time, however, an armed trawler patrolling down there was moving out from inside Hoxa Head, destination Switha and Gutter Sounds, which means it was heading to

320

cross that same stretch of the main channel — and would've triggered the loops too — but visible anyway, showing lights to *make* her so. Uh?'

'What's an indicator loop?'

'Loop of cable laid out on the sea-bed where an intruder's magnetic field sets up an electric current in it and triggers reaction in galvanometers to which it's connected. A galvanometer's a dial with a needle in it. Needle jumps, see. Anyway, the U-boat announced itself in this way, then must've turned back on its tracks and — well, disappeared. They think it must have spotted the trawler and turned away for that reason. In which case it's not likely to have been put off for long; when it sees the coast is clear it'll make a fresh approach. That's what we're hoping for.'

'And the trawler?'

'Oh, gone. Up what the Royal Navy sometimes call the tradesmen's entrance. That's Gutter or Weddel Sound, after Switha. Big ships using Hoxa Sound, small-fry relegated to the narrower passage.'

Sue asked him, 'Might the U-boat have any way of knowing it had triggered the indicator loop?'

'I don't believe so. And it's sort of my business, d'you see — why I'm here, a chance of seeing the system in action, as distinct from just an exercise. I say a *chance* of seeing it in action, I'm not taking any bets.'

Sam put in, 'He's a torpedo specialist. In our Navy — not sure it isn't the same in yours

321

— torpedo expertise takes in mines, electrical gear associated with all that, explosives and so forth. Whoa-up . . . ' Grabbing for support against the heaviest roll yet. 'Heck, maybe I shouldn't have dragged you two out in this!'

'Dragged us from a roaring fire and hot-water bottles waiting in our beds, incidentally. I'm still glad you did, though.'

'*Aren't* they something, Jack?'

'Sure are. And you don't have any claim on the little one, right?'

★ ★ ★

Landing at the Vincent Pier wasn't too easy. This was the northeast coast of Flotta, and the small offshore island Calf of Flotta probably did provide some degree of shelter, but not all that much, and the tide fairly sluiced through that channel. The picket-boat's coxswain knew his business, however, and they got ashore more or less dry. From there Ray had told him to take the boat 3–4,000 yards west, to the Royal Navy's re-fuelling base in Weddel Sound — between Flotta and Fara — where they'd have good shelter as well as telephone communication with the shack on Roan Head.

Fifty yards from the pier to the shack, someone had said, but by Anne's reckoning it was more like 500. The men had flashlights, anyway, which helped, and there was no rain or sleet at this stage in the gusting, icy wind. There had been, on the way over. The shack, as it loomed up ahead of them, could by its looks have been a milking shed. Had *not* been, was of fairly recent construction — stone, like everything else on these islands — but that sort of shape, long and low, flat-roofed — also fitted with double doors against the wind. Once through them you were in warmth and a glow of light, smell of paraffin from a heater somewhere in the middle. Windows on one side — the side facing seaward, east and southeast towards the Sound of Hoxa — with curtains of blanket material covering them; and against the wall on that side a table or work-bench with what looked like electrical gear on it, also hand-drawn chart-sections — in bright colours and much enlarged — a child's work, could have been. A loud-speaker on the wall above all that — wireless, maybe. No — loud-speaker . . .

Turning her back on all that anyway as three men converged from various directions — no, two converging, greeting Sam and Jack Ray, the other staying put, only glancing back over his shoulder. These two were a lieutenant with the wavy stripes of the Volunteer Reserve on the sleeves of his reefer jacket, and a warrant officer — slightly wizened — with a single narrow stripe on each sleeve. The lieutenant had small, rather crafty eyes — like a goat's, she thought — and had told them his name but she hadn't caught it; while the warrant officer, whom the lieutenant had introduced as Mr Showell, was a little stick of a man, jockey-sized with yellowish skin and thin, greying hair. Also a smell of whisky, she noticed, as they shook hands. The third member of the team, the one keeping his distance, was a leading seaman whom the lieutenant named as Derrymore. On one arm he wore a badge of crossed torpedoes with a star above them, on the other an anchor with a twist of rope around it. Except for him, they were all milling around, shaking hands and being affable, but he — Derrymore — was watching an assembly of clock-face gauges on the opposite wall. She wondered — studying them more closely — galvanometers?

There'd been a suggestion of making tea, but neither she nor Sue wanted any — there'd been rather a lot of it on offer at Mrs McGregor's and they'd felt it might be considered ill-mannered to refuse. Here in the shack the Americans weren't keen either, and Showell asserted that he already had tea practically running out of his ears. Special, high-proof tea, Anne thought, wandering over towards the leading seaman and asking him, 'Is that a galvanometer, by any chance?' He'd nodded. 'Six of 'em, Miss. There's six loops, see. Submarine triggers any one of 'em, tells us where it is, like. Then the chart-outlines on that work-top have the corresponding sections marked, mines an' all.'

A hand on her elbow then, as Sue joined her. Sam, Ray and Wroughton, the RNVR man, were on kitchen-type chairs around a desk that had telephones and what looked like instructional manuals on it — at the door end, but set more or less centrally. The hand on Anne's elbow was Warrant Officer Showell's, who was offering, 'Show you the scheme of it if you like, ladies. Derrymore 'ere needs to keep his eyes on them

324

gauges.' He'd winked. 'Hard luck, lad.'

'Mines, did he say?'

'Bless you, Miss, bloody *'undreds* of 'em!'

Nine thirty-five . . .

* * *

'Time now?'

Winter, hunched at the search periscope. Otto told him — from the chart, but referring to his own old silver watch, which for some reason he'd always thought brought him luck — 'Nine forty-two.'

'So we'll only have lost — what, hour-and-a-half, by the time we're through. No real setback, eh?'

Except that you'd lost rather more than an hour-and-a-half, and that both motors were at half ahead instead of slow ahead, using twice the amperage you'd been consuming an hour earlier. Could begin to look like a *very* real setback, if you got into any trouble inside. Or on the way through, for that matter.

Evading the trawler, they'd back-tracked for only about two miles, but on turning again, taking a chance on it having left the area by this time, had found the tidal stream working against them instead of for them, consequently were needing twice the power now to make the same headway as before. *Now*, Switha's North Traing (or right-hand edge) was still only about eighty on the port bow, Herston Head seventy to starboard. Hoxa Head when one picked it up would be about thirty degrees to starboard

— and you wouldn't see it at least until you had Herston abaft the beam. Had lost about an hour-and-three-quarters, therefore — as well as a lot of amps.

Which you were still losing, of course.

Winter said, 'When I find Hoxa, I'll alter to due north. Cut the corner until it's abeam, then go round to 020.'

Virtually shaving Hoxa Head, this would mean. But that second alteration wouldn't do. Otto, pencilling-in a revised track, suggested that 040 degrees, after Hoxa, would be better than 020.

'Otherwise you'd come too close to Nevi Skerry — that's off Roan Head on Flotta — and this other hazard northeast of it called the Grinds. Once past *them* — fine, you could come back to due north.'

Silence for a moment, except for the bison's hard breathing as he continued searching. Sound of the motors louder than it had been earlier, of course; before they'd had to speed up it had been a murmur, was now a thrum. The log's continual clicking unchanged — as long as there was way on her, unending. Winter's gruff answer then: 'Yes. Forgotten that skerry. Although . . . '

Although *what*?

He'd thought better of it, or was keeping it to himself. Nine-fifty. It would be ten-thirty before he altered to scrape past Hoxa Head, Otto reckoned. *Then* you'd be where you had been when the trawler had put in its appearance. An hour and forty-five minutes could seem like a bloody week, he was realising. Actually, *recalling*, more than discovering — one had experienced this kind of phenomenon often enough before; what made it more noticeable now was being on the sidelines, more or less a passenger. Frustrating — having run one's own show, made one's own decisions for quite some time. In UB81, as a prime example, only eight or nine days ago, for God's sake ... And what did particularly irk one was not having tried to influence Winter in the really basic mistake he'd made, the decision to press ahead immediately instead of accepting a delay of twenty-four hours and starting with the battery fully charged. Should have tackled him head-on, made an issue of it.

Trawler coming back now, for instance, you'd damn soon be in serious trouble. And not having argued the point made it at least partly one's own error. That was mostly what stuck in the gullet.

Too late for tears now, anyway. And — face it — so far *was* so good. No point giving oneself the bloody villies ...

The English girl's expression, to give oneself the 'villies'. In Berlin, in the place where they'd tango'd, when he'd made some reference to Kaiser Willi having banned German officers from dancing anything so decadent, she'd joked, 'If he could see us, might give *himself* the villies, mightn't he?' And *he'd* said, 'A heart-attack, no less! The way *you* dance it, might blow an imperial fuse!' Then he'd taken a bit of a grip on himself: the tango was one thing, subversive talk that might be overheard was quite another. 'The villies', though — she'd hit on pronouncing it with the 'v' sound, and found this screamingly amusing, had gone practically hysterical. Well, there'd been a strong element of that. Part of it — other than the fizz, as he recalled it — was that with his connivance she'd been passing herself off as German; there'd been a lot of anti-British feeling in Germany at that time, and an ingredient in her enjoyment of the evening had been the discovery that she *could* pass for a native — thanks to the Berlitz experience.

Despite her Spanish colouring, and all that blue-black hair . . .

But why think about *her* again, for God's sake?

Past ten o'clock. Winter growling, 'Herston Head's coming up abeam. Eighty-five on the bow, say.' Head back, blinking up at the bearing-ring. 'Eighty-six.' Back at the eyepieces. 'Where you spotted the trawler — almost.' Swinging left, then pausing to search again for Hoxa. Without success, evidently. Moving on, over to port to look for Stanger Head, which — assessing the position, from the log reading and the bearings he'd noted down — should be thirty-five or forty on the bow now, distance — oh, two miles, near enough . . .

* * *

'Not coming, is he?'

The warrant officer had muttered it. Showell

328

— old whisky-breath. Anne sighed: 'D'you think not?'

She heard Sam comment to the lieutenant — Wroughton, who had green cloth between his wavy stripes, labelling him as a specialist in some technical sphere — 'Surprising that he'd give up. Come this far, then be scared off by a trawler that hasn't even said 'boo' to him?'

'It's us as says 'boo'.' Showell again: quietly to Anne, who was beside him. Adding, 'Fritz is a funny beggar, ain't he, though. Speaking the lingo as you do, you'd agree with me there, I dare say?'

She smiled vaguely — enjoying the little man with his lined, parchment-coloured face and his attempts to entertain the visitors. They were at the work-table that had enlarged diagramatic chart-sections painted on three-ply and switch-gear and so forth all over it. Ten-thirty having passed, they'd had tea after all, she and Sue perching on stools and finding empty spaces for their Admiralty-issue mugs amongst all that. Sue had settled on Anne's left; she'd been chatting with Derrymore for a while, the torpedoman then retiring to the far end of the shack to smoke a cigarette while drinking his tea, Showell at that time shifting round to face the display of dials on the other wall, the galvanometers. There was another device, here where Sue was sitting, a box-shaped thing with a circle of brass studs and a pointer that could be twisted around, clicking over each stud in turn and — according to Showell, 'linking audial reception to this or that area of the sea approaches'. He'd added, nodding towards the loud-speaker on the wall between the curtained windows, 'Hydrophones we're talking about, of course.'

'So you'd hear it, as well as see the needles jumping.'

'One leads to the other, like.'

'Does it always work?'

'*Course*. No point 'aving it, else. Run exercises, don't we. With our own subs, when there's one 'andy.'

Needles all static now, though, and the speaker silent, except that on some circuits when they turned that thing around — which they did every ten minutes or so, checking each area in turn — there was the kind of sound you got when as a child you held a sea-shell to your ear. Sue had done it this last time — the instrument being more easily in her reach than in his, when she'd seen his intention and offered, 'Give it a twirl, shall I?' Showell then complaining over his shoulder to the others, 'Being done out o' me job 'ere, sir.'

Ten forty-three. She'd heard Sam asking Wroughton whether that trawler's primary concern would have been possible U-boat intrusions, and Wroughton's reply, 'Any kind of intrusion. Lots of back ways around these islands. U-boat might land saboteurs on the east coast of South Ronaldsay, for instance. Trek over with canoes, say.'

'Oh, surely — '

'If they had explosives with them? *Any* intrusion, though. Fast torpedo launches like CMBs, for instance. Hasn't ever happened, but

330

— can't leave back doors to a major fleet anchorage wide open, can you?'

Showell asked her, 'What made you learn German then, Miss?'

He kept calling her 'Miss', hadn't noticed the ring she wore. She'd wondered whether he was married, but didn't like to ask. She told him, 'Wanted to make myself more employable, and I already spoke French, so — '

'Get along well enough in English too, I notice.'

'Eh?' Glancing at him: realising it was another joke. His straight face and steady gaze told her nothing. She laughed — liking him, for some reason she couldn't have explained — and he added quietly, 'Lovely voice you have, if I may say so. Treat to listen to. Ever know a Fritz you took to, then?'

She nodded. 'A girl in the language school I attended. We were good friends.'

A nod: it occurred to her that when he smiled he looked like a tortoise. 'Dare say some of the *girls* is — '

'Loop B active, sir!'

Derrymore. The needle in the second of the line of galvanometers had flicked up from its dormant position and was quivering. Wroughton was on his feet with a telephone and its receiver in his hands, Showell muttering, 'Excuse *us*' as he lunged past Anne and Sue to the control-box of the hydrophone equipment: getting sea-shell echoes on the first click, then a sound of — undoubtedly, engine sound on the second. He tried the third as well, got nothing, clicked back

331

to the other. Definitely engine sound: and suddenly tremendously exciting. Wroughton was saying into the telephone, 'Section B, yes. Propeller noise too, but muted — as yet. Passing Herston is my guess. Yes. Yes. Searchlights then but no sooner — don't want him scared off again. But alert the Hoxa battery? Oh, and the Yanks.'

Showell muttered to Anne, 'Gun battery. Six-inch guns.' Forefinger stabbing at the chart-outline. 'There.'

'So where d'you think — '

'*There*.'

Sam's voice asked from the vicinity of the desk, 'Alerting guns on the assumption he might surface?'

'Less *assuming* than guarding against such contingency. If he's going for your ships, decided to come up and go hell for leather — '

'Hence' — Jack Ray's voice — 'Alerting the Yanks.'

'Exactly. Screws getting louder — notice?'

★ ★ ★

'Starboard five.'

Muller echoed, 'Starboard five, sir.' Eyes on the gyro repeater, long arms moving to spin the wheel and put that much angle on the rudder. 'Five of starboard wheel on, sir.'

'Steer north.' Bison's head pulling back from the lenses, Muller acknowledging, bison growling, 'I'd like Neureuther to see this. Would you mind, von Mettendorff?'

332

'Of course not. Good idea.'

COs would often give their second in command or other senior men a chance to see the results of their joint efforts. A sinking, for instance: Otto had several times offered Claus Stahl a quick sight of an enemy going down, had on occasion given 81's coxswain, Honeck, and her torpedo chief, Stroebel, the same treat. (The *late* Karl Stroebel, poor devil.) When there was time, and you didn't have an enemy right at your throat, why not? And this break-in to the Grand Fleet's hitherto inviolate lair was certainly an event worth witnessing. He put his watch in his pocket, heard Muller intone, 'Course three-six-zero, sir' as he started down the ladder.

Neureuther, also Leading Seaman Lehner and the Boy Telegraphist Rehkliger, all looked surprised to see him. At the hydroplane controls, Schnets and Napflein: Schnets prematurely bald, Napflein noticeably gap-toothed. Getting most of their names into his head had come easily enough: a physical feature or some characteristic or mannerism, to which you taught yourself to tie a name. In the hydrophone operator's seat, for instance, Telegraphist Siebertz, as usual chewing gum. Otto told Neureuther, 'Skipper wants you to take a look. Shortly passing through the narrows — spitting distance of Hoxa Head.'

'We're as good as *in*, then?'

He held up crossed fingers, but didn't answer. Aware of some considerable degree of unreality. Glancing around at this and that and the faces watching *him*, thinking, Because we *aren't* in

— not even 'almost', not until we're clear of that Hoxa peninsula and of Flotta's east coast. He'd been about to ask Neureuther whether he was happy with the trim, refrained because Neureuther was already on the ladder — anyway, he could take it in for himself pretty well at a glance . . .

Looked good. Depth exactly ten metres, 'planes more or less amidships most of the time, bubble half a degree aft. Telegraphs showing half ahead, and over the chart table the small winking light that matched the ticking of the log indicating steady progress.

Progress towards *what?*

In the wardroom he told Emil Hohler, 'Be as well to keep an eye on the trim. Neureuther's taking a look at the scenery up top.'

'*Jawohl* . . . '

Pleasant lad — open-faced and always cheerful. Otto sat down where he'd been sitting, telling himself, *Take a grip, man, you've been in tighter holes than this.* He nodded to Hintenberger, 'All right?'

A grunt. He'd been killing time with that novel of Neureuther's which Otto hadn't found all that absorbing; turning it open on its face now. 'How we doing?'

'Approaching Hoxa Head. Show you on the chart here?'

Shake of the head. Head like a bird's nest and face like that of an ape that had recently crawled through a hedge backwards. You could barely see the eyes — or expression under the matted beard. He asked him, 'Will you shave off some of

334

the undergrowth before attending my wedding?'

A shrug. 'Might trim it. Long as I get to kiss the bride.'

'One chaste kiss might be permissible. That is, if *she* permits it.'

★　★　★

In the shack, Derrymore had called sharply ''D' loop's active, sir!'

Hydrophone effect *much* louder suddenly: you could recognise it as twin screws thrashing. Wroughton was using the telephone again: on his feet with a view over Showell's and the girls' heads to the windows from which a few minutes ago Showell had removed the blankets and muttered apologetically to Anne, ''Fraid you might find it a touch draughty now.' Wroughton had said into the 'phone, 'Searchlights on D dog, please. He's on the line, entering from B baker. I'll give it one minute.'

In response to which, lights blazed in the southeast now, probing out from several points on what might have been half a mile of coastline, lighting a wide area of crinkly seascape, silver beams sweeping, searching. Hydrophone noise suddenly much louder, Wroughton having to shout to be heard, ordering Showell to 'Prime section D dog south' — which he'd done, apparently, was now back on his stool, telling her — as she took her eyes off that now lit-up area of sea — 'That's the beggar as'll finish 'em.'

Pointing at a switch with a large 'D' and a small 'S' on it, white capitals. Copper — a hinged bar about nine inches long, wooden handle. You'd push it over — Mr Showell would, his bony hand was ready to do so, close to it, right in front of her — to connect with a terminal that was also copper and shaped like a clip. There was a line of about a dozen similar switches over the full length of the work-bench; but this was the one that mattered now, he'd said.

Behind them, Wroughton had passed the telephone to Derrymore, had a stopwatch in his hand. Beginning suddenly — shouting again — 'Ten — nine — eight — '

Showell tilted his hand, inviting her, 'Be my guest?'

'What?'

Perfectly obvious, *what*. Pointing at it and nudging her with that elbow, whispering like a rasp of sandpaper, 'When 'e says 'fire' — shut it.'

Countdown continuing ' — four — three — two — one — '

★ ★ ★

Hintenberger put a hand on the novel he'd been reading or trying to read, muttered through the motors' steady thrum, 'Load of codswallop. Trying to hide in it, sort of thing, but — '

'Hide?' Otto's eyes on the small dark ones. 'From what?'

'Could've sworn I saw something like it in *your* noble visage, old friend. In fact right *now* — '

336

'Well.' Shake of the head. 'Truth is, I keep thinking about my girl being scared for me. It really hurts to think it's my fault she's going through this. Powerful urge to — oh, to hug her, tell her *don't* be — '

'If you were in a position to do that — '

'Of course — and the odds are she's flat out, dreaming — '

'Hear *that*?'

Bolt upright suddenly, eyes like gimlets, beard almost quivering, fists clenched on the table . . . Otto following the direction of his glance, then turning back. 'Hear what?'

'Something about searchlights?'

'Oh.' A shrug, and instant process of rationalisation — self-protective, but factual enough. Explaining to himself and to the engineer, 'They do have some around these narrows. Like as not burn 'em all night — and since we won't be surfacing — well, let 'em. What I was about to say — remember when we were on the bottom in 81, had the pump running and thought it wasn't having any damned effect at all, then suddenly she *did* shift — '

★ ★ ★

Anne still hesitating. Behind her, Wroughton's shout of '*Fire* the bloody thing!' Shutting her eyes, pushing it over, opening them to a crackle of blueish fire as the thing closed. The shout had been directed at Showell, of course: only the three of them at this work-bench — herself,

Showell and Sue — could have seen what had gone on.

No hydrophone effect now. Only a rolling burst of thunder — like a dam bursting, could have been — which Showell had reached to switch off.

'Christ almighty . . . '

'Ever see anything like it?'

Sam's and Ray's voices, from the other window. Anne on her feet, others around her grouped tightly, watching an acreage of sea in the southeast swelling in mounds of foam, dazzling white and silver where the searchlights fingered it, jet-black on the shifting slopes they didn't reach. Wroughton had binoculars on it, as did Jack Ray, who'd muttered, 'Like a submerged Vesuvius. Eh?'

'Nothing's coming up.' Wroughton, half a minute later. Taking the glasses away from his eyes and addressing Showell then: 'What took so damn long?'

Shake of the narrow head: 'Sort o' fumbled, near put me 'and across it. Sorry, sir.'

'If there's a next time, bloody *don't* sort of fumble!'

Ray had slapped Wroughton on the back. 'Unbelievable! And on behalf of the Sixth Battle Squadron — '

'Any time.' Wroughton laughed. '*Any* time!'

'Couldn't be any doubt you got him, I suppose?'

'None at all. There'll be divers sent down in the morning. No, don't worry, he's a goner.' Ray was coming to shake Showell's hand: pausing to clap Derrymore on the shoulder and thank him too. Anne asking Showell, 'Tell me why?' He shrugged. 'Make up for the long wait you 'ad. Something you'll remember us by, ain't it?' And Sue asked her in a whisper — five or ten minutes later, this was, after Wroughton had telephoned for the *New York*'s picket-boat to be sent back to the Vincent Pier — 'Weren't going to — were you?'

'Couldn't believe he *meant* me to!'

'I saw your face, though.' Still whispering — although there was no-one near them. 'Never *saw* such a look . . . Tell you what my guess is — if you hadn't known what's his name was already done for, you *couldn't* have — uh?'

'Perhaps *you* know what you're talking about. Sure *I* don't.' At least, didn't *think* she did. Was still keeping her hands out of sight so their shaking wouldn't attract notice. She'd felt she might faint, for a while. But Sam was drawing her aside. He'd been thanking Wroughton and the other two for having allowed him and the girls to clutter the place up — and congratulating them, and so on; asked her now, with a usefully steadying arm round her shoulders, 'Wasn't that right out of this world?'

'I was saying earlier, you *are* an extraordinary man.'

'What'd *I* do that's extraordinary?'

'How else did Sue and I get to be in this place, and seeing such a thing?'

'Why, opportunity happened to present itself, and — '

'Mrs McGregor and Mr McGillivray think you're my fiancé.'

'How come?'

'Sue told her. She was asking a lot of questions, and that was the simplest answer, I suppose. Then Mr McGillivray seemed to be under an impression that Sue and I were here for immoral purposes somehow connected with the US fleet, so I told him the same.'

No smile, no reaction at all for a moment. Then: 'They swallowed it, eh?'

'Why shouldn't they?'

'Couldn't get *your* mind around to the same concept, I suppose?'

'Well . . .'

'*Well?*'

She squeezed his arm. '*London*, Sam. Remember?'

Postscript

Sir Winston Churchill got it wrong, and so did C.S. Forester.

The attempt to enter Scapa Flow at the end of October 1918 was made by Kapitan-Leutnant Hans-Joachim Emsmann in UB116. His doing so was approved by the Wilhelmshaven U-boat Fuhrer Michelsen, and the boat was manned by its regular crew augmented only by one officer, name of Schutz, who'd sailed before with Emsmann.

In both *World Crisis* and *The Gathering Storm*, Churchill wrote that the U-boat was manned by a crew of officer volunteers, and Forester's play, *U.97*, made the same mistake, albeit in (presumably) a fictional treatment. But although the German High Seas Fleet had mutinied, the U-boat arm had not; no officers-only crew would have been needed or probably even thought of. Former submarine officers would agree with me, I think, that the performance of any such scratch crew might not have been all that impressive, either.

As far as I know, Forester's play was never staged in its original form; only after being re-written by a German, Karl Lerbs, and re-entitled *Germany*, was it put on in Bremen and Hamburg in the autumn of 1931. According to German reports it was well received. I have not read it or even seen it, but again, going by a

German review of that time, it seems that the fictional crew meet their deaths through oxygen starvation, not by being blown up in a shore-controlled minefield, as was the case. I should add to this, however, that Kapitan-Leutnant Emsmann's forlorn sortie only gave me the idea for *Stark Realities*, which is fiction from start to finish and only in the broadest sense a reconstruction of the historical event.

We do hope that you have enjoyed reading
this large print book.

Did you know that all of our titles
are available for purchase?

We publish a wide range of high quality
large print books including:
Romances, Mysteries, Classics
General Fiction
Non Fiction and Westerns

Special interest titles available in
large print are:
The Little Oxford Dictionary
Music Book
Song Book
Hymn Book
Service Book

Also available from us courtesy of Oxford
University Press:
Young Readers' Dictionary
(large print edition)
Young Readers' Thesaurus
(large print edition)

For further information or a free
brochure, please contact us at:
Ulverscroft Large Print Books Ltd.,
The Green, Bradgate Road, Anstey,
Leicester, LE7 7FU, England.
Tel: (00 44) 0116 236 4325
Fax: (00 44) 0116 234 0205

Other titles published by
The House of Ulverscroft:

WESTBOUND, WARBOUND

Alexander Fullerton

Late summer, 1939: The Clyde-registered SS *Pollyanna* sails from Cardiff on yet another tramping voyage — Welsh coal to Port Said is the first leg of it. On September 3rd, when Britain declares war, the *Pollyanna* is ploughing south through the Red Sea. One thing her crew hasn't heard about — because the BBC hasn't either — is that a fortnight earlier the German pocket-battleship *Admiral Graf Spee* slipped away into the Atlantic. Her mission is to seek out and destroy all the British and Allied merchant vessels she can find. This story, seen through the eyes of the *Pollyanna*'s third mate, Andy Holt, opens when the *Pollyanna* is westbound for Montevideo, Uruguay — which is where the *Graf Spee* too is heading . . .